Miss Adventures:
Abroad from Bangkok to Bali

by Ashley Percival

Misadventures Media- Ontario, Canada

All rights reserved.
Copyright © 2023 by Ashley Percival (Misadventures Media)
First Edition

No part of this publication may be reproduced in any form, or by any means, electronic or mechanical, including photocopying, recording or any information browsing, storage or retrieval system, without permission in writing from Ashley Percival (Misadventures Media).

Book cover design and formatting by: Black Cat Graphic Design

ISBN: 9798852443670 (paperback)

This novel, Miss Adventures: Abroad from Bangkok to Bali, is a work of fiction. Unless otherwise indicated, all the names, characters, businesses, places, events, and incidents in this book are either the product of the author's (Ashley Percival's) imagination or used in a fictitious manner. Any resemblance to actual persons, living or dead, or actual events is purely coincidental.

DEDICATION

This book is dedicated to my parents, Gary & Andrea: Thank you for loving me for me and helping to make all of my dreams come true. You are my world. I love you both with my whole heart.

Prologue

I wasn't exactly sure how I'd gotten into this predicament in the first place. Actually, I did know how I got stuck in this dreadful, sudden-death situation. It was because of a man – a very stupid, yet very sexy, man. Not just any man but a man whom I fell in love with, and who, inevitably, let me down, forcing me to flee the country. Okay, so he didn't force me, but he might as well have. Now, I was prepared to meet my maker. Not that I was overly religious or anything, but in a situation such as this, I thought religion, or at the very least, spirituality, could be vital to one's wellbeing.

    I contemplated my life, and the choices that I'd made, while I was trapped with two fellow travelers in a random, dark, broom closet somewhere in Kuala Lumpur, Malaysia. I heard the water drip down the damp walls as though it were a ticking clock, taunting me to make my next move. This small and humble closet was certainly not in the *Travel Guide's Top Ten Things to Do*, but I digressed. What I did know was that the closet door was the only thing that stood between us and a savage beast trying to claw its way inside and rip us to shreds. I saw its shadow lurking beneath the crack of the door. It paused, breathing heavily, before it continued its perseveration. Between you and me, I blamed the English girls whom I was currently trapped with.

"What are we going to do?" shrieked Emma in the shadows. She was the troublemaker who got us into this mess. This was something she should've thought of before she lured it in.

A shush silenced her in the darkness. It was unclear whose lips this warning emerged from. The temperature, and the drama, were rising.

"What are WE going to do? Don't you mean what are YOU going to do? YOU'RE going to go out that door and fend off that bloody beast whilst Poppy and I evacuate the premise!" Kate hissed at her friend. I envisioned Kate's claws emerging from her fingertips in the darkness, threatening to slice Emma's face.

To back track slightly, earlier in the day, we'd spent the morning admiring the Petronas Twin Tower and decided to take the scenic route back to our hotel. We marvelled at the futuristic architecture of the buildings, which were subtly hidden amongst the lush, jungle-like streets of the city. Unfortunately, our leisurely stroll soon turned violent when Emma decided she wanted to feed the beast – note to self, NEVER feed wild beasts!

We were lured in, as the song and dance goes. The beast had us right where it wanted us. What happens, you see, is that the creature lures you, encouraging you to welcome it into your comfort zone before it strikes.

To be fair, we were warned. Did we listen? No.

Like a wolf in sheep's clothing, you allow the beast, once in your presence, to nestle into your warm arms. The soft fur brushes against your skin as the beast breathes in and out while sucking your soul out of your body, unbeknownst to you. As you hold it, feeling safe and secure, you feel the humming of its vocal cords against your body. It's casting a spell on you. All you feel is comfort; it feels domination. You're becoming its mama and it's your baby. You're hooked in by the cuteness. It's winning.

Never let your guard down.

You gush how adorable it is, like a tiny baby. The large, dark eyes stare up at you as you cradle it in your arms. You catch a glimpse and think you've caught a smile. You feel sorry for it as the creature is out here all alone. You hold on tighter. You offer morsels of food as it hypnotizes you. You fall deeper and deeper into the trap.

It's too late. You've been bated.

It poses for photos before danger strikes. Suddenly, those large, dark eyes become devilish, like an animal seeing red! The cute and cuddly face morphs into a vicious creature, like a werewolf under a full moon, except here, you're under the boiling hot, tropical sun. Hair puffs over its body and suddenly, the creature is too big for your arms and falls to the ground. You witness the cute little paws hulk into giant pads with long claws that could tear into flesh – *your* flesh! Once the food supply runs out, the beast wants more. It wants the taste of blood. The beast begins to snarl and to gnash its teeth. It lets out a war cry and the hunt begins.

Emma, Kate, and I ran as fast as we could, our sandals click clacking down the road. We ducked and hid in a small, tourism office, broom closet as we'd nowhere else to go. Now, however, we were at the mercy of this beast. We prayed it took pity on us and released us from its clutches.

The hissing and shrill battle cry of the monster on the other side of the steel door made my heart race. As Emma and Kate battled it out as to who should exit first, I slid down the cold wall onto the floor, tears pouring down my face. How'd I get myself into this mess?

I'd packed my bags to come to Southeast Asia to get away from it all: work, friends, family, and a lover. Instead, I was pretty sure that we were about to get eaten. I already knew what my gravestone would say:

Poppy Beatrice Davis

1998-2023

Hopeless romantic who only knew how to run away from it all.

This seems pathetic, but at this point, I had decided to give up on love and relationships because of being jilted by my lover. I couldn't believe that I travelled halfway around the world to get away from a man who would never love me or return my feelings. Sure, we had our moments of love and passion, but now I was about to meet my maker because of Emma.

"Alright, let's rock, paper, scissors for it!" Emma

suggested enthusiastically.

"How the hell are we going to see who shows what, you thick wench?" From the tone in Kate's voice, it was clear Emma was about to get a rock over her head.

"Well, you could take my word for it, I suppose," Emma added. I could almost see Kate's eyes rolling in the darkness.

Just as they were about to fight to stay alive, the noise stopped outside. The clawing, the hissing, the threat of death, had all ceased. The door slowly creaked open, and as our eyes adjusted to the light, we saw a tall, dark figure looming above us. In the haze, it was evident it was all over, whether we were ready or not.

Chapter One

I liked men, which was part of my troubles. I liked tall men, short men, hairy men, bald men, athletic men, skinny men, and husky men. I liked men with tattoos, men with piercings, men with plain skin, men with motorbikes, men with bankbooks, and men without bankbooks. I liked spiritual men, religious men, rebellious men, strait-laced men, men with children, men without children, men with dogs, and men with cats. I liked men. My favourite thing to do was become entwined with a sexy man.

"Come back to bed," I purred like the cat that just got the cream.

"Poppy, love, some of us have to go to the office," John whispered in his soft and seductive tone as he brushed hair behind my ear, his fingers tracing my neck to my clavicle. He cooed like a famous, British playboy. I watched him move around my apartment with his heavy footsteps as he washed and got ready for the day. He made his usual pit stop at my place on his way to work after dropping his son, Oliver, off at school. Today, however, was his former wife's day to drop Oliver off so John stopped by earlier than usual.

I had a thing for his accent. I'd always been obsessed with the movies, television, and music from across the pond. It didn't matter if the man in question was a secret spy, a lonely shop owner, or a budding boy band member, I was into it.

My heart ached for John when we were apart. I always wondered if he felt that way for me. I was in love; his soothing voice and his tender touch hooked me. We were apart more often than I preferred. I was trying to be understanding, but it was a challenge. He was a single dad when we met, getting used to the routine of parenting alone. The custody case was ongoing and often added unneeded stress to John's life. Playing the supportive role to a single father was tough on me, too. I wasn't sure if he noticed.

"Fine," I whined. I slammed my hands into the plump, down duvet. The air from decompressing the fabric brushed against my face. "You can go, but I'd rather be in bed with you instead of that dreary little office. All I do is picture you in your birthday suit." A mischievous grin stretched across my face, one that usually made John crawl back into bed with me. My inner temptress was making a sacrificial offer.

He huffed to protest my request. John took a minute to compose himself as I studied his face. It was as if he was trying to decide if he should launch into a fight, or leave it alone. He had places to be.

"Behave," he growled. Clearly, he took the easier path. "Do you mind getting yourself to the office today? I'm picking up Oliver from school in an hour to take him to the dentist before I head into work." John struggled back into his black pinstripe suit. He jostled about, trying to get his damp legs into the inflexible fabric. He was always in such a rush; he never dried himself properly, an action that stripped away his sexy edge. I watched helplessly as his mildly muscular arms fought against the cloth. I much preferred his clothing to be in a heap on my bedroom floor, rather than back on his mid-thirties frame. "I don't know why she didn't just drop him off at school later." John fought to get his clothing on. "It's such a nuisance to interrupt my morning." He winked at me to smooth things over.

I wasn't fond of John talking about his ex-wife. It tended to monopolize our time together when he went on and on about what she did to disappoint or to frustrate him. How could a budding romance like ours grow when he focused on the past?

I also didn't like having to be so secretive. As a father, he was protective about what Oliver knew, and didn't know, about his personal life. I admired John for protecting his offspring, as you do when you are a parent. He didn't want his son to find out about us just yet. He also didn't want his ex-wife throwing wrenches into the custody battle. When we met, John assured me he was single; the technical detail that he was still married, although separated, was a secret he hid from me until I was hooked on him. I had stumbled upon a photo frame on his desk of Oliver and his soon to be ex-wife, and then the cat was out of the bag (more on that later as our story unfolds). I hated secrets. I was growing tired of our pre-work meetups or midafternoon 'business lunches.' Whatever happened to date night? That seemed like such an ancient concept.

I wanted to be John's wife. I longed to be a parent one day. I was sure Oliver would like me. Who doesn't like people with dogs? I often caught myself daydreaming about what we'd be like together – John, Oliver, and myself. I pictured making Oliver's lunches and packing his favourite treats. I'd add a bright sticky note with a smiley face on it, wishing him a good day and making him smile when he opened it at noon. His friends would tell him how lucky he was to have such a cool stepmom. We'd sing along to the radio as John, and I drove to and from school. I felt joy when I thought about having a happy little family. Maybe we'd soon expand our faux family from three to four. A baby would round out the dynamic perfectly.

"Earth to Poppy, do you copy?" I saw a blur of fingers pass before my eyes. Clearly, I'd been daydreaming, and John droned on, bursting the bubble of my fantasy.

"Of course," I said, pouting. I sat up on the bed, draping the linens around my bare body. "Shall I bring you a latte?" I hoped my offer to pick up his second addiction after me, caffeine, might earn me some brownie points.

"Ah, you're a sweetheart. Large latte with skim milk, please. No sugar this time, okay? I'm trying to watch my boyish figure. I'm not a young man anymore." He crouched down to whisper to me as he adjusted his tie. He pierced me with a wink. John's eyes were a soft blue, almost like a glass marble. They had the power to send shivers through my body like ice and warm me like a refreshing bath. He ran his hand across his buzzed blonde hair as his eyes connected with mine. When he was done donning his attire, he leaned across the bed to give me a soft kiss on the lips.

I don't think you could quite understand how sexy this man was – a six-foot-tall, two-hundred pound, mildly muscular hunk. His clothing clung perfectly to his body, as did I. His smile stretched into a small, boyish grin and had the power to draw me in. He always won. He'd have his way with me and then he'd leave.

I felt defeated as I walked John to the front door of my apartment. He kissed me goodbye as he tugged on the bedsheet that draped across my body. "How marvelous this is." His hands took one last journey over my curves before he headed out the door. "You should wear this to work every day." He cocked his eyebrows in unison as he turned and left. Loneliness washed over me. I was alone, again.

These days, I felt more like a lady of the night than the vixen I was when we first started seeing each other. Over time, things would change, and I would become nothing more than yesterday's news. I just didn't know it yet.

Chapter Two

Let's take a minute to rewind and learn the origin story of John and me; it's a doozy.

Last year, I applied for a job as a secretary after being fired from my previous position. You see, at the medical clinic, I had accidently mislabelled a vial, or two, of blood. Apparently, thirtysomething Eva Smith wasn't gaining weight due to a thyroid problem; instead, she was pregnant. Teenager Samantha Evans was told she was pregnant and had to tell her Christian parents she was expecting, but she was tired at school due to a wonky thyroid. The initials were so close; how was I to know?

After having Dr. Michaels whip three charts past my head, it was time to move on. I, however, had minimal references to provide. Unless my short-lived gig as a barista, my after-school job working at a hardware store, or babysitting my neighbour's kid when I was fifteen years old counted as a record of employment. I later found out Human Resources found that laughable. I'm sure there is a landfill full of my résumés.

My life revolved around daily soap operas and gummy bears for nearly three weeks after being let go from the clinic. Amos, my faithful black-and-white Chihuahua, and I enjoyed our alone time but even he was growing tired of me. Instead of cuddling in my lap, I found him slinking away to corners of my apartment so he could shield himself from my sobs. "How could Cory pick Alyssa? Didn't he know she was pregnant with their love child?" I'd scream at the television. It wasn't until I heard myself begging for characters to love each other that I knew I had a problem. I decided to make a change.

After much hunting in the want ads, I found a posting on the employment board of an accounting firm not far from my apartment and I decided to apply. Another secretary position so it seemed; Toronto was full of them. What did I have to lose?

The day finally arrived when I got the call for an interview at the firm. I spent hours rummaging through my closet looking for the most professional outfit I owned. I wanted something that screamed intelligent, trustworthy, working woman who didn't make mistakes – at least one who didn't make mistakes every day. No one is perfect, after all. I needed to wear something clean and tailored to make me stand out in a crowd. Poor Amos was buried under a pile of black-and-grey workwear debris before I made my final selection. I picked him up and kissed his head. He wagged his tail, signaling all was well. This would be a fresh start for both of us. He would finally have the apartment to himself.

The day arrived for my interview at the accounting firm. I made my way to the office, breathing in the cold, crisp, fall, morning air. It stung as I took in deep breaths to calm myself. Nerves overwhelmed me. I felt the armpits of my attire flood with pit stains.

When I entered the office waiting room, I was thrown into a crowd of people all vying for the job. Some individuals had their résumé encased in plastic folders. Others had résumés as thick as phone books if you can remember those. Mine was a mere one sheet, and slightly rolled up and poking out of the top of my purse. I tried to conceal it with my hand as I sat in the only empty chair.

From the far end of the room, a faint murmur announced the next candidate to enter. When the door of the office creaked open, and John emerged, that's when I first laid eyes on him.

From the moment I saw him, I couldn't keep from fidgeting. I didn't think he saw me, but I recall how he made me feel when I first observed him. I felt the temperature rise in my body, my blood feeling like it was boiling from lust and nervousness. I pulled at my skirt, wondering if its short length would help, or hinder, my chances of getting the job. I didn't want to appear to be using my twenty-something body for employment, but whatever works. Back then, I had a problem with seeking attention from men, and using sexy, yet professional, little skirts to achieve it. This was a behaviour I grew out of over time. We all evolve, after all; at least, that's the hope.

John stood in front of his creaky office door, in his

crisp black dress shirt with his silver gemstone cufflinks, and black pants. He was tall and handsome – not the image of an accountant that I'd conjured in my imagination. His blonde hair was trimmed like a military man. His cold, blue eyes stared right through me, and they popped against the dark frame of his reading glasses. If you aren't initially intoxicated by his sexy appearance, then you'll notice his boyish grin. I never knew if he was smiling at me, or if there was an inside joke I was never privy to. I was relieved when he opened his mouth; he had all his teeth, and they were shockingly straight. I swore they sparkled in the light. He had a gentlemanly demeanour to him that was, at first, lovable.

As I nervously awaited my turn, I tried to focus on my deep breathing. I made all possible efforts to relax. "I can do this," I said to myself repeatedly. I was ready for a change. I was ready for a job I wouldn't screw up, again. After I got a grip on myself, John re-emerged from his office with a woman. He held the door open for her and shook her hand. She was dressed in a grey pant suit with red-rimmed glasses. She looked very professional and, by the size of her résumé, was probably very experienced. My skirt paled in comparison. I should just go home. Why bother trying?

"Poppy Davis?" My name rang across the room. It was John. He was calling for me, searching the crowd for the body to match the name. He called again to the room full of secretaries, most of whom were on the edge of their seats. Apparently, I wasn't the only one ogling over the hot accountant. The women practically had their tongues wagging out of their mouths. A wide smile spread across my small, round face. Sorry ladies; it's my turn.

"That's me!" I said, slowly getting up, hot and flustered, as I didn't want to draw attention to my very short skirt. I felt his eyes on me, and he was smiling. As I walked towards him, I smoothed down my long, pin-straight, brown hair. I saw the blonde highlights catch in the sun's rays as I walked past the windows towards his office. I tried not to look directly at him when I walked by, but my cheeks flushed red as I felt him staring at me, as well as the daggers in my back from the other women in the waiting room. As John's office door closed, one of the suspenders on my undergarments broke free. Snap! The soft, silky stocking slunk down to the top of my knee. I tried to pull it up out of sight. Thanks for failing on me now!

"So, tell me about yourself, Ms. Davis," John suggested as he sat on the edge of his desk. He was perusing my résumé, which was single page and double spaced, filling in the gaps of the white page as much as possible. From my angle, I saw a small coffee stain on the top corner of the page. As John smoothed his finger over the crease of the stain, a slight smile spread and disappeared from his lips.

"Well, Mr. Daniels, I grew up here in Toronto and I have two brothers – " I was cut off by John, who was laughing to himself. He opened the top button on his dress shirt, getting more comfortable on his makeshift seat.

"Actually, I was referring to your work history. I see you used to work in a medical office, but I don't see a reference by your employer," he asked quizzically. His English accent much more pronounced than before.

I felt as though I was under a heat lamp in an interrogation room at the police station. Not that I had ever committed any crimes or anything – just nude in public once in college. We don't have to get into that right now. Doesn't everyone get naked in college?

"Well, Mr. Daniels, it's a funny story." My dark brown eyes grew to the size of saucers, trying to think of the perfect thing to say so that I'd land this job and get the hell out of the interrogation room.

"Is it?" He chuckled. "I always enjoy a good laugh." He took his glasses off as if to see me better. He locked his blue eyes with mine; I felt paralyzed.

I decided to confess my sins. "Well, I accidently mixed up a few labels and I was fired. I suppose having low thyroid levels is better news than finding out you're pregnant!" I tried to make light of my disastrous mistake, but no amount of humour could cover up the shame and embarrassment that I felt telling this potential boss that I screwed up. Maybe honesty isn't always the best policy.

He chuckled quietly to himself. "Marvelous story. Luckily, there are no vials to label here. We're all about numbers and spreadsheets," he said, raising both eyebrows in a cheeky manner, making me laugh and feel less foolish and at ease. He put his glasses back on to study my résumé, or lack thereof. He turned the sheet over, likely hoping to find out what made me qualified to work under him, or rather, for him. He raised his eyebrows and smiled a soft smile. He placed the paper on the desk and stared at me.

"Right then; shall we discuss the fine print?" He sighed as he walked behind his desk to sit in his chair.

"That would be marvelous." I felt a sense of relief. Amos and I wouldn't be on the streets anytime soon, I hoped.

We discussed details of my résumé and of the job. I thought the interview had gone well. As I got up to leave, John thanked me for my time. Our fingers brushed in that final handshake, and I felt the electricity scorching through my body. My heart raced faster than it ever had before. My confidence was crushed when I left the office John and repeated the same line to me that he had to the other lady, thanking me for my time and saying that he'd be in touch either way. As I walked towards the exit, he called out the next candidate's name. Is it possible to be disappointed and heartbroken over the same person at the same time?

Defeated, I walked home and wallowed in my pity. I didn't even notice my stocking draped around my ankle until I got home. So much for my attempt at professionalism! Perhaps the skirt worked against me, or at the very least, my poor judgment at my last employer did. It was time to go back to the old drawing board.

A week passed and I hadn't heard back about my interview. I was a little miffed, but not surprised that I wasn't successful. I pictured the woman with the red glasses working feverishly with Mr. Daniels, laughing, and making small talk between appointments with clients. I envisioned a group of colleagues clinking glasses together at happy hour after work. Maybe a wine or two and the woman with the red glasses and John would share whispers in the loud pub, laughing about something a client had said. Maybe they'd kiss.

I wished I was the one at happy hour with John. I fantasized about those blue eyes gazing into mine and sharing a laugh with him. I dreamt about his questionable wink and his smile, not knowing if it meant more. Perhaps we'd brush fingers under the table. I was jealous.

I'd spent the last few days ignoring the ringer on my cell phone. Only telemarketers called me these days. Emails weren't being responded to and most of the time, went straight into the trash. I wanted to be left alone. My mom, annoyed and frustrated by my recent behaviour, rapped on the door of my apartment early Friday morning to ensure I was alive.

Her intrusion began with three short knocks, all of which I ignored. I'd anticipated her tapping on the front door a fourth time but instead, I heard keys jingling in the lock. Damn, I'd forgotten that I'd given her an extra set. I heard Amos scurry to greet his grandma and to check if she had any treats.

"Honey, it's your mom! Where are you?" Her voice, typically as sweet as a kindergarten teacher, whispered loudly into every room. Amos followed along on the hunt. The little blood hound, and my mom, finally sniffed me out from under the covers of my bed. Later, the duvet would be used as a slinky backdrop for my lightly tanned skin, but for now, it was a camouflage while I tried to hide from the intruder.

I felt the weight of the small-framed woman sit gently on the bed next to my head. "Are you alright, Poppy? I've been trying to get in touch with you all week, but you're not returning my phone calls." My mom was always too sweet to be confrontational, but I may've finally struck a nerve as she thought that I'd died in my apartment. She probably thought Amos had gnawed on my carcass. I continued to ignore her in the hopes that she might eventually get the hint and leave.

"Will you please speak to me?" My mom's teacher voice morphed from sweet and meek to that of the discipliner who always scared my brothers, Myles and Peter, and me, shitless when we were in trouble. The she-hulk only emerged on rare occasions, but she was always lurking underneath. My mom didn't look scary dressed in her typical teacher clothing of lime green shorts and a simple, white t-shirt with an apple embroidered on it. Myles, Peter, and I would tease her mercilessly as most of her outfits consisted of either animal prints or embroidered popup decorations.

"I'm alive. Will you please leave now?" I yanked the duvet off of my head so that she could confirm my viable status and vacate the premise immediately.

"Well, what the heck is going on? Your dad and I

have been worried sick!" She crossed her arms, waiting for a reasonable explanation.

"I don't want to talk about it," I mumbled. My skin was pale from the lack of sunlight and my hair was dishevelled in a loose bun atop my head.

"I'm not leaving until you tell me. I want to help." Although my mom was still frustrated with me, she kept it together and soothed me like only a mother could. The disciplinarian could arise at any moment if need be; I was on alert.

"I don't think I'm ever going to be good enough. I'm a failure!" I wailed and threw the linens back over my head. Sometimes, I can be such a drama queen, FYI.

"You're being silly. So, you made a mistake, big deal. We all screw up. Are you going to beat yourself up over this forever? Run away and hide under your sheets?" My mom stroked the breathing lump under the covers to make me feel better, but only made me feel more pathetic. I was an adult who still needed her mommy.

During this conversation, Amos came barrelling into my bedroom from his post in the living room and leapt up onto my bed. The small stature of this Chihuahua may not look like much, but he is mighty. I strongly believe Amos thinks he's the same size as most other dogs. He is, however, mildly lazy and would make a terrible security dog. He sleeps soundly and he doesn't pick up on when other people are in the apartment as he is often fast asleep in his bed. This time, he wagged his tail and stole kisses from my mom and myself before curling into a ball at the foot of my bed, falling back into a comatose sleep.

Mom and I continued our conversation. "The other candidates seemed more appropriate. I don't know why Mr. Daniels would want to work with me. I'm hardly experienced or professional looking," I wept. I especially wouldn't be playing the supportive role as secretary, at least not now in my pink, panda print, pyjama bottoms and my ratty, old, gym t-shirt from high school. My mom extended her hand to wipe the tears from my eyes.

"We all have to start somewhere, and you'll grow into the person who you're supposed to be. Now, stop fretting and get up! Let's get some coffee. I'm beat. Your dad is driving me mad cleaning the house." My mom popped up off my bed and made her way into my closet to fetch me some more appropriate clothing. These pajamas were becoming fragrant, much like how I envisioned a panda to smell.

Defeated, I crawled out of bed and made my way into the shower for my daily constitutional. My mom sat in the living room, leafing through home decor magazines until I emerged looking human. She looked up from her magazine. Amos, too, in unison, turned his gaze from staring at the floor to look at his master.

We spent a good part of the morning drinking coffee and discussing the new floor plans for my parents' house that my dad had been preparing all summer. She was excited to finally have a quilting room. My dad was happy to have a man cave to avoid the latest quilters' gossip my mom brought home every week from her socials.

Eventually, I was able to laugh again and see how silly I was being chaining myself to my bed (and not in the fun way that I'd later become accustomed to with John. Pink fur handcuffs are definitely a thing). A job is a job and if this was meant to be, it would be. Get over it and enjoy life. Come Sunday morning, I'd started to circle the want ads so I could find something more fitting for me.

Friday evening rolled around, and I decided to curl up in bed with my favourite book. The pandas needed a break, so I put on a fresh, concert t-shirt and grey sleep shorts. My mom was right: I should stop putting all my eggs into one basket. I relaxed and readied myself for bed.

As I was turning off the lights in my apartment, I saw my cell phone had a message. The red dot was a beacon in the darkness. I pressed the play button, assuming it was probably my mom telling me not to worry; instead, it was a man's voice.

"Good evening. This is Mr. Daniels. I'm calling to congratulate you and to welcome you to my team. Please come to the office for work Monday morning at eight-thirty. There is no strict dress code, but please dress professionally. I find a pair of slacks, or a pencil skirt does the trick. Have a marvelous weekend. John."

My heart pounded out of my chest. I got the job! I immediately updated every social network I was on and called my parents and my friends. Forget sleeping! I had to find an outfit for Monday morning. Then, it hit me. Mr. Daniels noticed my skirt. My heart raced a little faster. Was he hitting on me, or was he giving me a helpful suggestion? It didn't matter; I would have time to figure it out myself.

Chapter Three

Sunday night was a disastrous blur. I tried to sleep, but I was continuously woken up by sirens, the recent heat wave hitting the city, and my snoring Amos. I tossed and turned all night until I finally fell asleep at five in the morning. This wasn't enough time for beauty sleep.

Amid my sleeping haze, I swore I heard another siren in the background. I remembered angrily hitting my nightstand in frustration. Then, it dawned on me that the sun was beating down on me. It seemed particularly bright and not like the usual sunrise this time of year. I was only used to this burning sensation after a night of clubbing when I would rouse in time for lunch.

I rubbed my sleepy eyes and looked towards my vocal pooch that had placed his head upon my pillow. As I rolled my eyes at the annoying sound of my dog's snoring, I turned my head to the left and blurrily saw 9:45 beaming at me from my alarm clock in hostile red lights.

"Holy shit!" I screamed, throwing the covers off the bed and Amos in the mix. I heard a little whimper and checked in the sheets to make sure the little prince was unharmed. He was cocooned in the bedsheets, but stunned at what had transpired.

I ran into the shower and hastily lathered my hair until my scalp was nearly raw. I scrubbed my face feverishly, getting grainy apricot pits into my eyes. After blow drying my body, I raced into the closet and searched for an outfit that I'd failed to set out the night before. I was too busy writing 'Poppy + Mr. Daniels' onto my note pad that I forgot to find something appropriate for working in the office for a very handsome accountant. Accounting didn't seem too sexy to me, but somehow he made a nerdy job go from a 3 to a piping hot 10.

I'd narrowed my search to a grey pencil skirt and a white blouse, or a green dress with a black cardigan. I'd finally settled on the pencil skirt, as I didn't want to steer away from the advice of the good accountant.

After throwing on my clothing and a poor makeup job, I ran down to the subway in my black high heels, dodging pedestrians along the way. Showing up to work with pit stains and sweat dripping down my face was most definitely not a smart, second impression. I didn't want anyone to think that I was a hot mess. I was sure he'd be glad he hired me after seeing my flushed, red faced and dishevelled appearance.

As I finally made it to my stop, I jumped up and ran towards street level. I couldn't help but panic. After all my previous screw ups, the last thing I wanted was to show up late for my first day on the job looking like a wreck. Pessimism washed over me, but it wasn't refreshing in the slightest.

I rounded the corner outside the subway station and looked up to see the shadow of the grey skyscraper looming overhead that almost eclipsed the sun. Just as I was about to enter the front doors, I felt a grip on my high heel. Before I had a chance to turn around and look, I fell in slow motion onto the ground and skid across the pavement. All I saw was blackness and all I heard was my heart thumping hard in my chest.

When I came to, there was a stranger above me. "Are you alright?" said the towering figure dressed in green, hospital scrubs. At first, I thought it was an alien. I jumped up, tugged at my high heel that had gotten stuck in a sidewalk grate, and bolted to the front entrance. I'd do anything to escape the man who would, most likely, take me to his leader. I realized later that it was probably someone who worked at the hospital down the street, not an extra-terrestrial who didn't wear tight skirts and high heels while they ran to their office late on their first day.

I limply made it inside the elevator and up to my floor. I unfolded the small piece of paper I had in my pocket with Mr. Daniels' office number on it. I was a bit more battered than I would've liked to have been, but at least I was finally at work. I had to start the day somehow.

Before I entered the office waiting room, I took a deep breath and told myself that if I got fired today, I'd treat myself to a glass of wine at the Vine-Yard Bar and look through the want ads with my vino in hand. No tears.

I turned the handle slowly and snuck into the office, closing the door quietly behind me, hoping not to get caught being late.

"Ah, there you are," announced a familiar voice. Shit, it was my boss.

"Sorry, I'm late; I ran into a bit of a – " I trailed off in my mousy voice, lowering my head towards the floor.

"What the hell happened? Sit down, you poor thing." Mr. Daniels pulled out my office chair and insisted I sit. What the hell, I thought, was the fuss about? I looked down and realized that both of my knees were skinned and bleeding.

"Let me fix you up. I know my way around a first aid kit," he cooed. I was hypnotized by his nurturing hands. He tossed his tie over his shoulder, winked at me, and began to flip through the box that was tucked away in my bottom drawer: note to self.

I watched in admiration while my boss got down on one knee and cleansed my skin. He gently unfolded the gauze to measure the appropriate length required and patched up my wounds. I didn't even notice any pain, particularly when he poured antiseptic on. All I could do was stare at his blonde head of hair. I leaned close to him to smell his odd, charming scent: him.

As I leaned closer, eyes closed, I felt a pressure on my shoulders. I opened my eyes to see what the matter was.

"Wow, miss, you must be very dizzy! You almost fell

on top of me!" He chuckled. "Come on. Let's get you to my office. You can lay down there and rest on the couch." I stretched my aching legs, trying to adjust to the patchwork on my knees.

The next thing I knew, I was being led to his small, cramped office. There was a black leather couch on one end and a small brown desk on the other. No windows, but the hum of the air conditioner filled the room. A few textbooks were placed neatly on the bookshelf and a picture or two on the desk in silver frames for display. I barely had a chance to catch a glimpse of the silhouettes before he led me to lie down.

He slowly placed me on the couch, swinging my feet up, and put a soft, quilted pillow of the union jack under my head. "My mum made that. It's just a little taste of home," Mr. Daniels whispered, helping me get comfortable.

"Now, I want you to rest, and don't think about getting up until you're good and ready. Alright, missy?" Mr. Daniels playfully scolded me like a little girl.

"Alright, Mr. Daniels," I agreed, cowering sheepishly into the couch, trying to hide as deeply as I could into the leather upholstery.

He settled behind his desk and began flipping through his files and crunching numbers, as I assume accountants do. As he worked, I didn't notice any rings on his fingers. Single: bonus.

"Oh, and Poppy, one more thing," he said as he looked at me with soft, caring eyes, "please, don't call me Mr. Daniels; call me John. We'll be working closely together, you know," he softly stated and went back to his files. My heart tore in two when he pulled his eyes away from mine.

Not a horrible first day, I thought as I closed my eyes. I might just make it here after all.

Chapter Four

Day two: I was feeling alive, which I was grateful for, considering yesterday's epic fail. I practically skipped to work today. This time, I'd be avoiding the nearly fatal grate that clutched onto my shoe yesterday. I'd try to revive the sassy number, but it might be headed for the bin. Aside from a mangled shoe, nothing could crush my spirits today, not even a sidewalk grate. As I approached the building, I made a pretend pistol with my fingers and pulled the imaginary trigger towards the ground as a means of saying, "not this time, bucko." I winked as if I was an urban cowgirl. Today, I wore flats, planning to change into my heels in the office, which was a safer bet.

After the elevator dinged, signalling that I'd arrived, I made my way down the abandoned hallway towards my office. My humming echoed in the emptiness. I reminisced about my new, favourite, top forty hit – some catchy, Latin beat about partying in the club. Perhaps, if I was this perky this morning from my radio alarm, I should start every day with a little Latin pop! I stopped for a second and started nodding to myself, approving this brilliant idea, and almost busting a move. I refrained, however, wanting to avoid a fatality on my second day of work. After I was done, I continued on my way, tossing my ponytail as I rounded the corner of the corridor.

I swung the doors of the office open and hopped in my seat. I was relieved to see that I was the first one here. Smiling to myself, I started singing the lyrics to the tune controlling my mood this morning and I must say that I rocked it.

I sat bent over, fiddling with my work bag, when I heard a voice above me.

"I've been expecting you," said the raspy, female voice. I searched my mental catalogue, trying to determine who it might be.

I froze for a moment, not sure how to respond. I slowly raised my head and peered over the surface of my desk towards the voice.

As I looked up, I saw a tall, slender woman dressed in a plain, light blue, pant suit. Her blonde hair, with thick brown undertones, was tucked into a ponytail. Her arms were crossed across her flat chest. She had dark blue eyes that pierced my body like knives. This intimidating posture left me frozen at my post like a timid animal lurking behind some bushes. I wasn't sure if I should remain hidden or pounce on this predator.

"Well, aren't you going to say hello?" she burst in a high-pitched voice. She uncrossed her arms and flailed them beside her. I was confused.

"Hello..." I said cautiously, not sure what to add after that. I slowly raised my head above my desk to fully meet the eyes of this wild woman. Better to accept the challenge than to shy away and admit defeat.

After I rose to my feet, the predator's body relaxed and her hardened face became calmer and more approachable: a chameleon, perhaps?

"Well, come on, and give me a hug already!" She darted towards me, wrapping her arms around me, and smothering me.

Confused, I mildly returned the hug with three awkward pats on her back. I was never much of a hugger.

"My gosh! I thought I was going to die with these nerds running this office. That is, until I heard you were coming." She hopped up and down like an excited child. "The last girl was dreadful. You should've seen the two-piece suits she wore to work. The girl never had a chance!" Her high-pitched voice remained, but instead of yelling, she began to laugh jovially. I slowly warmed to her. It was nice to have a new friend.

"I should probably introduce myself. I'm Casey Andrews, Mr. Evan's secretary. And you're Poppy, right?" She adjusted the front of her suit to regain her composure.

"Yes. Nice to meet you." I felt a little more relaxed at this point. She, however, plopped herself into my chair. I was cornered into conversation.

"What happened to you? I thought you were supposed to work yesterday?" Casey asked quizzically, crossing her legs as she sat in my chair, head cocked to the side. She continued to fiddle with the crisp, straight ends of her hair.

"I had a mishap with my high heel." I nodded, pointing to my scraped flesh.

"Don't tell me they were expensive!" Casey gasped with horror, hand to her chest. Her mauve lips formed the perfect shocked shape.

"No," I hesitantly giggled, "cheap, trendy ones."

"Phew! Don't want to waste those high-quality babies! Sometimes, I skip rent to get a designer pair." Looking at her, I noticed she was a mix of designer items and internet, beauty fails. Beauty is in the eye of the beholder, so perhaps I shouldn't be so quick to judge. I had been living in leisurewear for longer than I'd like to admit.

"Agreed. Well, I better check my messages. Get a head start before the boss gets in." I motioned for her to go to her desk.

"No doubt." Casey nodded enthusiastically. "Maybe we can grab some lunch and get to know each other?" She smiled and sauntered to her seat. She started clicking keys on her keyboard to signal her workday had begun.

"That would be great." I smiled. I smoothed my ponytail over my shoulder and started to figure out who John would be seeing today.

My animal senses kicked in and, without looking up, I sensed John enter and heard him whistling some eighties pop tune. I inhaled the scent of him as he passed by. I closed my eyes and envisioned our close encounter yesterday. But instead of disassociating, I returned to reality and continued to do my paperwork. He paused briefly on the way into his office.

"Are you alright? You aren't going to pass out on me, are you?" He smiled, and headed towards his door, whistling away again. He stopped and turned around.

"I have a bit of a busy day," he said, lowering his voice and his body towards me. "Do you mind picking up a coffee or two for me? There's a great little place around the corner. I'll give you money. Buy yourself one as well." His low voice put me into a trance. He stared at my bottom lip. I'd do anything he asked of me. I felt my face redden.

Before I had a chance to reply, he grabbed a pen and a piece of paper, gave me a little wink, scribbled something down, and handed it back to me. I barely had a chance to look at it. I was too busy staring at him in his gray suit with a uniform, crisp, white shirt. He handed me a twenty and headed to his office, adjusting his blue tie. The door closed behind him, and he disappeared out of sight.

I looked at the paper:

Large latte with skim milk.
Here's my cell number should you need me, for anything.

I didn't read too much into the note except that he wanted a latte. I entered the number into my phone and tossed the scrap into my purse. Back to work. It was too early for a break.

The morning flew by and after a quick lunch with my new colleague to get to know each other, I decided to bring the boss back a latte since I hadn't seen him come out of his office for hours.

As I headed towards the café he suggested, I rooted through my bag to find the little note with his order on it. Annoyed I couldn't find the request, I gave up and decided to text him. Hopefully, he'd get the message and get back to me; so much for a surprise.

Poppy: Forgot order, plz repeat.

I sat waiting on a bench with the sun blazing in my eyes. I thought about how well things were going but I didn't want to get caught up in this newfound success just yet. Sometimes, things are too good to be true. Pondering this, I felt a vibration from my hand and looked down at his reply.

John: Lrg latte with skim milk. Thx ☺

I smiled and sent a reply:

Poppy: Forgetful! Must have short-term memory loss.

Seconds later, I read:

John: 2 beautiful 2 have memory issues. X

'X' – what does 'X' mean? Poison? Danger?

I grabbed my order from the counter and headed back to the office. I was too dazed to even taunt the sidewalk grate. I stomped right over it as I was on a mission to figure out what was going on. Perhaps I was overreacting, but what was the meaning of this? Was this flirtatious? Friendly? Then again, if he was flirting, what's wrong with that? He's quite attractive, polite, and I'd clearly already fallen for the Englishman – both literally and figuratively.

Bursting through the office doors, I slammed the coffees on the desk. I startled Casey, but only enough that she acknowledged my presence. She smiled and returned to her filing.

I sat down and searched 'X' in text lingo on my computer. My search brought up a street slang dictionary, which outlined the use of the letter:

In modern pop culture 'x' represents different things depending on the size of the letter. Often a symbol used towards someone special.

$$Little \; x = little \; kiss$$
$$Big \; X = big \; kiss$$

"Hey, get a load of this!" Casey shrieked in her version of a quiet voice. She walked over to my side of the office. "My friend Deb is an emergency room nurse. Apparently, there's a guy sitting in the exam room with an inflamed piercing in his..."

"Casey! I'm busy. Do you mind?" I shrilled, trying to get a quiet moment to myself to decode this hieroglyphic message.

"Sure, but let me finish telling you what he has pierced!" she laughed.

I quickly shut her down and pushed her back to her side of the office so that I could be alone. I had a mystery to solve.

"You'll regret that!" I heard her yell as she fussed with the files. She stifled giggles. I may regret not hearing what she had to say, but I had a goal to accomplish.

I sat back at my desk, confused. John was a major hunk but he's off limits since he's my boss – my single boss. Maybe he didn't mean to send me an 'X'. Maybe it was an accident. Or maybe it wasn't.

Puzzled, I walked towards his office door, latte in hand. I knocked and he answered immediately.

"Ah, perfect. Thanks, love." John reached for the coffee and closed the door.

I stood there, frozen. Maybe the dictionary was right! It wasn't a kiss, but it was …something.

When I opened my mouth to breathe, I felt as though my lungs were filled with water. I gasped, trying to take in air. I realized that I might be in over my head. Shit, now what?

Chapter Five

From what I know about other cultures, the letter 'X' can be very affectionate, to anyone! My boss called me 'love.' Sure, it may've been a friendly English thing, or it could've been the beginning of so much more.

"It's very European to call someone 'love'," Casey reassured me the next day when we took lunch together. We sat on the front steps of the building, which had created unnecessary shade on this fall day. I unfolded the crisp edges of the sandwich wrapper and took another bite as I processed this information.

"I'm somewhat of an expert on men," gushed Casey. She leaned into me and nudged my shoulder. "I write a love column for a woman's dating website. It is very hush hush, but I get a lot of positive feedback. I'm one to pay attention to." Casey nodded as she noshed away on her wrap. "I'd write full time, but it doesn't pay the bills," she admitted. Not all work was so glamorous.

Over the next several months, Casey became a close

friend of mine, a confidant. Casey was good at giving advice on life's difficult situations. Most of the time, she was very helpful but other times, not so much. I think that she and I had different outlooks on men and love. She always had a boyfriend whom she seemed to find in all the wrong places – work, the internet, bars, a street fight after the bar, you name it. The last place I'd find a man for my liking is at an unofficial wrestling match on the curb, but Casey was a bit man hungry. She, at the very least, was entertaining. At the heart of it, she meant well.

As time went on, life got easier. I'd grown accustomed to the new pace of the job. I was making progress in my career, minus a few little errors along the way, such as faxing account records to the wrong business or forgetting to hang up the phone when I was done leaving a voicemail. When I made a mistake, John told me to call people to apologize and to not sweat the small stuff. I'm human after all and no one's perfect. This time, there's no blood work to be accidently switched and no one had the wrong diagnosis given to them. Arranging appointments and sending faxes was my norm. Life was grand.

I'd given up on the idea of the 'love' comment after a few months. By this time, snow had fallen on the ground, and Christmas came and went. John would wink at me, occasionally. On my birthday, he gave me flowers. I didn't obsess over the card he sent me as that little letter of the alphabet also made an appearance on a card he signed to his mum. I knew that it meant nothing for him to send the same thing to me. Things fizzled out and it was clear that he was only my boss.

Come February, I proudly put John out of my mind. Perhaps, secretly, I did wish he would fall for me. He was sweet, handsome, and sexy – very sexy. He, however, was not someone I could have a relationship with as he was my boss. A girl could still have a few dirty fantasies about him though, right? There's nothing inappropriate about that.

Just as I managed to push the thoughts of John out of my head, I felt as though I was getting in over my head, again. This time, however, it was in a look.

The building's heaters malfunctioned as someone, most likely me, had turned up the heat, and someone else, most likely Casey, kept turning down the heat so that her nipples raised the fabric of her satin blouse. She did this to lure her next man, even if it was one of our clients. This war went on for two weeks before we finally broke the dial. The heat in the office rose. It was so hot one day, John came out of his office after a consultation with steam on his glasses. He had to remove his designer eyewear to clean them off and asked me who was next. It sent us both into a fit of giggles and ended with him winking at me, as per usual.

Later in the week, we both came to work, scantily clad, to survive the temperature. John left his door propped open as it was unbearable to have it closed and he usually came out with sweat stains by lunch time. The repair man wouldn't be in until later in the week to fix the thermostat, so our problem persisted. I had been sizzling all day at my desk. I'd had enough of the sweltering heat, so I unbuttoned a few of the buttons on my blouse and leaned back into my chair to tie my hair up. After my hair was arranged in a messy ponytail, I finally felt the cool air from the winter wind blowing through the crack of the open window onto my neck. It felt good and I revelled in the moment. A smile spread across my face as I tussled with my locks.

When I opened my eyes, I looked towards John's door without thinking. I saw him quietly sitting at his desk, his eyes fixated on me, taking in my relaxed pose. He smiled, lowered his eyes, and resumed reading his report. I didn't know what to think of it then, but later I'd learn. His gaze had the same effect on me as a soft touch. That's exactly what I wanted.

As I packed up for the day, I was eager to go back into the cool air. There was no need for a coat. I needed to feel freshness on my skin. John passed by my desk and stopped. He looked around the office, back at me again, and then quietly said, "Has anyone ever told you how beautiful you are?" His accent was soft and calm in my ears, drawing me closer to him.

Instantly, I blushed. Finally, getting a nice compliment from a man whom I found so attractive was rewarding, but also embarrassing. His hand rose to my neck and gently slid up to my face. Time stood still. He cocked his head to the side and that boyish grin reappeared. He cupped my cheek and leaned in, but stopped just before his thin lips touched mine. I stood paralyzed. "I'm sorry, I can't." He lowered his hand from my face and turned around. He walked out the office door without looking back. For a moment, I thought Cupid was bringing my forgotten valentine in the mail; I guess I was wrong.

I didn't know what to do. This time, it simply wasn't about an 'X' or a look; it was something much more than that. One can't help but be excited, nervous, and scared when a man touches you, resulting in such a spark. He walked away. He's my boss – we can't be together.

Walking home that evening was a blur. I couldn't be bothered to take the subway. I walked to think, to not think, and everything in between. When I got home, I sat on the couch, dazed. Amos pawed at me to feed him, but I couldn't register anything that had happened. It was an hour or so before I realized that my phone had been vibrating. At first, there was one unread text message followed by two more.

John: So sorry 'bout earlier. Didn't mean to scare U. Please forgive me.
John: Poppy, please call me - want to talk to U.
John: Poppy, please. I'm sorry.

I didn't know whether to respond to him. I felt embarrassed to have a crush on my boss, and I felt embarrassed that he almost kissed me and then he walked away. Perhaps, I should make it right so that it wasn't awkward at the office. I picked up my phone and texted him back.

> Poppy: Don't be sorry. Nothing to be sorry about. All's forgiven.
> John: Thank U. I am your boss. I am truly sorry. I hope I didn't upset you.
> Poppy: Not at all, the moment got the best of us.

It certainly had. Maybe I should stop fantasizing about him. I didn't want to be the center of any office gossip.

> John: I do care about you.
> Poppy: I appreciate that. We're good.
> John: You're too sweet, never change.
> Poppy: ☺ Goodnight.
> John: Night X

I went to bed early that night. I was sad. On one hand, I was sad that John didn't kiss me, particularly as I'd been secretly pining for him since I started working there. And I was sad he felt guilty for almost kissing me. It must be hard for him being a single dad and a boss. It must be lonely sometimes. I turned a movie on and snuggled with Amos, falling asleep to the background dialogue.

Around 9:45pm, I was startled awake by my cellphone. More messages had flooded in. More messages from John.

> John: I've been thinking. I have a question.

John: Would U have kissed me if I had kissed U?

John: Forgive me, I shouldn't have asked.

John: I'm sorry.

John: Night X

My pulse raced, my eyes still blurry from sleep. I read the messages again and again. What do I say now? After a pregnant pause, I decided to tell him the truth.

Poppy: Yes.

The dots appeared and disappeared as I waited for John's reply. Finally, his message came in loud and clear.

John: I have to see U. Now.

The next thing I knew, I was giving him my address. Panic struck me. I flung the phone on the couch. What the hell did I just do? I had no idea. I paced the floor of my apartment. Amos was hot at my heels, confused, as if he thought we were going to go on a walk. Twenty minutes later, there was a startling buzz at my door. John had arrived.

I opened the door slowly, peering beyond the chain that stitched my door to the wall and saw John's light blue eyes peering back at me. His glasses were steamed again, making me laugh. He'd fought through the winter elements to make it to my place at the other end of the city. I unlatched the door and let him in.

"You poor thing." I motioned to him to take off his coat, but instead he just stood there. As he stared at me, water dripped from the edges of his coat onto the hardwood floor. His affect conflicted with desire and guilt.

"If you think this is wrong, I can leave." More silence, time to think. "I know I'm your boss, but I can't stop thinking about you," he whispered softly, moving closer towards me. Goosebumps dotted my flesh. I wanted nothing else.

"This is fine," I stuttered. I took a step back, hesitating. Neither of us wanted to cross a boundary but the line had already been crossed. I had one last chance to change my mind, but I followed my heart instead.

The next thing I knew, I was tearing his coat off, our mouths sealed together with kisses. It was something out of an epic bonk buster: my legs were wrapped around his waist as we fell passionately onto the bed in slow motion. I couldn't feel gravity, but I sure felt something else. Entwined and twisted with each other, and in the bed sheets, we explored each other as fast as we humanly could. It never felt like either of us had quite enough of each other.

We had been wrapped in our bodily cocoon for what seemed like hours. I think at one point, I lost feeling in my hands because I was so excited, or one of us was on top of them. Either way, it was exhilarating. Hot and sweating, we lay exhausted in bed. We looked at each other and laughed, hardly believing what had just happened, but not sorry that it had.

"So, will I have to go find a new job?" I asked out of breath, not sure myself whether I was joking.

"No. I rather think that I should give you a bonus!" John quipped. "All this exercise has got me hungry. Shall we go grab a bite to eat?" John asked as he propped himself on his elbows and brushed the hair out of my eyes. The bedsheets were barely covering us. I played with a small patch of chest hair he had as I contemplated the offer.

"That sounds wonderful," I added. This type of exercise always did rev up my appetite.

We put our clothing back on our warm bodies and headed into the cold. The snow had stopped, and we raced down the street towards an Italian restaurant around the corner that catered to couples. We were the only patrons. The piano player sat above us on the second floor churning out romantic tunes.

As the night flew by, John's low voice lulled me. The soft music added to the ambience, painting the perfect backdrop for two new lovers. He stretched his arm across the table and enveloped my hand in his. We spent the night getting to know each other, eating pasta, and drinking red wine. We talked about England, music we loved, and terrible movies we couldn't help but watch on repeat. Our childhoods played before our eyes like family video recordings, and we gave each other a play by play of the terrible pranks our siblings played on us when we were younger. John and I made plans for day trips and travels to faraway places we'd never take. As the conversation went on, the cloak on the night lowered. It was the perfect first date. I hated to think that at any minute, this night would end. I learned after a while to live in the moment and this lesson would mean more as time went on. Later, I would relive this seemingly perfect moment, a memory etched in time, and wonder if we were playing make believe.

We closed down the restaurant and John walked me back to my apartment. He held me close for another soft and slow kiss. This kiss was to savour and was burned into my brain forever. Cupid definitely had hit his target. As he walked away, I memorized him. His head hung low under the veil of the streetlights. I breathed in the night air. This would be the first of many nights like this. The moon was in my eyes but that's just how I preferred it to be, blinded by the light.

Chapter Six

The famous English woman with all the diaries had nothing on me, baby. I'd become a sex goddess. My days were filled with naughty texts, early morning, and late-night encounters, as well as candlelit dinners, which became the norm over the next two months. John and I would talk about ourselves, our passions, and our lust for each other's bodies. We moved past the shared guilt of the workplace relationship, and really began to enjoy each other's company. It seemed perfect. How could this not be love?

On an occasion or two, I'd come to the office early in my black lace lingerie, which was John's favourite. Carefully, I would tuck my naughty little gift under my workwear. I paired it with red high heels, the ones he preferred I kept on when everything else came off. I'd saunter into his office and close the door behind me. We had to shush ourselves as I let him unwrap me like one of the sweets he had sitting out on his desk. He was a hot nerd with an edge.

Casey had commented one day on all the commotion going on behind closed doors. I merely wrote it off as moving some chairs around to optimize space. We were optimizing the office chairs alright.

It wasn't all about romps. John had a tender side, too. He'd write me love notes and hide them in my apartment before he left. I'd smile as I brushed my teeth and read the cute messages. John would read song lyrics to me, as if it were poetry he'd written. I would smile as I nuzzled up against him, encouraging more affection. He'd send lilacs and daisies to my apartment. The sweet scents filled the last of the bleak winter.

I'd fallen deeper and deeper into this rabbit hole of love. A love affair, rather, had bloomed. It was exciting. It made my blood pulsate through my veins. It made my legs weak. It made my heart race. I fell so deeply, I wouldn't know how to get out of this hole even if I'd wanted to. I hadn't been this mad about anyone in years. Not since my kindergarten crush, the newspaper boy on my street, or even my high school boyfriend had I ever fallen so hard. There were a few bullets I dodged along the way, and I'll save those stories for another time. Love was blissful, maddening, and oh so yummy.

One day after christening John's office couch, I'd wandered over to his desk as I smoothed down my attire. I took a moment to gander at the items on his desk. I'd never done that before. I was always too busy exploring him.

As I examined the desk, I saw neatly stacked files on

the corner beside his outgoing mail. A container of blue pens and a sleek, black stapler were set out; it was all very practical. His desk was clean cut and in uniform, much like his daily suits. At the other end of his desk were three, silver, photo frames. I skimmed by fingers along the grain of the wood as I made my way to the other side.

"Who are in all of these photos?" I asked, picking up a frame and examining it with precision like a jeweller examining diamonds. John had just placed a new photo frame on his desk.

John came around the desk behind me and leaned over, kissing my shoulder as he buttoned up his dress shirt, tucking it into his unzipped pants.

"Well, those two dogs are my children Ben and Harvey." He pointed to the photo I had in my hand. "And the two little girls are my nieces, Annie and Beatrice. I'm also their godfather." He pointed to a photo on the desk. John walked away to grab his suit jacket off the couch. I wasn't done snooping. I placed each frame down to pick up the next to study it.

"Who are the woman and the little boy in the last frame?" I asked quizzically. I stared at the photo as if trying to retrieve a lost memory. I couldn't recall anyone else he'd told me about.

"No one to bother yourself with." John didn't look at me as he fumbled with his belt and cleaned his glasses off with the bottom of his tie.

"Is she your sister?" I grasped at any excuse I could at this point. I didn't want to accept reality, as in my heart, I already knew the answer.

John sighed and looked away from me again before saying with an icy tone, "No, she's my soon to be ex-wife. And my son, Oliver, is in the photo with her. I don't have any photos of just Oliver and I." I felt as though I had upset him with my question. Shock reverberated throughout my body.

My heart sank. The world stopped for a brief second. I gasped for air. I felt as though I was back on that sinking ship that kept reappearing in my life but this time, it kept dragging me down farther and farther. I didn't know whether to laugh, to cry, or to slap him. I could only sit there frozen solid in his chair.

"What do you mean, she's your soon to be ex-wife?" I asked dumbfounded. I feverishly recalled all our recent past in my mind. With the lovemaking and dates not once did he bring up still being married.

"We were separated when I moved to Toronto. The divorce has been long and drawn out over custody of our son. Nothing has to change between us, Poppy. The divorce has been so stressful on me. I've been putting on the pounds because of it." The suave man had now morphed into a pathetic, little boy.

Suddenly, I felt like I was the bad guy and for no good reason, John was the one who had kept a secret from me. I felt like an emotional, atomic bomb had just gone off.

"Of course, things change between us! You're still married!" My voice became shrill. John scrunched his eyes as if I'd pierced his eardrums. He tried to hush me with silent hands. Tears were welling in my eyes. I felt blindsided.

What luck I have. The first man I'd fallen in love with in years was married. Does this make me the 'other woman'? I'm officially a homewrecker. How about we add that qualification to my résumé?

"If you think that this is wrong we can stop." They were the exact words he had muttered the first night we were together. This time, the passion had disappeared from him. This felt more like a business transaction, or a secret.

"I don't know what to do. I can't even think right now." I walked out of his office and out of the building. I had to get away.

I spent the night alone, sitting in my apartment, crying. John's words, 'this is my soon to be ex-wife' haunted me, making me feel sick to my stomach. How stupid could I be? He texted me profusely, but I rejected his messages.

John: Don't be mad. Plz talk to me. X

John: I always wanted U. Nothing has changed. X

John: Going to bed, thinking of U. X

I began to hate the letter 'X.' It filled me with rage, and I never wanted to see it again, but then, it made me miss John. How is a girl to win? With every kiss, with every tender moment, I fell deeper into my own hell. I needed to get out.

Chapter Seven

For two weeks, there was a dull silence in the office. Not even Casey could drag me out of my funk. All of John's messages went unnoticed. Every time he walked past me, I felt his eyes taking me in, but I didn't give into him; instead, there was radio silence. I didn't want to become that person who bends the rules for others' happiness over her own. In this moment, however, my heart was a strong ruler. My brain would scream at me to run the other way. I had a hard time picking sides.

I was angry at this man whom I thought I knew. The sad reality, however, was that he didn't cheat on me – *I* was the other woman, an issue I couldn't wrap my head around as much as I'd tried. Even though he insisted I wasn't, I was. John was still married. Essentially, he was getting the milk for free from this dumb cow.

On the 15th day, the war was over. When I got to my desk early in the morning, there was a long, white box on my desk tied with a red ribbon, taunting me. The sender was a real prick.

Casey came up behind me and poked around the box. "Aren't you going to open it?" She picked up the box and shook it. Her long, hot pink nails dug into the sides of the box, nearly crushing the delicate contents.

"I don't know yet. I'm afraid of the repercussions of what lies inside," I pondered. The next thing I knew, her hand was leading mine towards the ribbon.

"Come on. Rip it off, just like a bandage. Or boxers; whatever your pleasure." Her glossy, pink lips spread into a mischievous smile.

Nervously, I pulled the bow off the box and lifted the lid. Inside, were twelve, perfect, light pink, long-stemmed roses with crisp, green stems. Something so beautiful was also covered with hidden thorns. You want to touch them, but you don't want to bleed. I was too busy stopping to smell the fresh scent of the flowers when I saw a note without a signature. I knew exactly who it was from:

My heart only belongs to you.
X

After Casey read my card, she sat on my chair, puzzled. "Who's this from?" She twisted back and forth on the rolling seat.

"No one for you to be jealous of." I turned and walked in front of my desk. I couldn't help but smile, even though I knew that this was too good to be true. The pink roses were my rose-coloured glasses when it came to John. Everything looked perfect on the outside, but cut flowers don't last.

The message on the card was cheesy, but it nudged me to reconsider him. I heard John's office door open a smidge and saw one eyeglass peeking through. I smiled and the door opened wide. He motioned for me to come to him. I didn't hesitate.

Behind closed doors, we shared our first makeup kiss followed by our first makeup romp. I wrapped my legs around his waist as he carried me to the edge of his desk. We kissed, silently taking moments to gaze into each other's eyes, and smiled. There were short, gentle caresses of the cheeks before I slowly unbuttoned the top of his dress shirt and kissed the peach fuzz-laden skin over his chest. His hands reacquainted themselves with my frame.

This time when we were intimate, I made sure the photo frames were out of sight. I was the only woman I wanted John thinking of in this passionate moment.

We slowly got back together, and with each date, I grew more and more attached to him. It took time to forgive him for not telling me about his separation, but the more he apologized and the more he tried to show me how important I was to him, I gave in. Kisses, romantic dinners, car rides in the country – and sex filled my days with John. I felt like I was someone special to him. No one's perfect, but I was finally happy.

One date night, during the height of our love affair, we decided to go for a romantic dinner at a tapas restaurant. It was a little out of our way, but promised a reduced chance anyone would see us – not coworkers, not friends, and not ex-wives. We'd use this as 'our spot' on occasion. We often requested a table in the back corner. It was dimly lit and out of the way of other customers. We could have private conversations and play footsies under the table. The tablecloth would shroud any naughty activities that occurred.

John told me that there'd been a change in plans and Oliver would be over in an hour. He didn't have time for our dinner date, but would come over to my house for dessert instead.

"What? We aren't going out? But I've been looking forward to this all week! I've barely seen you," I cried. Tears streamed down my face.

"Poppy, please," John started as he lay down on my bed. He stared at the ceiling with his arms stretched behind his head and his stomach peeking out the bottom of his button-up shirt. "I've already had one fight with her today. I just wanted to have a good time with you before she drops off Oliver."

I always had to hear about his former wife; I hated it. That's what I was, just a 'good time' to him? "You always do this. You never put me first!" I stomped through my bedroom into the bathroom. I needed to get away from him.

"I'm a father; I put my son first!" Amos, startled, sat with his ears perked up. "If you ever have children, you'll understand." His tone was sharp. He was no longer the 'British playboy,' but the headmaster of some stuffy, boarding school and I was his pupil. He made me feel like a child when I only wanted to be his equal.

I shied away to the doorway of my bedroom, trying to plan my escape. I didn't even want to be in the apartment with him. How could he be so cruel? Our relationship was a rollercoaster of emotions.

"You know I didn't mean it, love. Come here." He patted my duvet. I wasn't sure if I should go to him, or go to the kitchen and hope he would leave. John's eyes drew me in. They were warm and inviting. It always felt like a trick, so he'd get his way.

I went to him as I always did. I prioritized his feelings above my own. He never put me first. I often wondered if I was ever enough for him.

As I laid down beside him, he stroked my back. His hand worked down my thighs and back up my stomach. I knew what he wanted, but I wasn't about to give into him. When he sensed that he was not getting any action from me, he sat up in a huff.

"You know, I think I'm just going to go. I've had a long day and I'm sure Oliver and I will squabble over homework when he comes over."

"You don't have to leave."
"You don't seem to want my company." He got up and started to collect his wallet and cellphone. He was making his way to the exit.

"That's hardly fair! Sorry, I'm not in the mood. You just took out your problems on me!"

"That's what I get for picking a childish girl like you! I don't need two uptight women in my life!" His rage echoed as he slammed the door of my apartment and left.

Amos cowered in his bed and reluctantly made his way to me, his tail gently wagging, trying to determine if I wanted his affection. I surely did; Amos had undying love for me. Good days, and bad days, Amos was always there for me. I nudged him with my nose, and he licked my face as if to say, 'everything will be alright.'

I left my apartment and went for a walk to get a burger for dinner. No romantic meal meant that I'd have to fend for myself this evening. It hadn't even been an hour since John had left. I felt a buzzing in my pocket.

John: X

Nice try, I thought. There's no way I'm speaking to you after that ordeal.

When I got home, Amos was waiting for me. He raced to the door when he heard my key in the lock. I went to the kitchen to microwave the burger and frenchfries. Extra ketchup was also needed to balance the salt of the takeaway.

I sat cross legged on the couch and found some trashy, reality television to watch as I ate my dinner. Amos sat on the floor in front of me, patiently waiting for a fry to slip out of my hands and onto the floor. I'd glance down at my obedient bestie and toss him an end. He'd gobble up the greasy goodness and wait for the other shoe to drop. This was our regular routine, a little extra treat for a very good boy.

John: How long will u stay mad at me? X

Forever, I thought.

An hour went by, and another text arrived.

John: You know, you're so very special to me. X

How about an apology? I wasn't giving in. He hurt my feelings. He cancelled our date. He wanted intimacy from me. He left and he scared me and Amos. This wasn't okay.

Amos and I got ready for bed. I let Amos snuggle in my bed as I didn't want to be alone. My screen lit up one last time that night.

John: Guess it's over between us? You don't want me anymore.

This was something, much later, I'd understand to be a manipulation tactic. I, however, didn't recognize that at the time. Instead, I panicked. I didn't want it to be over; I loved John! I wanted to be his wife and Oliver's stepmom, when the time was right.

Poppy: It's not over. Don't be mad at me.

John: I was never mad at u. X

John: See u tomorrow at work. Bright n' early!

Poppy: Goodnight.

John: X

The next day at work, there was a bright bouquet of purple and pink flowers on my desk. The smell was intoxicating, signifying a fresh new start, but how many fresh starts can you give for bad behaviours? He had a pattern, and flowers couldn't solve everything.

The truth was, I felt childish and insecure – I wanted John to build a future with me and that image was slowly fading away. I felt like I was a background character in his life and that made me feel uncertain. I grasped at the flower stems, the proverbial olive branch, to stay in his life.

"Special occasion?" Casey asked as she filed her nails.

"No, not sure who they're from," I lied, pretending to investigate the bouquet for a card.

John emerged from his office. "Beautiful arrangement. Who's the lucky fellow?"

"Secret admirer, I imagine." I blushed.

"When you have a minute, Poppy, I'd like if you could help with some dictation in my office.

"Sure, I'll be right there." I adjusted my mini skirt and headed towards John's office. Casey's eyes followed me and lowered when I closed the door.

"Let's pick up where we left off last night," John said and grazed my leg above the hem of my skirt. It was the same old song we'd play like a broken record. Even a favourite song gets played on repeat, even if it makes you feel sad.

Chapter Eight

Our love affair flourished for a grand total of two months before it came to a crashing halt. The countdown was on. Everything is 20/20 in hindsight, as they say. The rose-coloured glasses finally came off.

Casey's and my workdays continued as they always had. She'd sneak over to my desk to discuss the latest gossip of the day, or what gross things her friend Deb was observing in the emergency department. Today, there was an eye superglued shut, buttocks bite marks from someone's ferocious house cat, and something about a turkey baster both of us couldn't figure out. Needless to say, we were cracking up laughing at the misfortune of others. I was glad that those incidents had nothing to do with me.

After Casey and I enjoyed our daily jokes, I sat at my desk, minding my own business. The weekly appointments had to be notified, but I could barely make the calls since my cell was buzzing due to a sexy accountant on the other side of the closed door.

John: Love the lipstick, come show me closer.
Poppy: Conducting serious business. Behave yourself.
John: That's my line! You're lucky I find you ....marvelous ☺
Poppy: Stop it ☺
John: What tiny knickers are you wearing today? Plz say none!
Poppy: Grannys!

Suddenly, a void of silence came between us. For ten minutes, I hadn't received a message. At first, I thought that he'd finally given up and let me go back to work. That was until I heard yelling from the other side of his office door. The commotion was so loud, Casey and I paused to look at each other, and some clients peered from over top of their magazines in the waiting room.

I slowly got up from my chair and tiptoed towards John's office. I put my ear against the door, a very reliable communication trick. Unfortunately, most of what was going on was muffled and I had to strain to hear.

A few minutes later, there was silence again. My desk phone rang. "You need to leave the office," John panted on the other side of the line.

"What're you talking about?" I couldn't understand what the fuss was about. I looked around in panic, wondering if there was a fire or an emergency of some sort. Everything seemed copasetic.

"She knows. My wife is coming to the office. Please, Poppy, I beg you, leave now! It's going to get ugly." He was breathing so hard, he was out of breath. "Apparently, she has been getting copies of our texts forwarded to her. I'd run for the hills if I were you!" John's voice was raised an octave I hadn't heard before. He genuinely sounded scared.

I was confused, as this was supposed to be his soon to be ex-wife. I said, "What does it matter? You're getting divorced." I thought I could assuage his mind.

There was a pause on the line. He said, "Well, we've been talking about the divorce and it's going to be too hard on poor Oliver. We're going to give our marriage another go," he confessed. A cacophony of emotions pulsated through me.

I felt like I'd been hit in the chest with the heavy stapler on John's desk. I was confused. When did this happen? Why did this happen? Right now, it really didn't matter. I didn't want my hide skinned. Before I knew it, I was running out of the building. I jumped down the front steps, landing flatly on the pavement. Just as I thought I was making a good get away, something held me back. Without gaining a good view, I wailed my arms and legs, ready to fight as though the real Mrs. Daniels had me in a boxing match over our shared man.

I realized that I was alone and not fighting for my sweetheart, the bastard. I was struggling to stand up. I was on the concrete, tangled in my clothing. What I didn't realize was that I'd caught my shoe in that damn grate again. It was like the universe was trying to tell me, 'don't work here; it's going to bite you in the ass.' And it did. I tugged with all my might and the heel broke, destroying the shoe. Serves me right.

I made it home safely and dove under the covers of my bed when the phone rang. I avoided answering it out of fear that it was Mrs. Daniels. The phone rang and rang, persisting for fifteen minutes. Finally, I caved and answered it.

"Hello?" I whispered cautiously. Sweat formed on my forehead.

"What the hell happened?" Casey screeched at the other end of the line. "As soon as you left, some mad woman came in looking for your blood. I told her I didn't have a clue who you were. Mr. Daniels came out and they had a big screaming match in the waiting room. Security had to drag her out. She said she would come back to 'talk' to you. Personally, I think she's going to kill you." I heard Casey's nails tapping on her desk in the background and the squeaking of her chair as she spun side to side. She was ready for me to spill the tea. I wasn't sure if I could trust her with the full information; I'd hidden a lot from her given the circumstances.

Great, just what I needed: a special 'talk' with my lover's wife. This was never supposed to happen. How did it get so messy? Damn, John! What the hell was he thinking, getting involved with me if he was still married? What the hell was I thinking, getting involved, and then, going back to him? What a conundrum.

"So, are you going to fill me in on you and the sexy nerd?" I almost heard the sly smile cross her face. She likely knew already; perhaps, we weren't that clever at hiding it.

"No, there is nothing to tell. Not anymore." It needed to end, now more than ever.

"Come on, we share everything!" Casey whined on the other end of the line. I needed to either give in or shut her up. My options were limited.

"Not this one. Sorry," I sniffled, trying to conceal my pain. I wanted this conversation to be over so that I could snuggle with Amos. He always made me feel better. Amos was my true 'ride or die.'

"Okay, but if you change your mind..." Casey trailed off. We said our goodbyes and I assured her I would check in with her later.

After hanging up, all I could do was cry. When I didn't cry, I tore up every love note he ever wrote me and threw the latest bouquet of flowers into the garbage. I couldn't stand to look at them. I could've sworn someone stabbed me in the stomach and continuously twisted the knife. The pain of my heartache radiated throughout my body. I felt used and useless. I'd no idea what I'd done to myself. I was back at square one, again.

The next day, I called in sick to work. Sick as in 'sick to death someone was going to pulverize me over top of my desk.' I was conflicted whether I'd done something wrong; my moral compass was spinning out of control. John told me that it was over with her. He told me they were getting divorced. He told me not to worry about her. Then, he told me they were calling off the divorce. He lied to me.

My meddling mom somehow caught wind of my sick day and decided to come over to tend to me. Damn, she still had her key. Why hadn't I taken it away?

"So, what illness do you have to warrant being off sick? You need to be punctual, so you don't lose this one," my mom chirped as we sat on my sofa drinking lemon tea. Amos snuggled on my lap, fast asleep. His snores, while usually annoying, were comforting.

"It's not that kind of sick, mom. I'm heartbroken." I lowered my voice, ashamed.

"Oh, honey, who is it?" she asked as she smoothed the embroidered butterflies sewn to her shirt. A look of concern crossed her face.

"No one you know. No one you'll ever meet. I'm just not happy anymore. I need a change." I sulked.

"What do you want to do? What will make you happy?" Mom asked as she patted my leg. Amos roused momentarily from his slumber only to fall back asleep after repositioning.

The unfortunate part of this was that I really didn't know. John had been a huge focus in my life. He'd given me a chance at a job that I enjoyed. For once, I felt as though I could accomplish anything. Being involved with him romantically made me feel alive. Now, those feelings had passed, and utter fear and shame took its place. Happiness came so quickly and was snatched away in an instant.

I couldn't tell my mom the truth even though she is so sweet and supportive. I was a home wrecker; how could I tell her that? He's the one who pursued me, despite having to answer to his ex-wife, or current wife; I truly couldn't keep up anymore. I couldn't help but accept some of the blame. I needed a breather. I needed to get out of Toronto for a while so that I could figure out who I was and what I wanted out of my life.

"Maybe I should go on a vacation. Just for a little while," I suggested. In the back of my mind, I pondered where it was I should go.

"That sounds lovely. Amos can stay with us; I'm sure he'd love it – right Amos?" He snuggled up against my mom, begging for her to pet him. Amos wagged his tail approvingly. My mom rang my dad and discussed the new plan. Tonight, I would decide where I would go and say my farewells to those who needed to know. I'd leave as soon as possible. The guilt swirled in my stomach like a flushing toilet bowl. I knew it was the right thing for me, and the right thing for everyone. It was time to get the passport out and go abroad.

Chapter Nine

Seven days, 20 texts from John with no reply from myself, and three phone calls from Casey later, I was ready to leave. My plane ticket was printed, and my bags were packed. There was nothing tying me to this job or to this city.

I had called my brother, Myles, a few days before to tell him about my trip to Southeast Asia. "Hey, punk," he greeted me on the phone, much as he'd done when we were kids. He'd gone with some friends a few years ago and I wanted his input.

"Where are you thinking of going?" he asked over the line.

"Well, I joined a backpacking trip. We start in Thailand and work our way to Malaysia, Singapore, and Indonesia." I shared some of the highlights of the itinerary. I recalled him telling me in the past, when he went travelling, to never go alone – there was always safety in numbers.

Myles told me tales of mischief and near misses of his own adventures in Southeast Asia. I heard the excitement in his voice when he talked about the spicy Pad Thai and the glistening ocean views. As big brothers do, he offered warnings, too.

"As much fun as traveling is, always be mindful of your belongings and never accept a tuk tuk; those things are total scams," he warned. I tried my best to take my big brother's advice since he was always looking out for his little sister.

My stomach lurched with emotions. I was excited to leave, but I also had to say goodbye and close the chapter on John so I could start a new chapter of self-discovery.

Early Friday morning, I went into the office before opening. First, my intentions were to toilet paper John's office but then, I decided against it. I needed closure, but I wasn't sure how to get it. One way was to write John a note to tell him goodbye. I struggled to find the right words but eventually, I settled on a simple explanation that I couldn't be around him anymore and I needed to leave. He could replace me as I wasn't coming back. I gently folded the note and tucked it under his computer keyboard. I took one last glimpse of his family. The photo frame now had a cracked sheet of glass across their picture-perfect family. I exhaled and the weight I was carrying came off my shoulders, knowing that leaving would be good for everyone and acknowledging that I hurt someone I don't even know.

After I left his office, I began to pack my things from

my desk. A few photos of Amos and a funny drawing of Casey and I got tossed into a bag. As I turned to leave, someone was standing between me and the door. The tall flesh of a woman towered above me; the same way we met was the same way we'd say goodbye.

"Running away are you?" Casey stood with her arms crossed and her body tense. Her warm tan, wrap dress clung to her body just as disapprovingly as her attitude towards me.

"I'm not running away." I continued to pack my belongings. "What're you doing here so early anyways? Thought you wrote in the morning?" I wanted to get my things and get out before John came in. I knew it was his day to take Oliver to school.

"That was put on hold today because I had to come in and review Mr. Evan's files for his meeting this morning. I don't think that man would survive without me. But back to the important question; why are you leaving me?" Casey pouted and her red lips almost reached down to the floor. She always had on a different lip colour to match her outfit.

"I'm looking for what's going to make me happy." I turned to face her, unsure if she understood the seriousness of the situation. The belongings were packed and ready to go. I just wanted to get out of the office. It was taunting me and tearing my heart in two.

"I want you to be happy here with me! We were just getting to know each other better. I'm going to miss our silly antics."

"I'll soon be replaced, and you'll have another friend

to play with." I tried to make a joke, but Casey's mood wouldn't lighten up. It was her turn to be sad.

"Actually no, some old broad will be replacing you. Mr. Daniels' wife is concerned about him banging another secretary. He's on close observation." Casey leaned in and in a hushed voice said, "In fact, Mrs. Daniels started random checks to keep her husband in line. Somewhat like a warden on jail rounds!" We both burst out laughing. "I guess he deserves it. No offense." She blushed. She still didn't know the whole story and she didn't need to know right now. Years later, I would find out that I was one of several women John bedded while he was married. He'd a history of playing this old trick on a lot of innocent women.

"None taken." I raised my hands in surrender. "Next time, I'll wait until the ink has dried on the divorce papers. I just had to try, you know?"

"I know. There won't be another you." Tears welled in our eyes.

Casey and I hugged as we said our goodbyes. I left the office feeling slightly more at peace than I had the last few days. There would always be another job when I returned. I would leave my troubles behind for another day. Adventure awaits!

Three hours later, I was on a flight to Hong Kong. It was a stone's throw away from Bangkok, Thailand, which was the first stop on my journey. I welcomed the gourmet meals and every complimentary, tiny bottle of wine offered to me. My glass flowed steadily with booze for almost the entire flight. I'd seen nearly every new release movie. I felt relaxed and ready to take on the world. What luxury I'd been missing out on!

After a smooth landing, we disembarked at the airport. Hong Kong International Airport was one of the largest and busiest airports in the world. It was a maze of terminals, haute couture designer clothing stores, restaurants, and a movie theatre, of all things. I'd felt as though I was at a mall rather than an airport. I spent hours exploring before my connecting flight.

Moving sidewalks transported passengers to their terminals and carts motored along, transporting luggage and workers. Airline attendants marched in unison in their glamourous attire, their hats perfectly pinned into place. Scarves flowed against their lightly perfumed bodies. They looked like they belonged in old Hollywood movies. Everyone cleared a respectful path when they saw them coming in formation. A happy flight crew meant a happy flight. I wondered where everyone was going and what journey they were starting, or completing. I wondered if they were content in their lives.

The light shone on my face through the gigantic skylights, awakening my tired soul. Jetlag had set in and maybe the aftereffects of the wine. Following a moment of rejuvenation, I lugged my day bag with me to the different stores, looking for treats and comforts. After settling with a familiar coffee brand, I sat at my terminal and waited for my plane.

One of the most exciting things about travelling is people watching. As I sipped my coffee, I saw fellow passengers talk with their loved ones, checking their boxes stuffed with food as well as other treasures, and others sitting quietly like me. In a deserted corner, there was a small group of people who were performing Tai Chi. I was comforted by the soft and fluid movements of their bodies. How beautifully people let themselves be free, wide open and out there, a feeling I longed to have.

When the time came, we were motioned to board the plane. Foreign languages alerted us to gather overhead. Standing uniformly in a line, the flight crew checked our tickets and passports, ensuring that those who were headed to Bangkok and those headed to Mumbai, were all boarding on time. Our plane would make two stops, and I'd be getting off at the first.

The second vessel was not as glamorous as the first. The seats appeared crowded and squished together. The plane was older, judging by the stained panels, outdated fabrics on the seats, and the noticeable lack of television screens. The noise and volume of people was overwhelming. I couldn't understand why there was so much turmoil. People had hardened expressions on their faces, and their eyebrows were furrowed. Skin as firm as stone that a smile couldn't possibly form without cracking the surface. People were yelling at their loved ones in unfamiliar tongues and gesturing towards luggage. My pulse began to race as I struggled to find ways to connect to those around me. There was a lot of content lost, but I tried my best to read their body language.

I slinked down into my seat and did up my belt. I may've said a few Hail Marys, just in case. Again, religion or spirituality can be helpful in times like these. As soon as the overhead safety instructions began, the passengers took their seats and sat quietly. Suddenly, my pulse returned to normal, and I looked around to see what was going on. It felt eerily quiet for the noise to stop so suddenly. I realized that I was experiencing some culture shock. All was calm again when everyone hunkered down in their seats, turning on their electronics or their music. As we took off into the night sky, I relaxed again and stared at the moon's reflection into the ocean below. In a few short hours, I would arrive at my destination and hopefully find the release that I was longing for.

Chapter Ten

Unknown Number: Darling, I miss you.
Message undeliverable.
Unknown Number: Let's chat. Maybe we can be together after all. It might not be the way we expected but I think we can make it work.
Message undeliverable.
Unknown Number: X
Message undeliverable.

Chapter Eleven

For several hours, I couldn't get comfortable. The humidity on the plane, the nattering of couples around me, and the lack of entertainment got on my last nerve. To add insult to injury, my knees dug into the seat in front of me. My seatmate laid his heavy head on my shoulder. Beads of his sweat dampened my shirt. I groaned in retaliation. We were two strangers, but his concept of personal space failed him. His snoring could've woken the dead. All I could do was reflect while I was trapped in my own personal hell.

Maybe I'd been too hard on myself the last few months. I wasn't hard enough on John. That prick deserved what was coming to him. Karma, she's a bitch. You're only as good as the information you're provided. He provided me no information about his wife at the start. I hadn't even known he was married! I kicked myself for remaining with him once I found out the truth. I shouldn't have continued when I knew they had not yet divorced. My heart was in too deep. How do you stop when you think you have the world in your hands?

I had been thinking about my self-worth, and that well had run dry. Sure, I fell for John, but I wasn't the only guilty party. I had a poor start at my career in the medical office. I made mistakes. I managed not to make many screw ups in my accounting job. And I managed to make a new friend, aside from my romance. That was a success! Why hadn't a job and friendship been enough? Why did I need to ruin it with a kiss? Because I didn't feel like I was enough until a man said I was enough. I boiled in frustration.

I wanted to be wanted, physically, but it should never have been at the workplace. I should've met a man at a post-bar brawl in the streets, like Casey suggested many a Friday night. Instead, I was lounging in bed imagining a fake life with a con man. He told me sweet lies to get between my sheets among other things.

Should I ever trust another man again? Should I just learn to trust myself and be enough for me? Being a lone wolf isn't bad, is it? There were too many questions and now was not the time to find all the answers.

Eventually, the humming of the engines cast me to sleep. I dreamed that I was in Thailand, on the beach. I imagined I was floating in the ocean with the sun beating down on my face. I felt the pearls of condensation from a fresh cold beer in my hand and heard, "Miss, you have to get off of the plane. We landed ten minutes ago. You're last. Get your stuff. We leave for Mumbai in five minutes. Go now!" An angry Thai flight attendant hovered over me.

Okay, okay, I'm done floating in the imaginary ocean! I didn't need to towel off, but I did need to get the hell off the plane. I grabbed my belongings and headed into the airport. On the moving sidewalk, I whizzed past groups of Thai girls laughing and greeting loved ones, kids chasing the random street dogs who snuck into the airport, and tourists, as well as business folks, heading to their next destination. I searched for the luggage carrousel. In the distance, I saw my big, red, touring backpack lurching on the ancient belt. The luggage danced in circles like a happy puppy waiting for its owner. My worldly possessions made their way to where I stood. I heaved my world over my shoulder and headed for the exit.

When I got outside, the air was dry and warm. It was the wee hours of the morning and the sun had yet to rise. I couldn't possibly imagine how much hotter it would become. Smells of cooking meat and spice loomed in the air beside the taxi stand. A man had set up a makeshift grill to cook for the tourists and taxi drivers awaiting their transportation. People stood around, dining on kebabs of barbequed meats. I was bombarded by a group of short, Thai men raising their hands and angrily speaking to me, "You want a taxi? I take you to the hotel. I give you the best price!" When ten men are shouting the same thing to you, particularly when you've just roused from a pleasant dream, reality feels harsh. As I scanned the crowd, I picked the gentleman with the biggest smile and who was bothering me the least; this trait would become the gold standard for the rest of the trip. He took my bag and hoisted it into the trunk with a loud thud. "Little woman, heavy bag." He made kind eyes as if he was trying to connect with me. I nodded sleepily and got in the back of the car.

After he asked me for the hotel's address, we were off. The airport was outside of the city centre, so we drove for what felt like an hour. We passed decrepit shacks, which I later learned were houses for people whose money was scarce. Social assistance was not necessarily provided here, and folks had to fend for themselves. We passed markets with the fresh catch of the day, stalls with plastic bags filled with cold beverages, and crates full of plump fruit all muted under the morning sun. There were endless stalls of men hanging fish on hooks, haggling with old women who got up early to come to the market to determine what they were having for dinner.

As we continued our journey into the city, we passed stray dogs by the dozen chasing each other in the street. We shared the road with families piled strategically on motorcycles, waving at us as we sped by. Men on their colourful bicycles heading to work wove in between cars. A group of tuk tuk drivers enjoyed their morning coffee under what small patch of shade they would claim for the day.

As we continued to drive, we eventually got closer to the city and the landscape dramatically changed. There were dozens of convenience stores, which I later learned would provide an excess of air conditioning and perfectly preserved chocolate bars. One must always sample the local fairs. There were rundown businesses nestled between apartment buildings. Modern skyscrapers sat next door to ancient buildings, two worlds one never thought would collide. The common outfit woven between all these features were the graffiti covered walls and torn bedsheets used as curtains that flowed out of select windows into the streets. There was something sad, yet very beautiful, about this city. I had only begun to scratch the surface.

We began to slow down, and my driver signalled to go down an alley. This couldn't be the correct stop. He pushed the buzzer, said some inaudible words, and the gate creaked open. We slowly proceeded down the alleyway and stopped in front of a hotel. The building emerged above us, cast in a dull, golden light. I sighed, relieved. The bellhop dressed in a yellow and red uniform jumped out of the doorway and ran down the side of the pool, which lined the front walkway, to retrieve my bag. I tipped my driver and thanked him for the ride. Finally, I had arrived.

While the building did not seem to be anything special, the room sure was. There were two queen-sized beds, gold-framed mirrors, a mini bar filled with familiar soda from home but in Thai writing, and prawn-flavoured chips! What delicacies. I couldn't wait to explore more but my tired eyes grew heavy. I managed to squeeze in a short nap before I got ready to explore the city. I still felt jetlagged, but I decided to push through and get used to the change in time zones.

As I cleaned up and got dressed, my heart began to thump. I was doing familiar things but in an unfamiliar place. I suddenly felt a sense of panic that I was a fish out of water. I didn't know the city and although I knew what I wanted to do, I didn't know how to navigate the strange, new world. I closed my eyes and tried to relax. "You got this," I told myself out loud. My breathing started to slow. I sat on my bed and opened my eyes. I looked around me and told myself that I came here for a reason. There was nothing to fear.

After catching my breath, I decided to listen to my inner voice. I wanted to see some temples today and damn it, I was going to. I found my confidence, grabbed my day bag, and headed downstairs. I asked the bellboy for a city map. He asked me where I wanted to go, and I said Wat Traimit. He looked at me, cast a side eye and scooted away. I heard the swish of his starched uniform as he made his way across the lobby. I waited for him, taking in the tropical pink, floral arrangements, and the never-ending supply of Buddha statues. It took a few minutes, but eventually the bellboy returned. He was not empty handed. Instead of a map, he had returned with a woman who was about my age.

"She's going to the market." He pointed to the stranger. "You're going to the temple." He pointed to me. "Go together and don't get lost." He was rather presumptuous that we would accept this blind date. We looked at each other, shrugged, and said, why not. We both introduced ourselves and hoisted bags on our backs. The bellboy beamed at his matchmaking skills.

"I'm Jane, from Australia. I'm headed to Northern Thailand with a group at the hotel. We meet up tonight." She extended her hand to shake mine. Loose strands from her blonde ponytail were frizzy from the humidity. Her skin was perfectly sun kissed, likely from the Australian climate. She had a dew of sweat forming around her forehead. Perhaps the climate here was a little warmer than she was used to.

"I'm Poppy. I think I'm with the same tour company, but I'm traveling Southeast Asia for the next month." We spoke for the next fifteen minutes about who we were and what we were planning to do on our trips. This was my first trip away from home and I felt intimidated in the company of a much more experienced traveller. My inexperience left me feeling as if I was left out of a club I hadn't yet joined.

My jean shorts had begun to stick to me. This exotic heat was suffocating, and it was only the late morning. The best part about travelling to a warm climate is that it's summer year-round. I picked the best time to leave Canada as spring was just creeping in from a winter's slumber. The downfall of being here was that I was not used to the temperature. It would take time to acclimatize.

The Australian and I mapped out our route, got acquainted with the city subway transit, and left the refuge of the air-conditioned lobby. As we made our way through the revolving glass doors, passing the plumes of jasmine incense, we waved goodbye to our bellboy. In planning today's journey, we agreed to go to Jane's market first and then back through the city to the temple I wanted to see. I had figured out how to get there on the map and felt confident in my navigation skills.

When we arrived at the market, we marvelled at the hundreds of vendors, unsure of where to start. There were rows of coconut water in plastic bags, glistening with condensation. The scent of grilled meats wafted in the air. Chunks of fresh fruit were skillfully being chopped with sharp knives for those who were watching the impromptu cooking shows. This was definitely a different version of fast food. I spent my change and feasted as we shopped. Jane and I took a minute to hide from the sun under the shade of a random umbrella. We savoured the local foods. We laughed as pineapple juice dripped down our chins. We bought bags of fruit cocktails and tried to wash the mobile courses down through the bottom of clear, plastic, lunch bags. We ate like royalty for next to nothing.

As we continued our walkabout, we passed stalls with knockoff label clothing, decorative masks, and woven baskets. In addition, there were stalls of beaded and wood-carved necklaces. People chased us down the road to haggle with us and see how much we'd pay. I didn't buy anything, but Jane was eager to get souvenirs for her friends. She felt sheepish at first to try to talk people down in cost, but eventually, she was arguing right back to the vendors. The corners of their mouths rose in a knowing look that she understood the game of haggling.

After we roamed around and felt satisfied with our stop, it was back to the subway and to China Town.

When we arrived at the second closest stop to the temple, Jane and I decided to walk. We might as well peek at what was being offered. Much of the same was seen in this area as we perused the shops. In addition to what we saw earlier, there was more fresh meat hanging in the open windows of the butchers, dried shrimps, and other interesting sea life that left a lingering smell. The scent polluted the streets and stuck to my clothes. I was sure it tasted great, but I wasn't brave enough to try it. Shop owners hung outside the window of their stores and lazily waited for customers to pop in, chasing no one.

We walked for about an hour through the hordes of people, careful to mind our bags from potential theft. I thought back to my conversation with Myles when I told him about my trip. He said pickpocketing was the second biggest issue next to tuk tuk scams. The blazing sun above us rose the sweltering temperature to forty degrees Celsius. I felt like my skin was melting.

"Are we close, Poppy? My feet are killing me, and I have to meet my group this evening," Jane almost whined. I still had an extra day, so I had no rush to go back to the hotel. I needed to remind myself to be more considerate to her.

We found a corner out of the crowd to pause and orient ourselves. "Let me get out my map to see." I unfolded the moist, crinkled map from my pocket; the edges of the map had turned into pulp. "Just down the street. Five more minutes," I informed her. The truth was, we were barely into China Town. And those five minutes quickly escalated into thirty.

As the sun blazed, we continued to trek, but our pace became slower and slower. Jane's blonde ponytail turned downward, and the ends of her hair were wet and plastered to the back of her neck. Finally, we saw the sign for the temple. "Thank, goodness!" Jane exclaimed. We paid our entrance fee and sat in silence, in the shade, admiring the beauty of the sights.

Towering around us was a sparkling, white temple. It almost felt like a mirage. The temple was adorned in terracotta red accents and topped with gold peaks. The twin staircase led us up to a shaded, massive, golden, cross-legged Buddha nearly five meters in height. Incense burned, offering a calm peace to each person present. It felt as though we were being offered an invitation to reflect. There was a small gathering of Thai men praying. Other tourists and I tried to keep quiet so we wouldn't interrupt their conversations with their higher being. Although I'm not Thai, I felt it was an opportunity to have a spiritual connection and to appreciate the values and beliefs of another religion. In the presence of Buddha, a figure I'd learned much about, I felt a momentary peace wash over me. I couldn't help but feel that I was being watched over and blessed with good fortune.

The time at Wat Traimit was short lived. Although we took the long path to get here, we had to head back to the hotel for Jane's meeting. Our feet and lower backs ached, so we decided to take a tuk tuk back to the hotel. A man with a toothless grin, driving a small, red tuk tuk, was waved down by Jane. He pulled up and jumped out of the contraption. He was dressed in green overalls, with barely a drop of sweat on him. He asked us where we were going. After Jane informed him where we were staying, he loaded our bags into the vehicle and started to drive us to our temporary home. I hadn't clued into what we were doing.

The motorized vehicle looked like a tin box on wheels with no doors or seatbelts. The red paint was faded, and sharp edges of rust encompassed the entrance into the vessel. Board at your own risk; I was glad I got a tetanus shot before the holiday.

I thought nothing of it as he seemed so kind and helpful, "but that's how they get you" I could hear Myles telling me, but I felt that this ride back to the hotel was legit. I put these thoughts of caution in the back of my head for a second. I was happy to sit down instead of having to walk back in this sweltering heat. I was pulled out of my trance when the driver said, "On the way to the hotel, we'll make a quick stop at a friend's shop. Jade makes a good gift." My smile began to fade. My eyes sprang open. I had fallen for it.

"Oh, no, sir, we just want to go to the hotel," Jane confirmed from our earlier conversation. She wiped the sweat from her forehead with her shirtsleeve. She'd expressed that she didn't want to be late for her group meeting this evening and at this point in the afternoon, she was getting anxious about arriving back on time.

"No, we go to the shop and then to the Tourist Authority to get a good deal on things to do tomorrow," our driver sternly stated as he continued. The rickety, red tuk tuk swayed on the uneven street, much like our fraying temper.

"No, sir," I stated, "we want to go to the hotel. Now!" I shifted forward in the seat, upset that he wouldn't listen.

"Two quick stops, then the hotel," he stated with an amused expression. As if this was a joke, he laughed. The tuk tuk trucked along, the engine making a sad, puttering noise as if it was almost out of gas.

In a sudden, whirlwind motion, Jane took off her shoe and knocked the driver on the shoulder with it just as he was about to take us down a deserted alley. Her instinct kicked in, afraid that something bad would happen to us. I was shocked and yet very appreciative of her insights. I was relieved after our tuk tuk came to a stop. She and I scrambled to collect our belongings and then, we shot down the street like lightening with a new sense of energy, not wanting to die on the first day of our trip.

"Hey! Give me money for the ride!" he shouted after us as he stumbled around in confusion. Jane threw a fistful of Thai Bahts at him, which amounted to less than a dollar. This was exactly what my brother had warned me about. Myles had forbidden me from travelling on my own, unless I went with a group. This warning was for events like these. Didn't I feel sheepish? I thought the toothless man was going to take us back to the hotel, but he wanted us to fall for his scheme. How was I going to last the next month when I couldn't handle being here a day?

When we got back to the hotel, we were exhausted, and Jane was a few minutes late for her meeting, but we were relieved we had made it back to the hotel lobby. The familiar surroundings, and most importantly, the air conditioning, were welcomed. Luckily, Jane's group was still waiting in the lobby and cheered as she entered. A greeting, I hoped, that would find me tomorrow night. We gave each other one last wave and headed our separate ways. I went to my room, exhausted, waiting to take on the next day. I collapsed on my bed until the sunlight of the next day began to break.

Chapter Twelve

When I awoke, the temperature was a scorching 43 degrees Celsius. I wasn't sure if I would ever get used to this. My pale skin had already formed a light tan yesterday. I'd need to invest in another bottle of sunscreen and an endless supply of water at this rate. I rolled around in bed, trying to find the cool side of the pillowcase before I got up for the day.

The plan for the next several hours was to take the river boat and scan the temples close to the water's edge. I got dressed in my most comfortable and sweat-resistant clothing, which was limited, I'll admit. I pumped up my self-confidence once more and headed downstairs. I strolled through the lobby, nodding at the bellboy, and made my way solo through the front doors of the hotel. I didn't need a chaperone today.

As I drifted down the street, I felt my shoulders rise and a smile donned my face. I walked confidently past men who offered tuk tuk rides; not today, scammers! The men didn't seem phased at my rejection and continued their discussions with the other drivers relaxing under a shaded tree. One foot in front of the other, I made my way; today, like every other day, for the rest of my life.

I walked past store fronts lined with fresh yellow and pink fruit marinating in their own juices. I stopped momentarily to gather supplies. Along the way, I passed fancy hotels that felt out of place for the rundown area of the city. I continued down a tiny path from the main street, which led me to a dock for the river transportation. You wouldn't think you were headed to a boat terminal based on this humble, little, dirt path. The river boat sat perched in the murky, brown water of the Chao Phraya River. The worn vessel bobbed in the water, waiting for the next group to board. It cost mere cents to ride. This acted like public transportation along the waterfront of the city, and was a safer way to get around compared to yesterday's events. The whistle blew, indicating that we would be pulling away from the dock to make our way along the river. After a brief ride onboard, I started my search for the Emerald Buddha.

Not far from the river's edge was the Grand Palace and Wat Phra Kaew, the Temple of the Emerald Buddha. It was free to enter for the Thai people and foreigners paid a small fee. When visiting the temples, it's important to be respectful. Women were given the opportunity to take scarves to cover their shoulders and legs out of respect.

The magnificent property was home not just to this Buddha, but was also strewn with white buildings outlined in golden trim, sparkling in the sun like gems. The blue sky beyond the temples only enhanced their beauty. Colourful roofs reached up high, making the structures stand almost as tall as the heavens. Buddha and praying bowls were like hidden treasures for those who dared venture inside. Intricate, coloured statues stood guard outside as if to launch an attack if provoked. As I walked around, I was led down perfectly manicured gardens. Rainbow scarves waved in the gentle breeze from their perch outside the entryways. They helped cloak the mats filled with shoes as people paid their respects. It took hours to walk around the property to take it all in.

I took breaks to sit cross-legged in the gardens and scroll through my camera photos to see if I took any masterpieces. The scent of roses filled the air, gently hugging those who lounged. I watched as tourists and families on an outing meandered around, peeking into windows, and taking selfies. It didn't happen unless it ends up on the internet, right?

As I began to set foot to find the coveted Emerald Buddha, the sky suddenly turned grey, and the rain poured down in sheets. People crowded together under various pergolas on the property, trying to shield themselves from the rain. In the rush to find shelter, I became surrounded by couples. Men shielded their partners with their jackets. They kissed and laughed as they took refuge from Mother Nature's rage. Being surrounded by these twosomes made me realize I was alone. I had had a somewhat happy coupling with John, but that quickly dissolved. I hadn't thought of him since I arrived. I was doing so well to put him in life's rear-view mirror.

After about fifteen minutes of reflective thinking, the angry rain stopped, and the clouds disappeared. People took their chances and began to roam the property once more. It felt almost poetic that I was alone and surrounded by lovers only to be left alone again. Perhaps this was a sign that focusing on me was my main priority.

I set out to find the Buddha. I had to search around the property for this carefully hidden treasure. I finally found the statue, as evidenced by a long line up outside of one of the temples. Once I got to the front of the line, I tried to get on my tiptoes to look into the small window. You were only allowed to look at the Emerald Buddha from a faraway spot. Other tourists were being sneaky and trying to put their cameras as close as they could without being caught for a better view of the golden, cloaked statue. You were not permitted to take photos, but people tried their damnedest to do so anyways. Being 5'5, it felt like a letdown as I couldn't see the thing. I finally gave up and searched for my shoes that I took off before entering. I ended up buying a postcard instead to make up for the disappointment.

Back on the road I went. This time, I ventured off to the neighbouring Reclining Buddha. So many Buddha, so little time. Visiting the home of the Reclining Buddha will bring you luck. Did I ever need luck now! This gigantic, 46-meter-long Buddha rested under the roof of a temple. You had the opportunity to roam around the statue while paying your respects. Some would wander and speak of the wishes they desired. The sound of chimes echoed in the silent space. The ever-familiar scent of jasmine filled the air. I would grow fond of it, and bring the scent home with me.

It took a good thirty minutes to circle the entire body. People formed a near single-file line and walked as if on a conveyer belt around the statue. I took my time and admired the feet of the Buddha, which were made of mother-of pearl with intricate swirls and etchings. After viewing the Buddha, and thinking about how I wanted my luck to change, I headed over to the 108 bowls along the wall, which are said to bring good luck. I took time to think about what I wanted for myself and other people as I placed coins in every few bowls. These were secrets I conspired to come true one day.

Escaping the sweltering hot sun was a lovely idea, but I knew that I had to continue my trek. I spent nearly the whole day exploring. It was getting late, and I still wanted to go to the Wat Arun and climb to the top for a good view of the city. I took my time to get to the boat and skipped across the river. Before I knew it, we docked, just in time for the setting sun.

I felt like an urban explorer. Signs were in a language I didn't understand and yet I was able to go to and fro on my own. I had conquered extraordinary new places the last couple days and learned about a culture I'd never been exposed to before. This was the beginning of a beautiful new confidence. I was an independent woman. Take that, Myles. That man has been trying to keep me safe since I was born, but a woman must learn somethings on her own.

Wat Arun sat on the bank of the river. As I studied it, it was clear that the temple was different from the previous temples I'd been to. It was darker in colour with one central peak. The fading daylight blanketed the cityscapes. Later that night, when the moon made its appearance, the temple would be covered in tiny, warm lights that made it stand out in the black backdrop of the night sky.

I made my way up and around the structure to the very top. I was out of breath, but I was excited for the vista. As I climbed, I passed colourfully decorated spirals, offering encouragement to continue my trek higher and higher. The steps of the temple were on a rather narrow, and slightly bent, curve. As I struggled to get my whole foot on the steps, a little bit would crumble beneath my feet. Pebbles made small cries as they landed below. Ancient paths are not always meant to be taken, it would seem.

When I arrived at the top, I forgot about the struggle to climb up, if only for just a few minutes, while I gazed over the city. I could see the tops of other temples that had emerged above the tree line. Scaffolding encased new buildings, which were being built amongst the older ones, taking up the skyline. The murky, brown river snaked through the city and faded out of sight. I had sat up there for a while, content with the day's events.

Carrying on, I made my descent down the stairs. Unfortunately, this was scarier than the way up. My heart sank as I realized how high up I was and how thin the steps of the temple seemed. The ground below zoomed into and out of view, much like in the movies. Heights are not my most favourite thing and I felt a rush of panic. I tried to get my footing to head down the steep stairs. With each step, I had to think twice as the narrow ledges seemed to weave into other tiers of the temple, making the trail to the bottom more terrifying. I'd be met at crossroads with other tourists suffering the same fate as myself. At one tier, I encountered a cute guy whose knees were knocking from anxiety.

"After you!" the Welsh tourist cautiously offered. His voice quivered. I saw the white knuckles form as his hands wrapped around the thin railing on the stairs. He was too frightened to continue the trek down, just like me. I assumed that he wanted to use me as a landing pad if he fell. I needed the confidence to take the first step and not tumble down the stairs – a metaphor in life, perhaps?

"No, after you; I insist!" I laughed as we were obviously too afraid to continue.

"Ladies first." He gestured with a quivering hand.

"You know, I wasn't raised to be old fashioned. No reason a gentleman like you has to wait for a lady." I smirked at him, challenging the patriarchy.

"Hey, now. Truthfully, I'm afraid of heights. I didn't realize that the temple was so tall, and these stairs," he gulped. I instantly felt bad. The man was trying to soothe his anxiety and I made him feel small.

"What's your name?" I asked, trying to offer a

distraction.

"Rhys. You?"

"Poppy." I surveyed the situation. "Tell you what, I'll go down first, and you may take my hand, okay?" The invisible olive branch was offered.

"Deal." After some slow maneuvering down the steps, we eventually made it down safely. We awkwardly shook hands before Rhys ran off to collect his dignity. After regaining my own composure, I decided that my day was done.

I hitched a ride on the river boat. The boat sank so low, the brown, sludgy water seeped in through the window cracks. People were ending their day and I was headed to my temporary home. Tonight, I would meet my travel companions for the next four weeks. I was excited and nervous for what lay ahead.

Chapter Thirteen

After returning to the hotel, I decided to have a shower and wash off some of the brown, river sludge that had made its way onto my body. As I rinsed, lathered, and repeated my hygiene ritual, I swore that the shower was cooler than the room I was in. When I stepped out, I decided to lie down on my bed and have a cat nap. Beads of sweat immediately formed on my body.

I'd set my alarm for 45 minutes, but when I awoke, my room was in total darkness. I sat up, startled, as I'd emerged from my slumber after longer than I'd anticipated. The sun had disappeared entirely, and the moon was slowly creeping in. I looked down at my watch with heavy eyes. The clock read 7:15pm. Holy, hell! I was late for my group meeting. I jumped into whatever clean clothing was at the top of my backpack.

I made my way to the lobby to see a group of people crowded around a single sofa. I huffed as I stopped in front of the large group and asked if this was the tour headed to Bali. Sitting on the coffee table, with his back to me, was a medium build man in oversized, beige, cargo shorts. He had a wet bandana cooling the base of his neck.

As I caught my breath, the man turned around and said, "Oh, YOU must be Poppy." His attitude stabbed me. So much for a good first impression.

"I'm so sorry. I feel asleep. This heat – " I trailed off, or more like cut off, by this bossy man.

"Yeah, everyone's hot. We've been sitting around waiting for you. The meeting started at 6pm." This man's words were sharp. He'd no time for my excuses.

"I'm so sorry. It won't happen again." I cowered to the back of the group. I felt like all eyes were on me. The last one here was the weakest of the pack. I felt embarrassed. The last thing I needed was for this group to hate me. The earlier confidence melted away.

"Always 'sorry' the lot of you. What're you, Canadian?" a female, English accent piped up from the back of the group, gesturing with her fingers as she said 'sorry.'

"Well, yes, I am," I mustered. My face reddened. Was there an issue with being sorry or for being Canadian?

"Then, instead of Poppy, we shall name you Maple." The woman peered her head through the crowd at me. Her short, brown hair fringed over her forehead. Her thick eyebrows arched up and down, making it harder for me to appreciate if she was joking or taunting me, perhaps both. More English people to try to navigate; I just finished running away from one!

"For those of you who missed the announcements, I'll review what we'll be doing over the next month," the buzz-cut man stated. Clearly, the comment was aimed at me. "My name's Paul Banks and I'll be your guide. Each evening, I'll let you know what will be in store the next day and what you'll need to prepare. Tonight, we'll have a short rest and pack our bags for a night train down to Southern Thailand. We'll be headed to the beach!" He roared, and the group cheered as we'd be enjoying sun, sand, and surf.

A night train, really? We just got here, and I hardly had any chance to sleep in a bed after my nearly 48-hour travel time. I was still jetlagged. When would the madness end? The last thing I wanted to do was to say goodbye to my air-conditioning and comfy linens!

"We really have to leave already? We can't leave tomorrow?" I queried. I felt myself sink into a sulk.

"First, she's late, then, she's sorry and now, she's unhappy," the English woman piped up. "Maple, go with the flow." A small number of people chuckled. My face reached a new shade of red.

"No need to be like that, guys," Mike, one of the travellers, interjected. He offered me a reassuring smile.

"Yes, Poppy, we're leaving at midnight. Buy some snacks and water. I suggest that you keep a daypack on you with a change of clothing and your valuables. The night trains are known for robberies, particularly targeted towards tourists," Paul stated, very factually. Clearly, this wasn't his first Thai rodeo.

I gulped in distress. Not only was I now having to pack my bag for an overnight train, but I may possibly get robbed. Wonderful. Just my luck, I'd be stranded in the middle of Thailand with no money or passport. The group may try to sacrifice me at this rate. They already seemed to be upset with me.

"We'll meet back here just before midnight. Bring your bags and don't be late." Paul made eye contact with me, fixing his gaze as if to get his point across to me and to only me.

I raced back upstairs and packed my bags. I had a small bag with some water and food leftover from earlier in the day. I was too scared to have a nap for fear of being late. Instead, I decided to text briefly with Casey, if she was free.

I opened our message string and sent her a brief text:

Poppy: Hello, darling. I miss you dearly. Still tired from my flight. Leaving tonight for the beach.

A few minutes felt like a few hours, particularly when you're missing the comforts of home. I dreamed of orange soda and dill pickle chips. I missed the sound of Amos' chain as he ran around my apartment getting his evening zoomies out of his system. I longed for that tiny heater hogging my pillow. I missed my intrusive mom calling and showing up unannounced. Her way of loving me, I suppose. I lay down and contemplated my choice of holiday given the events of the evening. As my stomach lurched with uneasiness I felt a vibration.

  Casey: Miss you too, silly goose! The beach! I'm jealous. Snap pictures of single men for me, please! I love exotic men!
  Poppy: You love all men!
  Casey: Busted! Are you having fun?

Loaded question. I was until I became the outcast of the group. I spent a few minutes reiterating the events of the last few days to my best friend. She felt sympathetic for me, but encouraged me to put it behind me as a one off. Perhaps she was right. It was an accident, after all. I wanted desperately to move away from the events of tonight. I was also desperate to move away from the nickname 'Maple.'

  Casey: Maple, I love it! Sweet like syrup!
  Poppy: Very funny. I'm the token Canadian on the trip, lucky me.
  Casey: That means you have something different to offer to the conversation, nothing bad about that.
  Poppy: I suppose you're right.
  Casey: I love you to pieces, but I have to go. Tell me all about the beach when you can! Miss you, love you.
  Poppy: Miss you, love you.
  Casey: Oh yeah, and if there are any hotties be sure to read my posts for dating advice!

And with that, my best friend's message bubble

turned off and I was alone again. I huffed at her comment about dating advice. That was the last thing I expected to do on this trip. I was here to move on, not to find another man. Men only got me into trouble.

I shifted in bed, trying to get comfortable. My eyes started to close, and my head began to nod. I forced myself awake. I decided to head down to the lobby and wait for my fellow passengers there instead of staying in my room. A couple hours passed. I spent my time listening to music and doodling in my travel journal. I leafed through the trip outline, and I refolded the clothing in my day bag. I was doing everything I could think of to keep myself awake.

As I finished the last of my packing, I saw Paul walk downstairs. He had changed into long sleeves and pants for the night's journey. He rested a plastic bag of coconut water on the counter. When he lifted the bag to his lips, I saw beads of condensation drip from the bottom of the bag onto his shirt. Perhaps he was collecting the last bit of nourishment before the night journey, or energy to deal with tourists like me. I watched as he spoke with the woman at the front desk, likely sorting out the bill. He ran his hands over the inch-long layer of sun-kissed, brown hair. His demeanour was calm. He looked peaceful and almost polite. Maybe he'd become less irritable with me over the next few weeks. Maybe he'd be a friend. Don't get too ahead of yourself, girlfriend.

He zipped up his bag and made his way out the front door to prep the taxis for the short trip to the train station. He negotiated prices in the parking lot to save time. Although he was short with me earlier, I admired the fact that he took the time to organize things so smoothly. I suppose that's what he was getting paid for. He didn't look to be bothered with the task. He also didn't seem to care. I felt invisible to him. It wasn't like he was paying attention to me.

The group slowly gathered. I was reading when I felt a hard plop beside me. I looked up and a sense of dread overcame me. Our group comprised of people from all over the world – Canada, The United States, England, Australia, Saudi Arabia, and Scotland. Such a diverse bunch of people wanting to explore this corner of the world.

"Well, Maple, you're on time, I see," the English girl commented. "The name's Kate. I'm from England if you hadn't figured it out yet." She crossed her long, lanky, pale legs and extended her hand. I wasn't sure if I should shake it or slap it given our previous interaction.

"Poppy." I extended my hand towards her. "But you already knew that." We shook on it and spoke for a few minutes about our journey here. Maybe the English girl wouldn't be so bad after all. I'd keep a close eye on any sketchy behaviour from her, just in case.

"There you are, Kate; I've been looking all over for you." A mousy female approached. She was a short, delicately tanned, East Indian woman with a slight, English accent. She rifled through a plastic, grocery bag and handed Kate a bottle of water.

"Good little thing, aren't ya?" Kate said to the new stranger. She pushed her short, brown hair out of her dark brown eyes. The woman plunked down beside us and opened the wrapper on a chocolate bar. Kate shook her head.

"I'm Emma," she said, barely audible. I found out later that when we spoke, I'd often have to lean in to hear her.

"Emma's my roommate," Kate stated. "We only just met this afternoon. English, too." They sorted their bags as the rest of the room was bustling with excitement.

"Alright, everyone," Paul bellowed, "it's time to get into the taxis and make our way to the train station. Make sure you have all your items." Paul only had a small backpack with him. He had no apparent need for these 50 to 75 litre bags we were lugging around.

We formed a line like kindergarteners on their first day of school and piled into the vehicles like sardines. Our taxi drivers zipped into and out of traffic. The night air was almost as muggy as it was throughout the day. Everyone had closed shop and were headed home. Tuk tuk drivers tried one last, lazy time to take people home for the night.

We arrived at the train station with an abrupt stop. Each of us climbed out of the cars and made our way inside. Lines formed and announcements rang overhead in Thai, and broken English, signalling passengers to board their trains. Paul corralled us into the centre of the building, warning us to get one last snack or toilet break before we got onto the train. Paul held down the fort as the nervous passengers scattered to find rations.

I decided to take a walk about, too. I had my

necessities, but I wanted to look around. The train station was grim. There hadn't been any updates to the building in a while. Expired posters of community events and politicians in military garb adorned the walls, faded by the sun. Kids ran circles around me, burning off energy before their long journey. Their parents happily allowed their shenanigans if it meant they would sleep tonight. Passengers rushed by, trying to reach their platform as the final boarding call bellowed.

    I roamed around the shops looking at familiar objects written in stern, Thai print. I wondered what it might be like being a regular here, to be someone who boarded the train for day trips or work. I closed my eyes and pictured this life as the fans buzzed and pushed around stale, smelly air. I imagined what it would be like to be immersed in this frenzy daily. In the background, the announcements blared. In my daze, I didn't hear Paul calling my name, alerting us that our train was boarding and that it was the last call.

    "I'm speaking to YOU, POPPY!" I heard my name called as I came back to reality. It was Paul, his voice rushed and impatient. His dark brown eyes pierced me like needles.

    I felt someone grab my shoulder and the next thing I knew, I was running as fast as I could. My feet fumbled as gravity revealed itself again. Like a flash from a near-death experience, I was leaping onto the train as the doors closed, narrowly missing my legs. The conductor looked down at me as I lay sprawled across the floor. He shook his head in disapproval. Paul got up off the floor; he had clearly lunged us both into the train. He didn't look at me, but got up and walked away. My touring bag had crushed my hips as it fell on top of me. No doubt, I would find some bruises later.

I made my way to my multipurpose seat. One of the girls on my trip, Rebecca, was my seatmate. She was a young, English girl, in her late teens. She helped me get my bag on the shelf. First impressions, she seemed kind and fun. I could tell she was sort of a partier as she wore a white, crop top with a glitter kiss on the front. Her hair was perfectly streaked brown and blonde. She had fingernails like a female rapper with bright colours and sparkling gems on them. Her smile lit up the entire train car, as did her voice.

"Wow, you really took a spill there, didn't ya?" she cackled. "Like a real football player, you are!" She laughed in between texting her friends, the fingernails barely able to hit the keys and the claws clicking the surface of the screen.

"Yeah, I suppose so," I sheepishly admitted. "I didn't know we were leaving so soon." I rubbed my hip as the pain set in.

"Ah, yeah, the man was calling your name. You could see the vein in his neck pulsate when you didn't answer him," she chuckled. I felt humiliated. I had a feeling I would become Paul's mortal enemy.

After an hour, Paul came around to show us how to set our seats into beds. He didn't look at me as he unfolded Rebecca's seat. He brushed past me and continued to help the other group members. Feeling rejected, I decided to set it up myself. My new vibe was independent woman. I reached up and lifted two panels down, forming my bed. Easy enough, I thought. Train bunk beds, how clever! I climbed to the top. Rebecca claimed that she had short legs and couldn't make it to such great heights. I rolled my eyes, but agreed. I tried to secure my spot in the bed as the train shook and took sharp turns on the track. I fastened my day bag to my arm and tucked it under my head to create a makeshift pillow. Paul's words rang in my ears when he stated that there had been robberies on the trains. He said that they'd come on and spray gas so that people would fall asleep. At that point, they'd rifle through their bags and take their valuables. I already made one mistake of not heeding my brother's warnings, and I wouldn't repeat that mistake again when a caution was given.

 I tried to fall asleep, but sleep wouldn't come. I was crippled with fear of being robbed or plummeting to my death from the upper bunk on a moving train. Both thoughts concerned me, so I lay awake, ruminating over these possibilities. I thought about leaving my life behind and all the mistakes I made. Maybe they weren't mistakes in the moment, particularly pertaining to John, but they were actions that broke my heart and left me feeling vulnerable. I still remembered laying on the bathroom floor, weeping for the man who lied to me. He could be cruel, and he wasn't always a gentleman. I found myself wondering why I had stayed. Was it love, or lust? Either way, John didn't deserve my tears. I felt like such a screw up, mostly in my own eyes. Coming here, on this trip, was a fresh start. I couldn't help but feel my first few steps in a new direction were clumsy. I didn't feel like I was making any friends yet. There would be plenty of opportunities to turn this around, I hoped.

At one point in the night, I decided to get up. My bladder had enough rocking and shaking. I made my way down the bunk, careful not to step on Rebecca. The dim lights from the train car and the screen light from people's cellphones lit the way as I made my way down the narrow aisle towards the toilet. The train shuffled and I steadied my gait with each step I took. At one point, I passed Paul, who was seated at the back so that he had an eagle eye of his passengers. We briefly made eye contact before he removed his gaze from mine. So much for friends. Disappointment swelled in my stomach.

I finally arrived at the toilet. The small, cramped room had just a toilet, but no sink. Thank goodness I packed hand sanitizer. I made my way to the toilet and lifted the lid. I was surprised to see no water in the bowl. At first, my groggy mind pondered how one would flush the toilet. I took a closer look. There was no water, but underneath it was rolling land! You used the toilet, and everything fell onto the ground! I supposed they didn't have to worry about transporting liquids. As I sat and did my business, there was a sign on the back of the door that read, "only use toilet when train in motion" and "do not use when stopped." I was puzzled.

I reached over to the toilet paper holder and low and behold nothing! My first experience with the train toilet and I was left stranded. I drip dried as best I could, steadied myself as I adjusted my clothing, and made my way back to my bunkbed. I was tired and frankly over this train ride.

The rest of the journey was quiet. I, unfortunately, didn't get any sleep along the way. Eventually, the sun came up and passengers started to rouse from their slumbers. Lucky bastards, I thought. The scenery along the way changed from an industrial city to greenery and, in the distance, I swore I could see water.

Paul made his way down the aisle, making sure we were awake, and provided us with a thirty-minute warning. When he arrived at my bunk, he made direct eye contact with me, and repeated, "30-minute warning, Poppy. Be ready." I cowered behind my makeshift pillow, much like Amos does when he knows he's in trouble. This clearly solidified that I was the group outcast, particularly as others looked at me and smirked.

The train rolled to a stop. We got off in single file and followed the leader. The group of sleepy foreigners made their way like little ducklings behind Paul to a roadside café. Paul instructed us that we had an hour for breakfast and then our vans would be here to take us to the hostel we would be staying at the next few days.

"I could really go for a coffee," Rebecca groaned. She sat in the shade with her sunglasses on. Kate and Emma decided to join us, too.

"I could go for some juice." Emma looked around for the waitress. She fiddled with the ends of her bedhead.

"You lot can have whatever you want. No use in

whining," Kate added, glaring at Rebecca, almost sizing her up. "I wouldn't expect too much here." Kate broke her gaze, and investigated the surroundings to cover up her passive-aggressive comment. We were the lone diners at a roadside café.

"No need to be short." Rebecca pulled her sunglasses down and glared back at Kate.

"I wasn't being anything, youngin, I'm just minding my own business. Perhaps you should do the same and shut your gob," Kate contended. Rebecca huffed as if preparing a rebuttal or to fight with her.

Paul walked by our table. "Ladies, how's everything?" He rapped his knuckles against the plastic tablecloth and shot a glance between the two he had clearly overheard.

The beverages arrived just as the women were beginning to cool off. "We're fine; nothing to worry about," Kate sneered at Paul. I felt uncomfortable with whatever was going on between those two, but I couldn't pinpoint any exact trigger that had transpired. Rebecca mumbled in agreement.

"Okay, let's keep it that way." Paul should add mediator to his list of credentials. We sat in uncomfortable silence when he left. Emma and I tried to make light conversation, which ended in silence.

Luckily, when the food came, we had something more positive to focus on. We feasted on familiar western world cereals, fresh fruit, and noodles. I had only had noodles for breakfast when I ate leftovers from lunch with Casey. I snapped a few photos of our random meal for her to see later. You got to embrace the culture.

"Hey, did any of you use the toilet on the train last night?" Rebecca and Emma shook their head 'no,' and Kate admitted to needing to use the loo.

"Why you asking, Maple?" Kate inquired between chews. The stormy interaction had settled between her and her trip mate.

"Did it seem odd to you that there was just a hole onto the train tracks? No water?" I moved around some of the remaining noodles on my plate.

"Yeah, that's common here. Was there a problem?" Kate's mouth was full. She washed the contents down with green tea.

"There was a sign not to use the toilet when it had stopped. I just wondered what that was about." Kate shrugged, and Emma piped up as high as her mousy voice would go.

"Splashing." Emma took a sip of her fresh mango juice. She looked at us nonchalantly as if we understood what she was talking about.

"Pardon?" What does splashing have to do with a bottomless toilet? There was no water to splash you. I was not clueing in on the obvious.

"When the train stops, there're people standing on the platform. You don't use the toilet because they don't want you to splash anyone." We looked at each other in confusion. "There are venders who sell food on the side of the platform. Do you really want a cup of fruit with a side of turd?" Emma dropped an unexpected joke. She also had to be extremely direct with this bunch of dim bulbs, myself included in that pack.

Rebecca roared, "Shit soup isn't on the menu!" Tears poured down her face. Others turned around to see what the fuss was all about. I had to admit, that made perfect sense. The contents got released on the train. Not everyone was into golden, or chocolate milk, showers.

After the meal, I decided to use the washroom, again, and prep for our ride to the hostel. Mike, one of the guys on our trip, held the door open for me and smiled sheepishly when it was my turn. He was kind of cute; who knows? It would be an hour or so until we would arrive at our accommodations. I was happy to see that there was a sink in the washroom so that I could wash to refresh myself. I was sure I smelt like a bouquet of roses – not! I turned around and was alarmed when I didn't see a toilet. I opened the door to check I was in the correct room. I looked around again, puzzled. I walked around, trying to solve this mystery. In the corner, there was a small hole in the floor as well as a pail of water. It was then that I realized that I'd come face to face with the dreaded squatty potty.

For other individuals who were brought up with the squatty potty, it is a rather hygienic and anatomically correct way to do one's business. For those who are not brought up with a squat, it is a delicate dance of lowering one's buttocks towards the floor while not peeing on your garments. The challenge is made especially difficult if the party using said toilet is experiencing traveller's diarrhea, an unfortunate circumstance many of us would fall victim to on this journey.

I decided that the best course of action would be to remove my pants. I found a hook and hung them on the door. I waddled over to the hole in the floor as I dodged pre-existing puddles, uncertain of what said puddles contained. I secured my feet on the tile grid and squatted as low as I could go without falling over. I closed my eyes and pretended that I was camping. After a few tries, I got the job done. I made my way to the sink, washed up, and in a careful, choreographed dance, I put my pants back on without any puddle interference. Last call of duty was to flush the contents of the squatty potty down with the pail of water and the short hose attached to the wall. I groaned as I finished this cleaning ritual. I longed for a toilet.

I made my way back to the group and we boarded the vans. The windows were rolled down as there was no air conditioning. The driver and Paul secured our backpacks to the roof of the vehicle. We made our descent to the beach. The glistening, blue ocean came closer and closer into view. This was the beginning of something beautiful; I could feel it.

Chapter Fourteen

We wiped the last of the sleep from our eyes as we received our keys from Paul in the lobby. We'd be staying in large, dorm rooms tonight at the hostel. I'd be sleeping with the ladies on the trip. Everyone raced to drop off their bags so they could get ready for the day's festivities.

Home would be a small, beach town, more of a layover town, with a view of the ocean – if you squinted hard enough. Our hostel was quaint. The large rooms housed a dozen bunk beds. There was a dining room and an activity room for people to gather. All you needed, really. This was a humble, three-storey building tucked behind restaurants off the main street. It was a strange mix of local and western world. Pad Thai restaurants were sandwiched between familiar fast-food chains. You could have a posh coffee with your noodles if you wished. Bars, cash machines, and small, open-air storefronts with souvenirs lined the streets. Not to mention, more tuk tuks.

The group was dressed in their finest swimsuits. Everyone was tired, but ready for a refreshing dip. Many of the group members still had pasty, white skin. A tan was certainly in order. Some of the girls had "pre-tans" from bronzing lotions or tanning beds in anticipation of their real holiday tans; odd preparation, but I can appreciate the logic of bikini ready. I should have thought of that, but others would have to suffer my pasty buns.

As we waited outside the hostel in the shade, Paul rallied the crew to explain what would happen today. Our first real adventure would be island hopping on a boat! We'd go to see the relished Patong Beach in Phuket, Maya Bay Beach in Koh Phi Phi, as well as Railay Beach in Krabi. These beaches were what dreams, glossy magazine covers, and movies were made of. We headed to the beach where we were greeted by three fishing boats. Bright-coloured strips of cloth in red, yellow, purple, and blue were woven together in different formations, making each boat unique. Our drivers waved enthusiastically to summon the group to board their vessels from deep into the water; no docks could be found.

We made our way through the clear, blue water, sloshing as we treaded deeper towards the boats, our belongings held overhead, trying not to get wet. Note to self: buy waterproof bags. The men laughed and hauled us onto the boats. The salt water stung my freshly shaved legs. I'd given them a quick, dry shave before we left. Big mistake. The morning sun was welcoming. There was a perfect breeze flowing through my hair. Paul warned us that the UV rays would triple today, so we should stay hydrated and lather as much sunscreen on as possible. I'd made sure to buy a couple of bottles at the store this morning before we left. This may earn me a few brownie points to share with the others.

The first stop was Patong Beach. The lush, white sand was a nice starter for today's events. We disembarked the boats, finding solitude in paradise. Some of us lounged on the perfect, soft sand that blanketed the shore and others sought shade. The entire beach was dotted with bright, beach towels and various shades of skin.

"I'll watch our things, love. Girl's got to get her tan on first." Rebecca waved to me as she oiled her two-sizes-too-small, bikini-clad body. She had a large, chain necklace on. She looked like she should be lounging on a yacht with a bunch of celebrities.

I plopped my stuff down and I ran into the water, diving and splashing around the shallow beach. Rebecca stayed on land to perfect her glow as promised. Others had made their way down the beach, opting for some alone time, or getting to know others in their small, newly formed cliques. I was still a lone wolf. Rebecca, however, was a good companion. I was happy to get to know her more. She took this little Canadian goose under her wing.

As I was wading in the water, I saw Paul in the distance where he'd remained on the boat. He was laughing and gesturing with the boat crew, seemingly having a good time. This was the first time I had seen him happy. His white teeth glistened in the sun. I stared at him and smiled, unsure why. Perhaps I was enjoying watching someone who looked happy as I longed to feel that way, too. I must've caught his eye as he suddenly zeroed in on me. He gave me a thumbs up and mouthed, "you okay?" This was the first time he had shown genuine interest in my wellbeing, other than lunging me onto the train. I guess that counted as a kind gesture. I grinned sheepishly and gave him the thumbs up in return. He smiled back, briefly, before continuing his conversation with the boat crew.

When Rebecca had enough of roasting her bod on the beach, she splashed in the water beside me, awakening me from my trance.

"A little taste of heaven, ain't it?" Rebecca sighed as she floated in the crystal blue, salt water. "You're looking fit," Rebecca commented on my bikini. "I think you'll get some fine attention if you keep wearing that!"

I laughed, continuing to enjoy the surroundings. We splashed around and soaked up the Vitamin D and when we'd enough, we staggered onto the beach. The sun beat down on us, drying our bodies with a thin layer of fresh, salt water. Rebecca pulled her shades down and announced, "Look at that tush!" as she stared at a tanned, six-packed hunk in a bright, yellow speedo.

"I'd peel your banana anytime!" she cackled. I nudged her shoulder, partially to stop her comments, but secretly to encourage the naughtiness. "I'd shag it!" she added. She was going to be trouble – the best kind of trouble.

After a while of rotating our bodies like rotisserie chickens, we decided to go exploring. Rebecca and I meandered, chatting with the street vendors selling jewelry along the boardwalk and sipping on freshly squeezed juice. We passed signs for nightclubs with free drinks for the ladies. Rebecca bopped to the music as I laughed at her silliness. This place had the best of all worlds to offer. Who'd want to leave?

After a few hours, it was onto the next stop, Maya Bay Beach. The boats skimmed the choppy water as we zipped around the curves of the mainland. We all made 'ohhs' and 'ahhs' as we slowed down to enter another out-of-this world location.

This area was significant for a couple of reasons. First, it had an amazing view. Towering rocks emerged from the water covered in bright, lush greenery. Topaz waters churned gently, guiding snorkelers along the unmarked paths of the currents. Tourists jumped off boats and dove into the water that resembled sparkling jewels. Everyone took their obligatory selfie in the landscape hoping others would believe they'd experienced such beauty.

The second reason this was a special stop was because it was described in a famous book that had been turned into a movie featuring a dreamy, Hollywood celebrity! It was a sheer definition of utopia, if only on the surface. Some guides said the area was compromised as there were so many tourists. The water had become polluted, and the oceanic wildlife had suffered over the years. I could see what the guides meant as there seemed to be more boats than tourists in the packed bay. There was, in the distance, garbage floating in the water.

I felt sad that my actions, those of a tourist, could've harmed something so beautiful, almost unknowingly. I sat on the edge of the boat contemplating this thought, feeling torn about allowing myself to enjoy being here. The next thing I knew, my boat driver emerged from the water with a sea urchin. My mood shifted back to joy and curiosity. We are allowed to feel multiple emotions at once. There was a lot of magic here to experience.

Not having a common language to bond us, the boat driver used his nonverbal cues to explain what he'd found. The dripping, wet mass rested in his hand, and he pointed to the sharp needles of the unusual creature. It was a rich, black, and purple lump with no evident signs of life, a camouflage perhaps. He motioned to his mouth that the urchin was edible. I opened my mouth in shock, and he laughed. The driver encouraged me to touch it. I eyed him and the porcupine-of-the-sea, trying to decide if I wanted to get pricked. I delicately extended my finger to touch it and then he pretended to launch it at me as if it were attacking me. We both laughed and he gently tossed it back into the water where it would settle on the ocean floor for a rest.

After our jolly encounter, he motioned for me to put on a snorkel set and follow him. Paul threw me the gear, underwhelmed. Paul returned to the shaded area of the boat and resumed his post watching his little ducklings. He seemed grouchier than before. I couldn't figure this man out to save my life. Not my circus, not my monkey. I rolled my eyes at him.

I followed my instructions and spit into the mask, swishing it around. I giggled at how childish this felt but I was excited to explore the sea life around me. The guide took my hand, and we dove to the bottom. In our underwater world, he showed me schools of neon yellow and blue fish swimming in perfect unison. We saw pink corals floating back and forth as well as bright green plant life. He dipped and dodged the furious feet of other snorkelers as he dove down to chase an eel. I was left alone. I looked around for him, but I couldn't find him. My breath quickened. Suddenly, I saw a propeller of another boat rev up, I panicked. I forced my way to the surface and became disoriented as my body thrashed through the water.

In my rush, I gulped some water. The salt burned my throat as I swallowed hastily, hoping it was air. The water made my eyes throb, making it challenging for me to navigate. As I flailed in the water, unable to find my way, I heard a splash and a voice call out my name. I couldn't see but an arm grasped tightly around my waist and pulled me. I was hoisted onto the deck of the boat, and I lay against the cool, metal surface, breathing heavily.

"Are you alright?" a familiar voice asked. Paul panted over me, drenched in water.

"I, I think so," I struggled to say, stunned from the events.

"Well, be careful next time. Can't go saving you all the time," Paul blurted out. He got up and resumed his position. He was the dutiful lifeguard with an attitude who needed to work on his bedside manner.

It wasn't like I was trying to drown myself on purpose! I couldn't feel more like a fool if I tried. I wanted to burst into tears. Luckily, it was just us on the boat; the rest of the group frolicked in the distance. The driver emerged from the water nearby. He looked around, surprised that I was resting on the boat. He motioned for me to come back in, but I shook my head no. He shrugged and made his way to find another tourist to entertain.

After the group collected, we roasted together on our respective boats under the midday sun. The heat of the sun made my skin tingle. I dabbed on extra sunscreen as per Paul's heeding. We chowed down on fresh fruit and the local beer as the boats lulled us into relaxation. We laughed and showed each other our photos. We described what we saw and expressed our disappointment for things we missed. You can't experience everything; it's important to live in the moment.

The slow boats lurked through the water until we reached the open sea. The motors kicked into high gear, and we danced atop the waves. The wind was so loud, we had to shout at each other, still not understanding what the other person was saying.

Railay Beach was our last stop of the day. It was a delight, and possibly the highlight of my day. Railay was equally as beautiful as Maya Bay Beach but with fewer tourists.

At this stop, I opted for land. After my near-death

experience, I thought this was the correct call. I walked up and down the beach alone, my sarong whipping in the wind. I stopped to snap photos of our colourful boats. I passed couples smooching under their beach umbrellas and others roasting under the afternoon sun, their skin turning a hybrid shade of brown and red, almost like a paint strip at the home improvement store. On my travels, I passed Rebecca who was trying to take a selfie in the water.

"Do you want some help?" I called out to her. Rebecca had changed into a leopard-print bikini. The sun glistened on the water as she splashed around to find the perfect pose. Her large breasts were hardly contained in the tight top.

"Would you, love?" she asked. And with that, I spent thirty minutes snapping various poses. Some of these snaps were for her social media while others were for dating websites. Rebecca wanted to show her potential, gentleman suitors that she had a worldly side to her. Some of her poses, I thought, belonged in a pin-up magazine. She was a wild beauty.

After our photoshoot, I sat on the beach. In the distance, I saw small specks moving on top of the rock cuts. People were propelling down the rocks after they had climbed to the top, much like someone summiting Mount Everest. I laughed in delight as people stood in a starfish pose at the top, much like that of a Christmas tree. Living their best lives, an accomplishment I was sure.

We swam towards the boat, ready to head back to

the hostel. On board, Paul helped people onto the boat. When he saw me, a smirk spread across his face.

"Didn't drown this time, I see," he laughed as he extended his hand towards me. His strong hand encompassed mine, pulling me up with all his strength.

I ignored him and nestled myself between Rebecca and Kate. I smiled at both of them, but soon realized they were scowling at each other. I prayed there would be no war. Not wanting to get into the middle of a cat fight, I asked Rebecca to show me her pictures from earlier, which diffused the situation. You can't get along with everyone.

Back at the hostel, we all washed up. Some people opted to stay up and play board games while others headed to bed, exhausted from the day. This was a crucial time in the early stages of the group as friendships, and lovers, formed. I decided to head to bed, happy to invite some solitude into my life. I didn't need a lover, but I was open to making friends. Tomorrow would be a new day to start all that.

As I headed back to the dorm room, some of my fellow passengers passed by me. Some smiled; others did not engage. It was early days, after all. And then I saw him: Paul. He was standing beside the glowing vending machine waiting for a soda to fall out. His outfit was stained from the sand, and his hair glistened with salt from the ocean adventure. "You staying up, Poppy?" he asked. He didn't seem annoyed, irritated, or bothered by me – just a general inquisition. I was taken aback.

"No, I'm going to go to bed; I'm beat."

"That's too bad. I was hoping to beat you at cards. Perhaps another time." He cracked his soda and took a swig.

"Maybe," I commented as I walked away, puzzled by this unexpected kindness. He was likely just doing his job, trying to build group cohesion for a tip at the end of the trip.

I made my way down the hallway. The dorm door creaked open, the light already turned off. I tiptoed my way towards my bed, hoping not to disturb the sleeping beauties.

"Good night, Maple," I heard Kate mumble in the darkness.

"Good night, Kate." I nestled under the single bed sheet for the night. Yes, friends were definitely in the making.

Chapter Fifteen

I woke up, bathing in a thin ray of sunlight. I felt like Amos basking in the warmth with not a care in the world. I lay there, enjoying the peace and the quiet.

I stretched my aching limbs. I felt the slight tightness of my skin, a mild sunburn from yesterday etched on my shoulder blades. The skin tingled briefly to the touch, but not enough to cause me any major discomfort. I lay in bed, thinking what a glorious day it was going to be. I daydreamed of either lying by the water or going shopping in the market.

My sleepy dream was disrupted abruptly. Like blinding headlights in the pitch black of night, I was startled awake by Kate.

"I can't see a bloody thing!" she wailed. "I need to get to the hospital right now!" She sprawled over the side of the top bunkbed, trying to find the floor below. Her long, previously pale, lanky legs were now a dark shade of red. Kate's face resembled a tomato, or is it 'tomatoe'? You be the judge. Her sleep mask, which was now plastered to her forehead, concealed a bigger issue.

"What you going on about?" Emma groaned as she rolled from her bottom bunk to help her friend. Watching them was truly a comedy of errors. Emma pulled at Kate, trying to get her to common ground.

Emma struggled over the bags and was finally able to get Kate down. She plunked onto the floor. As we helped her take off her sleep mask, we noticed that her face was entirely swollen like a balloon.

"What's wrong? Why can't I see?" Kate bellowed as she tried to make sense of the darkness. She swatted and groped at her inflamed skin, willing her eyes to open. Tears dotted her flesh.

"It appears your face has swelled," Emma said, carefully reaching out to touch the plump flesh. She pulled her hand back as if she'd been burnt on a hot stove.

"What do you mean, it's swollen?" Kate tried to pat her cheeks, but she winced. Kate delicately examined her eyes, her cheekbones, and her jaw.

"Oh, my god! What happened?" Kate tried to move about the room, but was not able to get far due to an inability to navigate the luggage landmines.

"Are you allergic to something?" I panicked. "Maybe you ate something?"

"No, Maple, I don't have any allergies!" Kate found the edge of the bottom bunk. As she sat down, tears streamed down her face. Kate winced as if the liquid were made of acid. "This had to happen now, didn't it?" she asked as if karma had bitten her in the, er, face.

"I'll go get Paul," Emma proclaimed and left to hunt down our fearless leader. She swung the creaking door open and made her way into the hall.

We sat in silence, not sure how to support her. What a strange thing to happen! After a few minutes, Emma returned with Paul.

"Ladies, what's going on?" Paul asked, knowing full well there was a crisis. "Are we all decent?" He hovered at the doorway with his eyes covered.

"Yes," we declared in unison.

"Alright, where's the patient?" he asked, removing his splayed fingers from his eyes, as he moved swiftly into the dorm room, dodging us ladies between the bunkbeds.

"Ah, a swollen face. You get in a bar fight last night?" Paul asked, concealing a smirk.

"A real comedian this one, ain't he?" Kate sneered. "When are we going to the hospital? I prefer not to die here." Kate still had a sense of humour, considering the current situation.

"Yes, that's a great idea. Get your wallet and let's go. I'll get a taxi." Paul made his way out of the room. As he passed me, he stared for a few seconds and then looked down. I felt like a leper to him, someone who disgusted him one minute and the next minute, he was kind. I'd no idea what was going on with him. Best not to read too much into it; I had a habit of misreading situations.

We watched from the front door of the hostel as Kate and Paul climbed into the yellow taxi. Emma trailed after them and swooped into the front seat just as they were about to leave. Rebecca and I stood in the doorway. Her shoulders shook as she tried to hold in a laugh. She did a pretty good job until the taxi door shut then she let out a howl.

"It serves her right for being such a wench!" Rebecca laughed so hard, she held onto her stomach, her golden highlights brushing against her cheeks.

"Don't be mean; she's not well!" I tried to defend Kate, but I soon joined in the chuckles. It was kind of funny.

"She's been mean to me. Maybe this will help her become more empathetic." Rebecca turned on her heels and skipped into the dining hall for breakfast.

"What's she done that's so mean?" I asked as Rebecca poured herself a bowl of tofu soup.

"Yesterday, she was mean to me at the café for no apparent reason. And on the beach, she made a snide comment about my bikini and my laugh. She's been sneering at me, as if she doesn't think I see her." Rebecca was visibly hurt. "I'm younger than her, but that doesn't give her the right to be cruel. I didn't do anything to her." Rebecca looked down at her polished pedicure. She was, in fact, the youngest member of our group. I hadn't been paying much attention to the things that had occurred between the two of them, but I could relate based on the way that I felt Paul was treating me.

"I'm sorry you feel that way, Rebecca. I'm here for you. We can stick together." I bumped into Rebecca's shoulder again to offer a playful gesture.

"Ah, Canadians! Gotta love them!" Rebecca's face lit up and she put her arm around me and brought me in for a hug. "The best of friends we shall be!" For the rest of the trip we would be bunkmates, roommates, and seatmates. We were truly attached at the hip.

The plan for the rest of the day was to hit the beach. The sun was bright, and it wasn't as hot as yesterday. There was a pure, white sand beach ten minutes from our hostel. It seemed like the right place to spend the day.

Rebecca also wanted to stop and grab a coffee from the coffee chain down the street, which seemed out of place here in southern Thailand. "Gotta get my mocha on!" she cackled. We kicked up sand with our flip flops as we walked the dusted sidewalk.

On route, we passed endless stores selling beach dresses, beer brand tank tops, and sunglasses. These would be the official apparel for the trip. This also seemed to encourage us to adapt to a carefree lifestyle while away. We stopped to try on a few tie-dyed dresses. Rebecca twirled in the warm air the fan was blowing. I swear we stopped in the stores just to cool off. I'd never admit that to the shop owner waiting patiently to barter with us.

As we got closer to our destination, we passed street venders selling grilled meat and dollar beers before noon! Street meat was considered a delicacy here. Men would swelter under the heat from the sun and the flames of the barbeque, serving fresh fish, shrimp, and chicken on skewers with chili sauce on the side. We sat on the edge of the curb and slurped our beers as we ate. When it got too hot, we'd dive through the front doors of any convenience store, as they were usually blasting the air conditioning at arctic temperatures. Food was inexpensive here. I was happy to get an ice cream to soothe my internal temperatures and as soon as we cooled, we'd head back on our way.

    The beach was near empty. Rebecca and I were the first to arrive from our group. Many of them didn't show for breakfast, either. Some were at the hospital and others were recovering from their hangovers. We spread out our beach towels and nestled into the warmth of the grit. When we got too warm, we swam and came back to air dry. Eventually, the others came to the beach. We swam, played cards, and drank beer. A good time was had, by most of us.

    There was one fellow who'd been making eyes at me from across the way: Mike. He was one of the Australians in our group. We hadn't had much chance to talk, but I'd noticed him looking at me at the welcome meeting, the café, and again yesterday on the boats. Maybe I should've stayed up late last night to hang out with him.

    "Whatcha looking at, Pops?" Rebecca withered over to me, protecting her vivacious bosom with her hand of cards and tilted her reflective sunglasses down to hone in on what I was looking at.

    "Nothing, don't worry about it," I stammered, looking down at my sand-covered feet.

    "Well, well, well, looks like we have a live one, mate!" Rebecca cackled. Her laugh was truly her signature.

"Are you playing or what?" someone snapped at her.

"Shut it. I'll be in when I say I'm in." She handed the attitude right back.

Rebecca was up on her knees now so we could huddle like two football players left out of the team play. "Right, Mike obviously likes you. I can tell these things about men. What you need to do is to flirt back. Don't go speak to him just yet. Bat some eyelashes, flip your hair. Men love that," she whispered coyly.

I tried to muster up some courage to practise these new moves. I'd been more of an awkward flirt, never understanding the art of seduction. The only time I was seduced was when it was blatantly obvious and usually left me up to no good. Either way, I liked men and craved the attention.

Around 4:00pm, the group turned to notice a figure, draped in black cloth, drifting down to the beach. The fabrics billowed in the wind. We looked at each other, puzzled. Was this someone heading to a funeral or the grim reaper? Alas, it was no grieving widow but Emma.

"Hello, all," Emma said as she sat with us. Her garments created a puddle that enveloped her. Her outfit took up more space than her actual body, knocking the game and the sand into our drinks.

Rebecca was lying on her stomach with her head cradled on top of her dark, tanned arms. She looked up and studied Emma. "What's that getup you have on?"

"Well, it turns out Kate had an allergic reaction to the sun yesterday. That's why her face is so swollen. Since we're both English, I was worried that might happen to me, too. So, I'm covering everything up," Emma stated matter-of-factly.

"Allergic to the sun? That's nuts! We're mostly English and none of us have blown up like a blowfish." Many of the group members laughed. I tried not to as Emma looked like she had tears welling in her eyes. It was a bit hard to tell under her cloak of darkness.

"Can't be too careful," I said to her, trying to offer an empathetic remark. She smiled at me, as if accepting my comment. "How's Kate?"

"She's resting in bed. The swelling has gone down so she can see again. She must avoid the sun as much as possible." That would be hard, considering the climate. "Paul got her a private room so she could be alone and tend to her facial care. He's been a real, good bloke." Emma appeared pleased with the care her friend was receiving. She'd been supporting her in spirit – girlfriends unite.

"I'm glad to hear. Hopefully, after some rest, she'll feel better," I tried to offer reassurance. It was a bizarre and unfortunate situation. No one likes to be unwell on holiday; the whole point is to rest and relax.

"Me too." Emma rolled out her beach towel that was somehow tucked under all the fabric, exposed her legs, and lathered on SPF 50. That was as risqué as she was getting today given her friend's current health status.

We decided to head back to the hostel around dinner time. We were intercepted by a large group of local children aggressively spraying water and tossing dried powder at each other, all with a smile on their faces. Malicious little things they were. The children darted around us, using us as obstacles as they launched their attack on the others. They laughed and chased each other until the other was unrecognizable, covered in white, wet chalk.

When we arrived in Thailand, none of us knew that it was technically the Thai New Year, Songkran, which is celebrated in the spring. New Year, for many, is a time to reflect on what's transpired and to move forward. This is exactly what I'd come here for: to start anew. Although I felt like I was having setbacks, I believed I was on the right track.

Seeing the children so happy, and so playful, filled me with a sense of joy. Water balloons were tossed in the air. There was much laughter and changing teams depending on who held the next pail of water and fistful of chalk. The next thing I knew, I was tossing water at children and running for cover. In fact, we all participated in this.

Laughing loudly and pleading with our newfound friends not to soak us with another drop of water went on for at least an hour. Many of us were drenched to the bone, happy to jump ship if it meant that we're not coated in more dust. We laughed hysterically at the ambush and how much fun it was. We retreated to the hostel, happy and defeated. Emma went to check on

Kate, and the rest of us took a number in line to shower and to change our clothing.

While waiting in line, I spotted my new crush. It was harmless to flirt a little on vacation, right? I shimmied up to Mike in line, hoping that he would turn around and notice me. I coyly made eye contact with him and darted my eyes away when he glanced in my direction. He'd looked at me in return. I tried to brush the hair out of my face with a seductive glance when he turned around a second time. I probably appeared like a crazed woman. Maybe he thought my brain had been done in from the sun, too.

At one point in my dance of seduction, Mike turned away with a look of confusion. I caught a glance of myself in the window and realized that I looked like a drowned rat. He was probably trying to figure out if I was a street rat or a trip mate; so much for my sexy interaction. I gave up on flirting. I proceeded to the stalls when it was my turn to clean up. After my shower, I headed back to my room to get changed. I sifted through my bag to find some decent clothing for our first group dinner.

When packing, I truly underestimated how much clothing I needed; therefore, I prepared on the light side and decided to do some laundry along the way. What I didn't know was that sweating so much each day led to multiple clothing changes, which meant that I was now out of everything but one fresh pair of underwear. I groaned and put on my last, semi-clean outfit. I made a plan to go out to get some cash to do laundry. Hopefully, I could get a load done before dinner.

I investigated the situation outside the hostel. I wanted to make sure that the coast was clear of any straggler children from the water fight. I walked down the alley to avoid common areas and headed to the cash machine. Once I completed my transaction, I headed back the way I came. I thought to myself that I had escaped the masses, and I could return unscathed. I smoothed down my linen shorts as I pressed on back to the hostel. I was dreaming of spicy Pad Thai when my thought bubble rudely burst.

Out of nowhere, I heard a small voice yell, "Freeze!" For a moment, I was afraid that I was being held at gunpoint, considering I just left the cash machine – another trap for tourists. I raised my arms in surrender and turned around slowly to face the robber behind me.

Scared for my life, I saw nothing in front of me. Confused, I shifted my gaze down to make eye contact with a pint-sized child. "Freeze!" he yelled again. The kid held a water pistol in one hand and a paper bag of chalk in the other.

I looked at him and begged, "This is my last clean outfit. Please, don't get it dirty." My plea meant nothing. I thought for a moment about offering him a bribe, but it was too late.

With a sonic boom, I was drenched, and my vision obscured with dust. "Damn, kid!" I yelled as I scraped the caked powder off my face. "As if!"

I made my way back to the hostel. Of all the people sitting outside to greet me was Paul. He was enjoying a drink alone. Great, him again. He's always there when I wished he wasn't.

He turned away when he saw me, likely to conceal a cruel face or a snide joke. "Poppy, you got a little something right here." He pretended to wipe his face. He went there, anyways.

"Very funny, Paul! A child attacked me! Attacked! I have nothing clean left to wear!" I shrieked.

"Well, it's Thai New Year, after all. Embrace it." He snickered and walked away, sipping his Bing Tang beer, his flip flops clicking as he made his way back into the hostel.

Luckily, Rebecca was able to lend me a black tank top and daisy duke shorts. Laundry would have to wait. This was not my typical outfit, but I was happy to wear something clean. I tugged the short legs down, trying to get more comfortable.

While I waited for my hair to dry, since I had to have another shower, I decided to ask my bestie for some dating advice. Given my flirt failure with Mike earlier, I thought it would be a good idea to get some advice from a professional.

Poppy: Need your help. Cute Aussie on trip. Tried making the eyes at him earlier. Fail! Please help.
Casey: Hmmm, send pic of outfit!
Poppy: Here it is!
Casey: Not what I envisioned but we can work with this. Try leaning over the table. Also slowly wink at him as you lean

Poppy: Okay, I'll see what I can do!
Casey: Report back. Love you, miss you
Poppy: Love you, miss you

"Time to go!" Paul yelled from the dorm room doorways. We headed out for traditional Thai cuisine. Kate decided to meet us. She and her doppelganger Emma were dressed head to toe in flowing dresses and black, swimsuit cover ups used as veils.

"Vampires, the sun is down. Did no one tell you?" Rebecca asked, studying her enemy from the other side of the lobby. Hurt or not, she wasn't going to take any crap from Kate.

"I wish to conceal my injuries at present time and mask them from the sun," Kate stated as she swayed around the room in her dress. Her feet were eerily invisible.

"I think you're safe to show your face." Rebecca tested Kate. "But then, again, maybe you're a minger," Rebecca added with a mumble.

"Now, now, ladies," Paul warned, trying to keep the peace. Between navigating the trip and the passengers, he really had his hands full, but I still didn't like him much at this moment.

Emma shot her tongue out at Rebecca after Paul turned around. This was her silent way to protect her friend. Rebecca saw and repeated the childish behaviour. I adored both of these women, but I didn't wish to get in the middle of this playground fight. Weren't we adults?

We formed our clan and headed down the street. When we arrived at the restaurant, we sat on simple, white, plastic, lawn chairs and mismatched tables formed a long, dining space for all of us to crowd around. Christmas lights adorned the inside of the restaurant and items from all over the world, mostly currency and postcards, formed the wallpaper. I was happy to have refuge from the children in the street. I hoped their antics were over for the night.

One of the best things about being here, aside from the amazing beaches, was the cheap food. You could easily have a three-course meal for ten dollars. The variety of Pad Thai, stir fry, and catch-of-the-day, grilled fish were endless. The sounds of freshly squeezed juices being squished and slushed in the back of the restaurant could be heard, and the sizzling of the meats on the grill made Kate jump. Perhaps she thought it was the sun scorching her face again.

We ate together, like one big family, laughing as we dined on seafood and slurped endless noodles from tiny bowls. We clinked bottles, celebrating our time together and looking forward to more of the same.

I'd purposefully situated myself across the table from Mike. Both of us were freshly laundered and buzzing from our beverages, so I decided to make my move. I inconspicuously lowered my top an inch down so that a bit more cleavage could be seen. I brushed the hair from my eyes and gingerly looked up to make eye contact with him. He looked at me, too, and smiled.

I began my mating call.

I looked at Mike, and attempted to take a sip from my straw. When I attempted to repeat this maneuver again, I slowly winked and lowered my lips to my straw. As I leaned down further, I miscalculated the distance and poked myself in the eye with the straw.

"Oh, shit!" I hollered as I launched backwards. As I prepared for liftoff, I leaned back too far and ended up knocking glasses off the table, and spilling bowls. I apologized profusely to my tablemates. I was so clumsy! What's wrong with me?

"You alright, Maple?" Kate stood to assess the damage. "There can only be one injured person on this trip and that position is taken." Kate slipped a spring roll under her veil. The chewing could be heard and not seen.

"Yes, I'm fine. It's a bit dark," I lied, trying to cover up the humiliation.

Near the end of dinner, Paul stood at the head of the table and proposed a toast. "To a New Year! May each of you receive all you desire."

Before I clinked my glass, I sat a moment and thought about what I wished to receive this year. I prayed for strength to move on from John and to find a career path I was passionate about. Above all, I wanted to forgive myself and figure out who I truly was. After I acknowledged my wishes, I cheered everyone else at the table.

"And cheers to a normal face!" Kate bellowed from beneath the black veil. We laughed and wished her the same, too.

After we settled our bills, we joined each other in the

street. In the distance, we heard music blasting and lights of all colours dancing in the background. Paul said that in the evening of the Thai New Year, there are celebrations. We migrated to where the party was to join in.

We danced for hours to top 100 songs, which had somehow gotten an Asian makeover as they were not sung in the voices we were familiar with. We looked at each other, puzzled, and decided to just go with it. We danced with some of those rotten children who'd ambushed us earlier. We tried to demonstrate our best dance moves while the children attempted to out dance us. Everyone was enjoying themselves.

At one point in the night, I felt a hand on my thigh. I turned around, concerned I was being pickpocketed, only to find Mike had decided to dance with me. He leaned down and I wrapped his arms around my waist. I leaned back and melted into his warm body. We danced and giggled, as if we were at a middle school dance.

Mike placed his lips on my neck and gently kissed my newly tanned skin. I took pause, and enjoyed the moment. I reinforced his hands under my own. In the background, I felt not just Mike up against me, but a set of eyes on me. I turned slightly to see Paul watching us from the sidelines. My smile disappeared slowly from my face, Paul's gaze not leaving mine. He took a sip from his beer, looked down, and walked away under the blanket of the stars that filled the night sky.

My heart sank.

What was with Paul? Was he jealous? An overprotective leader? My enemy? I couldn't understand this man. I needed to let go and have some fun tonight; I deserved it.

I released myself from my funk and carried on with the festivities. I couldn't remember the last time I felt such joy. I laughed so hard, my cheeks hurt. Rebecca had found some neon body paint and she had decorated herself in dots, stars, and hearts. Her body glowed under the shimmering disco ball. We all joined in the fun of painting each other. Forget about clean laundry, which could wait.

As Mike and I smeared neon paint over each other, our lips connected, and we made out on the dance floor. Passion ignited.

When we grew tired, we stumbled back to the hostel and into someone's bed.

Chapter Sixteen

The next morning, I felt a pounding in my head. My legs were cramped underneath me. I looked around and realized that I wasn't in my top bunk, but rather foreign territory.

I felt around the bed sheets. An empty water bottle crinkled under my knees. The corners of the bedsheets restrained me as they'd unravelled from their post. I felt a candy wrapper clinging to the back of my arm. I ripped it off like a bandage. I rolled over to see who was hogging the bed. Somehow, I had managed to find my way into Mike's bunk. We were entangled with each other, and he was still asleep, snoring.

Panicked, I looked around. Everyone appeared to be in a deep slumber, like a bunch of bears hibernating. I heard the whimper of a woman across the room, not from our group, trying to dislodge her arm from under an animal's grasp. We made empathetic eye contact as we tried to escape the den in silence.

I looked down and felt reassured that I remained fully clothed. A sigh of relief escaped my lips. A new year did not mean a new boo. A new year, however, meant a little more fun for me. I carefully unravelled myself from Mike's grip and slid off the bed. I was gentle, trying to ensure that I didn't wake him. I tiptoed towards the doorway and slithered into the hallway, shutting the door silently behind me. Breathing another sigh of relief, I headed through the hallway towards the ladies' dorm.

"Lost?" a familiar voice judged, echoing down the empty hallway.

My heartrate quickened, as I knew instantly who it was behind me.

"Just heading back from the washroom. Too much beer last night."

Paul wasn't buying it. "Uh, huh. The washroom is down the other end of the hallway, across from the ladies' dorm. In case you were wondering."

"Right, I must've got mixed up." Embarrassment flushed my face. I started walking, nay running, down the hallway.

"Wait a minute, Poppy." Paul stopped. "It might not be my place to say anything, but I just want you to be careful with the other guys on this trip." Paul looked down at his feet, kicking an invisible can.

"What do you mean?"

"Guys on holiday tend to mess around with a bunch of different girls. It isn't like anyone is dating. They're usually here to have fun."

"Mike isn't like that," I started defensively. "He's a nice guy. He wouldn't do anything to hurt me."

"Maybe not intentionally, but I saw him holding hands with Jessica on the boat yesterday. I don't want you to get hurt. You seem like a nice person, that's all." What did he just say?

My face flushed with both embarrassment and rage. "Feel free to mind your own business. It isn't like you've been nice to me these past few days."

"I'm not sure what you mean," Paul stuttered. Confusion spread across his face.

"Come on," – I crossed my arms across my chest – "don't pretend like you haven't put me down every chance you got."

"I don't know what you mean, seriously." He extended his arms in surrender.

I rolled my eyes, as if I had to explain the obvious. "The welcome meeting, the train, the boat…right now – " I'm sure if I thought harder, I could have pointed out a few more low blows.

"Wait, what are you talking about? I – " Paul paused as if in reflection. "Maybe I have been a little tough on you. I'm sorry." He looked down at his feet again, the invisible can still in motion. "There have been a few mix ups with reservations, and I find it frustrating. That and this group is hard to get to follow instructions." He grinned. "Especially you."

I had two choices, fight with him or let it go. "Ha, ha, very funny." I tried to lighten the mood. "I'm sorry things have been stressful. That sucks."

"Sure, does." The invisible can stopped moving at his feet. "I didn't mean any harm, truly. I will try to be more respectful."

"That would be nice. I don't deserve to be spoken down to. I just want to have a nice holiday." I felt liberated.

"Totally agree. I promise not to take my frustrations out on you, or the other group members." He made an x over his heart to form a promise. My stomach flipped a little at the reminder of John.

"Right, well I better get back. Big day ahead of us." I retreated towards my dorm.

"Get some rest. I'll see you soon." Paul disappeared into the lobby.

Sleepy and hungover, we boarded onto the crowded, oversized van. The van rocked as Paul and the driver hoisted our belongings onto the roof. The moans and the tightening of the straps could be heard out the cracked windows. Once our luggage was secured, we were off.

The drive felt long and exhausting. The van hugged the curb of the road along the way. To be honest, I preferred this to the previous train ride. I swear, with every twist and turn in the road, our vehicle lurched onto the two, side wheels. Groans echoed in the muggy, stale air.

When we got to the Thailand-Malaysia border, we all

unloaded from the van. Passengers collected their makeshift, sweatshirt pillows and were instructed to identify our bags, collect them, and have our passports ready as we walked across the border to meet our new drivers.

By now I had a system – large, touring bag in the back, day bag in the front. Sure, I swayed back and forth like a pendulum and couldn't see my toes, but I was organized, ready to run at a moment's notice.

We stood single file like school children waiting for recess. Rebecca, who was behind me, placed her head on my backpack, adding unnecessary weight to my luggage. Her hangover was not my baggage. While most of us stood in a similar fashion, some with more bags than others, Paul was at the front of the line with his small backpack slung over his shoulder. I couldn't help but wonder why he had only one bag, how he could fit everything he needed into one singular sack, and how he had so many clean clothes? I'd already needed one load of washing to be done and I hadn't even been away one week! I thumbed my passport picture page as I pondered this thought. I'd get to the bottom of his technique one way or the other.

"I'm hot," whined the hungover child.

"So, am I," Kate fanned herself from behind us. She stood shrouded in a new, beige sunhat and oversized glasses that concealed her face. A thin, long scarf was wrapped protectively around the remaining, exposed facial features. The puffiness of her flesh was slightly visible under the shading of the new accessories.

"You know, you don't have to wear all that," Rebecca added her unsolicited opinion.

"As I've told you, youngin, I'm protecting myself from further damage. I'd like to enjoy myself, thank you very much. It'll be a long trip if you keep sharing your insights." Kate huffed to the back of the line. Would this ever end? Rebecca shook her head and muttered an obscene name under her breath.

One by one, we made our way through customs. Our bags were placed on a rickety belt and buzzed through the scanner. Drugs were the border guard's main concern, Paul had previously told us. Weapons were a close second. The border guards would take our passports one by one and look through the pages. The guard looked at us each suspiciously, flipping the pages slowly, to continue his search. It was unclear what secrets he was hoping to find in the pages.

After we all made our way through the crossing, Paul collected us. He informed us that there would be good news and bad news. We looked to each other, wondering what could be worse than our cramped van with minimal air conditioning. When he told us we would have to split into three groups so that we could settle into our more spacious, premium, air-conditioned vans, we squealed with glee. Even better, there'd be movies available onboard, if we chose. Immediately, Rebecca looped her arm around mine, as if to lay claim to me.

"You're it! Let's go in the same van." As we settled onboard, we had enough room to stretch out comfortably. It would be a few hours to our next stop:

the metropolis of Kuala Lumpur where we were headed for a few days. After that, we would continue to travel, eventually making our way to Singapore.

People seemed more alive and refreshed as they settled into our new rides. The doors squeaked closed, and I heard, "Mind if I sit here?" I looked up from the book I had just opened and there, hunched over my seat, was Paul. I looked around to make sure he was speaking to me, and to also see if I could point to a free seat for to him sit in instead. After all, I wanted to stretch out, too.

After a brief look around, and no other free seat in sight, I turned to him, "Sure, no problem." I removed my bag and wiggled it between my feet. Paul sat down beside me with his mystery bag perched on his lap. I eyed the bag, curious to know its depths.

"What are you reading?" the unwanted guest asked. I'm not certain if he waited until the exact moment I opened my book, or he was just done his roll call. I was hesitant to explain to him that I was reading a self-help book. My mom had slipped it into my bag for me to read on the plane. When I noticed the deadweight, my heart sank into my chest. The last thing I wanted was to dig too deeply into my emotions, since my broken heart had not yet healed. I had shoved it to the bottom of the bag, hoping to forget about it for a while.

I shifted uncomfortably in my seat and decided to tell Paul the truth, or my brand of it. I didn't want him making fun of me. I explained that it was a book about self-empowerment and how to look at your perceived weaknesses as strengths instead. As I read it, I wondered if it would help me with my career path when I got home, I wanted to go in the right direction.

Paul stared inquisitively at the back of the seat in front of him for a moment. "Huh, that's pretty cool. What's the most insightful thing you've learned so far?"

I wasn't expecting a counter question. I panicked for a moment, trying to remember what I had read, and what I had read between the lines. "So far, to be yourself and not take shit from anyone." My affect was blunt as I delivered the punch.

A slow smile crept across his face, and he chuckled. "Truer words have never been spoken, Maple."

"Hey!" I playfully nudged into him. "Only the English girls can call me that!"

"I take it back; I won't use it again." Paul raised his hands in surrender.

With that, Paul rattled his bag around. My curiosity slipped from the pages of my book to the silver loop on the zipper. Slowly, Paul took his time to open the metal teeth. He didn't see me watching. Mindlessly, Paul opened the zipper enough to slip his hand inside, his gaze fixed to the roadside. I couldn't see inside. His hand re-emerged and in his grasp was a banana. I took a moment, puzzled, to figure out how he'd all of his worldly belongings and room for a banana in his bag. I looked at the banana and then back at him. He must have felt my gaze as he turned to look at me. He gestured his banana towards me after he took a large bite, his cheeks puffed like a monkey. I shook my head 'no' and leaned back into my seat, enjoying the cool air on my face.

A couple hours passed, and people were feeling rejuvenated, and a little restless, after the long ride. Many folks had still not quite worn off the jet leg, which didn't help.

"No, no, that's not how you play!" Rebecca winced. "It's like this. We make a list of five words, and these five words no one can say the entire journey to the hostel. Do you understand?" Rebecca bounced off her seat, preparing the passengers for an epic battle. "If you say the word, there'll be punishment!" She reached down below her seat. "This!" Rebecca pulled out a bottle of liquor from her bag. If you say the restricted word, you drink!" There was mixed emotions. Those passengers with hangovers were not too keen to continue their imbibing.

"Alright, what are the five words?" Paul asked. Somehow, a slip of paper and a pen emerged from said mystery bag while I wasn't looking.

"Let's put our thinking caps on, fellas." Rebecca concentrated. She rubbed her temples as if she was summoning a genie from a bottle.

"Beach, beer, toilet, cellphone, and-" Rebecca couldn't pinpoint a fifth word.

"Shit!" someone yelled.

"Oh, man, we'll all be hammered after this!" Rebecca roared. Her sparkly white crop top jiggled, catching the attention of other male passengers.

"We have our five words. Let's begin!" She clinked the side of the bottle with her fingernails.

"I'm watching you," my seatmate challenged. When

he leaned into me, goosebumps raised my flesh.

"You're on." Two can play at that game.

There was silence for about 45 minutes and then, the conversation started again. Some folks, inadvertently, dropped the ball and said one of the words as if they were casting a spell on the van, wanting people to play. Someone would usually point and loudly inform the van that someone was about to take a shot. Others purposefully said words, most likely because they wanted to get hammered on free booze.

"Don't be greedy, the lot of you. This has to last us to the hostel!" Rebecca shouted.

"You're awfully quiet over there. You scared?" Rebecca leaned over our seat from behind. Paul and I, in unison, turned around to look at our peeping tom.

"We're simply enjoying the written word," Paul poked. A small paperback had also emerged from his belongings. It was essentially a clown car with straps.

"Ya don't want to use that little device to send a message?" Rebecca was trying her best to trip one of us up.

"What device?" he said, making an ear of the page. He studied Rebecca's face.

"You know, that little thing," Rebecca mimicked, typing on the electronic device.

"What's she going on about?" He looked at me quizzically, pointing at our intruder.

"No idea."

"Ah, you know what I mean – your cellphone!" Rebecca stated as if we didn't understand. When she realized she'd said the word, she cackled, "Guess I better drink up!" With that, she took a giant swig.

"You two getting along?" She wiped her lips. Liquor had beaded at the corners of her mouth.

"I think we're surviving. We haven't been plagued with the drink yet, but we shall be victorious!" Paul announced.

I smiled and laughed. "We'll be the winners, after all." I high fived Paul. Maybe he wasn't so bad.

"Like van King and Queen?" He smirked.

I took a minute to think about this. He'd gone from loathing me, to tolerating me, back to being annoyed with me, to being a 'couple'? My, how things had escalated. Seeing the look on my face, Rebecca jumped in, "The only Queen I've pledged my life to was the one in jolly ol' England. God rest her soul!" Rebecca thundered and with that, some other passengers echoed her. "I'm still getting used to this King business," she concluded. Times do change.

"Back to your books, nerds." Rebecca slunk back into her seat.

The van periodically filled with laughter and booze, followed by silence. Everyone was having fun.

In the early afternoon, I was startled awake from my nap when our van took a sharp turn onto the side of the road. Our driver rushed to the side of the van and a small rug emerged. A loud voice could be heard over speakers that lined the side of the highway. "What's going on? Are we okay?" I nudged Paul. He groggily opened his eyes and tried to orient himself.

"What do you mean?" I took a moment to explain to him what happened. Paul looked down at his watch. "Oh, it's almost time for call to prayer. Our driver is Muslim, and this is a very important to him and his culture," he said nonchalantly and closed his eyes. Malaysia is a diverse country. Call to prayer happens anywhere, five times per day.

I took a minute to process the information. I'd heard the call to prayer before at home, but I suppose I didn't expect pulling over to the side of the road for prayer. I felt reassured there was no issue with the van.

"One of the best parts of travelling is learning about other people. Take some time to talk to others to learn about their cultures. You'll find out so many wonderful things. We may have our differences, but we are also very much alike." Paul closed his eyes and returned to his slumber. The mystery bag was a makeshift pillow.

I watched as the driver got up from his mat and smoothed the creases of his pant legs. He gently took his mat and tucked it back under the van. He boarded and continued the journey as if we had just filled up at the gas station.

One hour was left in the journey to our destination and I felt an uncomfortable pressure in my bladder. I wiggled in my seat. I wasn't sure if it was the sound of my pants or my bladder rattling around that must have woken Paul. "What's wrong with you? You're shaking the whole seat; I almost fell off!" Maybe Paul was the drama queen, not me.

"Nothing. Don't worry about it." The sweat pooled

on my forehead. I knew I needed to say, 'I need the toilet,' but I didn't want to say the word out of fear that I'd be forced to consume more fluid. Paul caught onto this little dance. "Do you need to make a request?"

The comment was pondered, but I decided not to reply. He was onto me. "No, I'm fine." Lies.

Paul smiled and reached down into his bag. My bladder was bulging and sore. I didn't even have a chance to look down. Paul pulled out a bottle of water. The sound of the lid unscrewing was loud in my ears, taunting me. The drizzling sound of the water being poured down his throat made my bladder palpate, causing further squirming. Paul sighed in satisfaction after he consumed nearly half of the bottle's contents. He wiped away droplets of the clear fluid from his plump, pink lips.

"You monster," I panted.

"All you have to do is say the word. One magic little word and I can help you out. So far, I don't know what it is you need from me." He turned and continued to leaf through his book, periodically glancing sideways at me. His side eye was enraging but also sparked something else inside of me, something I hadn't quite figured out yet.

Was I going to cave into my bladder or wait it out? As the van continued down the road, we passed a sign for restrooms about an hour away. "No," I quietly muttered.

"What's that? Were you speaking to me?"

I shot a glance at Paul. The decision was made "I. NEED. A. TOILET. NOW!" I raged, alarming my fellow passengers. People rustled in their seats to see what the commotion was all about.

Paul burst out laughing, his face soon covered in tears. "All you had to do was ask!"

The van halted to the side of the road and the door swung open. Paul gestured for me to get out.

"Here?" I panicked. I looked around for a washroom.

"Those who beg cannot always choose."

Feeling a sense of urgency, I pushed past everyone and launched outside the van. The driver took his jacket off his seat and made an impromptu partition. He'd likely done this many times before. He made sure to look in the opposite direction and closed his eyes as I juggled my belongings to undo my pants.

Embarrassed by the honking cars and the hooting passengers, I forced myself to 'break the seal' as they say. Bottomless railway toilets, squatty pottys, and highway hangs would become the new bathroom. The porcelain seat would not make a grand return for a bit.

Relief washed over me. Business finished, I boarded, red in the face. My bladder was stretched, but would eventually return to its original shape. Plopping down in my seat, Rebecca startled me. "Aye, glad the tank is empty! Time to fill it up again!" The van chanted for me to drink, Paul joining in on the action.

"Okay, okay. I get it! I said toilet!" They gasped and chanted for me to drink again. I contested and took another swig. Paul grabbed my shoulder and shook it, as if to say, 'that a girl!' I thought I felt my heart racing and time going in slow motion, all at once.

Rebecca laughed. She took a wordless minute to look

at me, to Paul, and back to me again. She saw something that I couldn't see. She winked and disappeared behind the seat once again. She was like the booze troll who lived under the bridge, only appearing to cause mayhem.

The rowdiness subsided. The van veered off of the highway and into a calm rhythm down a four-lane road. Surrounding us were tropical trees and skyscrapers. It was like we were in a modern, lost city, ready to explore and find our way through the jungle.

"Welcome to Kuala Lumpur," Paul announced. He provided us a brief history and promised a walking tour later that night so we would decide how to spend our next few days here. I was mesmerized, taking in the scenery, entranced with my new surroundings.

"Too bad the ride is over; it was so much fun." I exhaled, tucking my items away.

"Poppy, the destination isn't the main attraction. It's the journey that takes you there," Paul mused. With that, he leapt back into action.

Chapter Seventeen

Our hostel in Kuala Lumpur was more like a fancy hotel, well, a hotel, anyways. We were ecstatic when we learned that we'd be sharing rooms with four ladies instead of half the group of ladies on the trip. Paul went through the list of names and arrived at the last set of people. "Rebecca, Poppy, Jean, and Jessica. You'll be in room five." My heart sank. Jessica. Mike and Jessica. Holding hands with my man, Jessica. Jessica.

"Alright, let's get cracking!" Rebecca's voice echoed in the lobby. "We've got 30 minutes before we go on the walking tour, and I need my urban safari look."

I was too dazed to hear Rebecca.

"Hello, Earth to Poppy! Let's get our outfits on. Time to hustle and check out the local sights, and I do mean the men." Rebecca nudged me. She scouted around for new prey in our current surroundings.

"Yeah, sorry. I was thinking."

"'Bout what?"

"Nothing, it doesn't matter." I twiddled with the straps on my bag.

"Nah, nah, nah, you can't play me like that. What's up with my bestie?" Rebecca swung her sweaty arm around me, our flesh melting into each other.

I considered if I should say anything to Rebecca; I didn't want to cause any drama.

"Paul mentioned that Mike and Jessica were 'a thing.' Now, I feel silly for flirting with him." Crossing my arms, I turned away to hide my frustration. I couldn't help but feel like a plaything to my new man.

Rebecca nodded, processing the information. "Ah, well, there'll be others. He's not the only fish. Why don't we ignore them and have a good time?" She squeezed me.

"You're right." And she was. "We're here to have fun. I'm not going to let Mike and Jessica ruin my holiday. There will be other men for me to sink my teeth into!" With that, we made our way to room five to get ready.

The door scanned to open. The metal click of the door and the heavy hinge creaked. A flood of cool air washed over us; we relaxed in unison. We took our beds across from Jean and Jessica, all the better to keep an eye on her from here.

I generated a facade of happiness on my face. Jean had fluffed her pillow and closed her eyes. Jessica was on her phone, clearly texting someone. I watched her face light up when a sound notification went off. She giggled and tried to cover her mouth, but it was too little, too late. The dimples in her face popped.

"What's so funny over there?" Rebecca inquired as

she rummaged through her bag, tossing heaps of clothing onto her bed. I imagined her room looked like this: organized chaos. She'd have to suffer repacking her bag each time we changed accommodations.

"Oh, nothing," Jessica said shyly. More dimples, more giggles.

"Well, must be something amusing. Let's have a look and join in the fun!"

"No, no. It's private." Jessica turned off the screen and nestled the phone on the pillow beside her. She closed her eyes to daydream.

Not a few minutes later, the phone pinged, again. More dimples, more giggles. I grew irritated at this repetition. No answers. Jessica's phone was now safely tucked under her pillow for further protection.

"What do we think about this?" Rebecca pulled out a short, sleeveless, trench dress. "Is this suitable for an urban adventure? Or shall I wait for tomorrow to wear this?" Rebecca changed her mind several times, tossing more clothing onto the bed and the floor, before settling on jean shorts, a white t-shirt, and a vest for today's walk about. She paired it with a cheap tourist fedora she got at the airport in London. After she changed into her, as she called it, urban safari chic wear, she fixed her attention on Jessica. It was evident to Rebecca that I was still bothered by having to share a room with her.

If only Rebecca had a blow dart as an accessory.

"Now that I'm done getting ready, who ya chatting with, Jess? Inquiring minds do wish to know." She winked at her as she lay across her clothes-covered bed.

"Fine, if you must have it your way," she sighed. "I'm talking to a new guy."

Crickets filled the room.

"We figured that. But to whom do you speak?" Rebecca's irritated speech continued.

Jessica shifted on her bed, unsure if she should spill her secret. "He's a guy on our trip. I think he likes me. We had a chill day on the boat back in Thailand and a fun ride today." She shifted onto her stomach and crossed her legs behind her. The tea was being spilled. "But he hasn't really made much of a move yet. I'm not sure if he likes me back." Jessica shifted again to recline on her pillows, looking at the empty phone screen with no new text, and pouted.

Rebecca and I knew she was speaking about Mike. Rebecca looked at me as if to say, 'sorry I went there.' I took out my own phone. A pang of jealousy hit me. I was yet again reminded of John and his two women. I could rise above this. Jessica could have Mike if he's going to act like a player.

Poppy: Am trapped in personal hell.
Casey: What's up?
Poppy: The guy I like, Mike, I'm rooming with the girl he's apparently also into.
Casey: I thought he was into you?!
Poppy: So did I. They've been flirting too, more progress than I it sounds.
Casey: Are you going to just sit around to 'wait

and see?'
Poppy: I guess so?
Casey: No, if you want a man you have to throw yourself at him. Read my latest post 'When You Say We're Just Friends.' Basically, be wherever he is, offer to pair up with him, and don't let him out of your sight. He'll be charmed by you and be yours in a heartbeat!
Poppy: Not my style, Casey. I don't chase men.
Casey: Men love women who chase them! He wants you, trust me.
Poppy: Ugh, I don't know. I'd rather meet someone who is into me instead.

Just like that, the little chickadees headed out to see the city sights. Paul pointed out areas of interest we may want to visit the following day. We passed cafés, museums, and high fashion shops. I was sure Rebecca had whiplash from trying to snap photos of the places she wanted to visit, none of which were on the tourist map. I tried to keep pace with her. Against my better judgement, I tried very hard to follow Casey's advice about being near Mike to get his attention; after all, we'd had a fun night the other night. Maybe I misread the situation with Jessica.

We stopped and hid under the shade of tropical trees as Paul explained the cultural significance of the areas. I nestled in beside Mike. The first time I stood beside him and smiled at him, he smiled back. The third and fourth time, he began to look puzzled as to why I was always beside him, smiling like a fool. At one point, he moved away from me, and closer to Jessica. She was standing on the other side of him, her dimples popping. Game on, Jessica.

Once or twice, I lost count, I may've purposefully pushed Jessica out of the way to get to Mike first when we stopped to hear Paul's speech about a monument.

"Hey!" Jessica cried out when I zipped past, much like a football player trying to get to the ball first. Paul turned around to try to figure out what was going on. Puzzled, he continued with the tour when we began walking again.

"Maple, this isn't a race. We're all headed to the same destination," Kate chided behind us. She had on her large, brimmed hat with scarfs wrapped all around her. She looked as if she was at the end of a funeral precession.

"Sorry, Kate, I'm on a mission," I huffed, continuing to zip around others to get to my target.

"I see that, Maple." She fanned herself, likely boiling under the layers of fabric protecting her face. She looked ahead to see what I was focusing on.

As we continued our city travels, the heat got to us. This was something we were not used to. I grew frustrated as Mike never responded to my advances. He, however, was getting cozier with Jessica. It was as if my attempts repulsed him.

I felt myself giving up. Maybe Paul was right: be

careful.

Everyone was fanning themselves with the printed itinerary and city map Paul had given us. Some of us had completely zoned out. Paul, sensing our waning enthusiasm, suggested we take a detour to the Petronas Twin Tower before it closed. We would stop by a nearby mall on the way there to have something to eat for dinner first.

Everyone returned to life as we entered the refreshing mall. The smells from the food court wafted in the air. Flames from the grills danced from down below, mesmerizing us. Shops with foreign clothing intrigued us.

The food court looked much like that of a western mall. There were familiar, fast-food names mixed in with East Indian and Chinese food restaurants. As we took the escalator down, down, down into the three-storey food court we were amazed by the sights and sounds. Paul told us we had an hour and then we'd head over to the towers so we could go to the top before it closed. We all scattered like mice. I was a hawk, and I had my eye on the prey.

"What are you going to have?" I cooed as I rubbed up against Mike. He turned around, irritated to see me, again. So much for my method.

"Oh, I don't know if I'm very hungry. Jessica and I had a lot of snacks in the van."

Jessica. She was interfering.

"Oh, that's cool; me either. Maybe we can get one of those tropical fruit slushies instead. My treat?" I swayed, showing off my girlish figure.

Mike looked around as if he was trying to escape. "Yeah, I don't know. I was actually going to hang with some of the guys, if that's cool?" He placed his hands in his pockets and looked around for anyone to escape to.

Defeated, I shrugged and walked away. Mike headed off to sit with a couple of the guys from the trip who were huddled around a small, white table. I roamed around, hoping to find Rebecca or some ice cream to soothe my woes. I was a damn fool chasing a man; I knew better. What had happened to me?

"Ah, yes, madam! This is perfect!" Rebecca squealed. She had scored a shiny, purple bikini. I laughed. This girl's backpack was packed to the brim with endless items.

"You do know we won't be at the beach again for two weeks, right? Not until Bali," I reminded her.

"Ah, hush. Maybe there'll be a pool at our accommodations."

"Hostels don't have pools."

"Okay, maybe we'll meet some cute boys, and we'll hang at their pools!" Rebecca cackled. "Love, I need a few extra things. Mind if I meet you back at our room?"

"You're not coming to the towers?" I already felt low, and I wanted the cheerful company of my new bestie.

"I was hoping to hit a club or two while we're here. I didn't pack any club outfits. I'll see the towers tomorrow with you if you want to go then?"

Alone again.

"Sounds good." I didn't want to show my disappointment. "Don't spend all your money," I jested.

Rebecca was a kind soul; I didn't want to bring her down.

"Too late!" Rebecca cackled, her signature.

I walked around the mall and decided to head back to the food court. I thought that ice cream sounded good right about now. Circling the court, I found some chocolate, whipped ice cream that came in a fish-shaped cone. At the end of the court, Paul was sitting alone. He didn't notice me at first. Instead, I headed to where Mike and the guys were. I thought I'd make one last effort to get his attention. If I didn't, Casey would raze me.

As I moved closer to the table, I noticed that the group of guys had a new addition: Jessica. Mike and Jessica were laughing, and Jessica had one hand resting on his shoulder. He didn't flinch from her touch. I stood there, stunned. I watched in slow motion as Mike stretched his arm down and placed his hand on her knee, one of the most intimate gestures. My face turned classic red, and I spun around, trying to make a quick exit as the tears formed in the corners of my eyes.

As I tried to make my break, without my getaway car, I locked eyes with Paul who was emptying his tray into the trash can. "Are you okay, Poppy?" He brushed the wrappers into the receptacle.

"Not really. I made a total fool of myself today. You were right about Mike and Jessica," I confessed.

Paul looked down and placed his tray on the stack of soiled ones. "I'm sorry. That really sucks."

"Sure does. I came here with a broken heart. I didn't imagine it could break even more than it already had. I guess I'm feeling a bit sensitive. Sometimes, I don't recognize myself." I don't know why I decided to confess my tragic past.

Paul asked no more questions, just listened intently. He nodded as if he'd been there and experienced the same things before. After a moment, which seemed like a lifetime, Paul checked his watch and said, "No one seems to be interested in the rest of the city tour. Do you want to get out of here and explore?" No one had gathered to finish the walking tour after dinner.

I looked around. Paul was right; no one else had showed up.

"Come with me." Paul gestured to follow him. "I want to show you something I bet you've never seen before." I was ready for anything.

Chapter Eighteen

This time of year, the night comes quickly. When we'd emerged from the mall, the sky was dark. The stars above twinkled and competed with the Christmas lights strung along the street. A gentle breeze swept through my hair.

As we walked along the street, the cityscape changed. Instead of shops and restaurants, we entered suburbia. Families and tourists coexisted. As food venders pushed their carts, they called out for customers to visit them for a good deal. Their fares of cooked fish or dried fruits dangled down the sides of their squeaking carts. Children laughed and weaved in and out amongst everyone. The mood was light, and a smile formed upon my face.

Paul and I walked down the streets, getting further and further away from the city. The streets were now lined with tables of goods. Some people were selling beaded necklaces, small paintings, and exotic trinkets. Tables had towers of sweet and savoury spices. The colours danced and the aromas were intoxicating. I couldn't take my eyes away; at one point, I tripped as I was taking photos and Paul caught me, helping me up.

"So much going on, isn't there?"

"Yes, I'm loving this!" I squeaked.

"Here, I want to show you something." Paul grazed my forearm and slowly reached for my hand. This small act, although innocent, sent goosebumps up my arms and caused me to pause briefly. Paul turned around, puzzled.

"Everything okay?" he asked, his eyebrows arched in concern.

I stood there, frozen, as I gathered my thoughts. Something felt different suddenly.

"Yes, I thought I dropped my camera lens cover," I lied. We both looked down around our feet to investigate. "Here it is," I recovered. "I must've tucked it in my back pocket."

"No problem; glad you found it." He reached back for my hand again.

Our palms melted together. It felt calm and intense at the same time. I felt urges towards Paul I couldn't explain.

"Ah, here she is: my favourite woman!" Paul exclaimed. He let go of my hand. My heart dropped. Who was he referring to?

"You're back!" The petite, Malaysian woman danced around her table and cast her tiny frame around Paul. "I missed you. My best customer!" She kissed him dramatically on the cheek, hugging him again.

Paul laughed and hugged the woman back. "These are by far the best candied orange peels you will ever find. I have to come and get them every time I'm here." Paul winked at the nameless woman and dug a handful of change from his pocket. He picked through the contents of his hand and the woman gave him a bag of the treats. After the transaction was completed, he tucked the candy in his bag. "Come on, let's go get some other goodies."

"Bye, bye, handsome," the woman called out and waved as we walked away. Maybe she wasn't a threat after all. Paul was just a regular customer.

We continued through the market, hand in hand. For a bizarre moment, I felt like we were a couple, and this was just a regular date night for us. There was fresh fruit juice hanging in plastic bags, hot woks with sizzling oil, and noodles flipping in the air and crackling as soon as they hit the pan. Peppers and fresh vegetables simmered, and people ate them feverishly as they continued their journey for more sinful pleasures.

Paul pointed out different foods to me, such as dried shrimp, sardines, and some sort of jerked meat. The smells were conflicting between pleasant and overly pungent. He laughed at me. "Don't see much of the world, do you?"

I felt sheepish. "No, this is actually my first trip abroad. My family used to drive to Myrtle Beach every year, but that's the extent of my travel." I tucked my hair behind my ear with my free hand as we continued walking. I felt small.

Paul's face turned solemn. "There's so much beauty, regardless of where you are, even if you don't travel, isn't there?" He caressed my wrist with his thumb. His eyes met mine and they sparkled in the dark.

Paul no longer seemed to be judging me. He seemed genuinely interested in me. I wasn't sure what to feel.

"Tell me more about you. I'm interested to learn all about Poppy." We found a park bench and sat nestled under the night sky.

"You really want to know more about me?" I asked, genuinely shocked.

"Of course, I do. You're a mysterious woman." Paul opened the bags of fresh fruit and nuts. We had a makeshift charcuterie board on the bench. He also had two fruit juices and I reached for the coconut. "Good, I wanted the mango one!" Paul exclaimed, a sneaky smile creeping onto his face.

I laughed. "If you're interested, I can tell you a whole lot. You might regret it."

"Never." Paul opened his mouth, pretending to be offended.

That evening, we talked about our homes, our hobbies, and our interests. We shared funny stories about growing up and things we'd like to accomplish in the near future. Something had shifted, and just like that, we went from foes to friends.

Suddenly, Paul recalled the one treasure he had purchased, and he pulled out the candied orange peels. "Voila, madam, your dessert awaits!" I bit into a slice of orange. My mouth was filled with the refreshing and vibrant sweetness of the sugar, which contrasted with the bitterness of the peel. You could almost suck the simple syrup out of each chewy bite.

"So, tell me about your friend. What's her name? Cassidy?"

"Casey," I corrected him as I punctured the bag with a straw.

"You're a pro," Paul commented at my picnic skills.

"I've had some practice," I jived as our knees collided into each other.

"Casey and I met at work. She and I both worked for accountants. She's very funny and beautiful. She could have any man she wants." I looked down at my lap, as if defeated over being led on by Mike, only for him to end up with someone else.

"YOU could have any man you want." The pause between us was thick like fog. I didn't know what to say in response. I focused on my drink and waited out the awkwardness.

"Casey has been so good to me. She's helped me in some challenging situations, like starting a job," – I paused, unsure if I should tell Paul about the situation with John – "and out of a job. She's always been there for me. Her advice is, on point….sometimes," I laughed.

"What kind of advice?" Paul asked hesitantly. Timing is everything.

I shifted on the bench, unsure if I should drift into talk of romance. I bit the bullet. "Men."

Paul laughed. "She gives you advice about men?" He sipped on his mango juice. "Let's hear it; what's Casey's advice?"

I explained that Casey wrote columns on the side. Her advice may be questionable, but the intent was positive. Paul laughed at the antidotes that Casey prescribed me. I couldn't help but feel sheepish that I followed some of her more questionable advice.

"Good friend, but I'd think twice on the advice. Follow your own intuition," Paul coaxed. "The answer is always within you. You're a confident woman. You just need to get back up on your feet." He took another sip, refreshing himself.

I thought about his comment. I felt I should explain my past. The intent wasn't in a way to rationalize my actions, but rather to explain my truth and the ways I was growing as a woman. "I was with this man," I started, unsure of how to continue, "and he broke my heart. I haven't had many successful relationships and I thought what we had was special. He lied to me. He didn't make his intentions known. Casey was there to listen, and, in the end, to lift my spirits and to help me move on." I gulped. "I'm grateful for her friendship. She's blunt and to the point. Tear the bandage off, so to speak. I love her for that. She's kind of like my 'wife for life' if that makes sense?" I wasn't sure if Paul would probe further or leave the past where it belonged.

"It's good to have friends like that, people in your corner. I'm glad you have her in your life." Paul fell silent. We both peered in opposite directions, trying to decide how to change the course of the conversation. Paul continued, "I had my heart broken, too. I decided to become a tour guide because the woman I was with broke my heart. She told me I was the one. She told me that she wanted to marry me and have kids with me. I supported her through college. I helped renovate her apartment. Sad thing is, I caught her with another man. It tore me to pieces. There was a part of me that believed she was my soulmate." Paul chuckled, shaking his head, and looking up at the stars as if to contend that soulmates even existed.

"So, you became a tour guide to get away from her?" I asked inquisitively.

"No, I became a tour guide to find myself." There was a shared moment of clarity between us. "I had somehow wrapped myself up in the idea that I needed to be in a relationship to be happy. The truth was, I needed to find myself to be happy. Travelling can either give you an escape from the mundane, or it can open your eyes to an existence you didn't know was out there." He shook his plastic bag as if to summon more wise words, like a genie from a bottle. No further words came; they didn't have to.

A pause between us was like a gigantic, emotional, tidal wave. Paul stopped focusing on his juice and turned his attention towards me. The past didn't matter anymore.

"For the first time in a long time, I'm enjoying myself." His lips spread open to show his teeth. My heart melted.

"Me, too." I relaxed.

The moment broke. "Here, let's finish some of these treats before they spoil," Paul said as he unwrapped the plastic. He picked up more orange peels with his delicately callused fingers. He sucked the sugar off his fingertips. He extended his hand toward me and arched his eyebrows as if to say, 'open up.'

I opened my mouth and Paul glided the sweet sliver of fruit between my lips. A burst of citrus and memories of childhood sweets rushed through me. I closed my eyes to relive these moments of my youth. I felt the heat, not just from the night air, but the body heat of Paul moving closer to me. His hand rested on my knee and the side of his chest pushed against me. I contemplated kissing him. Paul wrapped his arms around my waist and drew me into him. I was almost sitting on Paul's lap, we were so close. In a daze, I found myself leaning closer until our lips barely touched.

I opened my eyes and heard a multitude of giggles coming from the distance. Paul dropped his hands. Two American girls from the trip had spotted this intimate moment and ran off when Paul and I caught wind of them. I feared the worst – that these girls would start rumours about me and Paul. That's the last thing I needed.

I looked at Paul in shock. "Don't worry about them, it'll be okay," he reassured me.

The last thing I had on my mind was more gossip. I'd had enough drama from John's wife finding out about us and the panic that drove me away from my job and Toronto.

"Are you sure? The last thing I want is rumours being spread." I buried my face in my hands. Paul reached over and caressed my back. "I promise, you're safe with me. I won't let anything bad happen to you." I believed this to be true.

Chapter Nineteen

I tossed and turned that night. I couldn't help but fluctuate between visions of our bodies wrapped around each other in bliss versus being ridiculed by other members of our trip. I woke several times in a cold sweat. I shivered with discomfort, my roommates none the wiser of what had transpired.

My brain swelled with confusion about what had happened between me and Paul. I felt heard and respected by him, more than any other man I'd ever dated. That list, however, was small and filled with mostly flings. I no longer felt that I was a nuisance to him. Something between us had changed. Maybe we had just misunderstood each other before. I longed for him. I wanted his fingers to graze my skin. I wanted to feel what it was like to have his lips on my lips. I imagined that his kiss was that of salty flesh, sweet and moist. I savoured him with my imagination as I painted memories like brushstrokes on canvas.

"You alright over there, Maple? The bed is going to come crashing down," Rebecca chirped, irritated with my squeaking bedframe.

"Sorry," I squirmed. "I can't sleep. I'm hot."

"Yes, Maple, it's frigging Asia. Get used to it." Rebecca emerged from her bed and drifted towards the bathroom, a huff of irritation escaping her lips.

The roommates began to stir. It was time to get up.

"What did you get up to, Poppy? We lost you at the mall," Jessica commented.

I panicked. I hadn't thought of an excuse quite yet. Jessica, however, was with Mike. What did she care what I was up to? Was she rubbing it in?

"I was just checking out the night market. What did you guys get up to?" I fiddled with the white sheet on my bed.

"Oh, we grazed around the food court and walked around. We found a nightclub and danced until 3am and came back. Same ol' same ol'," Jessica announced as she creaked in her bed, changing positions. Her phone screen lit her face to reveal her sleepy eyes. She was likely talking to Mike.

I rolled around in bed, confused. I focused back on Paul. Was this lust or something more? It was too soon to tell.

After I packed my bag, I headed out to the dining room for breakfast. I poured myself a bowl of sugary cereal and scanned the room for a place to sit. Paul, as usual, was on a perch far away from everyone. I thought twice about joining him. I scanned the room again.

Damn. There were those two girls from last night.

I didn't want to join them, not after how they treated us. I walked down the middle aisle and I veered away from Paul, and from the group of gossiping ladies who were now huddled together. There was a low murmur between them stifled with giggles as they presumably discussed their tidbits from the night before.

Humiliated, I found an empty spot and sat down alone. My gaze briefly met Paul's and we both looked away at the same time, hiding our secret. Rebecca clanged about the food service area and plopped down at the table across from me, her trench dress stretched at her bosom.

"You're as white as your bedsheet. Have you seen a ghost?" Rebecca asked.

My face deepened a darker shade of red. "No, it's just warm in here. You ready for the day?" I repositioned the tray.

"Ready as I'll ever be! Petronas Twin Towers, here we come!" Her excitement flooded the room.

I'd been looking forward to the towers. I glanced through the guidebook I'd brought with me to the table, examining the pictures. These two buildings dominated the skyline in this jungle-like city. They looked space aged, too modern for this background. Looking up from street level, they almost resembled two rockets preparing to launch into outer space.

I waited in the lobby as Rebecca finished getting ready. I savoured the last of the air conditioning before heading into the heat. In the corner of the room, Paul sat looking around and gathering his papers off the coffee table. He sighed, stalling, before walking over to me.

"Hey, Poppy. How was your morning?"

"It was great, yours?" Evading the question, Paul launched into what he was really looking to talk to me about.

"Look, I really enjoyed myself last night. While we shouldn't care what people think, it's important to remember that I'm paid to be your tour guide and those boundaries are important. I don't want to hurt you, or for anyone to hurt you. I really do like you a lot, Poppy."

Not only did my smile drop, so did my heart. "Oh, okay. I understand. I don't want you to get into trouble either." My palms were sweaty. I felt scorned by another man. When would I learn? I was above this crap.

"No, that's not what this is about," Paul stammered. It was too late. I raised my hand.

"It's okay. I understand. Don't worry about it." I glanced down at my bag, zipped my zipper, and headed outside to be with the others.

After breakfast, the group headed towards the Petronas Twin Tower. Kate's headwear was getting smaller and smaller as the tour progressed. The swelling in her face had come down and she was wearing brimmed hats and fewer scarves. Emma scurried behind her, trying to keep up. These two had been relatively quiet the last few days as Kate re-cooperated.

"What's with all the chatter I hear about you?" Kate quietly asked. She slowed down to walk with me as I tried to distance myself from the group.

"Nothing." I looked away. Kate glanced at me as if to say, 'spill it.' I gave in. "Some girls thought they saw something happen with Paul and I last night. They're wrong," I defended myself unnecessarily.

"No worries here, Maple. I just want you to know that I'd cut a bitch for you," Kate offered matter-of-factly.

I was a bit surprised at her offer. She was willing to defend me. Sometimes, I wondered if she even liked me! "I don't think that'll be necessary, but I appreciate the offer." I thought Kate has watched too many gangster movies.

"What's all this? I love gossip, too." Emma panted to catch up to us. She had left the hostel after us to have a second breakfast. She was tucking something into her backpack.

"Ay, no gossip here! We're just making some suggestions about how to spend our free afternoon," Kate covered for us. She gave me a knowing wink.

"Oh, there's an outdoor food court. Maybe we can try that! There are many nationalities of cuisine, I hear!" Emma suggested.

"We just ate, Emma. How can you still be thinking about food?" Kate chided. Their relationship mimicked that of a couple who had been married 50 years.

"What's wrong with food? It's part of travel!" Emma

softly fought back.

I left the two of them to fight it out as I caught up to Rebecca. Kate and Emma had developed some sort of non-lover's quarrel that was amusing to watch, but also slightly cringe worthy. There are all types on these trips!

"There you are, ma belle!" Rebecca linked arms with me, and we swayed as we made our way to the towers. I felt Paul turn around, on occasion, to glance sadly at me.

His feelings may've been hurt, but so were mine. Time to refocus my thoughts and work on becoming an independent woman.

As we made our way through the city scape, I marvelled at how urban and rural landscapes clashed so perfectly. Tropical trees and the songs of exotic birds chirped in the air. When I thought I was in a secluded paradise, a car would whip by, honking its horn.

The group roamed around the base of the towers. The silver twins reached up into the blue sky. The clouds faded around the glistening metal. A bridge walkway fused the buildings together. Paul provided background on the building and its significance. When we were done, we paid to take the elevator to the top to check out the view.

Most people had scattered, and I found myself in a small group with Emma, Kate, and Rebecca. I sensed Kate burning a hole in Rebecca's head. This would be an on again, off again theme in our trip; for whatever reason, these two didn't get along.

The two women danced around each other, trying to be polite and awkwardly offering to take photos for the other. There were dagger glances shooting back and forth, on occasion, when Rebecca's laugh pierced Kate's ears. They were giving each other mixed messages.

I gazed out the window at the world below. Palm trees swayed, fanning people who were walking around the pond. A refreshing thought.

"We all good here?" Rebecca studied the land below.

"Sure, let's get out of here and see what else's going on." We waited for the ding of the elevators to make our way back down. When we got to the bottom, we saw the backsides of other tour members dispersing themselves from the building into the jungle.

"Hey, how was the view?" Paul asked. He smoothed his shorts as he stood to greet us. Rebecca looked at him, and then at me, realizing something was off.

"Ah, you know, same ol', same ol'." Rebecca offered.

"Where to now?"

"Oh, maybe a little shopping, a little lunch. We'll see how me and my girl Poppy feel. Won't we, love?" Rebecca poked my ribs with her elbow.

"Sounds great." I looked down and away.

"Great. You ladies have fun."

"Wait up for us!" Kate shrieked, her hat flopping as she ran like a lanky gazelle towards us. I didn't want a repeat fight. I gulped hoping we'd keep the peace.

Rebecca turned into me and murmured into my ear, "We don't have to, do we?"

"Let's just have lunch with them and see what happens, okay?" I counteroffered.

"But the woman hates me! What've I done wrong?"

"I don't know. But let's just try to put it behind us and have a good time, okay? Please?"

"Fine," Rebecca huffed, "anything for my Canadian trip wife." She huffed again, getting out the frustration. "You bloody Canadians are too nice!"

Off to lunch the four of us went. We decided on curry, something Emma, Kate, and Rebecca bonded over. Phew! Finally, progress was being made. We sat at a lovely café overlooking a small park. Kids played while their parents prepared picnics. Things were working out alright until the bill came.

"I'm only paying for my meal," Kate quipped, "I didn't eat any bread." She rifled through her wallet to get some bills out. The rest of us glanced around at each other. I could've sworn she nibbled on a piece of naan when the breadbasket arrived.

"Yes, you did; I saw you," Rebecca pointed out. "I don't mind splitting the cost, but you did eat some! Don't lie!" Things were escalating again.

"It was a small piece. I surely didn't eat as much as this one." She pointed to Emma who was wiping the last of the curry sauce with an end piece. Emma's cheeks puffed like a chipmunk, and she went wide-eyed like she was in trouble.

"You still ate some bread! Please put some coin towards it." Rebecca shoved the tray with the bill back towards Kate.

"You did eat some," Emma suggested. Kate shot her a look as if to say, 'don't get involved;' the couple was at it again.

"I'll pay for it," I offered. I was disappointed to see that the peace was kept for a mere 60 minutes, although that was probably the longest they had gotten along all trip.

"Fine, never mind! I didn't want to eat lunch with you anyways. It'll be the last!" Rebecca got up and threw her napkin on the table.

"Same here!" Kate retorted.

"Ladies!" Emma hollered.

"It's fine; I know when I'm not wanted," Rebecca scooped her purse off of the back of her chair which teetered on the edge of the legs.

"Took you long enough," Kate growled.

I thought for a minute Rebecca was going to launch across the table towards Kate. I desperately wanted to get out and enjoy ourselves again.

"You know, I think I fancy some shopping."

"But what about the museum? I thought you wanted to come check it out with us?" I asked. I didn't want her to leave. Maybe we could get past this.

"Nah, I think I'll do my own thing. But you enjoy the day with grandma over here," she snarled at Kate.

"Rebecca, please?" I begged.

"Sorry, love. I didn't mean that. I want you to have fun, but I can't be around that one," Rebecca revealed as she pulled me aside. "I can't stand to waste my trip with someone who doesn't like me."

"Okay. Maybe we can meet up and have dinner together?"

"That sounds grand." After a quick hug, Rebecca

was out the door.

"Why do you do that to her?" I asked Kate.

"Because she's an asshole," Kate offered without consideration.

"But what did she do to you? You can't just call her an asshole."

There was a pregnant pause. No sound. No reason. Only silence. Kate was processing everything, but no conclusion was offered. Maybe Rebecca was right; maybe Kate was jealous of her. Rebecca was young, carefree, and fun. People instantly got along with her. She was assertive and not afraid to express herself.

"Why don't we head over to the museum? Check things out?" Emma broke the silence.

"Sounds good to me." I shrugged and headed off with the ladies.

Chapter Twenty

Emma, Kate, and I'd wandered through the city after Rebecca departed. We went to the museum and a couple art galleries. We excitedly shared our opinions of what we saw. Emma, once again, brought up visiting the outdoor food court and Kate finally agreed to it. I messaged Rebecca, hoping she would be able to join us, but I didn't hear back from her.

We veered into the park to enjoy the greenery. On the way to the food court we heard a rustling in the trees. We looked around and couldn't see anything. We walked a little further and heard it again. Suddenly, there was a crash as if something had fallen through the trees and bam! A small ball fell from the branches into the garden below.

When no movement could be seen, or heard, Emma tiptoed over to the garden bed to see what had fallen. She parted the branches of the lush bushes and a small, brown-and-grey head popped up. Emma jumped back as the little darling emerged.

"Oh, it's so cute!" Emma gushed. She reached her hand out to pet the curious monkey who was turning its head from side to side. Emma was mesmerized and mimicked the little creature.

Emma had almost touched it when Kate warned her. "You best not. You don't know where it's been!" Kate folded her arms, shaking her head at her ridiculous friend. Emma recoiled her hand. She decided, instead, to reach into her bag.

The monkey moved closer, grabbing the end of its long tail between its fingers. Curiosity brought the monkey closer and closer. Emma smiled as she pulled out a small bunch of bananas from her bag. That's what she was concealing earlier!

"Look what I've got," she called out as if it were a dog she was dangling a bone in front of. She slowly plucked the fruit from the bunch and motioned it towards the animal.

"Where'd you get that, Em?" Kate questioned, annoyed that she always had food on her mind.

"Breakfast. I thought I might need a snack along the way today." Emma had no qualms about sharing her rationale. Kate rolled her eyes.

"Maybe we shouldn't feed the animals," I offered.

"Don't be silly, a small snack won't hurt anyone." Emma began to peel the fruit.

"Famous last words." Kate strolled over and peered down at the fur ball as Emma extended an open banana towards it.

The monkey's ears perked up before it reached out to accept the gift. It seemed to be evaluating Emma to determine if she was a threat, because if she had her way, she would likely hug that monkey to death.

"See, no worries! It was just hungry." Emma handed the monkey another banana and it willingly accepted. This exchange happened until the last banana remained. The monkey sat there, peeling the banana with its teeth. I have to admit, it was a cute sight to see it eyeing us and the gesturing for a meal. With expert precision, it dismantled the fruit from the casing and enjoyed the sweet flesh inside. I wondered how many people it took advantage of everyday with its good looks.

"Never feed the wild beasts; didn't you hear Paul earlier?" Kate pondered. It was too late; the food was almost gone.

"Well, you want this one too, little buddy?" Emma ignored Kate. "Okay, I'll give it to you, but I want a picture first." She got the camera out and turned it on. I wasn't sure if it understood her request or not as I don't speak monkey.

The monkey took a cue from Emma who insisted on having a photo on a nearby bench. She sat down and the monkey jumped into her lap, likely lured by the remaining banana. Emma tossed the banana from hand to hand while telling the monkey to wait until the photos were done before it could have the remaining treat. The monkey didn't understand, obviously, and was growing frustrated by the dangling fruit.

Never let your guard down. It's too late. You've been

bated.

I struggled to take photos of the monkey as it wouldn't sit still for Emma. Eventually, Emma gave up and provided the final banana. It sat nestled in her arms until the photo was taken. The monkey looked up quizzically at Emma as if asking where the other bananas were.

"That's it, little fellow, all gone," Emma concluded. The monkey still perched upon her lap. It stood up, investigating over her shoulders and behind her for more snacks.

"All gone," she echoed again.

The monkey didn't believe her. It sat back down into Emma's lap, contemplating its next step. She began to stroke its head again. And with that, like a wolf in sheep's clothing, Emma allowed the beast to nestle into her warm arms. The soft fur brushed against her arm as she held it close to her. As an outsider, I could see the monkey beginning to morph from a cute, cuddly creature into a beast. As the beast breathed in and out, it began to suck Emma's soul out of her body, which acted as fuel for its metamorphosis.

Suddenly, those large, dark eyes become devilish, like a wild animal seeing red! The adorable face was now a werewolf under a full moon, except here, it was under the boiling, tropical sun. Hair puffed over its body, posturing. The cute, little paws seemed to hulk into giant pads with long, large claws that could tear into flesh – our flesh. The food supply had run out and the animal would have none of it. It demanded more. The sound of its growl started.

When Emma looked down, the beast bared its teeth up at her, saliva dripping down its front teeth. It either wanted more bananas or blood.

As it grew before us, it leapt to its feet. Danger was about to strike. It let out a war cry and started to chase us. Emma, Kate, and I ran as fast as we could down the road, our sandals clacking as we ran for our lives. We ducked and hid for cover in a small, tourism office broom closet as we had nowhere to go. Now, however, we were at the mercy of this beast. We prayed it would take pity on us and release us from its clutches.

As we were held hostage in this cold, damp closet, I couldn't help but think about all the steps that had led me here: a new job, new friend in Casey, a lover – John, a lost lover – also John, a passport, a plane ride, new friends, a budding self-esteem, a new love interest in Mike, then in Paul, and a lost love interest – in Mike, then in Paul again. Snap out of it, woman! I tried to tell myself.

My memories zipped through my brain. I was trapped in this closet because I was running away from a man to find myself. I didn't expect to find myself in this predicament. I prayed someone would help us. The last thing I wanted to be was someone's supper.

"Help us! HEEEEELPPP" Emma screeched. Kate forced her hand over her mouth.

"That will only make it more angry!" Kate hissed.

"It's a monster!" Emma cried.

"That monster is a bloody monkey! And it has us cornered, thanks to you. Do you have a better idea?" Kate asked.

More silence, except the sound of water dripping onto the tile floor beneath our feet. The silence was broken by the sound of claws against the door. The lurking shadow roamed back and forth, contemplating its next move. Occasionally, it would stop to bat its paw under the door, causing us to scream.

"What are we going to do?" shrieked Emma, the troublemaker who got us into this mess in the first place.

A shush silenced her in the darkness.

"What are WE going to do? Don't you mean what are YOU going to do? YOU are going to go out that door and fend off that bloody beast whilst Poppy and I evacuate the premises!" Kate hissed. I could almost *see* Kate's claws emerge from her fingertips in the darkness, swatting at Emma.

The hissing and shrill, battle cry of the monkey on the other side of the steel door made my heart race. As Emma and Kate battled it out as to who would exit first, I slid down the cold wall onto the closet floor, tears pouring down my face. How'd I get myself into this mess? I imagined that we'd die in this closet. My gravestone would read:

Poppy Beatrice Davis
1998-2023
Hopeless romantic who only knew how to run away from it all.

This seemed extremely pathetic but at this point, I'd decided to give up on love and relationships all because of being jilted by my lover. I couldn't believe that I travelled halfway around the world just to get away from a man, a man who'd never loved me or returned my feelings in the slightest. Sure, we'd had our moments of passion, but now, I was about to meet my maker because of stupid Emma.

"Alright, let's rock, paper, scissors for it!" Emma suggested enthusiastically.

"How the hell are we going to see who shows what, you thick wench?" The tone of Kate's voice made it clear that Emma was about to get a rock over her head.

"Well, you could take my word for it, I suppose," Emma added. Kate's eyes were probably rolling in the darkness.

Just as they were about to fight to stay alive, the noises stopped outside. The clawing, the hissing, the threat of death had all ceased. The door slowly creaked open and as our eyes adjusted, there was a tall, dark figure at the door, looming above us. In the haze, it was evident it was all over, whether we were ready or not.

Chapter Twenty-One

"What's going on in here?" The voice bellowed. It sounded eerily familiar, but I couldn't quite put my finger on it. We were too stunned to know what was happening. Were we about to meet our maker?

"Hello? Are you guys okay?" he asked again, his frame casting a shadow as it eclipsed the sun.

"I think so," Emma squeaked. She rubbed her eyes to adjust to the newfound light.

"Thank, God!" Kate moaned, "we were about to be eaten alive by that savage beast!" Kate clawed at the male figure, trying to move past him. Her hat had slid over her eyes as she groped for freedom.

"What're you talking about?" the voice asked, confused.

"That furry 'rodent'! He cornered us and we'd no choice but to seek shelter," Kate panted as she adjusted her clothing and took in sunshine again.

He laughed. I knew that sound. It was Paul. "A

monkey forced you into the closet?" He had one hand on his hip, and another held an apple. The sun shimmered above him.

We exited the safe haven and moved towards him. I relaxed, knowing we were rescued but my heart sank when I realized who had heard our cries for help.

"This fur baby held you hostage?" Paul asked again as he tossed the monkey a piece of his apple. The beast had returned back into the cute, cuddly creature we first encountered.

"I thought you said not to feed the animals," I pointed out.

"That I did, but I needed to lure him away from the door so I could see what was going on. For all I knew, he was trying to mate with an alley cat!" The laugh filled the street.

"Are you calling us alley cats?" Kate challenged. She did say she'd cut a bitch earlier.

Paul raised his hands in defence. "No, madam. I was just trying to suss out the situation."

"Well, thank you. I bid you a good day." Kate smoothed her skirt. "Coming ladies?" She regained her composure and started walking in the direction of the hostel.

"Yes, I am. I sure could go for some ice cream to calm my nerves," Emma suggested.

"Again, with the food!" Kate shrieked. She shoved her friend.

"I can't help it! I get hungry when I'm anxious!" Emma grabbed her stomach as if the hunger monster was brewing, too.

"What about you? You alright?" Paul asked when we were out of ear shot from the ladies, but not from the monkey who was still chewing the apple nearby.

"Yes, I'm fine. We had the situation under control." I shook the hair out of my eyes and brushed it behind my ears.

Paul was taken aback and smirked. "You sure? Didn't look like it." He crossed his muscular arms and leaned against a nearby tree, studying me.

"Yes, we were devising our escape plan. We're capable women, after all."

"No doubt. The screams, however, might suggest otherwise." A sly smile began to spread across his face." I hated that smile right now. He tried to cover his mouth with his calloused hand.

"I don't need your help," I roared, the lioness within me ready to attack.

"Okay, I got it. I was just making sure. I care – "

I stopped him before he could say anymore. I didn't want to hear what he had to say. I'd received too many mixed signals from him. "Thanks for your help, I guess, but I'm going to catch up with my friends."

I ran to catch up with them and left Paul in my dust.

I didn't feel like anymore adventures today. I went back to the room. All the beds were empty. It was obvious people were still out exploring. Rebecca's bed was a mess of discarded clothing she decided against for the day. I smiled, thinking what a mess she was but how cool she was, too. I wanted to be like her in a lot of ways – except for the chaos before me.

I couldn't help but feel badly that Rebecca went off on her own. She was an independent person, but I didn't want her feelings to be hurt. I also didn't want her to be trapped in the closet with Kate. The fate of the monkey attack would've been preferred instead of being locked in a closet with the two of them.

I put my jogging pants on after having a quick shower. It was a prime opportunity to bathe as I didn't have three other people to fight for the hot water. I curled up on my bed in the empty room. The air conditioner was a bit too cool, a sentence I may later regret.

I reflected on the day as I lay under the covers. I was happy to be safe. Today's events may be comical on another day. For now, I felt relaxed and played back the mental images of the tower, the fun lunch, and the tropical milieu. My eyes sprang open when I relived the terror of that fur ball.

I figured I needed some cheering up and a bit of distraction, so I texted Casey to see what was up with her.

Poppy: Casey, my dear! How are you?
Casey: Poppy! I'm great! I miss the hell out of you!
Poppy: I miss you, too.

Casey: What can I do you for? U having the best time?

Poppy: Trying. I'm having men problems!

Casey: Tell me about it, lady!

For the next half hour, I told her of my man drama with the two beaus on the trip. I reiterated all the thoughts I had about trying to move past John. The distance of space and time was helping me get over him. Casey always listened to me. She may not always give bang on advice, but her heart was in the right place.

I told her about the trip, too, as well as some of the upcoming highlights.

Casey: Here's what you're going to do. You're going to continue reading the book your mom gave you. You're going to carve out alone time to figure out who Poppy Davis is and tell yourself that you're a badass babe! You don't need a man! You're amazing, you have great friends (ahem, me!) and you're so talented. Figure out what makes you shine! You are number one, babe!

Poppy: You sure know how to make a girl blush!

Casey: I try. In all seriousness, try to forget about the lot of duds. Focus on you!

Poppy: Love you, girl!

Casey: Back at you.

I ended the conversation with my bestie and lay in the dark on my bed as the cellphone light faded to black. She was right, I needed to find out who Poppy Davis was. She's my priority.

Chapter Twenty-Two

As hard as I tried to stop thinking about John, sometimes he'd show up in my dreams, or nightmares. I was growing and moving past him, evolving, but images and stories of our time together intrusively entered my sleeping brain.

With John, it wasn't all tangled sheets, kisses, and stolen glances. We didn't have just bliss. We also had our fights. Lovers' quarrels. Doom's day. I think back to working with him, to our romance, and to all the hard work I'd done on myself to move on. How could I have been such a fool then? There were so many red flags I ignored. We do that when we're in love sometimes, right?

One red flag of John's, other than still being technically married, was that he had a temper. At work, the extent of it was him slamming down the receiver on the phone after a difficult call with a client, or a door he had slammed shut only to open it again and blame the wind, even when the windows were closed. When we were together, there were times we'd have screaming matches in my apartment, much like the one I often reflect back to. Neighbours would bang on their ceilings, signalling for us to shut up. John would leave my apartment and slam the door so hard it startled both Amos and me. What held me onto him was this idea that he was a doting father and gentleman. John's grand gestures of love and him idolizing my body like I was the most beautiful thing he'd ever seen did something to me. I was shy and introverted growing up. No one ever paid attention like that to me. I felt like he made me shine. Now, I'm the one who makes me shine, not a man.

Sometimes, we have our rose-coloured glasses on when we're in love. My prescription, in the rear-view mirror, started to change. The rose colour may be evident in some reflections, but not all. In the moment, we might feel like we're in love and we tend to ignore the demons creeping out from the closet.

Chapter Twenty-Three

A new day meant a new adventure. After spending several days in the city, we decided to move on. Today, we'd be leaving the humidity and heading for the hills. So long, monkeys; hello, butterflies and tea plantations.

Every few days, we organized our worldly possessions as we prepared for the next location. The four of us were quiet as we packed up our room. Rebecca sloppily shoved her mess, and her new purchases, into her bag. "We're done with urban safari; now, we are onto mountain woman!" she proclaimed. Rebecca held up a plaid shacket and tall black hiking boots. "I even got one of these beanies!" She held up a black, knitted hat.

"You mean a toque," I corrected her. We all laughed. The silence was finally broken.

"Oh, you Canadians!" Rebecca retorted. "But you're still wrong; it's a beanie."

"You've been having a good time the last few days

Rebecca?" I asked, hoping that she wasn't mad at me.

"Oy, yes, ma belle. I got these wonderful things. I even got another carryon bag for all my souvenirs. I've four siblings at home who expect gifts!" Rebecca had spent the last few days alone rather than with the group. I sensed she was avoiding her travel bully.

"That's generous of you." I folded my clothing and packed them in tight. My red touring bag was stuffed to the brim, the seams looking as though they were about to split.

"Yeah, we didn't have a lot growing up. My dad had a work injury, settled a lawsuit. He helped pay for this trip. He wanted me to see the world a little, more than the small town we live in. He's not able to travel due to his back. He's in bed most of the day. Least I could do is bring some nice things home."

Rebecca seemed somber as she told me a bit more about growing up. In my eyes, she seemed less of a partygoer and more like someone who was experiencing life, just like me, but for a different reason.

"Well, that's the end of that." I wasn't sure if she was referring to packing up her backpack, or finishing her life story.

"Same," the rest of us said as we hauled our bags out to the vans.

Paul was outside collecting the belongings from us lemmings and hoisting them to the roof of the van. The driver strapped the items to the top. I wondered how it looked from other vehicles, seeing a tower of luggage teeter.

"Alright, we ready for more adventure?" Paul cheered. Unfortunately, he only received a few murmurs.

"Well, it's only eight in the morning; I suppose we need some more caffeine first, yeah?" Paul said to basically no one. "Alright, in you get. To Cameron Heights we go!"

"Someone woke up a little too happy this morning," Rebecca mumbled. She lowered her sunglasses as if we were sharing a secret conversation.

We boarded the vans with the same passengers as before on each vehicle. I settled into the seat I was in before. I organized what I needed in the overhead bin above and plopped myself in my seat. The van swayed slightly as other passengers did the same. As I was getting comfortable, Paul boarded the van. He looked around and eyed the seat beside me where he'd sat before. I shifted uncomfortably. I didn't want to sit with him again, not after he made it perfectly clear that we were not going to be an item.

Sensing my discomfort, Rebecca leaned over me and said, "I love me a window seat. Move over, Poppy; I'm joining my trip wife!" She straddled my lap to claim her spot. "Can't leave my bestie alone, now can I? We've been apart far too much in the last couple days." She threw her purse open, rifling for her lip gloss and sleep mask.

"Sounds good to me." I was relieved as Paul continued to another seat.

He lowered his eyes, and he took the seat behind me where Rebecca had sat the previous day. This was for the best, I told myself. Give myself a little distance.

I pulled out my self-help book. Today's focus was on boundaries. This was definitely something I needed more guidance on.

"A little light reading?" Rebecca asked. I didn't want to explain my book again.

"Yes, ma'am."

"If you need me, I'll be catching up on my beauty sleep." Rebecca lowered her mask and mere seconds later, she was sound asleep. I was grateful for the silence and for the opportunity not to explain myself. I dove into the book and continued my self-care journey.

As we drove, we left the metropolis and were now well into the rural countryside of Malaysia. The two-lane roads twisted and turned through rolling hills. My stomach couldn't help but become a little queasy. Bright green hillsides lined the side of the road. It was almost as if someone had to bushwhack the way for us. Paul got on the mic to explain to us that these were tea plantations we were passing. We'd have an opportunity to go to one for a tour and afternoon tea service.

"Jam and biscuits, just like being home," Rebecca mumbled from her half sleep.

In addition to being in the hillside, we'd also have plenty of opportunity for hiking, trying Indian cuisine, and a chance to go to a butterfly conservatory. I couldn't help but become excited for this next part of the trip. We'd such an amazing assortment of beach, cityscapes, and now mountains. Soon, we'd be in an island country and venture towards volcanoes and an exotic giant lizard!

I bet my parents would be excited to hear about my travel stories when I got home. They got the travel bug when they retired.

In my book it challenged me to think about a time I felt happy. I closed my eyes as I reminisced about some of our family vacations of years past. Every March Break, we drove to Myrtle Beach. The journey took days. We'd stop at the homes of former presidents or heads of states. I found this a bore but there were some cool ghost stories and swamps we took boat rides through. I remember hollering in the backseat every time we passed my favourite chain buffet or a sign for mini golf. One time, I forgot my favourite stuffed animal and begged my dad to turn the car around so we could get it. I couldn't bear to lose a friend.

On one vacation, the last my brothers joined us, we decided to have a rousing game of mini golf. I was trying to act like an adult – my brothers, Peter, and Myles, were ten and twelve years older than I. They'd taken an interest in professional golf, and I thought that I'd show them some of my cool moves. I remember winding up with my club, as I'd seen the pros do on television. My brothers were snickering at my moves. I figured, at the time, they were jealous of me. In retrospect, they were making fun of me. How was I to know the difference? I was only a kid.

I remember how I grounded my feet and narrowed my eyes on my target of a clown mouth I had to shoot my ball through. I aimed, pulled my golf club back fast over my shoulder, gracefully lowered it down to the ground, and tapped my ball. It nudged the side of the clown's mouth but didn't go through. I sighed and turned around, waiting for one of my dim bulb siblings to have his go. When I turned around, however, my dad was laying on the ground. I somehow managed to hit him square in the forehead and there was blood gushing down his face.

I gasped. My mom got tissues out of her purse and cleaned his forehead off. I was banned from mini golf the rest of the trip, and the trip after. It felt like an unjust punishment at the time.

I stifled giggles thinking about these silly times. Youth can give us such blind confidence. Sometimes, I longed to feel that way again.

"What's so funny?" Rebecca woke from her slumber. She raised the corner of the mask to reveal one squinting eye.

"I was just thinking about my family vacations. I really miss spending quality time with my family."

"Nice to experience the world on your own, but I hear that."

"I could really go for some saltwater taffy right about now." My mouth watered thinking more about my seaside, childhood adventures.

"Hmmm, yes! Cinnamon!"

"Blue raspberry!"

"YES!" we said in unison.

After a brief break, Paul announced that we'd soon be in the highlands. Upon arrival, Paul handed out our room keys. I was prepared to room with the same crew, but to my relief, and a bit of horror, our roommates had changed.

"Emma, Kate, Poppy, and Rebecca. You'll be in cabin four." Paul blindly handed the key to Kate.

"Alright then," Rebecca sighed. We shared shy glances with each other, hoping that this wouldn't lead to a war again.

"Alright then," Kate echoed. "Shall we?"

We headed to our cabin and unloaded the bags. The ladies decided that they wanted to wander into town and check out the shops. I was hoping the idea of shopping would entice Rebecca.

"You know, I think I'm going to sit this one out. I didn't get enough shut eye on the van." Rebecca flopped onto her bed.

I looked at her sideways as if to say, 'come on, are you sure?'

"I mean it, you go have fun! I'll be here when you get back. Promise." She cozied up under her blanket.

"Come on, let's go have a look," Kate said. "We'll come back to see if you want to join us for dinner, yeah?" Kate suggested to Rebecca. An invisible olive branch was extended.

"Sounds good," Rebecca said reluctantly, unsure if this was a trap.

"Great, it's settled. We'll come back and check on our roomie." Emma gestured.

Kate rolled her eyes at Emma. "Come on, let's go before I change my mind."

Kate, Emma, and I decided to go to the butterfly

conservatory while Rebecca finished her slumber. I couldn't believe how much she sleeps!

"You really want to go in there?" Emma asked as we paid for our tickets.

"Of course! Think of the photo opportunities," Kate suggested as she mocked a group of girls who were trying to take a selfie. I couldn't help but laugh.

"Think about the beauty! So many different colours and designs on their wings! Check this out," I said as I pointed to a list of what lie behind the doors.

"Yes, beauty," Emma slowly stated. She was watching the doors closely. I wasn't sure at first why she was staring.

After we organized ourselves, we made our way into the entry. Emma inched in behind us with her back to the wall. "What's wrong with you? Need an ice cream?" Kate mocked.

"No, nothing's wrong." Emma breathed faster. Sweat started to form on her temples.

"Then, why're you acting like a nutter?" Kate questioned. The thin eyebrows on her mildly plump face arched.

"Truth be told, I'm a bit afraid of them." Emma crouched as she watched overhead for any attack by said insect.

"What do you mean?" I asked, unsure how this harmless entity could cause her so much distress.

"They're shifty. You never know where they are or what they're doing. They stay in a cocoon forever, plotting revenge." Emma seemed spiteful, as if there was some childhood story she was repressing.

I held my hand out and a beautiful pink one landed on my finger. I struggled to get my phone out so that I could take a photo. As I snapped a shot, I watched in slow motion as the dainty winged beauty fluttered down around Emma, a soft landing in the hopes that it would bring the visitor some joy. Wrong. It was like watching a shark attack.

And just like that, a blue butterfly fluttered down and landed on Emma's nose. Emma froze. I swore time stood still in this moment. Emma stood up straight and then fell to the ground, rolling around, as if she were on fire.

"I can't do it! I can't! It attacked me! Did you see it? Did you see the savage?" Emma wailed as she swatted at the poor insect. It took off so it wouldn't be further assaulted.

"What the hell have you got against butterflies, Emma?" Kate quipped.

"We have to get out of here! It isn't safe!" Emma yelled as she picked herself up and rushed towards the exit. Kate chased after her.

"I'm finally feeling better and now *she's* the patient!" Kate exclaimed.

With that, I was left alone. I puttered around the conservatory, taking time to sit and relish in the fluttering insects around me. As I gathered a silent moment of meditation, the bubble of calm was burst when Mike walked in, hand in hand with Karli, another woman on our trip. What a player! They were laughing and she was swatting his chest, saying, "You're too funny, Mike!"

How many women would he land on this trip? Paul was right.

They stopped to take selfies with the butterflies. Mike smiled as he walked past me. I couldn't tell by the mask of his smile if he felt guilty for our previous relations, or if he looked at me as another conquest. I smiled back, only to be polite. There was no use in holding a grudge.

On my way back to the cabin, I decided to keep up with the spirit of independence and have dinner alone. Cameron Heights is known for its East Indian influence and cuisine was part of that. I decided that I was in the mood for some Tandoori chicken. I walked around town until I spotted the perfect place to dine. Outside the restaurant, an older man stood over what looked like a clay pot with a fire inside. He had a long, wooden paddle in his hand that he used to flip something inside the pot. As I got closer, he ushered me to stay where I was. A few seconds later, the paddle emerged with a piece of naan bread on the end of it! He dropped it onto a table beside him, fanned it with his hands, and when he was content with the finished product, he motioned for me to take one half he'd just torn in his hands.

The naan was warm and fluffy and melted in my mouth. It smelled like a stone oven! I'd never seen or had fresh naan before. What a treat. He took a ball of dough and formed a flat circle. He then tossed it against the side of the pot to start the process again. I watched with delight as he made several more pieces before I settled on a seat to have my meal. I smiled and thanked him for letting me watch. He nodded in return. We may not speak the same language, but we bonded over food. Travel had that magic.

That night at dinner, I took a bit of time to reflect. I beat myself up a lot over John, but we both made mistakes. I shouldn't have taken him back as many times as I did. He took advantage of me. He made me believe I was special. "Never change," he would say to me. I wonder who else he fed that line to.

His poor son. His poor wife. His wife. Ouch. I thought repeatedly about how much I'd hurt her, not even fully appreciating how our actions impacted her. The more I thought about it, the more I realized how innocent she was in all of this. There were times that John would refer to her as his 'responsibility' and that he'd a 'duty' to take care of her. I thought he meant because they were divorcing but in reality, that was the reason he wasn't leaving her.

He told me how 'cold' and how 'callous' she was. John said that they hadn't shared a bed in ages before they separated. The first time we made love, he told me he finally felt alive as she didn't even want to touch him. I wondered how much more of the story there'd been that he wasn't telling me. I wondered how many other women there were. I wondered why they really were getting divorced in the first place. My guess was that he had not been faithful. John was good at acting. He was a liar and I fell for a con artist.

I needed to retell the story, even if to myself. I wasn't someone who wore the scarlet letter in this one. I wasn't the homewrecker. John wrecked his own home; he burnt his house down – not me. I did, however, take responsibility for staying involved with him, even after he told me about his soon to be ex-wife.

I felt myself becoming more confident. My shoulders relaxed and my head rose higher. I smiled, realizing that I was always able to share my story, to tell my truth, to stand up for myself. That was the new Poppy – a version of me I could be proud of. I was proud of.

Chapter Twenty-Four

The next day, I awoke due to a loud clang in the room. "Wake up, Maple! It's time for tea!" Kate screamed.

What the hell was going on? Why was Kate up my ass this morning? I hadn't even had coffee, let alone tea. "Isn't that an afternoon thing?" My eyes blurred as someone threw on the light switch.

"Today's the trip to the tea plantation! And we've to do our duty to England," Rebecca chimed in, standing tall and proud.

I didn't care about tea, or England. Was there something I didn't know about the importance of tea? As I woke, I came to realize that all three girls were helping each other secure fascinators in their hair. I felt like I was in a parallel universe, mostly because the three of them were helping each other.

"Do all the English pack fascinators?" I quizzed the girls. I found this to be a bit bizarre in the middle of

Southeast Asia.

"You never know when you're going to be invited to tea!" Rebecca cackled.

"Although you do know the royals won't be here," Emma offered.

Both Kate and Rebecca looked at each other and groaned in unison. Perhaps we were turning a corner after all.

"I feel left out. I don't have anything to wear," I whined jokingly.

"Ah, sorry, love, I only brought one." Rebecca examined the contents of her bag.

"Same with us."

"That's okay. I'm part of the Commonwealth, right? I'm still included?" I quipped.

"Always, ma belle!" Rebecca squeezed me in a tight hug. She gave great hugs.

We headed to the parking lot to join the rest of the crew. Noticeably, other members of the trip were not as lavishly dressed as my counterparts. Paul's jaw dropped when he saw the three girls in their best attire. "You bunch are two short of a girl band!" Paul laughed.

"Very funny," Rebecca commented.

"A real comedian." Kate rolled her eyes.

"Now, now, I was just teasing," offered Paul. "No need to gang up on me!" We boarded a bus, most of us not yet awake for our day's journey to the tea plantation. We huddled together, and the cold air outside mixing with the hot body heat in the bus fogged up the windows. We weren't used to this change in temperature. The bus rolled down the small hills and lurched up the large hills. We often had to share the roads with small cars and take turns on the narrow path. Rebecca adjusted her blue flowered fascinator after a big bump in the road caused it to come out of place.

We made our way to the bottom of a bright green hill and took a dirt driveway up an unmarked road. Surrounding us were chest-high bushes with refreshing leaves that swayed in the wind. Dotted amongst the bushes were darkly dressed figures. I couldn't make out what they were, but it appeared they were kicking up leaves behind them. As we got closer, they were people. Paul explained that the tea here was harvested by hand. Workers waded through the crops to chop the leaves with a machete and throw them into a basket they had on their back. This was the more traditional method of tea harvesting. He said we would have a chance to go into the fields later.

When the bus came to a halt, we got out and made our way into the building at the top for a tour of the plantation. They told us how they grade the tea leaves for sale and who their 'top secret' buyers might be, though they couldn't confirm. We ooed and ahhed when we realized some of us already purchased this product at home. Now this was 'farm to table'!

As the group made its way through to see how the fresh leaves were processed into tea, I felt a nudge at my back. I turned around to see Paul. "I want to show you something." He motioned for me to follow him.

I saw the group round the corner and the two

troublesome, American girls from the night market turned the corner last. "What do you want to show me?" I was reluctant to follow him, but I was interested in his secret.

"I want to pour you a cup of the best grade tea. I know the owner and he reserves a small portion for his favourite guests."

"Why me?"

"You looked excited when they were talking about how they harvest the tea. Plus, I feel like I owe you an apology. For everything." An apology, wow. This wasn't what I was expecting.

"You don't have to – " I turned to join the others.

"Yes, I do. Please let me do this for you."

"Okay," I conceded.

Paul poured the hot water into the bottom of the cup. To my surprise, he left the tea leaves loose. I wasn't accustomed to this, but I went with the flow. Light brown particles floated to the surface in my cup, only to sink to the bottom. Ripples of orange made the cup murky. A strong smell of lemon and honey wafted in my face. It didn't need the disguise of cream or sugar to make it enjoyable. The present company added to the intensity, too.

"My grandmother taught me how to read tea leaves." We took sips, savouring the hot brew. "When you're done your tea, I'll read your future." He spread his hand nowhere in the air as if gazing into another portal in time. We both laughed.

"I hope it includes employment."

"You never know what it might hold." Our eyes locked. We both nervously drank our tea. What would the future hold? Our future?

"Alright, let's see it." Paul took the cup and placed it so that he could interpret the leaves. I stared at him as he worked through his process. His face flushed a little. I wasn't sure if it was from the cold or the embarrassment that he had to complete a task he didn't know how to do.

"I see independence. I see happiness." He turned the cup in his hands. "Laughter, lots of laughter. I see love…" His eyes turned halfway towards me and darted back down to the cup. I wasn't interested in the love part, but the independence and happiness I could get behind.

"A job, yes. I see lots of money in your future! Maybe you'll give me some?" We both laughed. Just as we were finishing my reading, the group came back around the corner.

"There they are," said my two American enemies, Britney and Tiffany. I have never met a Britney or Tiffany that I liked.

"We're just having a tea break," Paul defended us.

"Would've been nice if we were included." Britney eyed Paul up and down. Was she also into Paul? I wasn't about to fight another woman on this trip.

"Yeah, I love tea," Tiffany added. She smacked the gum she had in her mouth.

"Well, we can all enjoy some tea and scones next," the plantation guide offered, redirecting us to the café.

"Are you coming, Poppy? Or are you getting a special tour?" Britney taunted me.

"Grow up, Britney," I challenged. I was tired of their immature behaviour. We weren't in high school anymore.

"She's coming with us." Rebecca butted in front of Britney and grabbed my arm. "No need to worry about her." And we went off to the café. Paul was left behind to clean up the mess.

We found a table at the front overlooking the hillside. The sun was shining, and droplets of water clinging to the bottom of the bright green leaves were visible. Emma, Kate, and Rebecca strode back from the counter with trays in their hands. "We're having an afternoon tea. It's a bit early here, but should be teatime in England now!"

Set on the table was a tower of finger sandwiches, crusts removed. Small squares and shortbread cookies were strategically placed between sandwiches. Fresh strawberries filled in the crevices on the tower. On another plate were tea biscuits. Kate explained that it was customary to have biscuits with clotted cream and jam. Emma was busy pouring cups of tea into dainty, flower-patterned teacups and Rebecca passed them around to each of us. As I sipped my tea, I was reminded of my grandma's fancy teacups. She collected one in every colour and pattern, mismatched elegance. Oh, how I missed her.

"To being independent women!" Rebecca toasted. We echoed and gently clinked our cups together. A perfect toast considering my good fortune, as per Paul.

Out of the corner of my eye, I noticed Britney and Tiffany whispering. They were basically identical in their white crop tops, torn skinny jeans and high blonde ponytails. Twin idiots. Again, you can't get along with everyone.

"Another party we aren't invited to," Brittney remarked. Why wouldn't she just go away?

"What makes you think you're invited?" Rebecca contorted her neck like an owl to glare at her, her eyes bugged out wide.

"Poppy seems to get all the special treatment, doesn't she?" Tiffany coyly added. She smacked gum theatrically in her mouth.

My eyebrows furrowed. It felt like steam was about to boil out my ears. Sensing my discomfort, Kate added, "Well, seems someone's jealous," and sipped her tea.

"Pardon?" Britney scoffed, her American accent hard on the vowels.

"You're just jealous of our Canadian Maple," Kate egged on the girls, ready for a row.

"Hardly," Tiffany exacerbated loudly. "She gets special treatment from Paul. Maybe it's because he thinks she's a good kisser." A sly smile spread across her face.

"What's she going on about?" Emma whispered to no one specific at the table. She looked around, waiting for someone to give her an answer. Emma always seemed to be left alone in the dark.

My face flushed, and the anger continued to escalate. I saw Kate, Emma, and Rebecca briefly eye each other, not sure the extent of what had occurred between Paul and me, but the foresight to protect me was evident. I relaxed slightly, knowing that they were in my corner.

"Button it." Rebecca got up from the table. She leaned towards the girls defensively. It was almost as if she had been in a pub fight or two back home.

"Watch it!" Brittney defended herself. The claws were out, only this time a different group were going after each other.

"Listen! There is no need for this," I started. "They saw me kiss Paul in Kuala Lumper," I confessed. The invisible weight lifted off my shoulders. "Paul is the tour guide and that's the boundary. That's that. We aren't a thing. Now, leave me alone!" My face flushed and a surge of confidence went through my body. I felt my spine straighten as if there was an invisible rod in it.

Emma, Kate, and Rebecca nodded in encouragement. Smiles of empowerment and pride stretched across their faces. I was proud of me.

"You heard the lady, buzz off!" Rebecca cheered. She lifted her teacup as if she was lifting a pint glass to cheers with us.

"Mind your own," Kate added between slurps of tea.

Britney and Tiffany got up from their seats and left the café. I'm not sure if this was defeat or annoyance from what'd just transpired. Instead of allowing them to tease me, I had told the truth and set limits. It felt amazing.

We were shown the signal that it was time to wrap up and head into town for an afternoon hike. As we cleared the table and made our way outside, Paul stopped me briefly. "I'm sure you don't need to hear this, but I'm proud of you for standing up for yourself. That couldn't have been easy."

"No, it wasn't. It needed to be done."

"You're amazing."

I batted my eyelashes at Paul and concluded, "I know," as I boarded the bus. I'm an independent woman, after all. I'd die on this hill before I told Paul 'thank you' for his support. He made his boundary; now, I had made mine.

On the bus ride back, I couldn't help but feel a little frustrated. Feelings take time to process. Did Paul's opinion of my courage matter, even if we did have a nice time sipping tea? Did the opinion of Britney and Tiffany really matter? No, but I let them get to me. I couldn't help but let this swirl around in my head after the hike, too. It consumed me all day.

After we got back to our room following our uneventful hike, I threw myself on my bed. I told the girls I just wanted to be alone. The three of them headed to the games room to challenge the others to a game of pool. Soon, my tears had soaked my bedsheet. I just wanted to have a nice time with my friends. Why'd those girls have to go and ruin everything? What did I do to them? Were they jealous or just being mean on purpose? Courage takes some vulnerability, and that was something I wasn't quite comfortable with yet.

Poppy: **I'm in hell. Two girls had it out with me today at the tea plantation.**

Casey: **Oh no, what did those two say?**

Poppy: **They accused me of getting special**

treatment on the trip because they saw Paul and I kiss. I feel mortified!

Casey: The tour guide?

Poppy: Yes. We had a brief thing. It's over now – he isn't interested in me that way.

I went on to tell Casey about what had transpired and how Paul let me deal with those girls on my own rather than swooping in to save the day. He had a bad habit of rescuing me when I didn't need it, and sometimes when I did.

I couldn't help but share a bit more about my feelings towards him and how there may've been a missed opportunity if those girls didn't see us. A moment of openness between friends was shared. I didn't want to feel like Paul's secret. I'd spent enough time being a secret to someone; no more! Poppy Davis was a high value woman!

I couldn't help but become a bit offended when Casey suggested that Paul did, in fact, rescue me when he didn't interrupt when those girls were picking on me. She suggested that perhaps he still had feelings for me. She reminded me that she was an expert in this matter.

Casey: Doesn't sound like he's not interested! Sounds like he likes you!

Poppy: He made it perfectly clear that he was just my guide.

Casey: Don't rule him out yet. He might be a good one.

Poppy: Whose side are you on?

Casey: Don't be like that! I'm on your side.
Poppy: Doesn't feel like that. We're over. Don't encourage something that's dead.
Casey: That's not fair!
Poppy: I've had enough. Goodnight.

I abruptly turned my phone off and headed to bed. I was irritated with Casey. I wanted her to be proud of me for standing up for myself. I didn't need her to defend Paul, or encourage me to keep an open mind about him. At this point, I was swearing off all relationship advice until I could figure things out for myself.

"Look what I found?!" Rebecca burst into the room and turned the lights on.

"What'd you find?" I was flooded with irritation.

"Vodka! I think we should wash down some of today's problems with a little drinksy poo!" Rebecca waved the bottle in her hands with a mischievous look in her eyes.

Kate and Emma strode in behind her with teacups in their hands. "We second that!" Kate offered me one.

"We're really keeping this afternoon tea thing going, are we?" I asked.

"Might as well. We're dressed the part, are we not?" Rebecca twirled in her pyjamas and fascinator.

"Why not? Let's do it!" I stuck my cup out and motioned for it to be filled with alcohol.

When Rebecca stopped, I gestured for her to keep pouring.

"So, tell us more about the kiss!" Emma begged. She

took a sip from her untraditional teacup.

I sighed and a satisfied smile spread across my face. I trusted these ladies, and I knew my secret was safe with them. "It was a great kiss. Paul has amazing lips." The ladies ooohed and ahhhhed.

We laughed as I told the girls what happened between Paul and me. We were forming a friendship and I might as well be honest. The truth shall set you free. In comparison, this felt so much better as John had been such a secret. I only felt comfortable telling Casey, after the fact. I suppose when you're someone's secret, you aren't that special. Being someone's secret should be considered a red flag – always.

"Well, he's a looker," Emma added, as she stuffed strawberries into her mouth. We giggled.

"Yes, but it can't happen. He's the guide and that's the boundary." Truth was, I wished something did happen. I felt a connection to him now. I, however, accepted the reality of the situation. "That's okay. I had a little fun," I confessed. I motioned for another swig of vodka.

"That a girl!" And with that, liquid spilt over the side onto my bedspread. I took three big gulps and closed my eyes. I stuck out my cup for more.

"If the lady does insist!" More, more, more.

"Let's keep it steady, yeah? We don't want to get you drunk off the bat!" Kate added.

"Better catch up!" I laughed.

The rest of the night swirled with laughter and libations. I forgot my confrontation earlier with those silly nobodies and I forgot my fight with Casey. I was sure she'd get over it. My feelings were hurt, and I decided to drink them away. Bottoms up!

Chapter Twenty-Five

The next day when I awoke, my head was spinning. The earth was tilted on an axis, and I wasn't able to open my eyes to restore equilibrium.

Memories of last night swirled in my mind. The anthem of "chug chug chug!" played on repeat. Scenes flashed in my recollection amongst bright lights as I held my eyes shut. It was a safe assumption that I had too much to drink. I heard tearing sounds in the room. I sat up, alarmed, wishing I hadn't roused so quickly.

"What's that sound?" a croak formed from my lungs. I couldn't bear to take in my surroundings.

"It's time to get up!" Emma jovially announced as she tugged the curtains open. The bright rays stung my eyes like sea water.

"What time is it?" Rebecca rumbled as a small landslide fell onto the floor from her bed. She'd been hibernating under a pile of clothing, too lazy to push them off when she crawled into bed last night. There may've also been an impromptu fashion show with her new purchases.

"8am on the dot; time for breakfast." Emma continued to turn lights on and rifle through every possible possession she owned, with the volume turned up.

"You couldn't bloody let us sleep in after last night?" Kate groaned. She threw a pillow towards Emma, slightly missing her target. She huffed and threw the bedding over her face.

"You lot kept me up last night with your tomfooleries. I didn't sleep a wink. Payback, as they say, is a bitch." Emma opened the last curtain, and the room was flooded with light.

"We'll remember this!" Kate hollered as she sat up. "I'll make sure we skip every ice cream stand from here to Bali!" She threw off the covers and ran into the bathroom. Faint sounds of clanging containers could be heard. Emma stuck her tongue out in retaliation.

I collected myself and headed into the dining room for some breakfast. I might as well get something else into me other than booze. I joined the buffet line and rubbed my temples. I admit, I was a bit dishevelled looking. I had on my jean shorts and a torn rock band shirt. I finished the look with a pair of sunglasses to hide my hungover eyes and shied my brain from making my headache worse.

"Went a little hard on the drink last night, did we?" Paul chided while we were in line for breakfast that morning. I think he made extra noise picking up his cutlery just to piss me off.

I scowled at Paul, unsure if he could see the full picture hidden under my coverings.

"Touché," he smirked as he headed down the line scooping scrambled eggs onto his plate. "You ladies were awfully rowdy last night. Too bad I didn't get an invite to the party." He continued to add fruit to his plate.

"What makes you think you were wanted?"

"An invite never hurts." He scooped some fruit salad and continued, "I'd like for us to get along. I do care about you. You make me laugh. I know we can't – "

"Look, I know. You're my tour guide. It's fine. We had our hot moment, and it's over. It's okay." He really didn't need to reiterate the boundaries; I got it.

"You thought it was hot?" He smiled for a moment. I thought about us sitting on the bench, connecting. I melted.

"That's not the point." I felt heat on my face, and momentarily between us. "My point is yes, we can be friends. Leave it alone. Okay?" I pushed my sunglasses back up and looked down at the food, my stomach lurching.

"Okay. Next time I'd like an invite to the party, please. Friendship sounds fun." And with that, he was off to join a group of guys on our tour. I tried to conceal a smile upon my lips. It felt nice to talk to him again.

"Ohhhhhhhh, I hurt, friend!" Rebecca threw her arm around my shoulder as if she believed that I was going to prop her up.

"Fend for yourself." I flung her arm away.

"Where's the love? Darling? And the cereal. I need my choco-puffs!" Rebecca sounded like an angry toddler, her fists firm at her sides. She scurried around, looking for her sugary addiction.

Kate and Emma entered the dining area next. Kate had broken out her sun hat from Thailand. The veil hid her pale complexion. When she had roused this morning, she put her head over the toilet bowl. Luckily, I missed the heaving. I don't 'do' vomit.

After breakfast, we gathered in the common room. Paul told us that over the next week, we would be steadily making our way through Malaysia to Singapore. Singapore was both an island and a country. Or a country that's an island; whatever. We'd another day to rest and explore here before we boarded the new bus the next morning.

Our journey would include a few stops in small villages to see different places of worship and to do some local cooking. It'd be more relaxing, and we'd have an opportunity to get to know the cultures of this country a bit better. This sounded fun, minus the long journey to Singapore. At least we'd be making stops along the way before the next border.

Bumpy bus rides to small towns nestled along the coast was the itinerary for the next few days. I enjoyed having some peace and taking time to wander around the various, coloured temples. As we gravitated through Southeast Asia, we came across Muslim, Hindi, and Buddhist places of worship. Cultures who you wouldn't think could coexist, were almost perfectly meshed.

Jasmine, rose, and sandalwood incense filled corners of the temples where people laid offerings. These might be wishes for people or for things to come. We tiptoed around those who took time for quiet prayer. I took in this experience, grateful that I was included. I might not understand everything that was happening, but I remained curious and asked questions.

When we weren't exploring temples, we were getting into messes in the kitchen. Cooking is a skill every person should participate in. My dad often says my mom burns water but hey, no one's perfect. One of my favourite activities was learning how to cook Nasi Lemak which is one of the national dishes of Malaysia. We stayed in a hostel and the owners let us help them make dinner for our group. It turned out that we were the only tourists they had for a while, so they were happy to teach us how to make local dishes.

We took turns making pots of fragrant rice, dousing it with coconut milk and a pandan leaf. We steamed local white fish to have with it. The dinner was both sweet and savoury. Mangos and sticky rice with sesame was served for dessert. I would never have imagined how delicious and fresh this would taste, but I soon became accustomed to all the rice!

Everyone was having such an amazing time exploring the small towns, making wishes at temples, and cooking. Rebecca and I wandered around the towns. I gave in to some pampering with her since she made the time to come to temples with me for some sightseeing. One day, after we visited a temple, Rebecca and I made a stop at a salon on the main street. She was desperate for a pedicure now that sandals were back on her feet.

Outside the salon there was a large tank of small fish. I leaned down to try to count how many of the greyish gold finned friends there were. I thought there must be a pet store nearby or, worst case, maybe they belonged to the grocer and would soon be someone's dinner. Rebecca had gone in to investigate how much her nails would cost. The esthetician brought Rebecca out by the hand and said, "Put your feet in here first, then come inside." Rebecca and I looked at each other in confusion. The lady appeared annoyed that she had to repeat herself in broken English. "Feet in the tank and fish will nibble your feet." The woman mimicked chomping sounds and laughed when she saw the horror on our faces.

"You want those fish to bite my feet?" Rebecca asked, dumbfounded, pointing towards the murky tank. This was an unreal request.

"Yes."

"Why?"

"The fish will make your feet soft to work with," the lady explained. "You do, too." The lady pointed to me.

"No, I couldn't." I smiled as I backed away.

"Yes, you both or no nails." What a bossy woman.

"Please, Poppy! I need nice feet!" I rolled my eyes at Rebecca and took my sandals off.

"Only for you." We hopped onto the bench. I took a deep breath and plunged my feet into the warm water.

It turned out that these were red garra fish, often used in beauty salons here. The idea was that the fish would make the feet soft, and cuticles easier to cut, as the lady had explained. They even suggested that it would help improve circulation, but I'm no expert. When in Malaysia, right?

I couldn't help but squeal when I felt the fish suck on my feet. I wasn't sure if this was a love bite or a piranha attack. We splashed our feet into, and out of, the water as we giggled. The esthetician laughed at us and ushered us inside once we were done our torture. We left that day with polished toes and a fun story to tell the others. I was learning the importance of trying new things and enjoying my adventures.

Chapter Twenty-Six

Singapore is a very clean and modern place. Paul told us how impressed we'd be with the architecture and the different activities such as a night safari, high end shopping (as if many of us could afford that), as well as an opportunity to try a Singapore Sling drink at the famous Raffles Hotel. As we made our way along in our new, large bus, Paul shared different laws that had existed in Singapore, one of which was about gum. With that last comment, some of the gum chewers around me ceased their chomping.

A puzzled look crossed Rebecca's face. "What do you mean, 'no gum.' What's wrong with it?" She squinted her eyes, trying to process what the big deal would be.

"It used to be considered illegal. People tend to spit their gum out wherever, right?" he asked the group. We nodded in agreement. "Well, gum gets stuck to everything. It costs a lot of money to clean the litter."

Rebecca nodded her head. "What happened when

you used to get caught?" The little rebel wanted to know the consequences.

Without skipping a beat, "Beheading," Paul answered. The group gasped. "I'm just kidding. It used to be a monetary fine."

Rebecca gulped. "What else?"

"What else? Durian fruit is a big no no." Paul explained that this peculiar food, which was spiky and almost as large as a pineapple, was banned from a lot of accommodations. When we asked why, he told us that while the fresh fruit was sweet and creamy, almost like vanilla or caramel, people thought it smelled. He said the smell was compared to dirty laundry, rotting food, or some folks said it smelled like sewage. I, under no circumstances, enjoyed the smell of any of these items. The scents were so powerful, it would get onto your clothes and work its way through the air system of the hotels and hostels. You couldn't even pretend you didn't have the culprit in your possession, it was so pungent. Paul told us it was even on signs that the fruit was not allowed. "You will definitely have a chance to try it," he said. "It even comes chocolate covered."

"Hmmm, chocolate-covered sewage. My fav," Rebecca chuckled, pretending to throw up in her mouth. I couldn't help but laugh. How could something so good tasting smell so horrible? I guess I'd find out.

The next day around lunch, we crossed the border. Hello city life, here we come! The countryside and small towns had been fun, but I was ready for more urban exploration. That and I had promised Rebecca we could do some shopping. I had to admit, I did pick up some cool souvenirs and a dress for myself.

Singapore City, Singapore. This was the last country we'd enter before our flight into Indonesia. This modern metropolis felt like a fusion of Toronto, Canada, and London, England as the buildings were beyond modern and built on the water's edge. There's also a splash of elegant history dotted in and around the city. I felt like I was in the past and the present. It was peaceful, clean, and refreshing.

Rebecca had failed to work through her supply of gum. I tried to reassure her that she didn't need to worry about a fine, or beheading, but she and I'd split up the remaining gum between our two bags just to be on the safe side. In reality, if Rebecca was going to get busted by the police, it would be for a fate far worse than gum smuggling.

A formal walking tour of the city would happen the next day. Some folks, tired from the travel, decided to have dinner on their own tonight. There's a casino in the city with a ship on the roof. Some folks wanted to go gambling and have drinks there. It'd be cool to perch overtop of the city and see the sights from high above. The rest of us wanted a fancy night out so we could dress up and rub shoulders with the rich and the famous. Dinner and then drinks at the infamous, elegant, and historical hotel were on the agenda. I wanted to be in the city and tonight, I wanted to be transported in time.

In addition to harbouring an unhealthy amount of gum, Rebecca had managed to give me a drinking problem and I felt as though my liver needed time to recuperate. I shouldn't have had so much the other day, but I wanted to let loose. My body would have a bit of time to recuperate. Drinks, however, were needed at the famous hotel. I'd do my best to pull up my bootstraps for the experience.

"What do you think we should wear for this fabulous hotel?" Rebecca held up garments and tossed the ones she didn't like behind her.

"Whatever you feel comfortable in." Tonight, Rebecca and I'd share our room, just the two of us, which I was looking forward to.

"I'm not so fancy, but I want to look nice. Maybe I'll meet some stud like Paul!" she arched her eyebrows, giving me a mischievous smile.

"Hey, remember – Paul's just the guide. We're NOT an item," I reminded her with a harsh glance. Even though we had decided to be friends, we had kept our distance from each other the last few days. There was no awkwardness – we just didn't seem to cross paths.

"Right, right. I just meant he's a looker. You're a looker. Two lookers together make a nice pair." She went back to sorting through her clothing.

"That's nice of you to say." I folded a few dresses I decided against. "Maybe I'll find a nice fellow here, too. I'd like to have a little fun myself!"

"That's my girl!" Rebecca cackled.

After what seemed like hours of rifling through clothes and applying makeup, we were ready to take on this city. Rebecca opted for a red satin, strapless dress. Somehow it had managed to remain wrinkle free in that disaster of a bag of hers. I donned a white Grecian beach dress that I had picked up in Thailand and I hadn't yet had the chance to wear.

When I was ready to meet the group, I headed downstairs. My hand grazed the banister as I floated my way down the stairs. I felt the humidity on my skin. Singapore reminded me of the jungle heat in Malaysia. The safe haven of the air conditioning would have to wait until we returned.

The others were at the bottom of the stairs, waiting for everyone to arrive. I had a little déjà vu from our first day of the trip. My, how times had changed over the course of our journey. As my eyes scanned the room for the ladies, I saw Paul standing at the reception desk, fanning himself. He was dressed in tan khaki shorts and a white linen shirt that was open at the collar. His tanned skin glistened as beads of sweat dripped down his face onto his chest and slid down his shirt, hidden by inconvenient material. My eyes lingered on him a little too long. I couldn't help it. He looked up at me and I turned away. He was handsome, yet we had to remain professional.

"Ready for an evening out, friend?" Paul didn't look up from the reception desk. For the first time, his face was red.

"Sure, am. I hear the Queen's Quey is amazing," I said, referring to our dinner destination on the waterfront.

"Are you enjoying yourself? I hadn't seen much of you lately." He shyly looked up at me.

"I've been busy taking in all the sights. I hope you didn't miss me too much," I cheekily offered before I joined my friends in the lobby.

The night didn't cool but the humidity stayed at bay, teasing us. Before heading to the hotel, we spent the evening as a group on the Queen's Quey savouring seafood and drinking wine. Twinkling, white lights lined the river front. Open air restaurants made room for guests to dine under the moonlight. The atmosphere had a romantic lull to it. We'd grown fond of each other, for the most part, and we were past the awkward stage of getting to know each other, so we could finally be ourselves without judgment.

"Right, well cheers to an amazing adventure!" Rebecca stood and raised her glass, her red wine sloshing in the stemware. She had to hike up her dress, which was slipping down her chest. A few gentlemen, or lack thereof, stared at her over the rims of their pint glasses.

"And to learning more about these great countries!" Emma chimed in. There were a few muffled giggles. Kate rolled her eyes.

"Way to be a buzz kill," Kate murmured.

"I think those are great toasts, and I second that." Paul raised his glass.

I glanced around the table as I clinked glasses. Mike and Karli were snuggled up against each other, kissing.

For a moment, I felt a pang of jealousy. I'd given it a go with him and at the end of the day, he'd found something in Karli he liked better than in me or Jessica. He was a dog, just like John. Best to move on; I dodged that bullet.

While we were eating dinner, I occasionally sensed that I was being watched from across the table. Twice, I caught Paul watching me when I was laughing. He had a soft, thin smile as he twirled his wine and when he sipped it, it felt like he was taking me in. For a moment, I thought that I was mistaken, but his eyes kept meeting mine momentarily. I looked around, but no one else seemed to notice.

After dinner, as we waited for our taxis to take us to the next destination, I wandered down to the water's edge and dipped my toes in. The air was warm and the water cool. I swept my toes back and forth for a moment of silence. I closed my eyes and breathed in the night air. I felt relaxed, free, and totally at peace. The stars above me shone like something out of a fairy tale and I wished to get back to my journey of finding out what would make me happy. I'd gotten to a point where I wasn't mad at myself any longer for the John ordeal, as that was in the past. Just as I finished my thought, I felt someone sit down beside me.

From the smell of his aftershave, I knew who it was. "I couldn't help but notice how lovely you look tonight." He took off his sandals and dipped his toes in. "Not your usual travel garbs." A moment of humour between two friends, I suppose. He continued to ramble, "What I mean is, you always look lovely. I just think that you look mystic in that dress, like something out of the heavens," he fumbled.

It was a little over the top, which made me suspicious, but it was a lovely gesture. "Thank you. You don't look so bad yourself," I returned the compliment; he did look good tonight. I created a ripple in the water with my toes.

"These old things," he laughed and playfully nudged me in the shoulder. Neither of us had been making much eye contact since he had decided to join me. We hadn't had this much body contact since Kuala Lumper.

The more we talked, the friendlier we became, and the closer we sat. It got so intense that he had playfully touched my hand while he was telling me a joke. Electric shocks pulsated throughout my body.

"Listen, I was hoping to talk to you," he started.

"Yes, me too," I cut him off.

"Come on you lot! Taxis are here!" someone bellowed from the road.

We both awkwardly got up and made our way to the cars. This conversation would have to wait. We ran up the hill and got into different taxis, respectively, like two boxers sent to their corners of the ring to regroup and figure out the next move.

Chapter Twenty-Seven

The Raffles Hotel was a bit of a legend. Initially, I didn't get what was so exciting about going to an older hotel for a fruity drink.

When the taxis pulled up to the final stop of the night, I had to squint in the darkness to see the white building with simple black letters of the hotel's name. The building was shrouded by large, palm leaves. We made our way around the back of the building, towards the courtyard, and followed a sign upstairs to the long bar. The intoxicating scent of flowers surrounded us as we ascended the stairs. Spanish music filled our ears as we travelled back in time to what felt like a cozy, Caribbean cabana.

"We double fisting tonight, Pops?" Rebecca nudged me as she eagerly made her way to the bar. The woman was clearly on a mission.

"One for me," I replied. I didn't want to get too wild. I was still nursing a sore head.

"On it!" she zoomed off to retrieve our drinks. She zipped through the crowd, dodging other patrons. "Coming through! Woman on a mission!" Rebecca's battle cry could be heard from the other end of the bar. I couldn't help but laugh at her antics.

Signs showing the hotel's history lined the walls. Most of the windows were open and there was a small porch lining the upstairs. Large, brown fans loomed overhead. The panels looked like palm leaves lazily swaying through the hot night. Small, rattan seats dotted the room. There was a stage where the performers played, and patrons danced. I wandered over to find our group seats, trailblazing through peanut shells on the way. People were cracking them open and tossing the shells on the floor. It was a bit barbaric, but when in Singapore!

"Here you go, ma belle." Rebecca handed me a cold, tall glass with the hotel logo on it. Inside, pink bubbles fizzed to the surface and a piece of pineapple, and a maraschino cherry were perched on the rim. The original recipe for this cocktail was created in this very hotel. The recipe, however, was lost, they say. Most bartenders make it with gin, sweet fruit, and soda water. It was a boozy, adult version of fruit punch. I liked it, but I knew it would be trouble as it went down a little too easily.

I'd barely finished my drink when I heard slurping through straws around the small group that had formed. Many others were delighted with the drink and went back for seconds. I enjoyed the cocktails, but I was on a budget, so it made me think twice before I got more. Rebecca offered to buy me another, but I told her I needed to wait a bit.

I stepped out into the courtyard for some fresh air in the moonlight. I thought that I was alone, but it turned out Paul had the same idea. Great! We couldn't get away from each other. I stood there and sheepishly smiled, still not knowing what to do or say since our earlier encounter. We had some unfinished business to discuss. I wasn't cold but I rubbed my shoulders as I tried to decide what to say.

"Cold?" Paul asked, and motioned towards me. My heart began to pound again, getting louder with every step he took. Suddenly, he was standing in front of me, caressing my bare shoulders. I was warm and him touching me, and standing so close to me, made my body heat rise. I wondered if I was the only one.

I looked up, not knowing what to expect, and our eyes met. I tried to look away, but I couldn't. I brushed a bead of sweat off his forehead. The man always had sweat pouring off him. I swear, I could feel the pheromones raging. Before I knew it, his lips were on mine.

So much for friendship.

His naturally salty, soft, plump lips traced mine. They tasted like the ocean. The hands that had momentarily touched my shoulders now drifted towards my waist, pulling me in closer. I felt our heat. The kissing intensified, and our hands couldn't move fast enough.

"Maybe we should stop," I interjected, pulling myself away. I didn't know that this would happen. I felt an attraction for Paul, and I also thought he didn't want me with the boundaries he'd set on our relationship. I chose to respect what he'd said, but maybe his feelings had changed.

"I'm sorry, we can stop." Paul stepped back and rested his forehead against mine as we tried to calm our breathing.

Paul tilted my chin up. "I'd never want you to do something you didn't want to do. I – I like you. I've been dreaming of kissing you."

Before my brain caught up to my mouth, I said, "I've been dreaming of you, too. I like you, Paul, even if you drive me crazy." I couldn't help but laugh.

"You drive me crazy too, Maple." Paul lifted my hand to kiss it.

"Hey, that's only allowed for the English ladies, remember?" I teased.

"Yeah, yeah. Maybe you can make an exception for me?" He winked before releasing my hand. I didn't want this to stop, but we still had to talk.

"About earlier, what were you going to say?" As if I had to ask. But asking was necessary to avoid misinterpretation.

"I was going to say that maybe we should give us another try. I don't want either of us to get into trouble but maybe, when the tour is over, we can continue what has been happening between us? Maybe we can start off as friends first, just to be on the safe side. I don't need anyone giving you anymore trouble."

Friends? We just kissed. I wanted to be more than friends. I mulled this over for a minute. Perhaps we could get to know each other now and figure the rest out later.

"Maybe, that would be nice." It was the truth. We could start off somewhere.

"Cool. We should get back, but can we talk about this more later?"

"I'd really like that." I grabbed my bag and decided that I could be friends. That felt right for everything going on now.

Paul and I headed back into the bar to listen to more music, excited for this new development. It was too soon to turn into an epic romance, but the kind and soft kiss, and the gentlemanly approach, were welcome. I felt respected and cared for. We'd have the luxury of being friends first, which was rare.

The rest of the night, Paul and I sat at opposite ends of the bar, our secret safe, but a good kind of secret. The music pushed through the pulsating sounds of the fan. The English ladies laughed, dancing about the peanut shell littered floor. They dragged me up to dance, too. The hem of my white dress swayed in the warm, night breeze. I would look over to Paul, who was seated with some of the other lads on our trip. He acted coy, glancing over at me and looking away to resume his chat with the guys. The Singapore Slings went to my head and attacked my pocketbook.

We walked home, tipsy. We linked arms as we stumbled back to the hotel. "One foot in front of the other," I repeated to myself out loud, while my friends poked fun at me. What else was new? I was used to it by now.

"Maple, I appreciate the direction, but stop pulling

on me!" Emma groaned. We all laughed.

Intoxicated on alcohol, and possibly budding love, I kept moving down the dark street, laughing all the way home. I was baffled no more by Paul.

Chapter Twenty-Eight

So long Singapore, hello Jakarta, Indonesia! Singapore was a quick pit stop before we continued onto the last leg of our trip. Yesterday, we'd had a free day to roam around and see the city sights before heading off to the next stop. Rebecca and I went to the night safari to see Malayan tapir, tigers, and elephants. It was magnificent to get to see these exotic animals.

Today, we had a late start getting to the airport as some people allegedly slept through their alarms. I think a few of the lot had partied a little too hard the night before.

At the airport we said goodbye to a few passengers who had to return home early. The majority of the travelers stayed with us, including Britney and Tiffany. We said our farewells, exchanged socials, and headed to our respective gates. After a whirlwind race through the airport, we got our new van when we landed. We skirted through the streets to our hotel near the city center.

The view wasn't anything special. It was the definition of a concrete jungle. Outside the window were tower upon tower of office and apartment buildings. The roadway was barely visible in the distance. The view was depressing considering the landscape so far. The adventure, however, would continue.

Rebecca and I shared a room again. I'd grown fond of her and her company. At first, I had thought she'd be a young, wild, party animal and there were times she could be. Who didn't want to have fun on holiday? But she was also sweet and sincere. She had a heart of gold. It showed me that you don't really know someone until you spend time with them.

I bounced on my bed to try to soften the stiff mattress. I thought about my last conversation with Casey, and I didn't like how we'd left things. Just like Rebecca, Casey was my confidant and someone who I initially judged, but who ended up being an amazing friend. Casey was special to me, and I didn't want to lose her. I fiddled with my phone before I had the nerve to click the screen on and text her. Apologizing was hard, but it was the right thing to do.

Poppy: Hey girl.

Tiny dots danced on the screen and quickly faded.

Poppy: Casey, I wanted to say I'm sorry. You were only trying to help. I see that now.

The tiny dots returned. Nothing. My heart sank.

Poppy: Please, Casey. Talk to me. I'll apologize forever if I have to.

Tiny dots. Suddenly, something appeared.

Casey: No need to be dramatic! ☺

Relief flooded over me.

Poppy: You've no idea how worried I was! I thought you hated me.

Casey: I could never hate you! I was worried you were mad at me. I was only trying to help.

Poppy: I know. No more fights?

Casey: I don't think we can promise that. But I'm happy to move on.

Poppy: Deal. You'll never guess what happened!

Casey: ?!

Poppy: Paul and I….

Casey: Slept together?!

Poppy: No, we kissed!

Casey: And?

Poppy: It was amazing. We decided we'd be friends for now.

Casey: Oh…Poppy: No, it's okay! We decided we'd get to know each other first and see what happens when the trip is over.

Casey: A globe-trotting romance! I love it!

Poppy: ☺

There was a knock at the door. Kate stopped by to tell us that the group was going out to pick up supplies and eat. I said goodbye to Casey, promising to talk later. I was so happy to make up with her. Good friends are hard to find.

We headed down the street to exchange our money into the local currency before we explored what the city had to offer. I found changing money to be a headache. Just when I learned how to convert one currency, we had to change it to another. When it was my turn, I handed over a stack of unused bills and a fistful of coins. The woman lowered her shoulders in disappointment when she saw she had some metal to deal with. Hey, I tried to spend it!

Her hands zipped through the cash like a card dealer at the casino. When she was done counting, she motioned for me to hold out my hand. I felt like I was 12 years old demanding my allowance from my parents. I was shocked when the lady handed me my money and said, "Here's your four million dollars," like it was no big deal. A million dollars?! I quickly checked my exchange app to realize that was a few hundred dollars. For the next bit, I would be living life as a millionaire! What would I spend my fortune on? Hey, it was funny!

Jalan Jaska aka Backpacker's Street was an area of the city designed for backpackers to gather for shelter, food, and souvenirs. Over the years, it had changed and was just a regular street. Jakarta used to be more geared towards tourists. It was a business capitol and layover for travellers now.

Paul had tagged along and wanted to show us all the places we could visit. He also wanted an opportunity for us to meet up with another group of tourists. We stopped at a restaurant to investigate the menu when a stranger approached us.

"Hey man! What's up?" A tall, muscular, American man fist bumped Paul and brought him in for a hug. He had short, brown, curly hair that was plastered to his head.

"Not much, man. How are you?" Paul offered in exchange.

"Just settling in for some grub. Grab some seats and join us." The man, named Eric, motioned for us to sit with his group. Eric worked for the same company as Paul, but they were travelling different areas with their groups. For the next hour, we uncomfortably mingled so Paul and Eric could catch up. Getting to know strangers is hard for some folks. We'd already mustered up courage to get to know each other a few weeks ago, so this was like starting all over again. After a few drinks and some games of cards, we were bonding like one big family.

"Man, I could tell you so many stories about this guy," Eric slurred as he wrapped one arm around Paul. He sloshed his beer in his hand, spilling the contents over Kate who sat on the other side of him. She wiped it off her arm and stared him down, her eyes casting daggers.

"Oh, no, you don't." Discomfort oozed from Paul's pores.

"Come on! All the adventures, the near misses, the girls." Eric laughed as he spilt some beer onto Paul's t-shirt. Paul looked down to evaluate the mess his friend had made.

"Really, man, it's cool. I think these guys aren't

interested in that!"

"Sure, we are. We want to know what a bad boy Paul is." That voice was Britney. When would she ever shut up?

"We love bad boys," Tiffany added as she leaned across the table to hear more dirt. Eric set his sights on them. The troublesome, Siamese cats were back at it, causing more mischief. I'd do anything to shoo them away.

Eric got up, wedged himself between the two of them, and said in a loud whisper, "Paul is quite the ladies' man. I think he's had more notches in his bed post than most." Tiffany and Britney looked at each other and sly smiles spread across their faces.

"Oh, really," they said in unison. Their wicked grins grew larger. They were clearly loving the drama.

There were audible gasps from around our table, mostly from the ladies. I felt like I was going to pass out. I couldn't look at Paul.

"No need to start rumours," Paul croaked.

"What rumours, man? I was there when we were in Bangkok last time. You went home with that Swedish blonde – " Eric was cut off of the booze and the conversation.

"Enough. Stop it, man." Paul got up from his chair. I wasn't sure if he was getting ready to rumble in the streets. The damage, however, had been done.

Paul summoned us to go back to the hotel. It was getting late, and we had places to go in the morning. Paul and Eric gave each other an awkward hug and exchanged some inaudible words – oh, to be a fly on that wall. Was Paul the person I thought he was?

Chapter Twenty-Nine

That night, I went to bed angry. I couldn't help but toss and turn. I liked Paul. I thought we were going to be friends, and then some. Now, this other tour guide basically said Paul was a player! Gross. I didn't want all the men I picked to be creeps.

The night moved slowly. I didn't want daylight to come as then I'd have to face Paul. But I also didn't want to close my eyes and dream about either of these people. There was a rumble coming from my nightstand. In the dark, I fumbled to find my phone. It had been vibrating non-stop. From across the room, I heard Rebecca moving around in her bed. Her mattress squeaked with every turn.

The light from the phone temporarily blinded me. As my eyes adjusted, I saw a new text message appear across my screen. My tired eyes tried to make out who it was from.

Unknown Number: X

My body momentarily paralyzed. I wondered if I was experiencing sleep paralysis like I kept hearing about in my ghost story podcasts. I was definitely being haunted.

I clicked the screen to darkness and placed the phone back on the nightstand. I don't know why I hadn't blocked him. Why hadn't I just now? What was I waiting for?

As my heartrate slowed down, I told myself that I'd moved on, and I didn't need John in my life. I was done with him. I closed my eyes and hoped to dream. I didn't want to relive that nightmare. His message was shit timing. Was the universe trying to test me?

Chapter Thirty

City life looked different in Indonesia than it did in other countries we'd visited. This morning, we went out in search of food before we made a long drive to see temples.

Crossing the street was much like a retro amphibian videogame – two steps forward, one step to the side, three steps back. Try again. Here, you didn't want to get quashed by a vehicle as that'd definitely result in a game over!

The famished members of our group gathered around Paul as he explained how to navigate traffic. He told us that our former idea of crossing the road didn't exist here. Good luck waiting for the crosswalk sign to light up. Instead, you had to become one with the traffic. We looked at each other, puzzled, trying to decipher the warrior move he was explaining to us.

"Uh, huh, so, 'master;' what does that mean, exactly?" Rebecca crossed her arms across her full chest.

She heaved with anxiety through her tight pink shirt. Her nails tapped against a wooden bracelet she had purchased.

"You enter into traffic when you want to cross the road," he explained, almost patronizing, like we didn't know how to cross a road in general.

"So, you wait for the cars to stop moving?" Kate added as she pointed to the swarm of traffic floating by.

"No," Paul cautioned, "you start walking through the traffic." More puzzled looks. We clearly didn't get it. "You see, they start to drive around you as you cross the road."

"So, they won't hit us? They drive around us?" Kate clarified.

There was a pause. "Most of the time," Paul countered. A sneaky smile crossed his face. Clearly, he knew how to play the game, but us newbies still needed to review the rules.

"What's that you say?" Kate leaned in. "I'm not really jonesing to go back to the hospital."

"Most of the time, they don't hit you," the group gasped, leaving little oxygen between us. I swear, some folks were about to faint. Maybe I'd just stay on my side of the street.

The roads were buzzing with cars, but the majority of the vehicles were motorcyclists travelling in all directions. Some motorcycles had one person on them, some had kids on their way to school, and some drivers were dressed in business attire and others leisure wear. The kids would point and smile at us as if they'd never seen tourists before. Paul explained that this part of

Indonesia didn't get as many travellers so we might look a little strange to them. I couldn't help but laugh when I saw families teetering on the motorcycles. Other drivers had peculiar items such as boxes piled sky high, ladders, and one even had a crate of chickens on the back! We'd made a travel game out of it to see which motorcycle had the strangest things, and the winner got a beer.

"Would people feel safer if they followed me?"

Paul was met with a resounding, "YES!" from the group.

With that, he acted as the captain and led his crew through the battle of sea traffic. You can call it a biblical parting or cultural instinct, but Paul was right. As we entered into the street, no one honked at us, and we didn't cause a catastrophic accident. Instead, as he suggested, people weaved around us and continued their journeys. When we safely made it across the street, we sighed in sweet relief. I lost my appetite crossing over, but I felt a rush of adrenaline through my veins.

"You alright?" Paul laughed as he squeezed my arm.

"I know how to cross a street." I caught my breath and looked around as the vehicles flowed back into their original formation.

Paul winked and checked on the other frogs. Perhaps he was right; he was growing on me. Something inside me had started to solidify feelings for him. Would a friendship be sustainable?

Today, we'd get to witness two significant temples near Yogyakarta where we were staying. For this adventure we had to ensure that our shoulders and knees were covered. For those of us who had short shorts on, we were offered sarongs to cover up out of respect for being in these spiritual spaces.

The first of the two, 9th-century, UNESCO World Heritage Site temples was Prambanan. It was one of the largest Hindu temples in Indonesia. The dark, stone structures loomed over us. Bright, lush palms illuminated the features of the temple, breathing new life to the ancient craftsmanship. A stone wall surrounded the temples. It was an abandoned piece of history, a quiet place for the higher entities to rest undisturbed. It truly had to be experienced in person to appreciate the beauty.

Paul walked around with us, explaining the art and architecture of the buildings. Each carving told a story. I ran my fingers over the ancient sketches, trying to connect with the people who put them there. Although I didn't understand everything that was written on the temple walls, I appreciated learning more about Hinduism.

As we walked around the space, we encountered a school group on a class trip. Girls in blue uniform skirts and cardigans giggled as they ran around the grounds, their teacher yelling at the students to slow down. A few times, I heard a click and turned around, but there was no one there and only the faint sound of giggles and scattered footsteps. Others heard this, too. Britney and

Tiffany confessed that a few of the students were taking pictures of us!

"That happens," Paul began. "They only see people who look 'like you' on television and in the media. To them, you are very different – exotic, even." Paul mentioned that those group members with blonde hair and blue eyes were considered the most exotic of the bunch as their features were the rarest.

We looked around and mouthed the word 'exotic.' Britney and Tiffany puffed their chests like they were celebrities. Cool it, broads. To me, the people of Indonesia were exotic. I would have never thought that they'd think that about us; it was neat to learn about different perspectives.

After an hour bus ride, we headed to Borobudur, which was the Mahayana Buddhist temple. We waited for Paul to arrange our entrance. The heat from the morning sun started to roast our sensitive skin and there was absolutely no shade here to enjoy. Some of us were fanning our sarongs, trying to create a breeze. Kate found a rock to sit on and gulped the last of her water. She held the bottle up to see if she'd missed any drops and tried to drink what she could before the rest evaporated.

Emma sat down near Kate as our group waited. "It's so hot," Emma whined. She pushed her thick, black sunglasses up the bridge of her nose. Kate looked at her as if she was going to slap her against her skull.
"Tell us something we don't already know, genius," Kate mumbled.

Reluctantly, we roused so we could continue to

learn, and to get back to the hotel for a rest. Upon inspection it appeared to me that the shape of this building was much like a pyramid with steps up to the top. It was one of the largest temples in the world. At one point, the temple was covered in volcanic ash, taking hundreds of years to refinish. I'd never seen so many different Buddha in one place before; each had a different meaning. As we walked up the levels, we were told that each level represented a different stage of enlightenment. We learned about the history of Buddha, not to mention other Buddhist tales.

At one point in our exploration, the group broke up and I found myself walking around with Paul. "So, what do you think so far?" He kicked a few loose pebbles at his feet.

"It's so beautiful here. I think this one's my favourite." I pointed to the structure around us. The sun was warming my face with its golden rays.

"Mine, too." We stopped walking for a minute. "And what about us?" His eyes met mine.

"What do you mean?" My breath disappeared.

"Us and our – friendship?" When he said it like that, I wasn't sure if he actually meant a friendship.

"Well, friends is a good word." Paul's smile dropped as I spoke. I continued, "Friends are honest with each other, right?" Paul nodded, 'yes,' to my question and I kept going, "What's the deal with Eric?" He'd no choice but to dig into what was shared last night.

"Him," Paul shook his head. He brushed a free hand through his hair and the other cast on his hip. "He's a good guy and all, but Eric parties a little too much."

I snorted in rebuttal. "It sounded like you partied pretty hard." Eric's words rang in my ear. I pictured Paul's bedpost with a tower of notches. I wasn't so sure I wanted to see his bed after hearing that.

"Don't believe everything. Guys like to exaggerate." Paul concluded. I wasn't so sure I was satisfied with his answer.

"And why should I believe you?" I sounded a bit more defensive than I'd intended. I relaxed my posture to help settle my nerves.

"Because I'm telling you the truth," he said as he looked me in the eyes. I believed him. "Yes, I've met some women on my travels. I may have taken a woman for a drink or even kissed some, but I'm not that guy." It sounded like he was honest with a sprinkle of scandal. I decided to take it at face value.

"I thought we were just friends?" Paul asked, trying to change the conversation with a grin. He studied my face, searching for my reaction.

Damn. Was I caught? "We are." Anxiety was brewing and it risked bubbling to the surface. "I just wanted to know about the company I was keeping, that's all." I shuffled my feet.

"Uh, huh. Well, 'friend,' go check out the top of the temple. It's the best part." He turned to walk away. "I have to go check on the others." He called back to me, "Don't forget to make a wish!" He disappeared out of sight.

"A wish?" I said out loud to no one in particular.

"Yes, make a wish on the way to the top. It will bring you good luck," a stranger said to me as she passed by. She stopped briefly to explain what she meant by that. It was good luck to touch the Buddha within each bell or stupas, to make your wish.

After I made my way to the top, I circulated around the stupas. I took a moment to close my eyes and decided what it was that I wanted to cast out to Buddha, the universe, and whomever was listening. I took a deep breath. When I opened my eyes, I sighed, letting the wish sink in. I felt like I was blowing out candles on a birthday cake, careful not to share my wish for fear it wouldn't come true.

I turned around to head back down the steps and I saw Paul. He smiled faintly at me. "What'd you wish for?" The sun was so bright, it caused him to squint.

"To mend my broken heart," I confessed. I decided to show my cards, and risk my wish not coming true.

"Did I – ?" Paul started, but I cut him off.

"Not you." I found the courage to share my deep, dark secret. "Before I arrived here, I was involved with my boss." I felt like I was at church, sharing my confession. "I got in over my head, hurt some people indirectly. I made a fool of myself. I want to move on."

"Things happen," Paul soothed. He didn't judge me, just listened.

"He was married, technically."

"Oh."

"He was separated when we got together, but legally, still married. He didn't tell me he was in a challenging divorce. I stayed longer than I should have." I brushed the sarong covering my knees. "I feel awfully stupid for being with him, but it's over." And it was.

"You're human; we all are." His lips formed an empathetic smile.

"Yes, I can't help but feel bad. I've been working hard to move forward. It's taken a lot of time, but I'm getting there."

"You're an admirable woman, Poppy. Keep your chin up." His comments made me feel strong and confident. I could change, and I was changing – for the better.

"I'll do my best." I brushed past his shoulder as I made my way back down. If I touched the Buddha and then touched him, would my wish come true?

At the bottom of the temple, there were some artisans selling their wares. I looked around and found a beautiful, graffiti-style painting from atop the temple. Streaks of yellow, blue, and pink spread across the rough, black outlines of the temple. The art would be a reminder that I could always make a wish and, with a little luck, and a little hard work, it might just come true.

We'd tried to huddle under a shady spot on the grounds, which was near impossible to do. Emma had slowly approached us, holding two, white, Styrofoam cups. She carefully tried to contain the piping hot liquid inside.

"How can you drink that? It's like a million degrees out." Rebecca fanned herself. She looked Emma up and down like she'd lost her mind.

Emma said matter-of-factly, "Hot drinks can actually cool you down." She blew on one cup. "Unlike you, who is making more energy by fanning yourself." Ouch, Emma! She could have a wicked tongue when she wanted to.

"Thank you, love." Kate extended her hand to accept the coffee. "What?" She looked at us, puzzled. "She isn't always thick. Sometimes she's onto something." Kate winked and took a sip.

"Thanks, I think." Emma scrunched her nose as she analyzed this comment. She shrugged and took a sip herself. "Who knew this coffee would be so good? Anyone want to try?" Emma looked around for any takers. Most people shook their heads 'no' I decided to take a mouthful.

As I took in the fragrant java, I couldn't help but notice a peculiar taste I couldn't put my finger on. "What's that flavour?" I pondered as I assessed my tingling taste buds.

"It's kopi luwak coffee," Emma shared. She tucked a bag of purchased beans into her backpack. "You might know it as cat shit coffee."

Kate and I spit out the horrid mixture at the same time. "You gave me shit coffee? What the hell is wrong with you?" Kate wiped her chin with her hand. She spit the rest of the contents onto the ground.

"Explain to me why you decided to purchase this particular coffee?" I pointed down at the cup. I was all for trying new things, but this was next level.

I heard Kate muttering in the background, "What a sicko."

"It's the most expensive coffee they have. Be adventurous! This is like liquid gold here." Emma stuck her nose in the coffee's steam. "Can't you taste the cherries?" Emma sat down to enjoy her drink.

"You know, I bet the cat who ate the cherries really enjoyed the fruit, but all I can think of is someone scooping my coffee beans out of a litterbox."

"The bag looked pretty." Emma held up the metallic, red bag.

"Oh, I'm so glad the bag was pretty. I hope I don't get E. coli!" Kate stormed off to get a bottle of water to rinse the rest of her mouth out. A stream of swearwords flowed, "What the hell is wrong with her?"

"Drama queen," Emma smirked and enjoyed her beverage.

After we were finished in Yogyakarta, we made our way through the mainland with the destination of Bali as the final stop.

Along the way, we had some interesting accommodations. In the inland, where travelers are scarce, housing for tourists was a bit sketchy to say the least. Our hostel, one night, backed onto a temple, where we heard the call to prayer with regularity. One night, it scared Rebecca so much that she leapt out of bed because the walls started to shake when the speaker kicked on.

Even though I knew how scared she got, I decided to play a trick on her. One stop, there was a motif of wooden animals outside our room in the stairwell. I took one of the wooden animals and placed it under her covers in her bed. When she got into bed, she shrieked when she saw the wooden figure, thinking someone else had crawled into her bed. I laughed to see her dismay.

Settling in under the covers, we heard a blast from the speakers. Everything in the room shook. The paintings on the walls jostled, our backpacks fell over, and the lights flickered. We'd be lucky to survive the night here. I felt like I was sleeping in a house of cards.

Suddenly, a green streak darted across the wall and then stopped moving. A gecko had emerged from its home behind one of the paintings. Before we had a chance to trap it, it took off again. We jumped on our beds, screaming.

There was a banging on the door. "What the hell are you two doing in there?" a female voice thundered. The door stormed open, and Kate emerged.

"There's a lizard loose in our room!" Rebecca screamed. Kate ran and got the wooden goose from the motif outside and swung it around trying to launch the uninvited guest out of our room.

"I used to play floor hockey. Let me at it!" The image was quite comical. We were screaming and throwing pillows and blankets around, trying to find our green friend. After all the commotion, it leapt down from the dresser and scurried out the door. We fell onto the beds laughing. It all seemed very silly for such a small thing. They say that you can eat spiders in your sleep. I didn't want to eat a gecko. Many of our nights were filled with laughter, sleepovers, and drinks by flashlight, as well as girl talk. When the location had a pub or a nightclub, we'd hit the town, too. Might as well let our hair down! Travel isn't all about sightseeing and souvenirs. The laughing and fun filled me with joy. My wish to move on was coming true.

Chapter Thirty-One

The journey through inland Indonesia ended with an epic hike of Mount Bromo. Indonesia is a magnificent land of temples, people, history, and culture, as well as volcanoes. "Don't worry," Paul reassured us, "not all volcanoes in Indonesia are active." We'd be spending a few nights in a mountain range to climb to the summit of a cluster of volcanoes.

After a rocky drive, we parked in front of a lone hotel. Our bus had gotten stuck earlier in the day and we couldn't finish the journey until well after dark. Paul and some of the others were covered in dirt after trying to dislodge the bus from a ditch earlier. The rest stood around and let the few brave ones do the hard work. Pushing a van wasn't on the top of my list of priorities.

We made our way into the hotel for the night as the moon rose high in the sky. Our host and hostess rushed out to help collect our belongings and offered to make us some tea. Tonight, dinner would be a warm beverage and bus snacks. Hey, sometimes it happens.

As we crowded around the family style, dining room table we heard a rumble. The hotel owners looked at each other and laughed when they saw how nervous we were. Paul glanced over at them and smiled as he told us what the next few days would bring.

"Tomorrow, you'll have a free day to check out the local town, meander around the property or sleep. Early the following day we'll meet at 3am in the lobby for those of you who want to climb to the summit." Audible groans were heard around the table.

"You serious, mate? 3am?" Rebecca tilted her head to the side, not sure if she heard correctly. She was usually the instigator for the question asking, challenging what Paul would lay out for us.

A long pause filled the room. Paul and Rebecca glared at each other. "3am," he repeated without taking his eyes off of her. A stare down had been initiated. First one to blink loses.

"You've got to be joking," Rebecca muttered under her breath. She looked up at the ceiling in contemplation, deciding if she wanted to get up that early. I wondered if it was worth the hassle of getting up early, too.

"Jokes are for kids," Paul smirked. Rebecca's face reddened as she had been overheard.

Another rumble made our cups of tea rattle, and the fluid ripple within the ceramics. What's that all about? Was there an earthquake?

"Say, what's that sound?" Emma inquisitively asked after raising her hand to speak. Sometimes, if felt like we were Paul's students and not his tourists.

"We're not in school, you nutter." Kate crossed her arms and stared down her friend.

"That sound? Oh, it's nothing." Paul laughed. He sifted his fingers through his short hair and tried to move the conversation along to the next topic.

Another rumble caused more ripples in our cups. We looked around, our eyes bulging. We weren't sure if we were under siege. "Alright, what's up?" Kate inquired. Paul better act fast or there'd be a British invasion.

"Well," Paul began, "that's the sound of the active volcanoes." Gasps echoed around the room. Panic filled the void.

"Excuse me for one moment." Kate lifted her fingers to her mouth to review mentally this new piece of data. She tapped her chin before continuing, "What do you mean, 'active' volcanoes?" She made air quotations in her speech.

"Just as I said, 'active'." Paul mimicked the air quotes.

Silence. Nervous eyes darted around the room. The panic continued to escalate. "Don't worry," our hostess started, unsure of how to continue, "there's a wall that surrounds the hotel. You're all safe." she smiled and nodded. She sipped her tea as if the answer sufficed.

"What? Are we going to die?" Rebecca wailed. She reached for my arm and held on tightly, her fingertips leaving imprints in my skin. I hadn't seen this side of her; it was rather shocking.

"You're not going to die. Mount Bromo is an active

volcano. The volcanoes here have the potential to erupt but I assure you, Bromo is safe to climb." Sighs of relief were audible in the room followed by "And it's safe to sleep here." He looked around at the wide-eyed passengers to ensure they weren't in danger. I wasn't sure, however, that everyone was convinced with this news.

Rebecca, Kate, Emma, and I lugged our belongings to our room we'd share tonight. Things could still get tense between Rebecca and Kate from time to time, but for the most part, had settled. We each snuggled under the covers of our respective, wooden, single beds. Rebecca sat up in bed and chugged a glass of water. She shuddered every time she heard the rumbling. The unnerving part was that we couldn't see anything going on; we could only believe that we're safe without any tangible evidence.

"A wall around the hotel will save us from an avalanche of lava. Right." Rebecca was trying to process this blind faith. She chugged more water.

"Are you going to be up all night in the loo?" Kate said with a sarcastic sigh. She unfolded the clothing from her bag.

"No, I can control my bladder. I'm not 80!" Rebecca tugged at her sheets. She looked as though she was a child afraid of the monsters under her bed.

I glanced at Rebecca whose eyebrows were furrowed with anxiety. She was tense and scared. I cocked my head to the side as Kate and I made eye contact. I was trying to telepathically tell her to 'be kind' to Rebecca. I thought she got the hint. Kate walked over to Rebecca's bed and sat down on the edge. She looked at Rebecca and said, "I was really worried when my face puffed up. Everyone assured me it would be okay." She patted Rebecca's leg. "I know it can be hard to trust others when you're so scared. It's okay to be scared." After an awkward moment's pause, Rebecca launched herself at Kate, wrapping her arms around her. Kate looked like a cat suffocating in a toddler's hug. Her eyes bulged out of her head. I stifled a giggle. Kate closed her eyes and settled into an embrace with her former enemy. Sometimes, you have to find a common bond and call a truce; enemies can become friends.

In the night, the rumbling continued, and it didn't stop the entire time we were in this village. We tried to gain some normalcy and settle into the feeling that, like it or not, the volcanoes were going to rumble. In the darkness, the morning of the hike, the alarm croaked at 2:30am. The machine shimmied on the nightstand from the buzzer and the vibration of the earth below.

We groaned as we got up. What fresh hell was this, getting up in the middle of the night for a hike? "Must we rise?" Emma rubbed sleep from her eyes. My thoughts exactly. Her tiny frame shook the bed as she made her way to a seated position.

"Yes, my dear. It's time to hike this bitch!" Rebecca, the lioness, roared. She'd a newfound bravery, thanks to

Kate. They winked at each other as Rebecca adjusted her headlamp. "What do you think about a morning disco?" Rebecca flicked her headlamp on and danced provocatively in the room.

"You best turn that off before I swat you!" I laughed, shielding my eyes from the faux light. "I'm not yet my best self. I need coffee," I grumbled. I dropped my bag on the floor as I summoned energy.

A faint knock on the door was addressed by Kate. "Rise and shine, ladies. It's time to get on top of the world!" Paul smiled brightly. He scanned the room to find me, and his smile widened. I blushed.

"That's a bit too much energy for this room, sir." Kate slammed the door in his face. His laugh was audible through the door.

"In ten!" Paul yelled as he made his way down the corridor.

In the dining room, we gathered to have a light breakfast before the hike. The porters were outside getting ready. While we're only taking small bags with us, they'd carry water and snacks for the summit. They'd also help us if we had any trouble along the way.

Kate was quiet as we sat at the table having some dry toast and coffee. "Do you think there are any animals on the volcano?" Emma queried. We looked at her, puzzled, as she chewed her cud.

"Why, you worried about a monkey attack?" Rebecca chimed in as she stirred her coffee. Rebecca looked her up and down. I wasn't sure if she was judging her or evaluating her interest.

"I didn't say that," she trailed off, embarrassed by her inquiry.

"Because I'll protect you," Rebecca offered. "I would find that monkey, approach him, and say 'oy you – buzz off. This is our mountain!'" Rebecca made self-defence movements, almost knocking our drinks onto the floor.

"Is that necessary? Can't we just tell it to shoo?" Kate suggested. Her voice was unsteady, and her posture tense. "I doubt we have to worry about a monkey attack, don't you?" she questioned her friend.

"I was just wondering if there are dangers. It'll be dark, you know." Emma was self-conscious for asking. She was a bit of an odd, lovable, duck.

"Okay, everyone. Let's make our way outside. There, you'll find our porters. You're welcome to hike, but if you don't feel comfortable, there'll be transportation to the top," Paul explained to the group.

"I'm interested in the transportation." Kate raised her hand, anxiety brewing in her voice.

"Come." Paul led her outside. In the dark, he pointed to a group of men with animals. "Take your pick." Paul pointed to the men.

Kate squinted. "Are those donkeys?" She studied the animals closely. She walked closer to examine the so-called transportation.

"Yeah, is that a problem?"

"No, it's just odd, don't you think?" Kate weighed her options, deciding if she really wanted to go to the top or not.

"They're not the most graceful animal, but they'll get

you to the top." Paul turned to walk away. He'd other nervous nellies to help.

Kate gulped. This wasn't what she'd had in mind.

"Alright everyone, follow the guides. We'll be starting the hike now." In unison, we all turned our headlamps on and started our journey with Paul leading the way to the trailhead.

I turned around to find Kate pacing. I wasn't sure what was wrong, but she eventually got on a donkey and made her way behind the rest of us. The terrain was rather rocky. We had to be mindful not only of the steps in the dark, but also paying attention to the sides and in front of us. Behind us, there were 'nays' from the donkeys. I turned around when I heard Kate yell, "Bloody hell!" She got off her ride, crossed her arms, and told her porter she refused to go any further.

"What's wrong? We got a monkey situation?" Rebecca turned around to see what the commotion was about.

"No, but Kate looks upset." I pointed to the back of the group.

Without hesitating, Rebecca marched down the hill towards Kate. "What seems to be the issue here?" Rebecca pointed towards the men and the donkey. She was ready for battle, as promised.

"It's just a bit uncomfortable." I'm sure it was. "I don't think I want to go any further." She clapped her hands on her pants to get the dirt off.

"I can see that. You're riding an ass up a hill!" Rebecca cackled. Both women smiled. "Why don't you walk with Poppy and me?" Rebecca pointed towards me. "We'll keep each other in line." Kate pondered the offer.

"No, maybe I should just head back down." Her face was defeated.

"And miss the view? No way!" Rebecca raised her hands and offered again for Kate to walk with us.

"It's just not easy for me," Kate stuttered.

"Why?"

"I'm afraid to get hurt again." The truth came out. "I've already had bad luck on this trip with my sunburn. And I'm not too excited to twist my ankle either."

Rebecca mulled this over. This was a moment of intimacy between these ladies. Last night, Kate supported Rebecca, and today, the tables had turned. "How about this," Rebecca strategized, "you get back on that sad excuse for a horse, and I'll lead you up. I'll try to find the less rocky parts." Rebecca looked down to study the ground.

Kate thought about this and nodded. "Okay, let's try and see."

"Worse case, you get off and walk, but I'll lead the way." Rebecca and Kate shook on it and tried to maneuver their new hiking process. Kate got back up on her donkey and they were off.

The first hour of hiking wasn't so bad, but into the second hour I was tired and mentally exhausted. Walking up the hill, I initially passed by other hikers and caught up to Mike and Karli. I zoomed passed them at lightning speed, so I didn't have to watch them hold hands. This situationship was lasting longer than Jessica and I combined; I wondered what Karli's secret was.

I kept pace with Paul for a bit and we talked about other hikes we might like to do one day. He told me how he always dreamed of climbing Mount Kilimanjaro, the highest point in Africa. I had to admit that sounded pretty cool, and also very intense. I was having a hard enough time hiking this volcano; I couldn't imagine hiking that! I found his other travel dreams to be interesting and I bet we'd have some fun adventures, as friends.

At one point, I felt my foot work becoming lazy and the path continued to get rockier. Suddenly, I felt a gasp exit my lungs and my feet slipped from underneath me. I fell backwards and skidded down part of the trail that was made of loose gravel. Paul stopped and offered me a hand to stand up. I took it and dusted my pants.

"Do you need a hand with the rest of the hike? I can help; I don't mind."

"No, I'm fine. I can do it." I rose to my feet to continue the journey.

"Are you sure you're okay? That was a mighty fall you took."

"I'm fine," I said a little too crossly. I instantly regretted it as he didn't deserve my wicked tongue. "Sorry," I offered. The offer of help was kind, but there were somethings a woman had to go alone.

"That's okay. If you change your mind, let me know." I knew he meant it. I smiled in return. One foot in front of the other, I made my way behind the others. My hiking boots were making indents into the skin on my ankles. I felt the blisters forming on my heels. The truth was my knee was killing me. A trickle of blood stained my hiking pants, but I'd be damned if I was going to turn around.

When we made it to the top, it was still dark. A faint hue of purple and grey painted the sky. The rumbling continued and was louder than ever. Our porters set up propane to heat coffee and they passed around muffins for us to enjoy. I guzzled the rest of my water and panted as I took my seat on a muddy rock. I was rather sick of rocks at this point, but it was the only seat available.

I'd taken some time to reflect on climbing to the top without assistance. Was I being stubborn? Likely. Did I care? No. I was an independent woman. I didn't want anything to get in my way. I was soon joined by Emma who'd just retrieved a piping hot cup of coffee. The scent of warm, cinnamon-spiced caffeine wafted into my nose and woke me up from my rest. "That was something, wasn't it?" Emma blew on her drink before taking a sip. I nodded in agreement with her.

"Look! There are the girls!" Emma pointed at two shadows huffing and puffing in the morning light.

"We did it!" proclaimed one of the figures. The singing continued, followed by a chant from an English football club that had Emma joining in. Soon, the figures revealed themselves to indeed be Rebecca and Kate. "We did it!" Kate exclaimed resting her hands on her knees. "We did it. I can't believe we made it to the top!" She took a few minutes to catch her breath. She waved off one of the porters when she was offered a muffin.

"Yes, we did!" Rebecca ran around in a victory circle.

"You dumped that ass only to find another one!" She shouted and both women cracked into hysterics.

"I did." Kate stood and looked at Rebecca. "I couldn't have done it without you. Thank you." Kate extended her arms for an embrace and Rebecca took the bait like a donkey to a carrot. Finally, the fence was mended. No one was really sure what the issue was in the first place – sometimes, different personalities clash no matter what we do, or don't do.

"Well, how's the view?" a familiar voice asked from behind. I had left the ladies to take in the surroundings as the sun came up.

"Not too shabby," I offered without turning around. I knew who it was the moment he stood behind me. In the distance, the sun revealed a sea of volcanoes. Brown peaks were visible in the distance. At the top, craters were exposed but even from this angle, darkness was in the centre, leading to the core of the earth. The rumbles were complemented by plumes of smoke coming out of one volcano, much like a boiling kettle. I smiled, looking below. I saw rigid paths along the sides of the volcano that were likely the routes of the lava. This prehistoric vista was a sight to behold. Such beautiful things exist when we open our eyes.

"This is one of my favourite hikes. I'm glad you made it to the top." Paul sipped his coffee. I turned to look at him, breaking my trance from my surroundings. "How's the ankle?"

"Better, thanks." I turned back to the view. "I appreciated your help earlier, but I'm happy to have made it alone. I needed to complete the hike for myself."

"Totally, I get it." He walked away to join the others. We still didn't want any further attention drawn to us. We're friends, and this was a comfortable place to be. I liked the way he was respectful of me and not interfering when I said that I needed to do things on my own. He respected my boundaries.

"Alright, everyone, it's time for a group photo!" Paul called out. We hustled together and tried to find a place to pose that wouldn't blind everyone with the rays of the early morning light. Paul stood beside me, and placed his hand on the small of my back. As the porter took our photo, I felt the flash on my face when I turned to smile at Paul. Our faces were captured on film, a special moment in his favourite place, solidified for years to come. Was this a look of love or meaningful friendship? Much like the voyage to the top of the volcano, the paths we choose in life can be rocky. The reward, however, can be meaningful if we make the journey.

Chapter Thirty-Two

We arrived in Ubud for a few days of rest. When I asked Rebecca if she wanted to go for lunch on a remote farm, she said, "Sod it!" which I took as a 'no.' Most folks didn't want to go on long journeys at this point; they were tired of being nomads. People wanted to unpack their belongings and rest, and I didn't blame them. For me, however, there was still some soul searching to do. I had blossomed on this trip, and I needed to figure out if there was a place for Paul in my life.

After everyone had found their rooms, I was left alone in the lobby. Rebecca, Kate, and Emma had gone to our shared room. I looked around to see if anyone was left to go to the farm. When I was done checking with the last few stragglers, I asked the receptionist how to get there myself.

As I was pointing to the map and asking for a ride, a voice said, "I know how to get there; I'll take you." It was

Paul. Was he always spying on me?

"You drive? Here?" What was he, a regular?

"Cars are nearly the same everywhere. You put the key in the ignition, it magically turns on, and goes from point 'a' to point 'b.' Strange, isn't it?" He smirked.

"Such a comedian." I folded up the map. "Fine, I'm hungry. You better be ready." I headed towards the door.

"Yes, ma'am." He followed me to the parking lot. He spoke to a gardener outside who handed him a set of keys.

"Trusting fellow, isn't he?" I placed my red sunglasses over my eyes.

"Ah, people know me. I'm kind of a big deal around these parts." Paul slid his reflective sunglasses down to wink at me. He fired up the car and took off down a dirt road.

We rolled down winding roads, the wind whipping in our hair. Dust kicked up behind us as Paul drove faster and faster towards our destination. The car jostled over gravel and craters. I felt alive and free. We slowed down as we found an unmarked driveway. Paul put the blinker on as he turned and slowed to a snail's pace. We were sandwiched between cascading pools of rice paddies in the Tegalalang rice fields. Palm trees dotted the terraced landscape. Workers were bent over, hats protecting their heads from the sun, as they tended to the crops. Kids ran and played on the wooden deck of the restaurant. Paul led us up the stairs and we were ushered to a private seat on an outdoor patio. The floorboards creaked as we made our way to our marshy oasis.

"This is paradise!" I marvelled as I settled into the wicker chair. I snapped pictures of the surroundings. I hadn't seen such beauty or felt as peaceful as I did here. And no one else wanted to come. Surely, some of them would have FOMO after this.

"It certainly is." Paul studied my face and adjusted a cloth napkin on his lap. I wasn't sure if he was referring to the backdrop, or the company. He made my heart flutter.

"How'd you know about this place?" I asked as I leafed through the menu. My body was in sensory overload with the fields and the symphony of scents in the air. The waitress delivered a glass of sparkling, pink juice garnished with berries and a bright, orange flower. My mouth watered at the bamboo, grilled chicken, and Nasi Goreng with a mix of grilled meats and vegetables with a fried egg on top.

"I used to work here when I first arrived. I helped wash dishes in the kitchen." There was a culinary side of Paul, or at least he was a man who knew where the dish soap was kept. Baby steps.

"Cool, I didn't know that." He kept surprising me.

"Yes, I wasn't always a tour guide. Everyone has to start somewhere. There's a lot of things you don't know about me, yet." He peeked over the top of his menu.

Yet. He did want to get to know me better. I was intrigued.

For the next two hours, Paul told me about adjusting to Southeast Asia when he arrived here. He told me about his days working in the kitchens, washing dishes, and learning how to make stir-fries and Pad Thai. I was amazed at all the wonderful things this man had done. He was so brave to travel to this corner of the world, alone, and make a new life for himself. Was this something I should consider? Was there any point going back to Toronto? Starting a new chapter didn't mean going back to your old life.

I appreciated that Paul and I'd agreed to be friends, which I'd come to accept. Today, however, felt like a date. Perhaps absence does make the heart grow fonder.

After dining and chatting, we decided to head back into town. Paul wanted to take me to the local market. On the way out, we passed a small box made from banana leaves with a stick of sandalwood incense burning. "What's this?" I asked, eyeing the potential fire hazard.

"It's an offering of gratitude." Paul leaned down to inspect the contents. "Some people put different things in here like money, rice, or flowers. Some put in coins or spices. It's a gesture to the Gods." I nodded, taking this tidbit in. Perhaps the rice and the money symbolized the request for good fortune for their restaurant. Maybe I needed to make an offering for my life, too.

When we got back into town, Paul and I headed out to shop at the market. In the streets were brick and mortar storefronts as well as open stall markets. I was in awe of the paintings being created on the sidewalk and patiently waited for a colourful creation to take home. There were beachwear and jumpsuits, carvings and necklaces, healing ointments and essential oils. Anything and everything you could imagine was available. I wafted the coffee-scented, essential oils, which smelt much better than the cat shit coffee we'd had. I recoiled at the thought of processing the java.

"Check this out." Paul held up a bag of hard, round fruits.

"What is it?" I examined the contents.

"Snake fruit." Paul pulled out a ball to show me. The skin of the fruit, which was the size of a tangerine, had skin identical to that of the reptile! He gave the man change and proceeded to remove the peel as we investigated the next vender. "Here." He motioned to me to take a piece. I took a bite of the flesh and there was an explosion of sweet and bitter juice in my mouth. Imagine a smoothie of pineapple, banana, and apple; that's exactly what this tasted like.

"Wow, that's amazing!" I chewed and took another mouthful. It was almost a tease trying these exotic things since you'd never be able to find them at home. I was trying to savour each moment, literally and figuratively.

"Sure is." Paul eyed me and focused back on his snack. We stopped at the next vender and Paul bought me some flowers. I was shocked when he handed me the fragrant, orange, and yellow bouquet.

"What's this?" I eyed the floral arrangement.

"I thought that they would complement your eyes." He brushed the hair off of my shoulder with the back of his hand. His touch sent shivers down my spine.

"Thank you." I turned away to smile. We continued until we exited the market, purchases in tow. We heard music in the distance in the park and decided to investigate.

When we arrived, we saw a traditional Balinese dance being performed. Drums set the tone as women danced in eclectic headdresses made of red, orange, and white flowers. The flowers were so fresh, you could get a whiff of the sweet fragrance as they spun by. Their dresses were bright, yellow, and pink plaid with bold, gold jewelry. Their hard expressions and body movements told a story of good and evil, fairy tales and history, among other stories. A cacophony of chimes, drums, and vocal sounds filled the air. It was hard not to let the emotions of the performance capture us.

I was mesmerized and I felt transported through the pages of the past and folklore. The dedication and connection to their culture felt so foreign to me, mostly because I felt a disconnection to my own history. My dad had researched our family tree, a couple of Canadian generations with much of my family being born in England. Not much was known about my mom's family. Not knowing where you're from makes you feel orphaned from history. In my own life, I was creating my own story, the pages vibrant and detailed with experiences as well as dreams for the future.

I was enchanted by the dancers. I didn't notice the night fall or Paul's fingers lace between mine. It was a secret shared between us. It was clear that we weren't friends, but budding lovers. Paul and I may have to keep it private for now, but it was only a matter of time before our own story would be written.

Chapter Thirty-Three

I couldn't help but hum to myself. Something was brewing inside me, the feeling you get when you fall in love. I had rested the bouquet of flowers Paul had given me the day before on the dresser in our room. No one had commented on it yet, which was probably for the best. I plucked one of the orange flowers and fastened it into my hair with a pin. I wanted to look like one of the Balinese dancers, and maybe a sexy offering for Paul – a secret shared between us.

I took my phone out to message Casey. I needed a little encouragement from my best friend.

Poppy: I think things are heating up between Paul and me!
Casey: Do tell…..
Poppy: We went for lunch and shopping yesterday. He bought me flowers ☺
Casey: Ekk!

Poppy: What do I do? We can't be out in public together, we agreed to be friends first.

Casey: But you're not his "secret" like with glasses here?

Of course, she was referring to John. My heart sprang into my throat. He was the last person I wanted to think about.

Poppy: No - nothing like John. I don't want him to get in trouble, and I want those dumb girls to leave me alone.

Casey: What do you think you'll do?

Poppy: Follow my heart. See how I feel in the moment.

Casey: Great idea, see what feels right.

Poppy: I think there's more to him and me than just friends.

Casey: I hope so! He sounds like a catch.

Poppy: Off to shop and to the Monkey Forest with the ladies. Love you lots!

Casey: Back at you, baby!

That morning, the ladies and I headed out to do some more shopping. We found the others and joined forces as we roamed the streets in search of treasures. The trip was winding down, and I was in desperate need of new clothing and some trinkets to take home to my parents. Our feet lazily glided along the sidewalks as we fanned ourselves.

After some shopping, we sat on a corner and had an

ice cream from the convenience store, one of my favourite pastimes on holiday. "Who wants to see some monkeys?" Paul asked, knowing there were a few in the lot who would groan and say no more monkeys. Bali was the land of gods and demons, and we'd found out on this trip that monkeys were the devil.

"I think not." Emma raised her hand. I was a bit surprised considering the fuss she made over them in Malaysia; then again, we narrowly escaped by the skin on our teeth.

"Anyone else chickening, er, backing out?" Paul laughed. All that was left were Brittney, Tiffany, Mike, Karli, and me. Not the dream team I was hoping for, but Paul was here, and that's all that mattered.

"I think we'll be doing some more shopping, and an early dinner." Emma eyed a shop in the distance.

"Aye, that's alright for me. I'd rather be electrocuted than to see another monkey." Kate stood and brushed dirt from the seat of her pants.

Out of the corner of my eye, I saw a familiar creature lurking in a nearby tree. I recognized that thin face with the furry, hollow cheeks. A long tail swished back and forth.

"It's back...." I sang to Emma.

She looked around. "What're you going on about?" Emma asked. I looked at her, smiled, and pointed to a monkey in a nearby tree. Her smile dropped when she saw the beast.

"Oh, no you don't!" And with that, Emma snatched Kate's empty water bottle and hurled it at the monkey.

She missed the fur ball but knocked the branch of the tree as it shook. The monkey screeched and jumped out of the tree, running for cover. Emma tore after it, yelling at it to get away from her.

"What's her problem?" Britney appeared out of nowhere.

Kate looked her up and down and said, "Monkey trauma." Tiffany and Britney shrugged, and walked away, asking each other why the English were so weird.

"It's the Monkey Forest; it's right on the sign. What was she expecting?" Kate shrugged and headed off in the direction of her friend.

Paul and I decided to risk our fate and walk into the forest. "Are you sure you're brave enough for this?" He rustled some bananas in his backpack.

"Why are you enticing them? Don't you remember what happened last time when Emma fed them?" I wasn't getting stuck in danger, again, over a damn monkey.

"They expect it. I always bring them treats and I've never once been attacked – unlike you." He winked as he hoisted his bag onto his shoulders.

"You're so funny." We paid our fee and entered the forest. This environment felt much different than Kuala Lumpur. This time, the monkey den was secluded in part of the city, rather than a jungle spread through an urban landscape. It's like the city was built around the forest so that the little monsters didn't lose their habitat. I thought they were cute, but their minds were pure evil.

"Here, want to peel one? Or are you too scared?" Paul gestured to the bright, yellow skin. We sat down on a bench under the canopy of trees. I took it begrudgingly from him. Truthfully, I did want to see the monkeys and snap a few pictures.

I heard some rustling branches as I cracked the fruit open to reveal the sweetly scented flesh. Out of the corner of my eye, a shy, little monkey inched closer and closer to me. Tufts of brown and grey fur sprouted in patches over its tiny body, a baby perhaps. It was like a little drug dog sniffing out the goods. The small, slender fingers cautiously reached out to take the banana. Once in its grasp, the monkey peeled the banana with its teeth and gorged on its meal.

Paul and I laughed as we walked further and further down the stone path. We were greeted by several monkeys waiting for their snack. They were like trolls living under the bridge, making us pay the piper. I sat down beside one and inched closer and closer until we were only a foot apart. I laughed as I kept handing out treats like it was Halloween candy. I noticed that Paul shook his head as if to say, 'no more food left.' I felt disappointed that the magic of the forest was over. We snapped a few more shots and got up to be on our way. When we were near the end of the path, a rather large monkey got in front of us, blocking the exit.

"Uh, oh," Paul sighed.

"What's wrong?" I wasn't sure what the issue was. There were tons of these 'rodents' all over the path; what was so special about this one?

"The male monkeys are not particularly friendly." He weighed his options. "We don't have any food left to distract him. We might have to run." He eyed my footwear.

"Why don't we just walk past him, like we did the others?"

"It's not that simple," – a deadly pause – "because these ones are a bit more aggressive."

And there it was. These weren't to be trusted!

"Let's just walk around it and move quickly until we get to the street" Paul grabbed my hand forcefully and pulled me down the path towards safety. I still wasn't quite registering what the big deal was.

We took a few steps, and I heard a huff and a growl behind us. Paul turned around and muttered something inaudible as he gripped my hand tighter and picked up the pace. I turned around again to see the large animal picking up speed, too, before it barrelled towards us. I pictured us in a bull fight in Spain, trying to get away from the horned beast with fiery, red eyes.

Suddenly, Paul and I started sprinting, and so did the greedy monkey. "Why's there such a monkey problem in Bali?" I screamed as we ran through the forest. I felt like I was being chased by the four horsemen of the apocalypse.

After we raced out of the forest, back to civilization, Paul suggested that we get something to eat. I struggled to regain control of my breathing, and laughed through the gasps. I agreed; near-death experiences made a gal hungry. "And maybe after dinner, we can go back to your room." I felt my pulse quicken while I waited for his answer.

"Sure, that would be great."

When we got back to the hotel after dinner, Paul led me through the darkness, by the hand, as we walked towards his suite. He jostled the key in the door and with the click of the lock, we finally had some privacy.

Chapter Thirty-Four

We'd finally arrived back at the beach. It felt like a mirage. We'd been traveling inland Indonesia for the better part of the last 2 weeks. I was looking forward to swimming and sunbathing, but that also meant being closer to the end of the trip. I had mixed emotions; it was, unfortunately, going to happen whether or not I approved.

For two days, our group sat pool side, and explored seaside temples with waves crashing against the ancient exteriors. We walked along the rocky beach as well as searched for trinkets and treasures. I enjoyed some time on my own, reading to further empower myself. I was getting stronger every day. I almost felt whole again.

Paul and I, when we had the chance, would wait until the others had gone to bed and sneak off to his room for a few hours. We continued our conversations in the dark to keep eyes off us. I enjoyed getting to know him. I wished more and more that we'd continue this momentum when the trip was over. It was safe to say, he was becoming my best friend.

On one night, Paul and I laid on his bed, our fingers intertwined. "You know, Poppy," he sighed, "I've been enjoying our time together." My stomach lurched, not knowing what he was going to say next. "The trip's almost over. Have you thought about what we are going to do when you go home?" This felt like the longest pause I'd ever experienced. I almost forgot the trip was nearly over. I didn't want this to end, but I didn't know how this was going to survive either.

"I'm not sure. I hadn't really thought about it. What do you think?"

He tapped his fingers on the back of my hand, and laid our hands on his chest. "Maybe you could use some vacation time to see me on my next assignment in Sri Lanka?"

"Oh, I don't have vacation time, I'm between jobs." Did he just want me to visit him because he would get lonely?

"Right." I felt the heaving of his chest. "I forgot."

"Yeah, it might be a while before my next trip."

"I was hoping…" He stopped himself.

"What?" I perked up, my head lifting to make eye contact with him.

"We could try long distance. I want to see where this goes if you do." I sensed his anxiety brewing. For the first time, I saw Paul feeling insecure.

"Can I have some time to think? I just got out of a relationship, and I'm not sure what I want. "

"I can appreciate that." He kissed my hand. "Take all the time you need, no rush." He leaned over and gave me a soft and simple kiss. He was tender and caring, a softer side in a man I hadn't seen. I felt safe and seen with him.

Regardless of my comfort level with him, I needed time to digest this information. Paul and I had a relationship of kisses and communication, pure and simple. Anxiety rumbled through my head and my body. How were we going to make this thing last? I liked him, but did I want to date him? I needed to think.

Paul led me to the door, kissed me once more, and I snuck back to my room unnoticed. I had a lot of thinking to do.

After all the hiking and slinging our backpacks around, Rebecca and I decided to go get a massage. We got our recommendation from Paul about a small parlour. One day, we decided to stroll down the dirt road into town to have a day of relaxation.

The door chimed as we entered the small shop. We were alone when we came in. A rush of air-conditioning blasted against our faces. We collapsed, taking in the refreshment. Rebecca immediately eyed the nail polish. She wanted to look fresh and clean for the final leg of the trip. "How about this one?" She studied the bottle.

I walked over to eye the colour "Neon orange? That suits you." I rested my chin on her shoulder, my turn to use her as a crutch.

"You getting yours done, too?" Rebecca shifted through the bottles. "How about this one for you?" She held a bottle of hot pink polish towards me. I scrunched my nose in silent repulsion.

After a few minutes of waiting, two women emerged from behind a thin, white curtain and they motioned for us to take a seat. "We're just waiting for our other guests to finish up," the one woman told us. As we sat and waited, a couple came out from behind the curtain, moaning and groaning as they stretched their tanned bodies. I looked at Rebecca, not sure what to think. Did they enjoy their massages, or did they emerge from a torture chamber? Rebecca shrugged.

"We're going to change the sheets and come back for you," the other woman commented. They disappeared behind the curtains again as the couple stumbled out the front door, the chime signalling their exit.

When it was our turn, we headed back with the women who introduced themselves as Indah and Kirana. They'd be our masseuses, or our torturers – the jury was still deliberating. They instructed us to get down to our underpants, or our birthday suits, whichever felt more comfortable and then get under the sheet on the table. The women had barely left the room and Rebecca had taken everything off and hopped onto her bed. "Ready when you are!" I quickly followed suit.

The tiny women entered. The curtain was closed, and a stick of jasmine incense was lit. I loved that smell so much. Plumes of smoke floated in the air, bringing peace and tranquility. Faint drums and strings from an unknown instrument filled the room. We were asked if we liked pressure during our massages and we nodded yes. After a minute, being lost in thought, I realized that I couldn't see their feet anymore. They were both standing on our beds, giggling. Rebecca and I locked eyes in confusion and before we knew it, the women had stood on our backs!

"Ohh!" We shouted as the women kneaded our bodies with their feet. "Ouch!" For a minute, I thought they'd let in a street cat, or a tiger, and we were being kneaded like cats making 'biscuits.' Except, these weren't cats; they're grown women, trying to break every bone in my body!

"Is this necessary?" I cried out, my voice muffled in the pillow.

"Yes, this will help get the knots out!" Kirana yelled. She jumped down and straddled me as she dug her elbows deep into my backside. They giggled as they continued their unique practice. After a few minutes of feeling like my internal organs had shifted, the women hopped off us and continued with a regular massage. Finally! I was terribly confused as to what had just transpired. I thought we were down for the count in a wrestling match.

For the next half an hour the women put hot towels on our backs and massaged essential oils of orange blossom and cinnamon into our skin. Their hands whirled around my back, soothing the aches and pains they'd created with their fancy foot work. The torture was over.

After the women left the room, we put robes on. "What the bloody hell was that?" Rebecca whispered. She tightened the belt on her robe, looking around the corner to ensure our captors were out of sight.

"No clue, but I'm conflicted if I liked that or not." I fixed the elastic in my ponytail and arched my back. I'd never experienced 'relaxation' like that before. I had to admit, I did feel like I stood a little straighter, but I'd likely hurt tomorrow.

We headed back out to have our nails done, a familiar self-care routine I was used to. This was a treat I didn't do enough for myself. I was feeling fresh and polished.

As I watched Kirana file my nails, Rebecca turned to me. "So, I have something to tell you," Rebecca started. Oh no, another surprise. I had barely handled the one Paul told me last night – this was a secret I was bursting at the seams to tell.

"What is it?" I gulped in anticipation.

"I met someone!" Rebecca wiggled in her seat with excitement. Her mouth opened wide in a gigantic smile that lit up the room. "He's a bartender. He's been working in Bali the last five months but will soon be returning to England, close to where I live." Rebecca's face flushed as she told me about her new man.

I was happy for my friend. Budding romance is magical, and it sounded like the stars had aligned for her. "What's his name?"

"Adam," she purred. "Rebecca and Adam. Has a nice ring to it, don't it?" she cackled as she daydreamed about her beau. The smile never left her face. She had a permanent glow.

Over the next two days, Rebecca was away with her new man after his shifts at the bar. I saw less and less of her, our friendship transitioning to online platforms as I saw her date night antics with her new fellow. I 'liked' as much as I could to let her know I supported her, and missed her. I'd spend my nights by the fire with Emma and Kate, and later under the veil of the night, with Paul before heading back to my own room. Loose ends were tying up. I contemplated my future with Paul and leaned into the idea of a long-distance romance. We could see where things went with no pressure like he said. When the timing was right, we'd talk about this more. Once I had a job, I could use my vacation time to come and see him in Sri Lanka.

I returned to my room the night before an excursion. Tomorrow, Paul, and I would head to Komodo Island National Park, with a stop in Flores before a boat ride to the island. We'd be going alone. I was sure people would talk, but Paul told the group that a licenced guide had to accompany me, and I was the only one who wanted to see the dragons. There were some snickers from Tiffany and Britney, but a quick glare from Kate soon shut them up. Until this point, no one seemed to catch on that we had feelings for one another, aside from the girls I shared this info with. We did spend late nights together, laughing under the stars and getting to know one another – and, well, share some passionate kisses, too. So much for friendship!

I couldn't wait to get away with Paul. Memories were being made, and a future was being considered. I'd grown so much on this trip. I was ready for anything.

Chapter Thirty-Five

It was an early morning rise for our grand adventure. Paul and I only took a small bag with us since we'd only be staying two nights. I still revelled at the mystery of the tiny backpack that held all of his worldly possessions.

He hailed us a taxi as the morning light was making its debut. Kate and Emma came out to say their sleepy goodbyes. Kate asked if she could have my hats if I should perish on the excursion. I told her that she could pillage my belongings if she must. I really felt the love there.

The morning sun shone down on us as we took the short drive to the airport. Paul slid his hand across the seat and squeezed mine. I rested my head on his shoulder as we continued our journey to the airport. I was looking forward to being out in the open with Paul; no hiding would be necessary. This would be like a trial run of our relationship.

Ticket booths, security, and finally, waiting for the plane was a process I'd grown familiar to. As we waited for our time to board, I couldn't help but notice that most of the people who were waiting for the plane were locals going home to visit family or continue on with their business. There were a few tourists who had the same idea as us to visit the dragons. I eyed Paul's bag once more. I was desperate to know the secret of the many contents in such a small sack. Moving closer to him, I asked, "What's the deal with the bag?" I motioned towards him.

"What do you mean?" A look of confusion spread across his face. I eyed him as he studied the outside of it, puzzled at the question.

"I've only seen you with one tiny bag of contents this whole trip, yet you pull so many things out of it like a clown car." The edges of my mouth rose. My fingers danced towards the zipper. He laughed and closed the zipper shut.

"If you want to know, you have to give me a kiss." He coyly moved his face towards mine, our lips inches apart, teasing me. Knowing no one else was around, I planted a small kiss on his lips. "The truth is, I do laundry a lot. And I leave a few things in some of the places along the way. Hence, the small bag of goods." He opened the bag to show me the contents. I felt foolish, but my curiosity had been satisfied, and no cats were harmed. I went back to reading more about the park in my guidebook while Paul closed his eyes to sleep.

One thing you should know about Komodo

Dragons is that they're allegedly the last ancestor of the dinosaurs – however, opinions on this are mixed. There are very few places in the world where this large lizard lives, and for good reason: they're fatal! One bite from it and you could die; it has so many bacteria in its mouth that it's impossible for people to survive.

GULP. Why'd I want to go here again?

From what I read, the Komodo Dragon lived in the trees of the island until they were a few years old. Then, they came out of the trees to roam on the ground. They could weigh a few hundred pounds! I was sure I'd make a tasty meal if the lizard was in the market for dinner. It felt like a special privilege to be able to come to the park, which consisted of a few islands, since this was a remote area of Indonesia. I'd been so lucky to travel, and I wasn't taking anything for granted.

When Paul and I landed, we headed to our hotel first. We'd have the day to go for a hike and then rest for our early morning departure. We met our guide, Joyo, who'd be with us the next few days. I looked at Paul quizzically. "I thought you were the guide on the trip?"

Paul looked at me and winked. "I was just saying that so we could have alone time."

I laughed at this, realizing that we're evolving past friendship. Cheeky man. I was falling for Paul, fast.

We headed out to hike. Today's goal was to hike around the island to find a cave with a million-year-old fossil. Joyo was very excited about this find as it was very rare. We hiked through brilliant, lush greenery. Plants, almost like large, palm leaves, shrouded our path. Joyo pushed these out of the way for us as we made our way on the trail. He told us about local animals and birds in the area, folklore of the island, and customs of the people. He told us funny jokes to distract us from the heat and the hills that we climbed. My thighs, however, were well aware.

Eventually, we stopped in front of a hill. "We're here," Joyo announced. Paul and I caught our breath, looking around to see where 'here' was. "Here," he said again pointing to a small opening near the ground.

"I don't think I understand," I trailed off. I felt confused, thinking I'd lost something in translation. I stood and arched my sore back.

"The fossil is in here." He pointed again. "We have to crawl into the hole for a bit. It may get tight." He motioned squeezing ourselves through the tunnel, so we understood. "But it's worth it." He stood with a proud posture, excited to show his treasure.

Paul and I looked at each other and nodded. Alright, this was part of the adventure! I wanted to see fossils. We finished our waters and decided to leave our belongings outside.

I stretched my back and my mind to take on this small space. I didn't like tight spaces. The more I pumped myself up, the more I felt my throat closing as if I was stuck in the cave without air. I tried to reason with myself that this was perfectly safe, but I had my doubts. Paul seemed excited and ready to go, I couldn't help but wonder if this wasn't for me.

"I wanted to share one other exciting thing about

this area." Joyo cleared his throat. "This past year the largest snake in Southeast Asia was found here on top of the cave." He pointed to the higher ground above us.

My heart stopped. Tight spaces was one thing, but snakes were another. "Pardon?" I croaked. I looked up to the top of the hill to see if the snake was looking at us, or rather eyeing us. I'd concluded that I'd be the dragon's dinner, but there was no way in hell I'd be the snake's appetizer.

"A snake," he paused, "very big," another pause, "largest python ever." He extended his hands to mimic the gigantic reptile's length. NOPE.

Perhaps, Joyo thought that this piece of information was a selling point on the trip. I disagreed. "No thanks." I started to back away from the tunnel. "I'll stay out here."

"What? Are you sure?" Paul was surprised I wasn't up for the task. He went to touch my elbow as I backed away from the entrance.

"Oh, yes. Given my luck, the snake that they found will be inside the cave." I pointed maniacally towards the opening of the death trap. "NO, THANKS!" I confirmed. I crossed my arms against my chest.

"Then I won't go in either." Paul was a gentleman, but I didn't want him to miss out.

"It's okay, you go ahead. I don't want to hold you back." He stood, thinking for a minute. I didn't want him to think that I was tricking him because I wasn't. He pondered this and I gave him another reassuring nod. Joyo looked at us in confusion but waited patiently for Paul to make his final decision.

"Okay, I mean, it's a fossil. Are you sure you don't mind?" He rocked back and forth on his feet. I knew he wanted to make sure I felt supported. I wouldn't want him to miss out on anything because of me. FOMO is a real thing.

"Go ahead; it's all good. I promise." And with that, the two men shimmied through the small opening. I stood guard, ready to attack if the situation called for it.

They seemed like they were in the cave forever. I wondered if they were the reptile's brunch. Once they returned, I breathed a sigh of relief. I was trying not to have regrets for not going into the cave, but I knew it was important to listen to my gut when I don't feel comfortable. You do you, as they say.

That evening, Paul and I sat on the patio of the hotel restaurant and had dinner under the setting sun. The sky was filled with pink and purple hues as the sun dipped beyond the ocean for the night. We continued to get to know each other. He told me about his family back home and different goals he had for his career. He shared some of his hobbies, like photography, and how he hoped to sell photos to publications to share the wonderful places he has travelled to. I smiled and told him that I'd love to write stories about travelling, which might help encourage others to travel. I'd learned so much about myself and the world from this holiday. I beamed with a sense of pride. We didn't yet talk about the long-distance possibilities; there was still time to discuss this elephant in the room.

Paul called it an early night. When he was done his beer, he headed to his room to sleep. Tonight was the first night in a few nights that we didn't spend more alone time together. That's okay; we'd have all day tomorrow.

I sat alone, drinking my beer. The darkness made it a bit chilly, and I rubbed my arms. The waiter passed by and asked if I wanted another drink. I said, "Sure." When he returned, he asked me where the man had gone. I told him he was my guide, and he went to bed.

"You want some company?" The waiter cleared his throat in anticipation and looked at me with a sly smile. He glanced around to ensure we were alone, which I had noticed.

I shifted uncomfortably in my seat. "No, thanks."

"You like women?" He leaned in to ask me, puzzled that I had turned down his offer. I felt the heat of his breath on my neck as he inched closer.

The heat in my face grew. I was beginning to boil. "No."

"You sure? I can show you a good time." He was relentless. I wasn't sure if he was a waiter or a gigolo.

"Forget the other beer. Goodnight." I got up from the table and headed to my room. I shouted at him to put the drinks on my room tab.

I shut the door, relieved that I'd escaped that awkward situation. That guy had the nerve to try to get into my pants! I settled into my pyjamas and got into bed. I texted Paul, "Goodnight," but he didn't reply. He must have gone to sleep. The screen faded to black, and I decided to call it a night, too.

When I rustled to get comfortable in bed, I heard a faint knock at the door. Maybe Paul was up after all and wanted to have a quick visit. I crept out of bed in the darkness and made my way to the door. I made sure not to make a sound, just in case, and I looked through the peephole. It was the damn waiter! I held my breath and tried to make it sound like I wasn't in the room. I looked again and he was still standing there. He had two beers in his hands. There was another knock. I tried to remain silent. "I know you're in there!" He sang towards the door. "I'm here to cheer you up!" Another knock. I panicked.

Suddenly, there were two voices, growing angry. I pressed my ear against the door so I could hear what was going on. "Leave the lady alone!" I made out, which was followed by, "I didn't do anything! I was just delivering these drinks!" A few more shouts and then it was quiet again. The silence was unnerving. Was there danger on the other side?

There was another knock on the door. I stood tall, confident that I was going to tell that creep to go away. Instead, when I opened the door, it was Paul. "What're you doing here?"

"I heard that guy knocking at your door. I didn't want him bothering you." Paul gently pushed past me. He'd brought a pillow and a blanket with him. "I'm staying here tonight, to keep you safe," he informed me. I didn't argue.

"Okay," I looked around, trying to figure out where he would sleep. I didn't want to be too forward and offer him my bed.

He planted a soft kiss on my lips. He gave me a hug

and stared into my eyes. As he held onto me, it felt like he was looking inside me, seeing my true self. Time stood still. Paul broke my trance when he kissed me again. He let go of my hand, taking a piece of me with him, as he headed over to the couch. He made a makeshift bed out of the couch and lay down.

"Are you going to be comfortable over there?" I asked, crossing my legs. I had other ideas in mind.

"Yes, this is perfect," he replied and closed his eyes. So much for being ravished by my Prince Charming. Isn't that what's supposed to happen when the damsel in distress has been rescued?

I moved back towards my bed and hopped in. I looked over at him longingly. I wished he'd gotten into bed with me. The temptation, however, was too great. I didn't want to move things if they weren't there yet. Truthfully, I enjoyed taking things slowly with Paul. I turned off the light and looked forward to the morning.

The sun rose and the alarm clock blared. It was time to get up. Paul went back to his room to get ready. We had a packed breakfast for the boat ride. Joyo was in the lobby waiting for us. We headed down to the local pier to find the boat that would take us to the park. The boat wasn't nearly as whimsical as the one we had in Thailand.

For several hours we'd be on this tiny fishing boat that still reeked of fish. We passed fishermen who were returning to the shore with their morning catch to sell in the market. My stomach tossed as the boat churned through the waves. I couldn't eat my breakfast. Paul leaned over and rubbed my back after I threw up over the side of the boat. As much as I appreciated Paul showing tenderness towards me, I wanted to get off this damn boat as soon as possible.

Joyo pointed out other islands with pink sand beaches that we could swim at if we had time on the way back. He screamed at us over the rumbling of the loud, old motor. Eventually, we made it to our destination, Rinca Island, where we'd be hiking to see the famous lizards.

Joyo helped Paul and I off the boat. He hurried to the tourist office to settle the bill for our entrance into the park. Paul and I slowly made our way up as I found my land legs. Paul held my hand as he led us up the rocky path to the tourist office. We'd get 'passports' for arriving on the island. I'd been looking forward to this the entire time.

I soaked in the surroundings. We were encompassed by rolling, green hills surrounded by water. You could hear the faint sounds of the ocean waves crashing against the shore in the background. Around us, there were small cabins for the Park Rangers to sleep in and a small café. In the distance, there was a small path with overgrown trees, likely one of the few paths we'd take to look for the dragons. A few Park Rangers stood around, waiting for the next group. I walked around the tourist office, looking for Joyo. I took a step back and I heard screams.

I looked around, panicked to see where they were coming from. What was the danger?

"Stand still!" someone yelled. I looked around to see what was happening. "Don't move any further!" I heard someone else call out. I started to panic inside as I didn't know what was happening. All of a sudden, life happened in slow motion. Someone ran towards me, scooped me into their arms, and ran to the side before placing me back onto the ground.

"What the – " I began. I was cut off before I could continue.

"You need to be careful!" Paul yelled at me, shaking my arms. His face was red, and he was breathing hard. He looked like he had just saved someone from an oncoming train.

"What're you talking about? I didn't do anything!" I hollered at him.

He stood with his hands on his hips, shaking his head. "You almost stepped on a Komodo Dragon!" He pointed to a greyish green, camouflaged mound in the grass.

I squinted to look closer, and I saw one lying in the grass in front of the tourist office. I hadn't noticed it before. Everyone else saw it and had yelled at me to get away. They likely didn't want to test how deadly the creature was. In the commotion, Joyo emerged from the tourist office. He clucked his tongue in disappointment over what had happened. "Must be careful, Miss Poppy," he said. Joyo was with a Park Ranger. This tourist guide thing got me so confused. Paul had fibbed to come to the island with me, and Joyo was our guide for the hike and the boat ride, but we also needed another Park Ranger for safety.

The Park Ranger led the way through the park. We pushed through the overgrowth of the bush. He had a whistle, a bottle of water, and a stick the length of a broom. On the end was a dull piece of metal. Like that would protect us from the dragon, I huffed.

We were told more about the lizard's diet, what it was like to be around them on the island, and ways people were trying to protect them. He told us to look up in the trees for the young dragons while also looking down towards the ground for the larger ones. I felt all eyes on me when the safety tips were explained again. I know, I know! I was accident prone. I got it. Thank goodness for travel insurance, was I right? We roamed around, spotting dragons of all sizes. We snapped photos and admired this beast. Other people may see these in the zoos, and I was lucky to see it in real life, out in the wild.

At one point in the hike, I heard a crack in the branches. The Park Ranger looked around quickly to determine where the sound was coming from. The sounds grew louder; whatever it was, was quickly approaching. I gasped and started to run down the trail. I didn't want to be eaten alive! I heard everyone yell at me to stop running, but it was too late. When I thought I was a safe distance, I caught my foot on a tree root and smashed my body into the ground. My ankle swelled. Paul, Joyo, and the Park Ranger ran over to me and helped me up. Paul shook his head at me, again. I felt like we were right back at the start of the trip when we first met; how he hated me then.

We walked back to the main gate in silence. Joyo took me to the medical clinic to get me checked over. There was no other damage, but my ankle would probably be tender for a couple of days. Luckily, I was able to walk. I sat alone as we waited for Joyo to call for the boat. There wouldn't be any time for the visit to the pink sand beach. I felt sheepish. Paul was clearly mad at me. I didn't know where Paul had gone, but I was happy to have a few minutes alone to myself. I was sure he needed to blow off some steam.

As I sat waiting, I took one last look at this amazing island before we would head back to Flores. What I saw surprised me. One of the ferocious beasts was being fed leftovers of grilled chicken by the Park Rangers. I thought that they were dangerous creatures roaming hidden, ancient lands. Their very existence could wipe a human out with one bite! I looked at the dragon and shook my head. Should I have been so scared if they were being treated like pets? I think the chicken was tastier than my sun-screened legs.

The boat ride back was silent. Paul and I sat on opposite ends of the boat. My hair blew in the wind, tears staining my face. Why was he so upset with me? I didn't understand him.

When we returned, Paul headed back to his room without even talking to me. I got washed up for dinner, ready to put the day behind me. As I was about to head to the restaurant, there was a knock at my door. It was Paul. I opened the door, and he marched in past me. His etiquette could use some work.

"What you did today was foolish!" he yelled. He paced the wooden floors of my suite, the wood creaking angrily beneath his feet.

"What are you talking about? How was I foolish?" I defended myself. I had no idea what he was talking about. All I could focus on was the throbbing of my swollen ankle.

"The dragons! You almost stepped on one and then you ran away from us! You don't listen!" The veins on his neck pulsated. He was unnecessarily angry at me; both incidents were accidents.

"What's your problem?" I huffed, "why are you being so controlling?" I headed towards the bathroom to give myself some space from him. I'd had enough of men yelling at me.

"Controlling? You could've died today! I'm trying to protect you!" Paul was angry at me, but this was displaced anger. He was concerned about me, but he was also overstepping, I didn't ask him to rescue me.

"Protect me? I don't need you protecting me. I'm an adult!" I shook my head in frustration. Who did he think he was?

"You almost stepped on a dragon today; they're deadly. There's no cure for their bites," Paul breathed, trying to relax. He ran his hands through his hair. His t-shirt clung to him. It was clear he hadn't towel dried well before putting his shirt on.

"But I didn't!" I walked towards him. "It probably wouldn't have even bit me – they're basically pets!"

"It isn't that simple," his voice raged on.

"Then, what is the big deal?" I cast my arms out. I gave up trying to understand what his issue was.

"Because you're important to me! I don't want anything bad to happen to you! I care for you, okay?"

"I care about you, too!" I raised my voice back. I thought for a second. "Paul, why are we arguing? This makes no sense!"

"Because I was worried about you!" Paul looked up at me and into my eyes. "Poppy, what I feel for you is real. You're magical to me. You make me feel like no one else has ever made me feel. I think I'm falling – " and before he could get a word out, my lips were on his. I knew what he was going to say, and I didn't want him to say it, not yet.

In front of me, now, was a man who cared for me, who protected me, and who was presumably falling in love with me. What more could I ask for? Still, I didn't feel ready for love as my heart wasn't fully whole yet. Not until I loved myself more, could I let real romance come into my life. I wanted to be the best version of myself before I had another partner.

I ran my hands down Paul's body, feeling his firm thigh muscles. I traced my hands up and down the sides of his ribcage and I felt the goosebumps form under his cotton t-shirt. We kissed and moved our mouths over top of each other's, feeling our lips and tongues intertwine. He held me closer, protecting me, caring for me, wanting me. We pulled apart, momentarily, looking at each other and smiled, knowingly, that this was a special moment to let our walls come down and to be with each other.

Paul took my hand and led me towards the bed. I turned the lights off and followed him in the moonlight. He looked back to see if I was still there, and he smiled. We spent the night together. We took our time and gave in to what had been building between us. He was a gentleman and made sure I was feeling safe and comfortable, which was definitely a first. That night, when Paul was fast asleep, I stared at him, and his body under a thin sheathe of the beige bedsheet. I caressed his chest and, without opening his eyes, he smiled a sleepy, half smile and held my hand. I shifted over to nuzzle up against him and he kissed my fingers. We fell into a lull that night. The best was yet to come.

Chapter Thirty-Six

The morning after being together for the first time could be awkward. Paul and I had gone from enemies to friends to lovers. It was a wild ride. I couldn't quite believe how fast things had progressed. It was an amazing feeling, even if I was still figuring out who I was.

We lay in bed. I traced my fingers on Paul's chest as he slowly opened his eyes. Paul yawned, brushing the sleep from his eyes. "Morning, sunshine." He rubbed his hands over the shape of my thigh, concealed by the bedsheet.

"Morning to you, too," I said back, burying my head into the bedding, sheepishly.

"What have you got to be shy about?" Paul pulled me closer towards him. He nuzzled his chin into the crook of my neck. I broke out in goosebumps and giggled as his stubble tickled me. It felt wonderful to curl up with him like this.

"I have dragon breath," I said as I cast a stream of

hot breath towards him. He laughed at me and playfully patted me with a pillow.

"Well, I guess I do, too. Komodo breath!" He scooped me up in his arms. We were entwined in the bedsheets, and I had no desire to leave. We laughed and tumbled about without a care in the world. We were in our own private reverie.

He stopped mid tickle and held me close to him again. He locked eyes with me, and moved his head closer. Our lips touched and he kissed me again and again. These lips were like a hug: he wrapped me into him. It was, however, time to go. We had a flight to catch.

Paul and I made our way to the airport. It was difficult to leave the hotel after the night we'd had. We sat in the one room terminal waiting for our flight to be called to board. Paul paced the room, looking out windows. I sat and texted my bestie back home.

Poppy: It finally happened. Paul and I did it!
Casey: OMG! Tell me everything!
Poppy: It was fantastic.
Casey: LOL as long as you liked it, that's all that matters!
Poppy: I did. I think he could be something special.
Casey: Time to plan a wedding?

Poppy: Don't get ahead of yourself!
Casey: Okay. Am happy for you!
Poppy: Thanks ☺

"You're texting up a storm," Paul whispered over my shoulder, one last public kiss as he planted one on my neck. I could get used to this.

"Just texting Casey, telling her about the dragons."

"Sure, you were." Paul laughed, knowing I was talking about him. Guilty! I didn't need any blush on this morning. My face was already pink. I would call this look 'beyond satisfaction.'

"What are you implying?" I playfully nudged him. Paul shrugged, not wanting to publicly give away our secret. I pressed into him under the caress of his hand, and I closed my eyes. I enjoyed the smell of his skin and the warm air being blown onto us from the fan above. He played with the brim of my hat. Eventually, we were summoned to the plane to head back to reality. Our love was a secret once more.

The flight back to Bali was rocky. The plane was old, and I worried whether it would even take flight, kind of like an overfed bird – I was excited when it finally took off. Paul and I collected our backpacks and headed back to the hotel. When we arrived, everyone was lounging around the pool, trying to decide what to do with their free day. Most people commented that they were tired of temples and craved some excitement.

"What's up, lizard people? See any mighty dragons?" Emma giggled.

"Very funny, and yes, we did, as a matter of fact." I spent the next half hour sharing our tale of the mighty Komodo Dragons. I tried my best not to let on how scared I was. I told them Paul rescued me from an ill-fated death. The group gasped and praised Paul for his heroism. It was the least I could do after his worry last night. I still don't believe I was in any danger, but I decided to rescue his feelings instead. He looked away shyly and said that I was clumsy at the best of times. I didn't tell the group about the night of love making, or that morning of love making, either. Sometimes, it's important to keep your private life private; not everyone needs to know everything about you. Things near and dear to the heart are sacred.

As the others chattered about how they wanted to spend their day, I dipped my feet into the pool. My sunglasses shaded my vision as I daydreamed about Paul. I took a deep breath and closed my eyes, letting the sun absorb into my skin, bringing back familiar heat to my body. I heard Paul's voice saying my name. His voice was quiet, growing louder with every motion, every movement of our bodies against each other. I heard the quickening of his breath as I ran my fingers down his body, touching every delight. The pool water cooled me down from these hot thoughts.

"Maple, what do you say? You in?" Kate inquired.

Her body loomed over me, bringing me back to the current moment. I shook my head to orient myself to the present. My sexy thought bubble was burst.

"What are you going on about?" I wiped the sweat from my forehead. "What am I in for, exactly?"

"These Canadian girls are thick in the head, aren't they?" Kate asked Emma as they giggled.

"We're going clubbing tonight. You in?" Kate asked, as she danced around the pool. I hadn't seen this side of her before. She was ready to let loose.

"Alright, I think I can manage that." I smiled and looked around. Most of the group was discussing some Irish bars in the town. Paul was at the other end of the pool, chatting with some of the other guys. He looked over at me and smiled. My cheeks reddened. I could pass off the redness of my face from the sun.

After what felt like an eternity of staring at my lover, our gaze was stopped by the entrance of what can only be described of as a 'bro.' Paul leapt to his feet and shouted, "You're here, man? I wasn't expecting to see you!" He embraced another tanned man.

"Yeah, man, our group changed some dates and we're here for a couple of nights. So good to see you! Are we going to party?" the strange man asked. Immediately, I didn't trust him. There was something slimy about him, but I just couldn't put my finger on it.

"I think we're headed out tonight, if you want to join us?" Paul offered. He provided the stranger our details for tonight's fun. How dare he let this stranger crash.

"Sure, we're going to unpack and hit the beach. Text

me later?" the stranger suggested.

"Yeah, man. I will," Paul said. "Good to see you, bro." The two embraced and grasped each other's hands like it was some sort of secret code. I'd had enough secrets.

I got up out of the pool. My footprints trailed behind me and quickly evaporated as I walked over to the vending machine. I needed something else to cool me down and the chlorinated water wasn't doing it.

"Who was that?" I inquired of Paul. He had followed me and was inches behind me. He brushed up against my sun-kissed shoulder. He looked around to see who was in the immediate vicinity and then, he leaned down and tried to kiss my shoulder. I jerked away before he could plant his lips on my skin. "Hey, not here where everyone can see!"

"Sorry, I thought it was safe." I didn't mean to shame him, but I still didn't want everyone to find out about us.

"It's, I just don't want people to talk about us." The can of soda tumbled to the bottom of the machine. "I like my privacy." I cracked open the can and slurped my first sip.

"I get it. I'm sorry."

"Nothing to be sorry about, I shouldn't have snapped. Forgive me?" My doe eyes shone up at him.

"Forgiven," Paul said, as he bit his lip. I knew what he was thinking.

"Who was that guy?" I broke the sexual tension. I wanted to get to the bottom of the 'bro' situation.

"It's another tour guide. His name's Tony." Paul got a soda from the machine. "He's from California. He works for one of the rival tour companies. We have similar itineraries. Sometimes, we happen to be at the same place, at the same time. He's cool," Paul offered.

"Right on, bro," I teased. My stomach twisted. I thought back to Eric, that creep from Jakarta who made Paul sound like a dog. I had finally gotten over that and I didn't want it to be true, especially after last night. We were advancing, a future together on the horizon.

"Yeah, I get it. I sounded like a douche. Sometimes, you have to meet people where they're at. It's part of the business," Paul said as he pressed up against the vending machine. He cracked open his cold soda and beads of condensation dripped onto his bare chest. I wished I was one of those liquid drops.

"Don't look at me like a piece of meat," he joked.

I broke my gaze. "I wasn't looking at anything," I lied. Paul wrapped his pinky finger around mine. He let go of my hand, moved away, and went to spend time with the others. I was left alone with my thoughts. I headed back towards my girls.

Chapter Thirty-Seven

The sun had taken its time setting in the afternoon. One by one, our group members left the pool for refuge in their rooms to recuperate from the scorching rays. Emma, Kate, and I ran out for some fast food and headed back to our shared room to get ready. Many western world chains had local offerings on their menus too. We could even get a big, meaty burger, familiar from home, with fried shrimp and mango juice. The toy was still the same, but the cuisine made it an exciting, new adventure.

"What does one wear to a Bali bar?" Kate asked as she held up various beachwear garments from her luggage. Most of her space was taken up with sunhats and long-sleeved shirts she needed for her freak sunburn. She had two tank tops and a couple of sarongs to choose from.

"I think anything that barely covers your tits is enough," Emma chided. Kate and I looked at each other, shocked. It was such an unexpected response from this mousy woman. "What did I say?" Emma shrugged, completely clueless. We all giggled. Emma had pulled out a red crop top and was fussing to put it on in front of the mirror.

Rebecca had insisted on her own room tonight. She said she was adamant she was going to have some fun with her bartender beau. She wanted to see if there was a love connection before she invested in a long-distance romance, and I didn't blame her.

We got dressed. The three amigos, from different parts of the world, were ready to take on Bali. We strutted out of the hotel like three misplaced angels. Kate was dressed in a yellow bikini top and a matching sarong. Emma donned her red crop top and black shorts. And I wore a silky purple tank top I had picked up at the local market and jean shorts, which may have been cut a bit too high. You're welcome, Paul!

We walked out to the lobby where everyone had gathered. People were chattering, excited for a night out on the town. I overheard people commenting on what raunchy named shots they were going to have first when they got to the bar. Most of the guys were dressed in generic khaki shorts and short-sleeved dress shirts. The girls were in their finest beachwear, made over into evening attire. It was important to improvise when the laundry was running out.

I noticed Paul talking to his 'bro,' Tony. He took one look at me, and I swear his jaw dropped. I thought he must be impressed with my look. I made sure to look nice for myself, and it was a bonus if he found me attractive as well. Everyone started to pile into the taxis that Paul and Tony ordered. Downtown Bali was a trek from our hotel. I made sure that I was last to get in so that I could sit beside my new lover.

"You look beautiful tonight." Paul squeezed my hand and kissed my shoulder. I leaned into him to feel his body heat. We enjoyed our silent company on the way to the bar. I took in every moment we had together. Maybe long distance would work; he was worth it.

"We're here!" Paul put his head out the window and shouted. He rushed out, squeezing my leg with his hand and winked at me. "I got the bill, guys, just head inside," Paul offered. I jumped out, too, to join the group inside.

The music inside the bar was loud. Of all places, our first stop was an Irish bar. An Irish bar in Bali, who would have thought? The Celtic music was bumping with such force that I swear I felt the floor move. Everyone was laughing and having fun. Australian tourists, who were unfamiliar to us, joined in and were hitting on Emma and Kate. They laughed and giggled at the flirtatious efforts of the young men. They knew full well they would let these guys buy those drinks and head back to their hotel rooms, alone...well, some of them anyways.

"There you are!" Rebecca shouted at us over the music. "I didn't think you guys were ever coming!" Rebecca sauntered over to us with a glass of white wine in hand. Beads of condensation dripped off of her glass onto her strapless black mini dress. She wrapped her free arm around my waist and then spun me around.

"Looking sexy tonight, Ms. Davis!" She bumped into my hips. "You got your eye on anyone here tonight?" She looked over in Paul's direction. She had a vague idea that something besides friendship had progressed, but she didn't push me. She saw us together in Ubud, but she never rushed the conversation. I smiled in response and instead of providing an answer, I took a sip of her liquid gold.

"Hey! That's mine!" Rebecca playfully tapped my arm. "Come with me and meet Adam. I came by early to hang with him before you lot got here." I was excited for Rebecca. It was thrilling for her to meet someone who gave her that spark only romance can provide.

As the night progressed, we danced, laughed, and drank. We took turns getting everyone on the dance floor, purchasing rounds of drinks, and going outside to fan ourselves off and to find a quiet corner to chat. I danced to the drums, enjoying the freedom of the night. I swayed and felt the music move my feet, the breeze move my hips, and a hand on my ass.

"Hey!" I jumped at the disruption of my vibe. "What do you think you're doing?" I accused the stranger with the long, curly hair who had his hand planted firmly on my backside.

"I'm just having a good time, mate!" he yelled through the air noise.

"Well, I'm not interested!" I swatted his hand away.

"Everything alright here?" Paul's voice boomed. He was coming to my rescue, again.

"Everything's cool. I'm on my way," the man

commented as he backed away.

"Are you okay?" Paul took my hand in his.

"Yes, I'm fine. No need to worry. I took care of that guy before you even came over," I reassured him with a slight air of defensiveness. I pulled my hand away to ensure we continued to have our privacy.

"Some guys, they see a girl looking like you do, and they – "

"What? Are you slut shaming me?" I was aghast. I recoiled from him. I couldn't believe that he was accusing me of bringing this attention on myself. Did I even know Paul? Did he think I was some dumb broad who couldn't take care of herself? How dare he!

"No, I would never imply – " Paul stuttered, thinking about how to clean up his verbal mess. I didn't really care for whatever excuse he was conjuring. He had already insulted me.

"Well, it sounded like you were implying something!" I yelled at him over the music. My anger was enough to get the attention of some clubbers who stopped to listen in. Perhaps they were expecting some sort of brawl to place bets on.

"No, Poppy, I swear. You look beautiful. It's no wonder guys would hit on you. That's all I meant. I'm sorry. I didn't mean to upset you." Paul turned to go back to his friends, a cowardly retreat.

Did that guy think I wanted to go home with him? I don't believe that women bring negative attention themselves. Maybe I did misunderstand Paul, but I didn't need him to be so protective of me. I was upset with him.

Before he teased me and made fun of me. Then, he loved me and made love to me. And now, he was overprotective. I look a long look at myself in the mirror, fixed my makeup, and headed to the bar. I wouldn't be told what to do by any man.

"I'll have another beer, please," I called to Rebecca's bartender beau. He located my preferred beverage and cracked the cap off. I placed the cold bottle against my neck. I wasn't sure if it was cooling the heat or the anger.

"A beer and no shots?" Tony, the 'bro' from the hotel, asked. He looked me up and down before speaking further. "How about a tequila and we get to know each other better?" He leaned in closer to me. Not this again.

"No thanks, I'm taken," I said, looking around the room for my Romeo.

"I don't see you with anyone and, in fact, it looks like you're all alone." Tony turned on the barstool to face me.

"I'm seeing someone in my group. It's kind of private. We don't want everyone to know." I hoped that piece of information would throw him off my track. No such luck.

"Ah, a secret romance." He leaned in and whispered, "Do tell." Tony wouldn't take his eyes off me, summoning me to share my secrets with him.

I looked around, making sure no one was in earshot. "Well, since you are 'bros,' Paul and I are a new thing. It just started." I turned away, my face reddening with embarrassment. I blew our cover.

"Paul?" Tony laughed. A quizzical look crossed his face. "Are you sure? That's not really the tour guide's way to fall in love." He laughed again and spun on his stool. "You seem like a nice girl and all. I hate to break it to you, but guys like Paul have a girl on every stop of the tour." He sloshed his drink in his glass. "There's someone in every town, every city. He has someone to keep his bed warm almost every night. No offence." Tony took another swig of his drink. "For example, tonight I'm going to meet with Indah, a beautiful woman who works in a massage parlor here. She really knows how to work her hands, if you know what I mean." Tony ran his hands through his hair as he made eye contact with another woman who brushed passed him on the way to meet her friends. "Paul has been to her, too." I flushed with jealousy. Indah had been my masseuse when Rebecca and I went the other day. I felt the reality of the situation set in. Maybe Tony was right, maybe Paul wasn't really 'in love' with me after all. Tony continued to run his mouth, "Next week, I will meet Fitri, and let me tell you, she is not pure!" Tony let out a menacing laugh and took a final glug of his beer, pointing to the bartender for another round. "It's a lonely life as a tour guide. We aren't in any spot long enough to get to know anyone, so we might as well get to know everyone and have a little fun."

I felt not just my heart, but my body, break. Not another failure. Had I fallen for another man who would hurt me? I couldn't take another heartache; it was too much! I returned to the dance floor and spun in circles. I drank more and more. I wanted to feel numb. I had fallen for another man who wouldn't love me the way I wanted to be loved. I was a damned fool!

"Hey, are you okay?" Paul asked over my shoulder. No tender kiss this time. I shrugged him off me. I was done with him.

"I'm fine," I slurred. "Don't worry about me! Go hangout with your friends; I bet they're more fun than me."

"Okay. You just look like you've had enough, that's all." Paul suggested he call for a ride back to the hotel. I scoffed at him. How dare he try to end my night. Did he want me out of the way so he could find someone to take back to his room?

"Don't tell me what to do!"

"Poppy, I'm just trying to help."

"I don't want your help! Go away!" I stormed off. I needed some space from him. Tonight was all too much for me to process.

"Oh, Maple!" Kate called. "There's a party at these ol' boys' hotel. Wanna come?" Kate said as she clung to one of the Australians. She made eyes at him. She definitely had a wild side to her!

"Why not!" I laughed and clung to Kate's arm.

"Okay, but first, we're going to another nightclub! Get your purse!" Kate pulled me towards the front door.

"I'll be right there!"

Out of the corner of my eye, I saw Paul talking to a young woman from Tony's group. He laughed as she grabbed his arm. I stared at him, hoping he would look over. He appeared fixated on his conversation with her. Momentarily, he turned and locked eyes with me, and looked away to continue talking to this girl after his affect turned solemn. Was he upset with me for arguing with him, or was he trying to make me jealous?

I had to admit, I felt like a jilted lover seeing Paul talk to this other woman. He wasn't even trying to stop me from leaving. Sure, our budding romance was private. Our connection had escalated last night when we slept together.

Maybe last night was a mistake.

We headed out the door and into the taxi to the club. More fun and drinks needed to happen tonight. I needed to get Paul out of my head.

On the drive over, I lowered the window in the front seat. The ladies sat in the back, giggling about their new men. I was enjoying the sound of the wind and the passing cars. I sighed and felt the warmth of the alcohol on my breath. I was intoxicated by the fun we were having, and the booze added to that, too.

"You looking to have a good time?" the driver asked, glancing at me in the darkness.

I turned to him and said, "Yes, we're having fun." I closed my eyes to enjoy the breeze.

After a moment of silence, he suggested something I couldn't hear. I asked him to repeat himself. He coughed and asked, "You want mushrooms?" His eyes darted around the vehicle to see if anyone else had heard him. Was he referring to shopping for groceries?

"Pardon me?" I was confused at the offer.

"Never mind," the driver conceded.

"I would hope not!" I finally clued into what he was suggesting. Drugs! Never in my life would that be a good idea to have drugs on a trip in a foreign country. I'd seen too many Hollywood movies to know that that's a terrible idea. I would never make it in a foreign jail! Or worse, execution in some countries!

"What's going on up there, Maple?" Kate peered into the front seat. She adjusted her bikini top as she had been spilling out of it.

I took a moment to consider if I wanted to tell her what I was just proposed. I saw beads of sweat form on the driver's brow.

"Oh, nothing, just our driver offering us mushrooms!"

"What variety? I'd love to try them in a hot pot while we're here." Emma fantasized about her next meal.

"You daft cow, she means drugs, not food!" Kate swatted at her.

"What are you doing offering tourists drugs? Don't you know that could put us in jail?" Kate shouted at the driver and hit him on the shoulder with her purse. The car swerved and cars honked at him. She continued her rant as she didn't want to have to call the Embassy to bail her out. The car finally screeched to a stop, and we got out as fast as we could. I would never last in jail. I couldn't imagine being someone's prison bride let alone a real one.

Our next stop was a discotheque nightclub. Mirrored

balls glistened through the cracks of the front door as the vibration of the music jostled our feet. We stood in formation as the bouncers checked our IDs. Some folks ahead of us were turned away. One of them exclaimed that she had paid too much for her fake card and it still didn't work in her favour.

I gulped hard as we approached the large, toned man. I was of age, but I didn't want to get turned away. I needed to dance! He took the card out of my hand and studied it. He rubbed his large, callused finger over the plastic and stared into my eyes, or rather stared through me, before he continued to investigate my card. After a few seconds, he handed it back to me. I waited as he studied the others' cards and, without saying a word, he unclipped the end of a red velvet rope that separated the outside world from the party inside.

Inside the club, there was a sea of people dancing to the electronic beat. A DJ sat on a pedestal high above the partygoers. Strobe lights flashed and illuminated the glow necklaces and sticks people were pumping into the air. Everyone wore bands with the club's name around them like warriors in a retro action movie. Waitresses circled the dancefloor like hawks, their trays of feel-good juice held high above them, trying to avoid losing one single drop. The waitresses were dressed in outfits so short that if they sneezed, you'd see their crowned jewels. Some of the waitresses were dressed in drag attire and their crowned jewels may be different gems. Everyone should live their truth and be who they are.

"Let's get out on the dance floor!" Rebecca took my

hand. Somehow, in the commotion, she had landed herself a bunch of glow necklaces and put one over my head. We got into the motion of the music, and I felt my mind separate from my body. As weird as it sounded, my body danced to the music and my mind went somewhere else, freedom from thought. No care in the world. No more Paul. No more problems.

We danced with Kate and Emma, and their male sidekicks. I had wished, for a second, that Paul was with me doing the same thing, but I was upset with him. He was being too overprotective to the point of insulting. Then, I found out he's a scumbag. I hoped he enjoyed his time with whatever her name was. He's probably going to go home with her, much like Tony suggested.

As the dancing continued, so did the drinks. We waved down the waitress as she went by. She wore a feathered headband. Her eyes were surrounded by glitter and stick-on rhinestones. Her gold, sparkling lipstick shone like fireflies under the club lights. I was dazzled by her beauty. I wondered if she dressed like this every night. When she came back, she happily passed our drinks around. She got down on one knee and we followed suit. Her black, see-through dress was sky high and one of the guys tried to peek underneath. I gave him side eye and he quickly shifted his gaze. As we were shitfaced, we continued to follow what the waitress did. She said a cheer, downed her shot, and she raised her free hand to her mouth, making a howling sound. This ritual went on for one too many shots. More and more, I felt myself propel towards an all-too-familiar hangover. That would be a tomorrow Poppy's problem.

The world around me felt like a kaleidoscope. Images of my friends dancing and drinking swirled into beams of coloured lights. At first, these visuals changed slowly and then started to spin into one, blurred image. I laughed and laughed as I spun. The air was hot and reeked of sweat and sweet cocktail mixers. The fans above barely made a difference to cool us off. Sweat glistened on our bodies. We were happy, and we didn't care.

I felt hands come and go around my waist. For a moment, I thought it was Paul. I decided to forgive him, but only for the rest of tonight. We'd talk later about what happened. Relieved, I squeezed the man's hands and said, "I'm so glad you're here." I felt a kiss planted on an unfamiliar nook of my neck and I opened my eyes, realizing that it wasn't Paul. Then, I felt force releasing me of the grip. The hands vanished into thin air. Faint sounds of Rebecca telling people to "go away" echoed in my head. She had been dancing with a woman dressed in a sultry, police officer's outfit when she saw what was happening. I would later learn that men had been coming up to me, touching me, and offering cocktails that they'd bought me. She had been protecting me from these vultures.

Sometimes, ugly things can happen. I've had girlfriends back home in Toronto tell me that people drugged their drinks at the club. Some people's idea of a good time was coercing others. Consent should always be taken seriously. Being on this trip opened my eyes to some new dangers. Sure, I was in a group of people, but what if I got separated? What if the well-intentioned man turned out to be a creep? What if I got trapped in a room and couldn't get out? Or went to his hotel alone and not know my way back to where I was staying? These were lessons I would need to learn for my safety and the safety of others. Thank goodness I had a group of friends looking out for me. I would do my best to protect them, too.

"Alright, time to go!" Rebecca dragged me off the dance floor, her skin hot and slippery from perspiration. Emma, Kate, and their brood of men followed suit. Our clothing was plastered to our bodies, making my silhouette more obvious.

"We're headed to the guys' hotel for a late-night swim! Want to come?" Emma offered Rebecca. Rebecca studied us, trying to determine if we'd had too much to drink and should head back to our own hotel for the evening, or let these guys host their pool party.

"We'll be fine," I whispered. She looked at me, unsure if she should trust me. I was sure the alcohol was oozing out of my pores.

After a few minutes of reflection, she said, "Fine, but no more drinks." I nodded in agreement. She patted me on the shoulder and said, "I'm going to sit this one out. My man is getting off work and I want to go for a walk with him on the beach. You'll let me know when you get back to the hotel, yeah?" Rebecca confirmed.

"Yes, I will," I agreed. She hailed us another taxi and sent us on our way. As we pulled off the curb into the streets I saw Rebecca hustle across the street and vanish into the darkness with only the faint glow of her necklace in the distance. She was off to find her man and enjoy the rest of her night in peace. I was looking for peace, too. My head spun and I would really kill for something to ease the budding headache.

After five minutes, we pulled up to the front of their hotel on the other side of the island where the Australians were staying. In the darkness, we headed over to the pool. Someone dared us to skinny dip. I said I'd be sitting this one out to relax on the edge of the pool. I contemplated life while the others got in their birthday suits to do cannon balls.

Kate dove in, frolicking with her flavour of the night. I couldn't see Emma, but I heard her giggle. I was glad someone was having fun. My mood took a nosedive after the club. I couldn't help but ruminate about my failed relations with Paul. So much for the dream of romance.

I leaned back against the concrete and closed my eyes, the alcohol setting in. There was silence around me. It was hard to escape my worried mind. I would open my eyes to try to make out the dark figures comingling in the night. These were momentary lovers. Lips locked. Bodies entwined. The silence was broken when a female voice suggested someone was receiving a special job in the pool. We all laughed, and my mood shifted slightly.

"Want some company?" I tried to adjust my eyes to

see who was talking to me.

"Oh, I'm just sitting and enjoying the water." I replied.

"I see that." He inched closer to me, and I felt his hand on my knee. An older version of me might hop onto this one-night stand but the new me didn't want to get entangled in any further drama. I had shit to figure out.

"I could help you keep the party going." He leaned in to kiss me on the cheek.

I brushed his hand off of my knee and inched away from him, so we were no longer touching. "No thanks, I'm not interested." Growth! I stood up and walked away. He huffed and called me a bad name under his breath. I smirked and moved over to the other side of the pool to be alone again.

I might be in some type of 'situationship' with Paul, but I wouldn't want to mess around on him, even if he was playing games with me or he was a player. I needed to figure that out.

After some splashing in the pool and other hidden make out sessions, Kate suggested we head back to our hotel. She had enough of her man. "Sure," I said, disappointed Paul hadn't come to join us. Maybe he was in bed with the woman from the pub, repeating the same sweet nothings he had said to me. 'Never change,' I mimicked to myself, some shit John used to say to me. After all, Eric and Tony implied Paul was a jerk, and they were probably right.

"Time to go, lover boy," Kate told her sweetheart for

the night. She gave him one more kiss and said, "It's been fun, but it won't last. Thanks for the drinks." Savage! As she rose to dry off, a look of confusion passed over the young man's face. Maybe he thought that he was getting lucky tonight. He thought wrong.

"Where's Emma?" Kate asked as she tapped me on the shoulder. "I haven't seen her in ages. I hope she's alright." It was Kate's turn to be concerned about her friend.

We both got up and started to look for her. We asked strangers if they were her and the dark shapes said they weren't and hadn't seen her. "Emma!" Kate and I called out. No response.

As we walked around the property, we heard rustling in some bushes near the main sign for the hotel. It better not be a snake or some other creature of the night. Kate and I paused. We looked at each other, trying to telepathically decide what to do next.

"Hello?" Kate called out in a small voice. "Anyone there?"

The rustling stopped momentarily. We remained silent, waiting for the onslaught of dripping fangs to attack us. We held our breath. The rustling started again. We stood there, shocked. It didn't sound like a wild animal. We nodded at each other and took a few steps closer. I swore I heard a moan.

Looking a little farther ahead, I squinted. I thought I saw shimmering material dangling from the corner of the hotel sign in the middle of the roundabout located right in front of the building. I could have sworn I saw two pairs of shorts and a polo shirt hanging in a nearby tree.

More moans. Multiple voices.

As we inched closer, who was making these animal noises but Emma and her gentleman traveller. They were tangled together, naked, in front of the hotel sign with five, big spotlights on their naked bottoms barely shrouded by the tropical flowers.

"Oh, hello, you," Emma said, unfazed as we stood over her and her new friend. Kate and I put our hands over our mouths to stifle our laughter. "We'll be done in a minute," she said to us. Her new friend looked down at her in shock. I wasn't sure if he was shocked because Emma wanted to continue what they started, or that she was so nonchalant about the whole experience. Either way, Kate and I ran down the road to give them some privacy. Perhaps Emma was the new, wild child of the group!

We waited for ten minutes before Emma made her way down the driveway. Kate was leaning on a tree eyeing Emma up and down as she made her way towards us. Emma adjusted her top.

"So, you were shagging in the garden in front of the hotel sign?" Kate asked Emma to validate our findings.

"Where else were we to go?" Emma asked.

"Doesn't the bloke have a room?" Kate pursed her lips in mock punishment.

"Yes, but he shares it! We wanted privacy," Emma defended her location.

"You wanted privacy? I reckon you didn't select the right place!" Kate burst into laughter. "Epic. Well, that's one for the travel journal!" There were shushes in the darkness and we tried to contain ourselves.

Kate hailed a taxi, and we are off with our saucy, little minx. Moments seemed to last forever. My head swirled with disappointment, alcohol, and bad choices. I begged the taxi driver to pull over and he didn't at first. I wasn't sure if he didn't hear me or if he was anxious to drop off us drunk gals. My stomach turned. I felt a lurch brew in my stomach, and I hurled into my black purse. I heaved and I heaved, releasing all the contents inside of me.

Everyone groaned. Kate reassured him it was all concealed in the bag and demanded he keep going. I felt drips of my bile run down my bare leg. The smell of vomit slowly seeped into the air. We arrived at the hotel. The red break lights of the car shone on our path back to the lobby.

As I made my way towards my room, Paul appeared out of nowhere. "Are you okay? I was worried about you."

"I'm fine," I said as I wiped water away from my lips. I had chugged a bottle on the way back to avoid a hangover tomorrow.

"Are you sure? I was looking for you." Concern washed over him.

Yeah, right. I fixed my gaze and looked ahead. The woman from the bar was seated in the lobby, looking over at us. "I think you were just fine on your own." I didn't break my gaze. "Looks like you have company." I nodded towards her.

"What are you talking about? Samantha? She's on the other tour," Paul said, looking confused.

"Yeah, right. I bet you meet up with her every time you're here." I poked at his chest.

"Stop it. You've been drinking. Let's talk tomorrow."

"Whatever. Have fun with Samantha." I called her name a little too loudly as I wobbled back to my room.

"What was all that about?" Kate asked as she struggled to take off her clothes and get into her pajamas.

"Who knows? Paul is such a control freak," I offered as I plopped onto my cool bedsheets. "He was fussing about me, but he was with Samantha." I said her name in a mimicking voice.

"Who's she?" Kate added.

"Someone on Tony's tour." I fussed with my bedsheets, not quite comfortable. "Two guys have commented that Paul is a player. What am I to think?" I huffed, my head swelling.

"I thought you were just friends?" Emma questioned as she exited the bathroom, patting the water from her freshly washed hair. I didn't want to give away all the secrets. I hated gossip.

"We are, for now. I just don't want to get close to a guy, friend or not, who uses women. It's gross."

Kate and Emma exchanged glances, as if they knew something else was up but didn't want to go there with me tonight. We settled into our beds and Emma shut the light off. Maybe tomorrow would bring clarity.

Chapter Thirty-Eight

I woke in the middle of the night to the sound of my phone buzzing on my nightstand. A vibration was preferred so that I didn't wake during my beauty sleep. I rubbed my tired eyes and squinted as I tried to focus on the text.

Unknown Number: X.
Unknown Number: Miss you, babe.

My heart raced so hard, I thought it was going to pop out of my chest. That's no 'unknown number'- that's John.

I closed my eyes as hard as I could. Maybe this was just a nightmare. Maybe this wasn't real. I took a deep breath and decided to open my eyes again. My head ached from last night's events. I tried to focus on the low light of my cell phone and yup, it was him. His words glared at me, begging for me to respond. "No, no, no!" I shouted as I threw off the covers. I leapt from the bed and paced my hotel room, my feet banging hard on the floor like hooves.

"Keep it down! Some of us are trying to sleep!" I heard someone bellow under a pile of blankets. I forgot that I wasn't alone.

"Bite me, you wanker!" Clearly the English were rubbing off on me.

What should I do now? Reply? Ignore him? Delete him? I didn't want John, not after he humiliated me. I didn't deserve this. Paul and I had just slept together, and I thought I was falling for him. But then again, he had a woman at every stop on the tour. My anger rose.

Unknown Number: Come home, babe. I need you. X

I couldn't handle this. The wound of my broken heart opened. I felt rather vulnerable after all the new info about Paul. Maybe I needed John instead. Just as I started to work up the nerve to form a reply, there was a loud crack from across the room. Kate had shimmied to the edge of her bed and was awake, adjusting her eyes to the light.

"I'm so sorry. I didn't mean to wake you. But I got a text from HIM," I emphasized as I pointed down at the screen she couldn't see. "He won't stop!"

"Who is 'him'?" Kate groaned, half awake. "A text has got you so worked up, you're waking up the hotel, Maple? No man is worth MY beauty sleep." She fluffed her smooth, brown bob, then smoothed down her plaid pyjama shorts. She struck a model pose, then began to chuckle. "Show me, Maple. I haven't got all day. What did the bugger say?"

Hesitantly, I handed Kate my phone, in fear that she may decide that she would rather smash it than read my messages.

Kate sat down on the end of my bed. She sighed and crossed her legs. She tilted her head to the right and then to the left. Emma had woken up somewhere in the midst of things. She crawled in behind us and peered over her shoulder. After they read the messages, they both looked at each other and nodded, then looked at me. I had told them and Rebecca a little about John somewhere between Singapore and Mount Bromo.

"So, what the hell's this about then?" Kate inquired. She waved the phone about. I was sure it was headed for an open window.

"I mean, it's vague. He's a prick, yes?" Emma chimed in.

"Woah, Emma, watch the language. Canadians don't swear; they're too polite." Kate gave Emma the side eye and stifled a giggle.

"I don't know." I felt confused and just as devastated as I did when I left Toronto. I plopped down on the floor, legs crossed. I buried my head in my hands.

John was lust, excitement, and danger. Was I ever in love with him? I didn't know the answer. But whatever it was, it was definitely one sided. I was the repeat victim of unrequited love. "He wrecked me; he really did. But I loved him, and maybe part of me still does." I felt embarrassed and stared at the peeling nail polish on my toenails. My ponytail dangled as I looked downward.

I felt torn as I began to move on, to be my own person. But travelling, while it can help a person grow, could be an escape from reality. I wasn't home and I wasn't going to stay in Bali forever. Eventually, I would be going home, away from these fun ladies, and away from Paul. Even though Paul and I felt a spark and a budding relationship had occurred, it didn't mean that we were meant to be. We were just living in this moment in paradise, one that would soon be over. The idea of a long-distance romance now felt dim.

Kate and Emma sensed my hesitation. Kate validated some of the crappy things I had told them about John. They felt my pain. Even with the pain, there was a momentary longing for something familiar, perhaps, or something to take away the pain of Paul.

"Listen, Poppy, if you like this man and you have unresolved business of the heart, then perhaps it's necessary to talk to him. See what he has to say." Emma offered.

Kate shook her head in disagreement. "Be brave, kitten! You worked too hard to go back to that sod of a man." Kate's eyebrows furrowed as she tried to talk some sense into me. "Paul fancies you! That's worth something." She was right. I had felt something different for Paul than what I felt for John, or anyone else for that matter.

"Maybe he and Samantha will end up together," I whined, wiping tears from my eyes. "Not like we would be able to make long distance work, anyways." We still hadn't figured out the logistics, but given Paul's encounter with Samantha, maybe he wasn't so attached to the idea of us continuing to see each other.

"Perhaps that's a miscommunication, missy. Don't you think you should talk to him?" Kate suggested. She adjusted her fuzzy, grey, sleep mask over her bangs. The last thing I wanted to do was talk to two men. Kate didn't know half of the feelings I had for Paul.

I looked down. "Right, let's resume our slumber and then go for some breakfast, shall we?" There was more of Bali to see before this trip was over.

We all stood up, looking awkwardly at each other as this was the most heartfelt we'd been all trip. Instead of an awkward hug, they motioned towards their beds. Emma turned back briefly and gave me a sympathetic, yet knowing, smile, that part of my work of moving on was closure from John.

After we snuggled into our respective beds and the lights were off, I felt alone again. I smoothed the hair of my ponytail and took a deep breath. Whatever happens, happens, I told myself. I clicked on the home screen and selected John's number.

Poppy: Hello, John. How are you?
John: Hello, sexy. I missed you. X

I knew I was in trouble. I gave myself a pep talk. Don't be a fool, Poppy, you've worked too hard. You travelled halfway around the world to get away from him. *Don't. Give. In!* I shouted to myself in my brain.

Poppy: I have been thinking about you, too.

In my heart, I had one last glimpse of the life John and I had shared together, and what I wished would have happened. I pictured his Cheshire cat smile oceans away. I swear I could feel his hands, and lips, all over my body. My head, and my heart, knew what they wanted. I felt the blood pulsate through my body and my face grew hot. I daydreamed about coming clean to John, saying all the things I never got a chance to say, but maybe he didn't need to hear it. Closure was a bitch.

My brain made a brief appearance to remind me of the damage John caused. I took another deep, confident, breath.

John: Come back to me.

Poppy: Why would I do that?

John: **The divorce will be finalized in a month. Oliver will go to boarding school and we'll split holidays. Now you and I can be together.**

Too little, too late. I took a moment and thought about Paul. I wanted something that wasn't a secret. I still believed he could be fooling around with many others, and I was just a pawn.

John: Come back to me, Poppy. I need you.

My heart broke for both John and Paul, for different reasons. My eyes swelled with tears.

Poppy: **Let me put this into words that you'll understand.**

John: Yes?

Poppy: Piss off. It's over, John. I never want to see you again.

And with that, I blocked John's number. Good riddance. I threw my phone across the room into a pile of clothing. I was done with this crap for tonight.

Chapter Thirty-Nine

The last day in Bali, we decided to sunbathe around the pool. I had my yellow bikini on. After I slathered myself in SPF 30 and tanning oil, a dumb combination Kate told me on several occasions, I took a selfie lying down with my legs crossed, bikini top cast to the side. I tried to work on my tan before going home.

"Need any help?" Paul asked, trying to make amends.

"No, I'm trying to even my tan line before I go home," my voice was harsh and quick with my emphasis on 'home.'

"Oh, yeah, right. Home. Only a few days away, isn't it?" He seemed saddened by the realization that the trip was nearing the end. "Have you given more thought about a long-distance relationship?"

He'd crouched down beside me. I avoided eye contact as I felt that it would make me too sad to look him in the eyes. I kept looking forward, shuffling my playlist, trying to find the right summer beat. I ignored his question. He seemed defeated, sighed, and stood up to socialize with the others. He was always trying to make sure we were happy and taken care of; that was his job.

I peered over the top of my oversized sunglasses. I watched as he smiled out of the corner of his mouth. His body moved out of my line of vision. He turned back momentarily, as if he noticed that I was looking at him. I quickly looked down and rested my head on my forearms to work on my tan.

Paul walked away. I felt guilty, but what should I feel guilty for? I wondered what notch I was in his bedpost. Perhaps, I should just be single for a while. A partner felt like it might not be the best idea, given I had dying feelings for John. The last of the embers of our relationship flickered to ash. I, however, felt liberated to reject John. He wasn't worth another chase.

Later in the afternoon, we decided to get washed up and do some last-minute, souvenir shopping. I decided to go out on my own as I wanted to escape the interrogation by Kate and Emma. Rebecca was off with her new man. I was happy that she was enjoying herself, but I was going to miss her.

I ventured into the town with my flip flops and my sarong on over my bikini. My black, oversized, brimmed hat protected me from the blazing sun. I passed by the different merchants. I rubbed the fabric of the sundresses between my fingers and imagined dancing in the moonlight. I saw trinkets and blankets, things that I was sure my mom would show off to her quilter friends.

"So, that's it then?" I heard a panting voice from behind me. "I'm not much of anything to you, am I?" Paul squinted in the sun.

"What are you talking about?" I tried to pretend, but I was certain I gave myself away.

"I thought we had something special, Poppy. Don't you want to continue it with me? See what happens?" Paul looked desperate, his eyes trying to search mine through my sunglasses, but he couldn't gauge a reaction from me. I stood still. I tried to process what it was that I wanted to say to him. I struggled.

Part of me truly fell for Paul. I wanted to give in, ignore the red flags that I had collected. I wanted to tell him that I wanted him, too. But reality slapped me across the face and said differently. "Like I'm the only woman you've fallen for on holiday. Like I'm something special," I mocked him.

He stood there in the alley, shocked, as if I had blown his world apart. "You are the only one, I told you so."

"I'm sure you say that to ALL the girls!" I yelled at him. I threw my hat onto the ground. I had sent myself into a rage. "I have no doubt you've said that to more than one person. Do you think I'm a fool? I know better than to trust a man like you!" I turned and tried to run in my clumsy footwear.

"I think you're mistaken," Paul stated as he grabbed my shoulders. "I only want you." With that I broke free of his grasp.

"Liar!" I accused, and I tore down the street towards

the hotel.

"Poppy, wait! I don't understand what's going on!" Paul called after me.

My brain tried to interject, to make me stop and to think about what just happened, but I didn't want to stop and process it. I just wanted to leave. I had other places to be.

In my room, I showered and changed. My phone buzzed. A text popped up on my phone. I couldn't breathe. What if it was John again?

Casey: **Nice buns babe, but I'm not into chicks!**

Baffled, I looked down at my phone. Crap! I had accidentally sent my bikini bottom photo to Casey!

Poppy: **I'm so embarrassed! That wasn't meant for you.**

Casey: **Who was it meant for? Paul?** ☺

I needed a minute to think, to reflect what I would say to my best friend. Ultimately, it was my decision to have who I wanted in my life. It wasn't John, and right now, it wasn't Paul either. I grazed the flat surface of my phone with my fingers.

Poppy: **Paul and I are over. I'm sure he will be onto another international flavour next**

	week. Paul was just a fling. I needed to get over John.
Casey:	You sure? You seemed really into him.
Poppy:	I think I told myself some stories. It wouldn't work out, I know it.
Casey:	Too bad to hear. But who is this photo for?!
Poppy:	Just me ☺ I wanted to remember the trip. Wasn't meant for anyone.
Casey:	I see. Sure it's not for John? He's been moping around the office since you left. I could hear him singing sad 80s pop tunes again. It's a truly dreadful noise. I brought in earplugs. The English have such strange tastes in music.
Poppy:	Don't I know it! Has he really been sad?
Casey:	Yes, after you left the wife blew through here like a hurricane. She even accused ME of having an affair with him! They had tried to sort it out for a couple weeks but it was obvious that they were over. He told her he wanted you.
Poppy:	ME?! Ha!
Casey:	Positive. He asks me daily when you're coming back.
Poppy:	He messaged me last night and I told him we're done.

Casey: Good for you! Player can't have his cake and eat it, too!
Poppy: I felt liberated.
Casey: Gotta run! Spin class. Love you.
Poppy: Love you more.

And with that, my bestie had helped me to solidify my plan. I was an independent woman, travelling the world, becoming more and more confident and choosing the people I wanted to have in my life.

I set my phone down and headed out to meet the girls for poolside drinks. I didn't need my phone; real fun was to be had.

Paul: Poppy, I feel badly about earlier. Not sure what happened but can we chat, please? I'm in love with you.

As the daylight faded, the night began to blanket the sky. Everyone had congregated on the beach. We decided to have a bonfire as the weather was beautiful. The guys dressed in their tackiest tropical shirts and the ladies in their sundresses. Everyone stood around, laughing, and drinking Bintang beers. I decided that it was necessary to get a Bintang tank top as a memento. Rebecca and I got matching ones and spent one of the afternoons on our trip taking selfies on the beach in our new threads.

I made my way through the crowd and found my

friends. Kate handed me a chilled drink, toasting to a night in paradise. "Nice tan, Maple," she complimented me as we clinked bottles.

"Glad to see your face is back to normal. I hardly recognized you!" I laughed and nudged her shoulder with mine.

"Ha, ha! You Canadians think you're so funny, don't you?" Kate laughed playfully. We had come a long way on this trip. She was definitely a friend, not a foe like I had originally thought. People can surprise you.

"So, what did you decide to do about that bloke?" Emma asked. She had appeared out of nowhere like a ninja.

"I told him we're done. And then I blocked him." I took a big swig of my drink.

"Good on you!" Kate high fived me.

"I bet that was hard," Emma empathized. "It sounds like you did the right thing."

"I did. It's for the best." I tried to find a smile. "Back to single life I go!"

"You don't have to stay single; Paul wants you," Emma pried.

"It won't work out between us," I cut her off.

"But – "

"No, we're done. End of story."

"Okay, okay." Kate smoothed her hair down.

Emma looked at me, puzzled, but nodded in agreement. "Whatever works for you; you deserve to be happy." She was whisked away into the crowd by the beat of the dance music.

After having contact from John, and then deciding that I couldn't trust Paul to continue to see him, I booked an early flight home. I was going to make a French exit. I didn't want to ruin anyone's fun. As Emma moved away the crowd parted ever so slightly. Through the throng of people, there was Paul stoking the bonfire. This seemed ironic as a few days ago he was stoking the flame of my heart. He had khaki, cargo shorts on, one size too large, and a yellow and orange flowered shirt. The flowers looked like the ones he had bought me in Ubud. I shook my head and rattled my opinion of Paul. Don't fall for it, Poppy. You can't trust Paul.

I continued to watch as Paul fumbled with the logs trying to stack them into the fire. I saw the frustration build in him. Someone finally came over to help him. I heard his laugh, which was intoxicating. I had to break free of his moment. I was in too much pain. He would move on and find another woman. I would be a distant memory to him soon enough.

As he turned around to glance at me, my back was already towards him, walking into the crowd. After getting into the celebrations, Rebecca stormed the beach. "What's a party without me?" She hollered, holding a large bottle of liquor in her hand. People turned around and cheered. Her smile was infectious.

"There you are. I didn't think you'd show up!" I wrapped my arms around her. Rebecca's skin was still warm from being in the sun all day, her tan visible in the moonlight.

"Ah, yes, the man has to get ready for work. We

were enjoying cocktails on the beach loungers today." She cracked open the bottle and found some empty cups. "We went on a dolphin boat cruise earlier this morning. It was magical." Rebecca told me all about her adventures with her new love.

Rebecca really was a friend for life. Even though we'd soon part, I had every intention of keeping in touch with her. I didn't want to say goodbye to her; I wanted to remember the fun times and not cry because the trip was over. Travelling brings together people you may never imagine being friends with or even meeting in daily life. I was grateful for her.

"A toast," Kate started. She towered over all of us as we sat at the makeshift, dining table on the beach. "To holidays! May work be more bearable with paid vacation!" Glasses were raised in the air.

"Here, here," we echoed with our cheers.

"And to booze! May it make tonight memorable, or not! Whichever you prefer!" Rebecca added.

"Here, here," echoed the group again.

Platters of fried fish, shrimp, rice, and vegetables were scattered across the table. We reached across each other to grab at dishes and washed it down with wine and beer. We laughed and playfully teased each other, just as families do. Paul had taken on the role of a single dad on this vacation, looking after his riffraff children. In reality, he was only a couple of years older than us and had no business being in charge of a bunch of unruly twentysomethings.

After dinner, we headed towards the bonfire. We

circled around it like it was a shrine. The alcohol warmed my body. I closed my eyes to enjoy the moment. As the fire began to die, the visibility of the patrons reduced. Some couples could be seen kissing in the dark, like Mike and Karli, while others moved away from the fire for privacy.

From across the flames, I saw two people shrouded under the moonlight by palm trees. I squinted to try to make out who the figures were who were embracing in a passionate kiss. As I looked harder, someone walked by them, temporarily shining their flashlight on the twosome. When I finally realized who it was, I gasped. Tiffany and Britney were sharing a kiss! They were a couple. Maybe they were teasing me to take the heat off people realizing they were together. I quietly laughed to myself. This all made sense now. Love is love. There was no reason to hide their romance, and there was no reason to treat me like shit either.

As I closed my eyes and enjoyed the breeze, I felt a light brush against my shoulder. "I haven't heard back from you. Are you ignoring me?" I broke from my trance to face whomever had nuzzled against my neck.

"I don't know what you're talking about."

"My message – you never replied." Paul raised his lips to my ear, barely touching it. The heat of his breath sent goosebumps over my body. "I'm sorry if I did anything to hurt you. I want to make this right."

I wanted to believe him, desperately, but how many men can you believe? "It's just better if we go our separate ways. What we had was fun, but it's over now." I didn't know if I truly believed it, but at this point, what other choice did I have? I was about to head home to Toronto.

"I want you, and only you. Please, can we make this work? I'd do anything. I could come see you every month. You're worth the 36-hour flight." There was desperation and fear in his voice. Paul inched his fingers towards mine in the sand. He lightly intertwined them with mine. He raised my hand to his lips and gently kissed my fingertips. He didn't seem to care who saw us. His gaze met mine, fire reflecting in his eyes. I felt the passion for him again, if only for a second.

I wanted to kiss him one last time, but I pulled back when he leaned in. Truthfully, I could hear the words spoken about Paul by the other guides. "I can't, Paul. I can't," I softly spoke into his shoulder.

"I don't understand." After a moment of silence, he unlaced our hands, got up, and walked away. This was for the best, I thought. Forget about me, Paul. Tonight, I was headed home.

Chapter Forty

As the fire died down, the crowd departed. I snuck back into my room and grabbed my belongings. I had packed after my shower, hopeful and optimistic about my future. I'd be starting anew, alone.

I turned my porch light off and headed towards the front desk. My bag was heavier than before, mostly from all the stuff I bought to take home. Kate had joked that I was the fancy backpacker as I purchased a 100% genuine, fake brand label bag to carry my purchases in. Somewhere between Bangkok and Bali, I'd made a few too many purchases. I was just as bad as Rebecca!

As I headed down the pathway, a small voice alarmed, "Where're you going?" Emma stepped out from the shadows, arms crossed and holding a lit cigarette.

"Emma, you smoke?"

"The mood called for it," her mousy voice rang. Emma was a surprising combination of a caring friend to Kate, a woman who had a neurotic fear of butterflies and monkeys, and bit of a sexy vixen. "You're leaving us?" She blew a steady stream of smoke as she inspected me.

"Yeah, I decided to head home early," I managed to say sheepishly.

"You're going back to him?"

"No, it's over between me and John," I concluded.

"You sure?" She wasn't buying it.

"Yes, I'm done with him," I said, which was absolutely the truth. I had no desire to go back to that scum.

"I don't quite understand the need to leave. We've a few days left." She took another puff of smoke, and me, in.

"I have nothing left here. It's time to go." I felt bad to say this to my friend. She looked disappointed. I valued her, and the others, but when things fell apart with Paul, I felt there was no reason to stay.

"What about Paul? He's in love with you, I reckon." She flicked the ashes from her cigarette. "I've seen the way he looks at you; that man loves you."

"No, he doesn't." I wanted to laugh in her face.

"He does, but you can only see what you believe. That man has been pining for you."

I huffed, unable to answer her. I didn't need to be confused about any feelings right now. My mind was made up. I was leaving without him.

"It's the truth." She snubbed her cigarette out on the path. "You have to do what you feel is right for you, no judgement." She unfolded her arms and hugged me. I felt loved and supported, even if Emma didn't quite agree. I wanted a fresh start on my own.

The next thing I knew, the taxi pulled up. The trunk light shone in the darkness as the driver loaded my luggage. We bartered the price of the lift to the airport and slammed the doors shut. As we made our way down the dirt driveway, Emma stood in the glowing red of the taxi's light waving goodbye to me.

The cool air blew through the car as we made our way out of the city towards the airport. A small offering plate made of palm leaves was on the dashboard filled with coins, orange, and purple flower petals and freshly burnt incense. It was an offering the driver made to have plentiful fares. Hot tears stung my eyes. I was sad to leave my new friends, to say goodbye to this glorious place, and to return home to the unknown. At least I had Amos' sweet kisses to look forward to. I suppose I could circle want ads as Amos ran around in the dog park.

For a minute, I thought of Paul. What if Emma was right? I relived those tender touches and kisses with Paul. The silly selfies we took in the street. Fleeting moments of pleasure that helped me to heal and to grow. I would be forever grateful to him, but this was not our love story; it was my own.

Chapter Forty-One

Casey: You know, Poppy. I've been thinking.
Message undeliverable.
Casey: Maybe you shouldn't make any decisions in a state of vulnerability. Stay and enjoy your trip.
Message undeliverable.
Casey: Crap, are you on the plane?
Message undeliverable.
Casey: Look, maybe Paul is your match! I love the way you talk about him. He sounds special. Give it another go!
Message undeliverable.
Casey: Please give this some thought before you give up on Paul.
Message undeliverable.
Casey: I support whatever decision you make.

Message undeliverable.

Casey: Damn it! Technology sucks.

Message undeliverable.

Chapter Forty-Two

I sat in the darkness with my complimentary white wine in hand. I had made it on my third, and final flight, home. I couldn't hear or feel anything other than the faint tapping of my fingernails against my glass. My thoughts were interrupted, and I quickly came back to reality when my seatmate cleared his throat. Startled, I looked around and make eye contact with him and smiled in embarrassment that I had been noisy.

"Nervous?" he asked in a soft, English accent. Another English man with a sexy accent. Just my luck, I couldn't help but snort. His question seemed particularly genuine and an excuse to get me to stop tapping.

I squirmed in my seat as if someone had found out about a deep, dark secret I had been hiding. "Yes, I've been travelling for about a month in Southeast Asia. I'm going home to find a new job. I've left my friends and my 'something' to come home early." I truly didn't know what to call Paul. Suddenly, I felt panic that I had left a trip that was bringing me so much joy, without discussing the possibility of a future with Paul. What had I done?

"Hmmm, a 'something.' I've had a few of those. Was it worth leaving your trip early? You've been away so long," he asked quizzically as he scratched the stubble on his chin. The gentleman then placed his clasped hands over his crossed legs, waiting patiently for my answer.

I felt a lump form in my throat. "I hope so. I left Toronto to get away from a bad 'something' and I did well to move on. He ended up contacting me during my trip, AFTER I met a new 'something,' but I told him to get lost." As I made air quotes around Paul's nickname, my new 'something' now was a gone 'something.' A gulp of wine flushed down my nerves. "Then, I left my new 'something' because I couldn't imagine how we'd make a long-distance relationship work, particularly after the gossip that he was a player."

The gentleman raised his eyebrows in unison. "This is getting good." He shuffled in his seat, preparing for me to spill the tea. The English do enjoy their tea. "So, what happened? What about the new 'something'?" The stranger made air quotes, imitating me. "What makes him a player?"

"Well..." What a complicated answer. "He was my tour guide," I was filling the tea pot. "We were enemies at first, then got along, then enemies again, and finally decided to be friends." The tea was steeping. "We shared a passionate kiss, roamed around temples and cities, and climbed a volcano together." The tea was about to be poured. "We er – 'did stuff,' but I'm sure he 'does stuff' with other tourists, too. Lots of them from what I heard. The lifestyle, you know." My face turned red. "Now, we are no longer anything," I concluded, out of breath and emotionally exhausted. The teacup was spilt.

The man, clearly embarrassed, too, shuffled in his seat. "Right, I'm sure that's the way for some tour guides, but surely not all, especially if he became your new 'something'. What makes you think he's all bad? Sounds like he wanted a future with you?" My unofficial therapist was making me regret my decision to leave. Should I have given up on Paul? Oh, shit.

The truth was, I didn't know anything for certain. I thought about it. My thoughts were interrupted as I dove deeper.

"Well?" he said, "Why was he bad?"

For the next fifteen minutes, instead of telling this strange man all the things that made Paul bad, I spoke of all the ways that he was good and kind. I spoke in depth of our adventures, our hopes, and dreams for the future. I spoke of how he challenged me and helped facilitate my growth over the last month. I even mentioned the way he helped me let go of my past. And then, I stopped myself. Regret took over my brain.

"He's wonderful. My confidence was broken when we ran into another guide, two different guides, actually, and they made comments about him getting frisky with other women. Many women, to be exact, at every stop. I'm sure he finds a lover on every tour." I felt angry that Paul would or could ever be a scoundrel.

"That's a hefty accusation, especially if he didn't tell

you he was seeing other women." He sighed and thought about his reply, searching for a kinder answer. "In my experience, men don't make the effort you are describing for 'something' who isn't important to them. A man goes to great lengths and efforts for a woman who makes his heart race. A coward would only, er, do things with you, not make you feel special as this new 'something' made you feel special. Maybe it's worth reconsidering. Is it too late?" He searched my eyes for an answer.

"Maybe, but it's too late. I'm headed home to start over."

"Ah, I see. Could I give one last bit of advice?" I nodded. "Sometimes, a fresh start doesn't need to start alone. I do hope you find what makes you happy." With that, he pressed the call bell and summoned the steward. He took his earplugs and placed them in his ears before I heard the final sigh to indicate that he had fallen asleep.

What had I done?

Chapter Forty-Three

I had drifted to sleep in the night. I was woken by the faint light of the morning sun and the wheels making their wobbly landing onto the airport runway. That old, familiar feeling came over me of the gentle dip of gravity, the rumble of the airplane's engine, and the wheels touching the ground; the soft clicking of the flight attendants' heels as they sauntered down the aisles getting ready for everyone to disembark; and the passengers eagerly standing too soon and tearing their items from the overhead bins before they zoomed back to their everyday life or dashed to their next flight.

"Well, we're here!" my seatmate said cheerfully as he adjusted his tie, his neck pillow still tautly secured. We shifted in our sardine-like seats, trying to be polite and accommodating to our fellow passengers, but also wanting to get the hell off this plane to take in some fresh air.

We handed our bags to each other as if our moment

of bonding last night never happened. We were strangers once again. The gentleman and I glanced at each other and made our own separate way down the aisles, past the rows full of discarded blankets and magazines tossed haphazardly across seats. The flight attendants smiled weakly as we passed, no doubt looking forward to our departure so they could find a soft pillow to place their heads.

I followed my former seatmate, not meaning to, down to arrivals and through customs as we fumbled to put our chicken-scratched claims forms into machines instead of talking to real humans. I didn't want to talk to them anyways and risk intense glares as they tested to see if I was lying about bringing back forbidden goods. They didn't need to know about the loose-leaf tea or those wooden figurines that could have been a home for termites.

Down, down, down we went through the bowels of the airport. I followed the man to the luggage carrousel. The sound system alerted us to carrousel number five and the red sirens flashed, signalling that the belt would be parading our luggage in circles for us to collect. The passengers watched hopefully, and impatiently, for their luggage to make its debut on the line. Everyone made a formation outside the perimeter of the conveyer belt, and be damned if you didn't launch yourself into the circle to collect your belongings.

I watched as the stranger grabbed his suitcase and made one final passage through security towards the arrival section to greet loved ones. I tried to catch up to him as best I could. I was not sure what I wanted from him – more advice on what to do? I had the support of my friends, but I didn't have my own support. The stranger had provided a false sense of caring only close quarters provides. I saw him in the distance as I received my last stamp of approval to leave security. As the doors opened, he was greeted by two people, a petite blonde woman, and a young girl. He wrapped his arms around both of them, wide like a net. He didn't care about creasing his dress clothing or tearing his jacket. That hug meant everything to him. The family relaxed when they embraced as he was finally at home and safe. He got down on one knee to face his daughter. She wanted to show him her stuffed teddy bear. He made a fuss of it and hugged it, too, like a cherished family member. His smile could not be any bigger. I watched them, the happily reunited family, drift into the abyss of the other loved ones waiting for their traveller abroad to enter through the doors. Before I knew it, he was gone.

Clumsily, I grabbed my backpack. The bright, red canvas was worn with small holes from the pushing and pulling on top of luggage compartments, vans, buses, and trains. The canvas was dusted with dirt from being shoved under beds, into cramped lockers, and used as a pillow and a makeshift footrest. Old red knew her place in my life. Patches were like tattoos, cherished memories of where I'd been, and also like bandages, helping to hold off on repairs. Faint marks of blood were visible around the patches where I pricked myself with the needle from the hotel room sewing kit, perhaps a reminder that this mess made me stronger.

I got my backpack on, stumbled through the last set of security, and held my breath as the doors opened to the arrival area. I closed my eyes and made a wish: I wished someone was waiting for me, purple balloons in hand and a sign to welcome me home. Instead, no one was here: no Paul, and no friends. I was alone, again, amongst the chaos of strangers. Eyes formed on me, feeling sorry for me, that I left the airport alone. I made my way towards the exit, bags in tow. Head down, defeated, I made my way back home.

The sun started to rise higher and higher into the sky. The air was crisp, not quite warm, as summer had not yet arrived. I swore I saw the final signs of cool morning air as my warm breath left my mouth and disappeared.

The taxis zoomed by with lovers, families, and friends, eagerly making their way back into Toronto or a destination close by. I tried to hail a taxi but had no luck. It was too cold to try to show off some leg to get a ride. Not even one taxi driver felt sorry enough for me to stop. I made my way to the rail line, which would take me back home. Tired, I rode the rails and rested my head on the windowsill, watching the sun.

I finally arrived back at my apartment building. Another old familiar sight I had longed for. I had so many happy memories, mostly with Amos as he raced me out the front door for the nearest fire hydrant to mark, or our daily cuddle sessions. I dropped my sack from my back onto the sidewalk. I ached, still sore from the journey. I took a moment and then I dug around for my keys in the outer pocket. The key had pierced a hole outside the canvas. I'd need another patch to cover this up. I found the keys and made my way upstairs. I turned the lock of my apartment slowly. I felt saddened by my revelation that the holiday was over, and it was time to move on. Part of me felt happy to put it all behind me, but there was still an ache.

The hallway was quiet; everyone had left for the day. On the other side of the door, I heard a faint barking sound. Confused, I wondered if that was a neighbour's dog barking. I felt half asleep and was likely imagining things. Then, all of a sudden, a smile appeared across my face. That's not the neighbour's dog. That's my Amos!

I burst through the door and a dog with a jack-in-the-box tail sprang into my lap! "Amos! Mommy missed you!" Before I knew it, I was covered in kisses from a happy little Chihuahua. Finally, I felt like I was home. Too bad I didn't know when I stood in the airport that this woman just needed her faithful mutt to make her feel special.

"I tried to keep him at the house, but he was bugging your dad with his constant need for attention." My mom appeared from behind the half wall leading into the living room. "I hope it's okay we have been staying here the last week, trying to get ready for your return home." She smiled at me, enjoying the embrace with my fur son. A quizzical look plastered her face. "Shouldn't you still be on holiday?"

I wasn't sure what to say, so I just said, "I got homesick. Decided to come home a few days early and surprise you. SURPRISE!" I said with arms wide open. My mom came in to share a tender embrace with Amos and me. Amos gave a little growl, signalling that he preferred his reunion with his mom alone. He had had his time with his grandma.

"Well, I'm glad you did. We sure missed you." I put Amos down. With that, my mom embraced me in the warmest and biggest hug. I knew she missed me. Amos cried at our feet. "You already had your turn," she said to him, as if he knew what she was talking about.

"I'm just surprised," she said, still hung up on why I wasn't still in Bali. "I thought you were having a nice time with those ladies and your new friend."

"Ma!" I said as I smiled and rolled my eyes at her. "I did have fun. But all things must come to an end." I plopped myself down on my couch and hugged a cushion. Amos jumped up beside me and diligently placed his sympathetic head on my lap.

"And what will reality bring for you?" Mom asked as she took a perch on the arm of the couch.

"Well," I sighed, hoping it would buy me time, "I guess I start to circle the want ads. Someone's got to need a secretary. I'm excellent at answering phones and fetching coffee."

"All this time away and you still decide all you want to do is to be a secretary?" She rose off the couch and held the traditional mother stance with her hands on her hips. "I thought this trip was going to give you some insight and clarity how to proceed with your life." So much for gabbing.

"I mean, I did enjoy travelling. Maybe I could look into some courses on how to become a travel agent or maybe some travel writing. Share my experiences with others." I felt a ping of confidence in my recent choice. The words had fallen out of my mouth. I had discussed the idea with Paul, but even then, it had felt like a silly idea. It was likely a desperate way to tether myself to him, so we didn't have to leave each other.

"Tell me more." Her stance softened.

"Everyone has something they want to get out of travel. For some, it's an escape. For others, it's to learn about new cultures. Some travel to make new friends, whether they be temporary or for a lifetime. And, for some, it's to learn about themselves. I want to help facilitate those things, directly or indirectly." I couldn't help but peacock, feeling pride in my new life path, though the path did need some trailblazing.

"That's my girl. I'm so proud of you." She had my cheeks in a firm pinch, much like she did when we I was a child. When she let go of my flesh, two white spots remained. Slowly, the blood flowed back and gave me my rosy complexion.

"Thanks, you're my biggest cheerleader." I laughed and tugged at her leg.

"I try. Now, I just have to work on your dad. He leaves his dirty plates all over the counter. If only he would clean up once in a while, then I wouldn't have to plot his death."

"Ma!"

"I'm just kidding, sweetheart. Take a joke!" She

grinned at me. She picked up her coat and purse. After saying her goodbyes to her grand-puppy, she was out the door. Amos and I were alone in the peace and quiet.

The want ads and educational brochures on travel agent studies could wait a few days. I needed sleep. I felt a sense of confidence return, as well as some jetlag. This was my future. I felt okay with this path. I rested my eyes after I had plopped down on my bed. Amos curled up beside me. The heat of his body lulled me to sleep momentarily. I was alarmed by a slight buzzing at my hip. My pocket was vibrating, or rather, my cellphone.

Unknown Number: Poppy, I'm outside. We need to talk.

I thought I blocked him. Not this, again.

Chapter Forty-Four

I was not awake enough to deal with this. Why was John back? Couldn't he take a hint?

Great, just what I needed. I told John we were done. What more was there to say? I didn't have any of his old records or his favourite sweatshirt. We weren't together long enough to share an apartment or own furniture together.

As I was pondering what the British worm wanted, the buzzer rang. Amos perked up his ears. I tried to ignore it, but the more I pretended I wasn't home, the more obnoxious the ringing got. Could this man not take a hint?

Poppy: John's at my apartment! How does he know I'm back?!

Three little dots came to life and disappeared.

Casey: I'm sorry – I let it slip you were coming home today.

Ugh! In reality, it was inevitable John and I may run into each other, which I hadn't quite prepared for, but to show up at my door? This man had balls, just when I assumed he hadn't any.

Poppy: What do I do?
Casey: Hide?
Poppy: He's texted me three times now, and keeps ringing the buzzer. I can't hide.

Amos had hidden in the back of his crate to get away from the constant sound of buzzing. I wish I had some hole to crawl into, too. My text exchange with Casey was interrupted by an intruder:

Unknown Number: Please let me in, Poppy. I missed you.

Bullshit.

Poppy: How is he even texting me? I blocked his number!
Casey: The wife was in yesterday. She said she found some questionable text messages and she smashed his phone. I'm a little afraid of her, but she's also kind of a badass!

She'd have to be a badass to put up with John's shit. All I wanted to do was to go to bed and sleep. That wouldn't happen until I dealt with my nightmare.

Poppy: I'm going to talk to him, and then send him on his way. I need this man out of

> **my life! I can't escape to another continent to get away from him.**
>
> **Casey:** **Do as you must! Keep me updated! Love you.**
>
> **Poppy:** **Love you, too!**

With the fifth, and final buzz, I answered the call, "What do you want?" I growled. I wasn't sure if I qualified for vixen status anymore, but I was definitely an angry bear.

"I just want to talk to you. Please let me in," John pleaded. I stood with my back against the door, summoning strength. I hadn't faced him since the day he told me to run for my life when his soon-to-be ex-wife was about to storm the gates of the office in search of my blood. With every breath, I dug deeper, looking for my confidence.

"I'm not sure we've much more to say," I huffed into the receiver.

"Please, one more time?" I couldn't stand that coo. Before I knew it, I pushed the buzzer to let him in. A few minutes later, there was a soft rap at my door.

I guess there's no better time like the present. Deep breath, door open. The devil stuck his foot in the door.
I couldn't look at him at first. A multitude of emotions bubbled over, ones I didn't know still impacted me. The wound healed but the edges were brittle.

"These are for you." He extended his hand towards me: red and white roses tied together with a perfect, black ribbon. "Welcome home." I took them from him. Once his hands were free, he took one step closer to me, then another. Soon, we were touching toes. I didn't lift my eyes to his; I couldn't. His hands reached for my waist, and I recoiled like a snake.

"Don't touch me." I stepped back. "What makes you think you can smooth over everything with flowers?" I tossed them onto the coffee table. Amos backed into his crate and started to growl.

"I missed you. I want us to get back together," he whispered to me as he leaned in closer.

"I don't believe you." I took a few steps back and headed into the living room. "You always seem to have your own agenda."

"I'm just trying to be nice." He rolled his eyes. I guess the gentleman demeanor wasn't going to last too long. The charade was already over, and this round had only just begun.

"Nice? Nice?" I paced the apartment to get away from him. "Nice would have been telling me you had a wife when we got together!" More paces, more words. "Nice would have been telling me the truth!"

"Come on, Poppy. Let's move on. No need to be dramatic." His sideways smile formed on his face. He wanted to play, but I wasn't going to play nice with him, not again.

"I'm not being dramatic. You lied to me! I wouldn't have gotten with you if I had known the truth." I paced around the other side of the couch. "You were married!"

"What difference would it have made?" He started to morph before my eyes. "You came back to me once you knew I was still married!" He laughed like I was the villain.

"How could you be so cruel?" Tears welled in my eyes. I had told myself to be strong, but even confident people falter.

"News flash, Poppy, you're not the marrying kind." He moved closer to me and placed his hands on my shoulders. "You need to learn to take what you can get." Shock rippled through my body. Did he think he was the best I could do? Talk about a slap in the face! How dare he speak to me like that!

"Get out!" I roared. I became someone I didn't recognize; a new confidence and fierceness that was buried deep down came to the surface. John's face was stunned. He stumbled backwards with every roar that escaped my lips. "I said, get out!" He grabbed his coat and fumbled towards the doorway.

"You'll be back, Poppy. You always come back." I wasn't sure if this was him taunting me or threating me. Either way, the hell I was going back to him. I slammed the door in his face and slid down onto the floor. I crumpled over myself in a heap and the tears pooled around me. I felt like I was drowning in emotions, but I knew now that I could sure as hell swim.

Chapter Forty-Five

For the next 24 hours, I lay exhausted on my bed. I ignored calls and texts as I was in emotional turmoil and still jet lagged. When I had left Toronto, I was a mess. I didn't know who I was or what I wanted. Now, I returned home a more confident woman in control of her own destiny. Sometimes, a confident woman stumbles, but then, she gets right back up again.

Once I groggily roused for the day, I took Amos outside to read the dog mail as my coffee percolated on the counter. When I returned to my apartment, the aroma of cinnamon and vanilla java wafted through the air. I thought back to the lazy trip mornings without a care in the world. I wished I was still on holiday.

I finally got around to checking my email to see college applications for travel and tourism. I couldn't escape this epic hint from my mom. I smiled to myself, thinking of the wonderful, new possibility in front of me. A new career path sounded exciting and just what I needed.

My morning thoughts were interrupted by an abrupt, and repeated, ringing of my phone. Annoyed, I rolled my eyes and looked to see who was calling; it was Casey. In the mix of things, I hadn't returned her messages either.

"Hello?"

"Why have you been ignoring me? Didn't you see the SOS message?!" Casey shrieked into the phone.

"No, it's been a rather intense homecoming. What's up?"

"I've got some news," she gasped into the phone, desperate to get her message out. "There seems to be an uninvited guest at the office who refuses to leave," she said in a low, muffled voice I could barely understand.

"Who is it?" I asked, puzzled, as I had already seen John. Maybe it was his wife. I panicked, my pulse quickening.

"It's a man named Paul. I believe he was your tour guide. Your lover," she cooed.

My heart sank. "What? What's he doing here?" My mind spun. This couldn't be true; the trip was only just ending today – how did he get here? There must be some mistake.

"He said he wants to talk to you. I don't think he'll leave until you come." There was a silence on the phone. "Poppy, he looks heartbroken. Give the poor guy a chance."

I hung up the receiver, and petted Amos on his head. "What should I do, Amos?" He huffed and rolled over for me to rub his belly. "Some help you are." I threw my head backwards onto the pillow, trying to decide my fate.

What was Paul doing here? I tried to get dressed as fast as I could. I fumbled through my closet, trying to get something on. I never thought I was going to see him again. I'd been so mean to him. While I did feel some regret for up and leaving him, I didn't believe there was going to be a future between us. How could there be? He'd always be travelling. When would we see each other? I don't know if I could trust him.

Casey: Are you coming? I can't stall him anymore. Now he is asking me where you live!

Oh, no. I couldn't have him come here. I already felt as though I had kicked him like a puppy; no offense, Amos.

Poppy: Yes, I'm planning my escape. How can you let someone down twice nicely?

Casey: Stop – just see what he has to say!

I put a comb through my hair and checked my face. Good enough. I patted down my blouse in a lazy attempt to smooth out the creases. Why bother dressing up? I was only going to break Paul's heart again.

I raced down the street, zipped through people traffic on the sidewalks, and narrowly avoided a bicycle messenger. I panted as the sun shone between skyscrapers. The rain from the day before had lifted. I dodged puddles along the way, keeping my last outfit clean. I shivered as I thought of Thai New Year and the chalk fight with the children.

I was almost at the office now. I stopped across the street from the building. I folded over, out of breath. I needed to catch what was left. I needed to figure out what I was going to say to Paul. He didn't outwardly hurt me. I had this strange feeling as I turned to face my former workplace. This was the building where I fell in lust with 'someone,' not love. This place had given me a purpose but then that was taken away from me and I felt like nothing. It was the place I was given the title of an adulterer, a scarlet letter where an ex-lover was likely working. This was the place another ex-lover stood waiting for me. How much worse could it get?

I stood up tall. I remembered that those actions were ones of the past. I had evolved. I had travelled to the other side of the globe. I had tested myself and tried new things. I had forgiven myself and let the past go. I shouldn't fear this place; I should own it. I put one foot in front of the other and crossed the street. I took one deep breath and held onto it. When I saw Paul, I would know what to say. My heart would speak. I took wide strides towards the revolving front door. I waited for the chime of the elevator and got in.

The stops between floors were tedious. Could this car move any slower? If I was going to break his heart in another country, I would at least like to get it over with and move on fully completely. I don't know what was going through his head to chase me here.

The doors finally dinged, alerting me that I had arrived at my final destination. It was the last, bloody time I hoped to be in this place. Why couldn't anyone let me move on?

As the doors opened, Casey burst into the elevator. "Hello, lovey, good to see you!" She grabbed me and held onto me as hard as she could. She was in a short, white lace dress, which flared perfectly at the waist. Her bright, dewy skin shone in the florescent light. Her grin was made wider with her fuchsia lipstick. Girl was never afraid to be bold.

"I missed you, too." I stood back to get a good look at my best friend. I felt relieved to see her, but also so emotionally exhausted, I could have stayed in that hug all day.

"So, what's the game plan? Do we love him or send him back to the airport where he belongs, on the other side of the world?" She stared at me, and squared her hips. She was like a football player waiting for the coach to give her the play. She always had my back.

"I don't know. I think I'll decide when I see him. I thought I had ended it." I paused, thinking. She stood examining me. My mind flip flopped back to Paul being a potential love interest. "I'll hear what he has to say, but I promise nothing." That was the truth. I couldn't promise anything as I had no idea what I'd do. I looked down at my hands, which were still entangled with Casey's. Casey, even though she gives advice, knew when to let my heart speak to me instead of her.

The elevator dinged again. At this very moment, she and I stood facing each other, holding hands. It looked like our souls were connecting with each other in a romantic moment, or a pose from a Kama Sutra book. Different strokes for different folks, I say. As the doors opened, two doctors in their white lab coats looked up at us from their clipboards, seemingly confused whether they should enter the elevator or take this girl-on-girl action?

Casey stared at them and barked, "She's my heterosexual life partner! Stop staring, pigs!" And with that, the doors closed. We burst out laughing as hard as we could. She definitely was my partner for life – the best partner a person could ask for. We pushed the button for our floor again. When we arrived, Casey asked, "Alright, then, shall we?"

"We shall." I offered a faux curtsy in her direction.

We walked towards the office and there he was. "It's you," Paul stuttered after a few moments of silence. He was dressed in the same outfit I had left him in that night on the beach. This time, his attire was stained with sand and obvious sweat marks under his armpits. It may have been nerves, the sweltering Indonesian sun, or three plane rides – all of the above, perhaps. He inched a step closer to me and paused, waiting for my reaction.

"It's me," I said. "And, it's you." We were as awkward as two people could get. More silence. I shifted my weight over each leg, buying time.

"You never gave me a chance to speak." Paul took

deep breaths. He stood frozen for a minute and then, suddenly, there he was, my shining star. "You never gave me a chance to tell you that you're the one. I want to share my life with you. I was more than happy to try long distance with you. You didn't listen to me." His breathing grew stronger. He took another step towards me. He hulked in his confidence. My eyes grew as wide as saucers in the cartoons. This was a turn on, a side of Paul I'd never seen.

He walked a few steps closer to me. "Near the end of the trip, I was offered a contract here at the head office." My jaw dropped. "I accepted. I was going to tell you in Bali. But you stopped speaking to me. I don't know what I did wrong. All of a sudden, you gave up on us and shut me out. How much clearer can I be?" He raised his voice, not to me, but to the room. His shoulders collapsed in surrender. His smouldering eyes stared back at me. He was fighting for me, and for us.

I saw a collage of images before my eyes of us holding hands, having long, midnight conversations under the stars, sharing tender kisses like we could understand each other's soul, sharing what we wanted in a future, and in love, us living life, us together now, and us, at our worst as well as at our best.

Out of the corner of my eye, Casey inched out of the room. Maybe she took a hint from Paul that we needed to be alone together. She peered from behind the corner of the wall. I gave her a knowing glance that it was okay for her to leave, and she disappeared. She may be gone but she was always near when I needed her.

"I know I didn't end this well. You deserve better," I confessed. "But you'll find another woman, maybe several, and you'll get over me." I tried to turn this around, turn him away from me after what I had done to him. I felt embarrassed that I had broken his heart.

"What are you talking about? I don't understand why you keep bringing up other women. I have been very clear," he spit through his teeth, his passion rising. "I WANT YOU!"

"Eric and Tony said you get with other women on your tours. You have women at every stop. That's what most guides do, I was informed." The truth was finally out. I felt relieved. The cards were on the table, and we were both showing our hands, but I was still protecting my heart. Perhaps, I should have told him everything in Bali. He could have saved his money and took on another tour rather than uprooting and moving to Canada. Part of me, however, felt that my insecurities got the best of me. I suppose I had never truly felt wanted by a man.

Paul paused for a minute as he processed the words. His eyes fluttered back and forth, searching his memory. Then, suddenly, he blurted, "THOSE PRICKS? Not EVERY guide is a dog! Did you think I was rolling around with other women in bed? Is that how little you think of me?" He almost howled like a dog at the moon.

I found my power. "What about 'Indah,' hmm? Tony said you'd been to see her, too." I crossed my arms. I was prepared to fight.

Paul took a minute and laughed. "Indah works at that massage place, the same place I sent you and

Rebecca to. You had a massage from her." He crossed his arms. "I had a massage from her; I didn't sleep with her."

"What about going home with different women every night? That's what Tony said," I shot another accusation at him.

Paul sighed. "That's what Tony does. It doesn't mean that's what I do."

"Eric said something similar. What about that?"

"I've had some romantic interests on trips, yes," he started, "but those fade away. I get hurt because people come and go. Sometimes, I click with another guide, or traveller, or shop owner along the way, but it is always temporary." He looked down at his feet. "You're the first, and only, tourist in my group I fell for. I mean that. I was about to move here for you!"

I felt so foolish. The words, now spoken by Paul, felt too silly to even hear. Paul had not done anything wrong; in fact, he had been the perfect gentleman. He told me his truth, and had been all along.

I couldn't find the words. I felt like something had struck me: reality, perhaps. I'd made a mistake about Paul. I judged him based on something I hadn't even confirmed. I made an assumption. Communication, or lack thereof, could be the devil.

"Look, I understand you've been hurt. You moved on from someone else and I'm sure the last thing you needed was me showing up here. But I want you – only you. Please, give me a chance." He got down on both knees, as if to surrender, possibly even beg.

I heard Emma and my seatmate on the plane echo

inside my head. Why not him? Give the man a chance. "I suppose you're right. I just assumed travel guides got lonely. I assumed you were like the rest of them and just wanted a warm body at night, not a girlfriend." My face was burning hot, like someone had struck it with a fiery poker straight from the flames. I couldn't look at him.

He didn't reply. He stood up and studied my face, which only made me more nervous. My heart raced. When I have feelings on the spot, I simply can't shut up. "I'm imperfect. I make mistakes, I learn from them, and I grow. If you can accept that I'm not perfect, then, well, maybe we can start over again. You flew all this way for me. I'm sorry." A small smile crept across his face.

"No one's perfect. Give me a chance, too. I love you, Poppy Davis." He cupped my face in his hands and gave me the softest, most tender, kiss. This kiss was my confirmation that he had picked me. He wanted me. He would do anything for me. A lover's kiss sealed the deal.

"Awww!" was accompanied by a soft clapping. Casey was still peeking out from behind the corner wall.

Our lips parted. We looked at each other and giggled. Paul brushed his hand against my forehead, moving the hair away from my face.

"We see you," Paul teased. "You can come out now. It's safe, right?" He looked at me for validation.

"I'm just going to leave you two alone," Casey stated. She was walking backwards and fumbling towards her desk without breaking her gaze with us. She was so fixated that her best friend had found a man who was worth holding onto.

Ah, it's okay. We should go. I need a shower. I haven't bathed in days." Paul smelt himself and made a face of humorous disgust.

"I concur," I laughed.

We stepped away from each other and tried to process what just happened. Paul collected his things, and we headed back towards the elevator.

"I'll be here if you need anything!" Casey shouted from her desk. I turned to wink at her as Paul and I held hands. She'd still be my wife for life, no doubt. I hoped Paul would accept our complex relationship.

"So, you thought I was some sort of travelling alley cat, did you?" He smirked.

"I suppose, in a way. Shut up!" I laughed, trying to hide my embarrassment.

The sun was hot and welcoming as the rays touched my skin. I felt brand new – ready to begin a new chapter in my life. I'd need to find a job. I needed to support Amos; those biscuits didn't buy themselves.

"So, how did you know I left? Who told you?" I interrogated my new boyfriend.

"Oh, those English ladies. They can't keep a secret to save their lives." Paul smiled and held me closer as we walked side by side. "Rebecca, Kate, and Emma send their love, by the way. They really miss you."

"I miss them, too. I'll keep in touch. I think I got a few messages from them."

"Yes, I think they're planning to come see you. They said they want to play drinking games with the maple syrup."

If anything, this entire experience taught me that I was whole on my own. I didn't need a man to feel complete. Being with someone and falling in love, regardless of who they were, was just the icing on this cake called life.

THE END

Epilogue

Three months later, my apartment had been taken over. Moving boxes teetered in a flimsy tower. I heard Amos' whimpers, and I searched through the rubble to find my faithful companion.

"I know, it's an adjustment." I stroked his head. He brushed his ears through my soft fingers. "Everything'll be okay." I kissed his furry little head. He sighed, defeated.

"That's the last of them! I think we are done." His voice echoed through the hallway. Finally. I hated moving. I never thought this day would come, but times change.

"Should I get a head start on dinner, sweetheart?" Paul set the last box down and wrapped his sweaty arms around my waist. Amos let out a little growl. He hadn't quite gotten used the new roommate, but he was warming up.

"Down boy," Paul smirked, kissing my forehead, and heading towards the kitchen. He tore a few boxes open to look for his gourmet pots and pans.

"He's only protecting his human," I mused, stroking

my very good boy.

As Paul found his place in the kitchen, I sat down at my computer. I put the finishing touches on a freelance article I had written for a travel magazine. The idea was to promote travel for young women. The magazine was pleased to read about my recent journey and there was the potential to submit more work. A new beginning for me – for us. What else could I ask for?

"What would you like for dinner?" Paul called out across the apartment.

"Forget dinner; I'm in the mood for dessert." A mischievous smile spread across my face. We raced to the bedroom and closed the door. Life was heating up.

One thing's for sure: adventure's calling.

Acknowledgements

I want to thank my parents, Gary, and Andrea, for giving me an amazing life. You have supported all of my endeavours, even if you haven't always agreed with them.

Jason and Matthew, thank you for your torment throughout my childhood – it adds to my writing material. Just kidding! Thank you for being fantastic big brothers, always looking out for me. I hope the boys get the travel bug one day, too.

Melanie, you've always been my top supporter and there for me no matter what. You challenge me to be the best possible version of myself. Thank you for loving me, for me.

To my friends, particularly those whom I confided in that I was writing a travel novel, thank you for believing in me and encouraging me to continue with my passions. I did it! Now, all of you please buy a copy?!

A special thank you to: JG MacLeod for the beta reading and editing, Rebecca Yelland with Black Cat Graphic Design for the cover design and the format editing, and Jim Kost for the beautiful author photo. I've learned so much from your crafts. Thank you for the attention to detail and for helping to create this project.

To you, the reader – I hope you have wild adventures and experience the world. I hope you find out who you are, and who you want to be. Don't give in to what others tell you is 'right' or 'proper.' Don't focus on the invisible, ticking clock of life. Follow your own heart and create your own path. You're not alone.

ABOUT THE AUTHOR

Photo by Jim Kost

Ashley Percival is a dreamer and a romantic. When she isn't travelling, she's telling tales of her own travels abroad and fantasizing about her next life adventure.

For Ashley, travel has helped her to learn about herself. Travelling tested her limits by putting this shy, introverted person into circumstances she never thought possible. In her life, she has taken the road less travelled, which has opened her eyes to the most magical people and places.

Thank you for taking the time to read this creative work. It has been a lifelong goal to publish a fictional version of her worldly travels.

Ashley Percival resides in Canada.

Find Ashley's social media here: https://linktr.ee/misadventuresmedia

Manufactured by Amazon.ca
Acheson, AB